SECRET
OF THE
CORPSE
EATER

TY DRAGO

Month9Books

The Undertakers: Secret of the Corpse Eater by Ty Drago
All rights reserved. Published in the United States of America by Month9Books, LLC.

Edited by Erica Rose
Published by Month9Books
Cover illustrated by Zach Schoenbaum
Cover and typography designed by Victoria Faye
Cover Copyright © 2014 Month9Books

Month9Books

In loving memory of two amazing women:
Debra Ann Head, dear friend and sister-in-law, taken too soon;
and Bonnie Virginia Drago, mother, advisor, and loyal fan.

Thank you for everything you both gave me.
You will never be forgotten.

"There can be beauty even in monsters,
if one knows how to look."
—ANONYMOUS

TY DRAGO

CHAPTER 1
A MORNING'S STALK

This is my life.

I remember thinking those words as the three of us stood on that South Street rooftop, looking down into the lifeless, upturned faces of hundreds of the walking dead. Many of them were smiling. There's nothing worse than a smug Corpse.

They knew, as *we* knew, that they had us trapped.

Um … I'd better back up a little.

It started with the poster.

Harvey's Open Air Tours!
Knowledgeable Guides!
Custom-Made Open-Air Limos!
Leaving PROMPTLY at the Top of Every Hour!
See Philadelphia in Comfort!
Just $15 per Person!

I read it—memorized it, really—but not because I cared about some Philly tourist trap.

You see, when the target you're stalking looks your way, it's important to not just appear innocent, but to *be* innocent. Suddenly, I wasn't Will Ritter, Undertaker. Instead, I was just a thirteen-year-old kid in jeans, with my face buried under a hoodie and my attention glued to some random poster slapped onto the window of a closed shop.

So I read the poster. Then I read it again. And again. Until my peripheral vision told me the target had turned away. Only then did I let out the breath I'd been holding.

If I got caught now, I was *dead*.

Tracking prey through city streets is hard enough at night, but it's way worse in the daytime.

My target moved along South Street, heading east, with me about a half block behind. It was a little before eleven a.m., not a prime stalking hour.

South Street's a pretty big deal in Philly. With its clubs and bars and stores, it's a major nighttime hot spot. In twelve hours, these sidewalks would be choked with people. There'd be lights and music and drunken laughter.

But *now*, blanketed under a gray, April-morning sky, there were few enough shoppers that I'd be noticed if my tracking got too obvious—and yet too few to use as camouflage.

My target abruptly crossed the street and continued along on the other side. Not exactly hurrying, but with definite purpose.

I crossed the street too. Tracking 101. A newbie might think it better to stay on my side of South and follow catty-corner. Mistake. People look around while they walk. It's safer to stay behind them, where you can react fast if they pull what Sharyn Jefferson, co-chief of the Undertakers, calls a "Crazy Ivan." That's when your target pauses without warning and looks back—like mine just did.

I think it's a movie reference.

My target stopped. So *I* stopped too, ready to play innocent again. Then she knocked on the door of Quaker City Comics. I didn't know the place.

A few seconds later the door opened and she went in.

A few seconds after that, I peeked through the glass frontage. A sign said the place wouldn't open for another ten minutes, which explained why the target had knocked.

It was hard to see much inside: a cashier's counter, a little snack shop on the left, and shelves upon shelves of comics. A pretty cool place. I tried to remember the last time I'd read a comic book—and couldn't, though my roommate back at Haven, the Undertakers' HQ, kept a bunch of them.

I just had no time for stuff like that anymore: *X-Men*, *Batman*, *The Avengers*, *Green Lantern*.

My old life.

I spotted my target swapping words with a twenty-something dude dressed all in black and sporting a nose ring. He smiled and pointed toward the rear of the store. She nodded and headed back there, disappearing from view.

I tugged on the door handle.

Locked.

Normally, this wouldn't have slowed me down much. I carry a tricked-out pocketknife, which can pretty much pick any lock. But before I could even reach for it, the nose ring guy was there. He yelled, "Not open yet!" through the glass, his voice muffled but understandable.

I faked confusion and pointed at my ear.

With a visible sigh, he unlocked the door and cracked it about six inches. "We're not open yet."

I stuck my sneaker in the gap. "I need to come in for a minute."

"Look, kid—"

I shoved the door with my shoulder. The guy wasn't real big, but then neither am I. If my roommate had done this, he'd have sent the dude flying. But the best I could manage to do was force him back a step, and that was more about his surprise than my muscle.

"What do you think you're doing?" he demanded as I stepped into his shop. The place smelled of crisp, new paper—a musty but not unpleasant odor.

"Sorry," I said, meaning it. "This'll only take a sec ..." Then I sidestepped him and headed toward the back of the store.

He grabbed my forearm. "Look kid, I don't know what you're trying to pull. But get out now before I call the cops."

I put my hand on his, found his pinky and yanked it the wrong way. He yelped and let go. I didn't. Instead, I forced his wrist back until he dropped to one knee, grimacing in pain. "Call whoever you want," I told him. "Like I said, I won't be long."

He nodded feverishly.

"Don't worry. Everything's cool," I said, wondering if that was true. Well, I'd know in about a minute.

I released his hand and went on my way. He muttered something after me, but I didn't catch it. Just as well.

I found a narrow hallway leading to a small mudroom that had been turned into storage. Boxes lined one wall. On the opposite wall stood shelves of graphic novels—

obscure anime, according to their spines.

At the rear was a blue door with the word *EXIT* painted on it. And on a box right beside it sat Helene Boettcher. She clutched a sheet of paper in her hands and was reading it so intently that she didn't notice me right away.

Helene was also an Undertaker. In fact, it was this thin, brown-haired girl who'd first brought me to Haven, having come to my rescue during an eighth-grade math class early last fall. That had been the day I'd found out monsters were real.

Another story.

Helene was one of my best friends. Except she was a bit more than that, too. I knew it but, so far, hadn't done anything with the knowledge.

Frankly, I hadn't yet figured out what I *should* do.

Helene, however, met my eyes and, as usual, knew exactly what to do.

She got up and took a swing at me.

I ducked.

She threw another punch. I blocked it. Then she pivoted and jabbed me in the chest, near my left shoulder. It hurt, but I knew from experience that it wasn't half as hard as she was able to hit.

"What're you doing here?" she demanded. Her cheeks were red, and I noticed for the first time that there were tears in her eyes.

"Ow!" I yelped, rubbing the spot where she'd punched me. "I ... followed you from Haven."

"You *what?*"

"You've been doing this a lot!" I snapped. "Sneaking out on Saturday mornings. You think nobody noticed?"

Alarm flashed in her eyes. "Who else knows?"

"Well … just me."

Her visible relief did nothing to help in the anger department. "You've got no right to be … spying … on me!"

I started to say something—maybe argue, maybe apologize—but I didn't get the chance.

Both of us jumped as someone pounded on the comic shop's back door. Then the knob jiggled, loud and urgent. But of course it was locked.

Helene and I swapped looks.

A morning delivery, maybe? I glanced over my shoulder toward the front of the store, but I couldn't see Nose Ring Dude. Maybe he was calling the cops. Maybe he was in the bathroom running cold water over his hand. Either way, he didn't seem to have heard a thing.

A moment later, the pounding returned, though this time it sounded farther away. Whoever-it-was was running along the alley, trying each door in turn.

I stepped around Helene and pushed the blue door open.

At first I saw nothing but the cracked pavement of your typical alley. Then someone yanked on the other side, tearing the knob out of my hands with tremendous strength—and I found myself face-to-face with a dead man.

CHAPTER 2
PARADE OF THE DEAD

I knew the next few seconds counted—big time.

We call them Corpses, not zombies. We do that to remind ourselves that unlike the movie monsters, these dudes are far from stupid. If I gave away that I could See this guy for what he was—a rotting, walking cadaver, he'd peg me as an Undertaker.

Then he and his dead peeps would kill me.

He glared at me with milky, seemingly lifeless eyes. Behind him, I spotted at least four more deaders hurrying east along the alleyway, heading toward 6th Street, maybe chasing whoever had just knocked on Quaker City Comic's back door.

He was a Type Three. That's a grading system based on degree of rottenness. Threes are around a month dead. Their juices are drying up and their bodies are bloating from all the trapped gases. Worse, by now the bugs have settled in to stay; this dude had maggots crawling around inside his cheeks. I could see them wriggling.

And don't even get me started on his *smell*. Threes

7

radiate a stench that would make a bucket of vomit smell like roses.

In the early days, I'd have lost my breakfast, but those days were long gone. Still, it was an effort to keep my voice steady when, as innocently as possible, I said, "Somebody knocked."

"Ain't your business, kid," the Corpse growled. He had a raspy voice; his vocal chords were drying up.

For just a second, I crossed my eyes and had a look at his Mask. It's a Seer trick—a knack that can take a while to pick up. But once you've got it, you're able to see a deader's illusion: the false face that each of them somehow projects to the rest of the world.

This guy's Mask looked about forty, with thin brown hair, a pointed nose, and an acne-scarred face. I often wonder why some Corpses project ugly Masks. I mean, if you're going to fake being alive, why not fake being halfway good-looking? But many of them don't. Just another of their little mysteries.

"Okay," I said, trying to look intimidated. It wasn't hard. "Sorry."

I started to pull the door shut. For a few seconds, he kept holding it, suspicion in his eyes. But then a shout from farther along the alley caught his attention.

We both looked.

A girl in a blue blazer darted around the corner at 6th Street, heading north, with at least a half-dozen Corpses in pursuit.

Dead Guy let go of the door. I shut it.

Then I turned to Helene. "They're chasing a Seer!"

We ran back through the comic book store to find

Nose Ring Guy gazing out the front window. "Weird," he muttered.

"Gotta go, Doug!" Helene announced. She waved a paper at him, the one she'd been reading when I'd found her. "I'll get back to you with the reply."

He looked at her, then at me. His eyes narrowed.

"Sorry about the hand," I said.

"Everything ... okay?" he asked Helene.

"Sure!" she said. "See ya!"

We pushed through the door and out onto South Street...

... and froze.

The dead were *everywhere*. The street, all but empty just five minutes ago, was now thick with Corpses—a parade of them, all heading the same way. Some wore jeans, others suits, others dresses. A few were in uniform: policemen, firefighters, even mailmen. No rags for these walking cadavers. Corpses shopped for clothes just like anybody else, held them up in front of the mirror, and tried them on for size.

I've seen it. It isn't pretty.

Hundreds of them crowded the narrow street, choking off what little traffic there was. Car horns blared. Angry human drivers threw curses out open windows.

The deaders ignored it all.

"Oh my God," Helene breathed.

"You armed?" I asked her.

She shook her head. "You?"

"Just my pocketknife," I replied. Then, after a pause, "I wasn't expecting this."

"Me, neither."

"I saw the Seer cut north on 6th," I whispered. "She might still be on South Street...or she could be headed north toward Market."

Helene said, "This looks like a reverse Number 23 to me."

"Yeah. A big one."

Undertakers have moves, and most of those moves are numbered—pretty much in the order that somebody thought them up. A Number 23 involves a bunch of Undertakers chasing down a running Corpse. Yeah, occasionally *we* do the hunting. The bulk of the team makes chase, cutting off as many routes as possible, not giving its target any chance to double back—all the while driving them right into the arms of the smaller force, who finishes them off.

Helene had it right. This was a reverse Number 23, and on a huge scale.

"So what do we *do*?" she asked, sounding hopeless. I didn't blame her. There'd be no fighting these guys. The direct approach—usually my favorite—was suicide.

"We gotta get ahead of 'em," I whispered. "But be subtle about it. If we just take off running, they'll make us for Undertakers before we get twenty yards."

A slow smile crept across Helene's face. "So let's not run."

She turned back into the store, leaving me standing in the doorway, gaping at the tide of deaders marching east toward Penn's Landing and the Delaware River. I couldn't imagine where they'd all come from—or why Lilith Cavanaugh, the Queen of the Dead, would risk sending so many of her cronies to one place like this. She didn't like to draw so much attention.

Whoever the girl in the blue blazer was, Cavanaugh wanted her *bad*.

Behind me I heard arguing. Then pleading. Then more arguing. "They're two hundred a pop, Helene!" Doug was saying.

"I know. It's just a loan."

"I can't loan you these! They're limited-edition collectibles! Numbered! My boss would have my head! What do you even need them for, anyway? Has it got something to do with that flash mob out there?"

Flash mob. That was almost funny.

I went and stood beside Helene, though seeing me didn't do anything to improve Doug's attitude. I said, "Our friend's in trouble out there and we need to find her…fast. Please. Seconds really count here."

He glowered. "You assault me and then you want a favor?"

Helene smirked. "You'd be surprised how often he does that."

Doug was an adult, if only just, and he didn't have the Sight. This wasn't surprising, as the only person over eighteen who ever *could* see the Corpses had been dead for going on three years: Detective Karl Ritter of the Philly PD—founder of the Undertakers. My father.

And Doug wasn't *him*.

"Look," I said calmly; whining rarely works on grown-ups. "I swear this isn't a prank. Whatever Helene needs, give it to her. I promise, we'll either return them or pay for them. But we need them right *now*." My pocketknife was in my hand, my finger poised on the **2** button. Pressing it would release the Taser—yeah, it's got a Taser—which I'd use if I had to.

"I'm sorry, dudes," he began. "I can't —"

Helene said, "February 14, 2002."

Doug's face reddened. "You've got to be kidding me."

"You owe me," the girl pressed.

"We had a deal! You promised!"

"And I'll keep it. But I'm calling in the favor. Right now."

Doug wasted precious seconds deciding. Then his shoulders sagged and he fetched two long boxes, which he dropped onto the countertop.

Skateboards.

Cool.

Then I noticed Fergie's face smiling up from their footboards.

I glanced at Doug. "The Black Eyed Peas? Seriously?"

"They're collectables. Take 'em," he said, sounding furious. "Bring them back if you can. Get me the money if you can't. I need this job." His eyes fixed on Helene. "But this squares us."

"Totally," she said. "Sorry."

"And find someplace else for your letter drops."

Helene's face went pale. "Doug…"

"I mean it. We're not friends anymore. Now get out of my shop!"

Fresh tears shone in Helene's eyes. I had about a million questions, but this wasn't the time. Instead, I wordlessly tore open one of the boxes and pulled out a Ripstick DLX—a serious board.

I was new to boarding. Sharyn had been making everyone on her crew, Helene and me included, work some jumps and turns on these quarter pipes at a public skateboard course in Fairmount Park. Other Angels—

that's the name of Sharyn's crew—were better at it than me. But I was improving.

And Helene had been right—it *was* better than running.

"I'm really sorry, Doug," she said again. Then she pulled out her own Ripstick as we dashed out the door.

"Let's do this," she told me.

We kicked off and hit our boards, jumping the curb and slipping into the "parade" of deaders. They barely noticed us and, as long as we didn't show that we could See them, that would continue. These dead guys were on a mission—all of them—to hunt down one girl in a blue blazer.

I didn't want to think about what would happen if *we* didn't find her first.

CHAPTER 3

CARVING UP CORPSES

We headed east, following the flow of the deader hoard. Helene led the way, weaving in and out amid the uneven parade of Corpses, calling out shouts of "Coming through!" and "'Scuse us!"

I followed her, wheel for wheel, shifting my body weight just enough to skirt around the next obstacle. The smell was horrific! These dead dudes were at all levels of decomposition: mostly Type Twos, Threes, and Fours, but with a few Fives mixed in as well. Fives are way far gone, so dry and brittle that they can barely walk. The entities inside these stolen bodies, the *Malum*, are always looking for fresh cadavers to inhabit. But there's a caste system with Corpses, and lower classes lose dibs on the better host bodies.

I didn't see any Type Ones at all and, despite the situation, that made me smile—because I knew why.

At 6th Street, the hoard split, with some turning north toward Market Street and some south, toward the stadiums. The majority kept going straight and so we did too, hoping—praying even—that the girl in the blue blazer was still running along South Street.

Not that we didn't have our own problems; if this deader mob wised to us, we'd be torn apart in seconds. As we continued along the next block, I had to keep damping down my heebie-jeebies.

But at least we were gaining ground.

We passed Cheesesteaktees, a Philly memorabilia shop, Olympia Sports, Game Stop, and Lady Love, a lingerie place my mother would never let me set foot into. All the while, people—regular, living people—paused in their Saturday morning shopping to gape at the inexplicable river of single-minded men and women rushing past them.

Without the Sight, the whole thing must have looked as if someone had spotted Elvis at Unica Footwear!

When a particularly huge Type Two loomed in front of me, I crouched down at the last second and rolled right between his tree trunk–sized legs. He was a giant, six-foot-six six at least, and host cadavers that big were hard to come by. Curious, I risked a glance upward and crossed my eyes.

My heebie-jeebies throttled up into full-blown panic.

Oh no…

I *knew* this particular dead guy. I'd fought him just a few months back. If fact, I'd driven a sword through his skull while he'd been trying to choke Helene.

Small world.

Corpses tend to have expressionless eyes that don't give much away and this dude was no exception. But his Mask told me volumes. *He* recognized *me*, too.

Before he could make a grab for me, or even yell a warning, I straightened up and called out, "What is this?

Some kind of 'Occupy Philly' thing? Where're all you dudes going?"

"Shut up, kid!" This came from a nearby Type Five, his dry skin the color of parchment and his eyes so sunken that they were hard to spot. With his every step, I could hear the crunch of old tendons and when he talked, his jaw sagged to one side. Shiny, black beetles bumbled out from between his teeth. He was a mess.

He was also shuffling along right in front of the giant.

Faking a wobble on my skateboard and sudden alarm, I cried, "Watch it dude!" Then I put my hand on the Type Five's fragile shoulder, as if scrambling for support. A shove was all it took. He toppled over, hitting the curb with a loud crunch that only a Seer would have heard. Then his head snapped off, tumbling across the sidewalk.

I moment later, as I rolled clear, Dead Giant Guy tripped over Headless Gutter Dude and crashed thunderously to the street.

I called back, "Sorry, man!" Then I scanned the mob for reactions.

There were none. All of them—except the fallen giant, of course—had bought it. For now.

Believe it or not, I hadn't *killed* Headless Gutter Guy. Killing deaders isn't that easy. All I'd done was "break" his stolen body. The *Malum* inside the decapitated cadaver would be trapped, immobile, until one of his buds decided to help him Transfer to a new host.

Dead Giant Guy, however, was nowhere near immobile. In fact, he was already on his feet—and *seriously* pissed.

Except he didn't raise the alarm—not in English and not in Deadspeak, the weird, telepathic language that

Corpses sometimes use. For a moment, I didn't understand his silence. Then I did. I'd humiliated him the last time we'd met. This was his chance for payback.

Great.

The hoard crossed 5th Street, still headed east. Helene was abreast of me now, several yards to my right, skirting the curb. Fortunately, we'd cleared the frontline of this "reverse 23" search party—and ahead of us lay a city block's worth of nice, empty South Street.

I could hear heavy footfalls on the pavement behind me, the giant in pursuit. But I wasn't worried. With open space in front of me, the Black Eyed Peas and I could outdistance a jogging dead man.

Ahead I spotted Blue Blazer Girl sprinting down the center line. She was tall, with black hair tied into a neat ponytail. Her jacket looked like thin polyester, not great for a chilly Saturday morning. I couldn't help but wonder where she'd come from and why she was dressed like a hotel maître d'.

I'd have to ask her once we caught up.

Then, just as Helene and I got ahead of the hoard, a *second* wave of Corpses spilled in from both ends of 4th Street. Dozens of them. They flooded the intersection like an incoming tide, blocking the way ahead.

Blue Blazer Girl was boxed in. And so were we.

A Number 23.

I heard Helene curse

Ahead, the girl stopped in her tracks, with the eastern wall of Corpses thirty feet away from her. I glanced over my shoulder. The western edge of the deader mob had stopped, too. Hundreds of pairs of seemingly sightless eyes fixed on the girl.

Only now, they were fixed on *us*, too.

Deaders aren't stupid. A couple of skateboarding kids being rude on South Street was a tolerable annoyance. But this new turn of events smacked too much of Undertaker.

We'd been made.

Then, as if to drive the point home, Dead Giant Guy pushed his way through the ranks. His head was watermelon-sized and just about as hairless. His skin was blackish-gray and his teeth, when he smiled, were the color of rotten eggs.

He waved at me.

"Oh crap," I muttered. Then, as I braked my board, I did something I'd *really* hoped I wouldn't have to do. I started talking into my wrist.

"Haven? This is…um…" No mission name "…Will."

There was a long pause. Not a lot happened with the Undertakers on Saturday mornings. We are kids, after all, and most of our fighting is done at night.

At last, an almost absurdly deep voice said, "Will?"

"Hi, Dan."

Dan McDevitt was a Chatter, one of the crew that managed communications with Undertakers who were out on one mission or another.

"You on mission?" his baritone asked. "I don't have a profile."

I glanced around. Helene was watching me. The Corpses were watching me. The girl in the blazer stood statue still, about a hundred feet away—probably frozen with terror.

"Not exactly," I said. "Listen, Helene and I are on South Street, between 4th and 5th. We've pegged a Seer, but there are deaders on us."

"Jeez. Okay, I'll wake Sharyn. How many deaders are we looking at?"

My gaze bounced between our crowded flanks.

"Um … kinda looks like *all* of them."

CHAPTER 4
THE RUNNING GIRL

"We're on our own," I told Helene.

"I figured," she said. Then she kicked off and rolled down the street toward the Seer. After a moment's hesitation, I followed her.

Blue Blazer Girl didn't even glance our way until we stopped beside her. Her attention was fixed on the wall of Corpses filling 4th Street. They'd started marching toward us, murder and triumph in their collective, ghoulish expression.

"Hi," Helene said.

The girl turned. She was older than I'd thought—maybe sixteen—with brown eyes and delicate, pretty features. She wore blue trousers, a white dress shirt, and of course the blue blazer, which I now saw sported an official-looking pin that I didn't recognize.

But there wasn't time for intros. So instead I recited the *Terminator*-esque line that Helene had used on me the first day I'd gotten my Eyes. "Listen ... I know you're scared, but if you don't want to die, then come with —"

That was as far as I got.

"You Undertakers?" she asked.

Helene and I swapped looks. "Yeah," I said.

"Great!" Blue Blazer Girl exclaimed. "Try to keep up!"

Then she turned left and bolted down South Leithgow Street.

Now Leithgow isn't a "street," but more of an alley running between Auntie Anne's Pretzels and Beyond the Wall, a poster and art store. The road is narrow and flanked by three-story buildings. Cars *can* squeeze through it, but only barely.

Maybe the girl in the blazer was hoping the Corpses had somehow missed that potential escape route. But I knew better.

"Wait!" I called, but she ignored me.

Helene cursed again. Then the two of us kicked off after her while, on both of our flanks, the walls of Corpses surged forward. Every deader in town was chasing us, and we were running into what was basically a canyon between man-made cliff faces.

Seriously stupid!

Ahead, Blue Blazer Girl picked up speed. She was fast, and that gave me a flicker of hope. If the three of us could squeak through before—

Then more Corpses appeared at the far end of the block, spilling into the narrow street like sand pouring into a funnel.

We're dead.

Seeing them, Blue Blazer Girl changed direction, making a beeline for a head-high brick platform that stood against the right-hand wall, supporting an air conditioner. Bounding upward, she caught the platform's edge with the tip of her left shoe.

But instead of climbing atop the air conditioner, her right foot connected with the appliance's thin, metal surface just long enough to redistribute her body weight—backward. Then, before our eyes, she executed this crazy leap, riding her own momentum through a long arc that carried her clear to the other side of the narrow street.

At the last moment, she somehow twisted in mid-air and grabbed a protruding window box that formed part of the opposite building, latching onto it with her hands and the balls of her feet. There she hung for a half second before launching upward again—this time from the top of the lower window to the ledge of the upper.

Bending her knees like coiled springs, she kicked up and back, vaulting across the street a second time and somehow catching the lip of the roof with one hand. Then, again using her own momentum, she swung up and over the rooftop, disappearing from sight.

Helene and I stood frozen, our mouths hanging open.

Ahead and behind us, the hoard stood frozen, their mouths hanging open, too.

Then Blue Blazer Girl's face appeared over the edge of the roof. "Come on!"

"She's freakin' Spider-man," I said.

"Sorry, Doug," Helene muttered.

We abandoned our boards, running to the brick platform and scrambling up onto the air conditioner. There we stood, maybe seven feet off the ground, looking helplessly up at the building's smooth brick wall and distant roof.

Footsteps flooded the street. The Corpses were moving in.

And we had no place to go.

Overhead, the girl sounded exasperated. "Hasn't Tom taught you anything?" This unexpected reference to our chief, Tom Jefferson, staggered me. But we didn't have time to figure it out before she called down, "The drainpipe!"

We looked to our left. A thick, black drainpipe was mounted vertically along the wall beside the air conditioner.

Helene looked at me. I looked at her.

"You first," I said. She didn't argue. Grasping the pipe with both hands she hoisted herself up, bracing her feet against the bricks on either side of it. Then she climbed— one hand, one foot, the other hand, the other foot.

I waited until she'd made it up maybe six feet, until the dead were crowded around the air conditioner and grasping at me with gnarled, rotting fingers, before I followed. Swallowing back a wave of panic, I tried to mimic what Helene had done so smoothly. And I managed it—sort of. I'd like to say it was harder for me because I was a little heavier.

But the sad truth is that Helene was better at *most* things.

I cleared the Corpses' reach barely in time, ignoring their frustrated moans and focusing on what I was doing. One mistake and I'd drop like a stone. Then, if I was lucky, I'd break my back on the air conditioner before the hoard ripped me apart.

My heart trip-hammered. My palms sweated.

Above me, Helene reached the roof. I still had about

ten more feet to go. Then eight. Then six.

That's when the pipe started shaking—hard.

Hugging it, I looked down. A new face had appeared amidst the sea of cadavers. Dead Giant Guy grinned up at me, head and shoulders above the rest, his huge hands around the pipe, his bloated, purple fingers working to pull it free from the wall. Any second now, I'd lose my grip and drop right into the big wormbag's crushing arms.

The giant knew it, too. His grin widened.

Then a brick hit him in the face.

It struck end-on with terrific force, turning his already rotting nose to mush and planting itself deep between his eyes. His facial bones shattered and his cheeks caved in around the brick, until the dead dude's pupils were looking directly at one another.

Dead Giant Guy staggered back, flailing his big arms and sending the nearest of his peeps flying. For just a few precious moments, everything was pandemonium. But those moments were enough.

I climbed. I won't say it was any easier, but fear's a great motivator. Within seconds, I felt Helene's hands grab my forearm and pull me up the last couple of feet.

Then I dropped gratefully onto the flat tar roof, my hands and face lathered with sweat.

"You okay?" Helene asked me.

I nodded. "Nice throw…with the brick."

"Wasn't me."

I turned to Blue Blazer Girl. "Thanks. I'm Will Ritter."

"You're welcome, Will," she replied. "Jillian. Jillian Birmelin."

"Beer Mellon?" I asked.

"Birmelin," she said.

"Sorry."

She shrugged. "Nobody gets it right."

Standing up, I peered down at the mass of deaders filling Leithgow Street, and thought about the hundreds more who choked every road and alley for blocks around. Sooner or later, they'd figure out how to get onto this roof.

And that's when I thought: *this is my life.*

Well, it is.

"Okay...now what?" I asked.

"I don't know," Jillian admitted, sounding frightened for the first time. "There's *so* many zombies!"

"Don't call 'em zombies," Helene and I said in perfect unison. It was embarrassing.

"Why not?" the girl asked.

Helene started to explain, but there wasn't time. So, instead, she turned my way and said, "We're trapped."

"Yeah. I get that."

"Um...this is usually where you come up with a really good idea."

I rubbed my grimy face with my grimy hands, thinking furiously. I hated it when she put me on the spot like this! How was I supposed to dream up a miracle with so many—

Wait a second ...

"How do you feel about a really *bad* one?" I asked.

CHAPTER 5

THE ROOFTOPS OF PHILLY

The rooftops around us formed a landscape of sharp angles and weird, boxy shapes. Sheer walls rose from lower roofs to higher ones. Narrow service alleys ran between buildings, creating treacherous gaps that you couldn't see until you were right on top of them. There were chimneys, some brick and some metal, industrial-sized air coolers, sheds, vents, antennas, and even a small greenhouse. Some of the roofs were flat, others sharply pitched. Some were tarred, others graveled, and still others shingled.

I took all this in. Then I looked at the rooftop across the street, and considered the mass of eager, scrambling dead between us and it.

"Any chance we can get across Leithgow?" I asked.

Helene frowned. "No way."

But Jillian said, "Sure."

We both stared at her.

She rolled her eyes. "It's called *parkour*, the art of movement. You *never* got any of this from Tom?"

We shook our heads. "That's how you got up here the way you did?"

Jillian nodded. "That was a combination of Wall Pass, Tic Tac, and Precision Jumping."

Helene asked, "Where'd you learn it?"

"Later," I said. Any minute now, the Corpses were going to find a way up here. "How do we use it to get across the street?"

"*Parkour*'s about harnessing your momentum, your balance, and your environment to navigate obstacles as fast and efficiently as possible," Jillian explained, sounding like she was quoting someone. "See that upper roof?" She pointed to a building on our side of the gap that rose maybe ten feet higher than this one. "Do what I do."

Then she ran straight to the wall—and *up* it. Through the whole thing, her upper body stayed straight, so that all of her weight remained neutral. At the last second, just before gravity took her, she vaulted upward using the traction of her shoe against the bricks, grabbed the lip of the next roof with both hands and pulled herself onto it.

"Looks easy," Helene remarked.

"It *does?*"

"Sure. I've been running up walls like that since I was ten. Just never knew it had a name before! Let's do it!"

Helene went first and nailed it. She wasn't as smooth as Jillian, but she got there without breaking her neck. Then both girls looked at me.

Great.

I put everything I had into it, and got farther than I thought I would. As my sneaker hit the wall, I leaned into it a little and was surprised to find that I *could* run partway up. But then my foot slipped and I'd have dropped like a rock if the girls hadn't caught my arms.

"See?" Jillian said as they yanked me up onto the higher roof. "Easy."

"Easy," Helene echoed. "Was that a Tic Tac?"

"No. That was a Wall Pass. Tic Tac's pretty advanced." She looked at Helene. "You're a natural." Then she turned to me. "You're *not*."

"Thanks," Helene replied.

"Thanks," I replied.

Jillian said, "From here, the roof across the street is lower, so gravity becomes our friend. Just do what I do and we'll get there, okay? But…"

I looked at her. "But?"

"Well…what's the point? We'd just be trading one rooftop for another!"

"Except *that* rooftop borders 5th Street."

Helene blinked. "So what?"

A loud bang made the three of us jump. About twenty feet away on this higher roof stood a kind of wooden shack with a heavy door built into it—a door that had just crashed open.

Two Corpses emerged.

Jillian gasped.

Their eyes locked on us like laser beams. They were a pair of Type Twos, reasonably fresh and very strong. I wondered why there were only two of them, but then figured that the hoard, however it was organized, had sent a couple of hunters into every building on the block, looking for roof access.

And these wormbags had just hit the jackpot.

Showing their rotting teeth, they charged.

"Will!" Helene exclaimed. "I'm not armed!"

I held up my pocketknife. "I am. Let's show Spider-Girl what we *are* good at. Number 16!"

"Got it!"

As we both ran forward, I hit the **2** and **3** buttons on my pocketknife together. This was a new trick I'd learned. It popped the Taser out of one end and a five-inch, razor-sharp knife blade out of the other.

Where'd I get this thing, you ask? Again, that's another story.

Being so armed wasn't as good as having a super-soaker loaded with saltwater, which messed with the way deaders controlled their stolen bodies—or, better yet, or a crossbow fitted with Corpse-slaying Ritterbolts, but it would have to do.

As the deaders attacked, I noticed that both of them did so with half a milky eye pointed behind us, at Blue Blazer Girl. After all, it wasn't Helene or me they wanted. For reasons I didn't yet understand, Jillian Birmelin seemed to be the guest of honor at this ridiculously well-attended murder party.

But, their distraction *was* an advantage.

The one on the left swung at Helene, who arrived at the fight just a step ahead of me. The sweep of the deader's arm hid a lot of power behind it. But Helene ducked at the last instant, letting his own force whip him halfway around. Rule number one of fighting Corpses: *never* let them hit you. They're strong and they don't care much about the body they're in, so they don't hold back. A hard hit can knock you cold. A really hard hit can kill you.

Best to not be there when the blow lands.

Coming in right behind her, I took advantage of Dead Guy One's unguarded flank to tap him with my Taser. He stiffened and crashed to the rooftop. At this point, I *could* have stayed with him. If I kept my Taser pressed against him for fifteen or twenty seconds, it would trash his host body's nervous system, rendering it useless. But in this instance, I held back.

Number 16.

Just in front of me, Dead Guy Two stepped into Helene's path and lunged for her, his black-tongued, maggot-riddled mouth opened wide. This one meant to bite. They do that sometimes, another weird trait they have in common with their movie cousins. Steve Moscova, the Undertakers' science expert, thinks that hands and teeth are the way they fight in their home environment, wherever that is. It might explain why they never use weapons, like guns or knives, even if they're available.

Fortunately, Helene saw the attack coming a mile off and dipped backward—*Matrix* style—a sweet move that used their competing momentum to carry her under the deader's grasping arms. Once behind him, she pivoted and slammed the blade of her foot behind his knee, making it buckle. Then, as he fell backward, I came up alongside him and brought my blade up from underneath, nailing him in the "sweet spot" at the base of the skull where the brain stem meets the spinal cord.

His limp body hit the rooftop like a sack of wet rags.

In case you haven't figured it out, a Number 16 involves an unarmed Undertaker distracting the attackers just long enough for an armed Undertaker to deliver the "kill" shots. Not that these guys were permanently dead. The Corpse I'd Tasered would soon recover, though the one I'd knifed would need a new host body.

Still, it was one for the "win" column.

"Nice work," I said.

"You, too," she said.

We ran back to Jillian, who'd gone right to the edge of the roof and was peering down at the deaders filling Leithgow. Every eye was turned upward. All were baring their teeth. Many—too many—were smiling.

"Time to do whatever it is we're gonna do!" Helene exclaimed.

Jillian nodded. "Okay. This is a little tricky and we're only going to get one shot, so you need to pay attention. See that flower box down there?" She pointed to a brick outcropping beneath a third-floor window partway down the wall, maybe six feet below us. "You're going to launch off the roof at a sharp angle using your left foot and hit that outcropping with your right. The second you do—and I mean the *second*—you shift your body weight and leap for that window ledge across the street, the one that's sticking out toward us. It's about twelve feet out and maybe ten down. Long, but doable. You'll want to catch the ledge with your hands and tuck in your feet to absorb the impact. That's called a Cat Grab. Once there, use your legs to push yourself high enough to grab the edge of the far roof." Then she looked at us. "You both got that?"

"We'd better," Helene muttered.

I said nothing. No *way* was I going to pull *this* off!

"Watch me!" Jillian yelled.

She jumped. Her right foot hit the brick flower box perfectly. An instant later, her body seeming to *float* above Leithgow, with a hundred pairs of dead eyes wordlessly following her. At the last second, she lifted her feet and caught the window, her fingers clutching its sill. Then with a final heave, she sprung upward, snatched the rim of the roof, and pulled herself onto it.

Flight time: Maybe three seconds.

"Can you do this?" Helene asked me.

"We'll find out," I said. "Go!"

She launched herself—and missed. Oh, she hit the flower box okay, *and* cleared the alley. But her feet slipped on the opposite window ledge and she *almost* fell, dangling by the strength of one hand. As I watched, terrified, the deaders below her jumped and snapped like crocodiles. Then Helene's sneakered feet found purchase on the brick wall and she was somehow able to pull herself the rest of the way up.

Jeez. If that's how she did ... I'm screwed!

Five more Corpses exploded through the broken doorway at my back. They ignored their fallen buds and came for me—fast.

I jumped.

The flower box rushed up to meet me, way faster than I would have imagined. Still my foot landed on it more or less correctly. Then, gulping, and I shifted my weight and pushed off with everything I had.

Now, I'd done a lot of scary things since becoming an Undertaker. But nothing came close to that second leap. The whole world seemed to open up around me. I saw the faces of the hoard beneath my feet, smelled the stench of their decaying bodies, and heard their moans behind the rush of the wind past my ears.

Then I hit the window.

I mean, I *hit* the window.

And smashed right through it.

Stabs of pain sliced up my forearms, which I'd thrown up in front of my face at the last moment. Then I hit carpet, rolled, and slammed into a heavy dresser. For a split second, I was sure I was dead, *minced* by broken glass.

But I wasn't. With a gasp, I climbed to my feet and looked around.

An old woman sat in an armchair, watching television. She looked at me in shock, her mouth open to speak, maybe to scream.

"Sorry," I said. "Um…roof?"

She gaped at me. Then she replied, "Hallway."

I stumbled out of there, limping but mobile. Blood ran down my arms, and I could feel more cuts on my stomach and legs where shards of window glass had pierced my clothing. But, right now, none of that mattered.

In the narrow hallway I found only one other door. It was locked and, while my knife was in my pocket, I had no time to use it. So I kicked the door in. That's not as easy as it sounds, but I managed it.

Inside was a staircase, which headed up.

I took the steps two at the time, fumbled the top door open, and staggered out onto the rooftop. "Helene!"

"Will!"

The two girls stood peering over the roof's edge, maybe a dozen feet away. At the sound of my voice, they both whirled around in obvious astonishment.

"You okay?" Jillian asked, sounding shaken.

"He's always okay," Helene told her, though she looked worriedly at my bloodied body.

"Kid," Jillian said, "you're living proof that luck's better'n skill."

"I get that a lot," I replied.

Across Leithgow Street, more than twenty Corpses now glared at us from the opposite rooftop. A couple tried to jump the gap. Corpses are good jumpers, but not *that* good. They dropped like stones. Unfortunately, a glance over the edge showed me that the hoard below—those not flattened by falling peeps—had decided to pull out all the stops. Deaders tended to be cautious by nature. This whole flash mob thing was totally new for them, so I guess they'd been reluctant to show their whole hand, at least within view of an already confused and curious public.

But our leap had convinced them otherwise.

They started clawing at the wall of our current building. Climbing.

They didn't move like Jillian, of course. No fancy acrobats for these dudes. Instead they just tore their way up, digging dead fingers into the mortar between bricks, breaking windows and tearing off wooden frames as they came.

"They want you *bad*," I said to Jillian.

"I know," she replied with an edge of despair.

Time to go.

"The southwest corner!" I exclaimed. "Now!"

We sprinted across the roof, vaulted over an alleyway between two buildings, climbed from a lower roof to a higher one, and then dropped down onto a lower one again. Jillian moved with perfect grace. She always knew where to put her feet and, while Helene seemed able to follow her steps, I had to struggle to keep up.

Behind us, the dead streamed onto the rooftop, a hideous wave of cadavers half a hundred strong and growing.

Jillian reached the southwest corner first—big surprise—and gasped in fresh horror. As Helene and I joined her, I saw that we were only one story up, atop South Street's famous Johnny Rockets burger place, low enough to maybe reach the ground with a little creative thinking.

Except for the dead.

They choked the sidewalk and, hearing Jillian's gasp, turned their grotesque faces upward. Some attacked the wall, trying to claw their way up to reach us. Others flooded into the restaurant, looking for roof access.

Meanwhile, the mass of Corpses at our backs advanced like a tidal wave.

"We can't get down..." Jillian whispered.

Helene looked at me pleadingly. She was counting on me to have a way out of this. She was counting on me to save the day.

And I was counting on Harvey.

I just hoped I remembered the route map right.

"There's our ride!" I exclaimed, pointing at the long, touring car that was making the turn from South Street onto 5th. It was a roofless stretch Cadillac, obviously custom made, with a place for the driver and seats for a dozen passengers. Despite everything, I couldn't help but wonder how well Harvey's new tourist attraction was doing profits wise; his "Open-Air" city tour car was only half full.

But at least he was punctual.

"You're right," Helene said. "That *is* a bad idea." But she was smiling.

Neither she nor Jillian waited to be told what to do. The open car swung around and slid past the front of Johnny Rockets, its occupants staring with uneasy curiosity at the mob of, to them, normal-looking folks who seemed to be trying to tear down the restaurant. As they did, the driver slowed—just enough.

With a hundred Corpses converging on us, Jillian jumped. Then Helene jumped.

Then I jumped.

And that's how I broke my leg.

CHAPTER 6
THE THIRD HEAD

The creature *thought* it had three heads. After all, three different Selves worked independently within its tortured psyche, and each separate identity had its separate personality, separate goals, separate fears. Given all that chaos, what was it *supposed* to think?

Simple math. Three identities equaled three heads.

And right now, the First was in command

Keeping out of sight, clinging by four of its many claws to the huge, passive face of George Washington, it gazed down at the circular room far below. The creature knew this huge room quite well—at least, its second head did.

The Rotunda.

During the day, there were dozens of people down there: men, women, and children from distant places who gawked at the statues and artwork. Many gazed up at the huge mural, which occupied the very pinnacle of the room's ornate dome.

At such times, however, the creature hid. It knew how important it was not to be seen—at least, not by humans.

Humans are not the enemy.

That was the Second talking. Its second head always defended the humans, perhaps because it had once, itself, *been* human. Whatever the reason, the First was glad its second head was asleep.

Because now it was night, and night was for hunting. Prey approached, the scent of it strong and sweet, and the priority tasks of feeding and—of course—revenge, had taken hold. It was killing time. The Second didn't like killing.

Then, of course, there was the Third.

The third head was always awake, always alert. But, unlike the other two, it was not *part* of the creature, at least not physically. It was—elsewhere. Disconnected. Lost. The creature yearned to find its third head. Doing so, in fact, was its *highest* priority. More important than feeding. More important even than revenge.

But, while the creature could sense its Third, could *feel* it, it didn't know where the missing head was. So, for now, it had to content itself with listening to the third head, hearing it clearly, despite the distance between them.

"Hello, sister," the Third was saying.

"That is not how I'm to be addressed." This was spoken by someone else, someone that the First thought of as the Stranger. Not part of creature at all, but a completely different person—and a menacing one at that. The two speakers, the Third and the Stranger, were talking, but they weren't together. As it listened to them, the First didn't understand how it knew that, but it did.

The two speakers were in the *Szash*.

"I'm sorry, Mistress," the Third said, though it—she— didn't sound sorry at all. "It's sometimes hard to forget that we were once hatchlings together."

"Try harder. I can't be forever reminding you of your place, Lindsay."

The third head sneered. "*I'm* to be addressed as Senator Micha...Mistress."

"I'll address you however I please. The only reason you hold that absurd human title is because I gave it to you."

"But it's mine now, and it suits me. Imagine: the hairless monkeys occupying this world believe they understand the art of politics. But we know differently, don't we? They're all so easy to manipulate."

"Lindsay..."

"I've obeyed you...stayed away from media cameras. But I haven't been idle. I've made connections, whispered the right words into the right human ears. When necessary, I've...dealt with...any potential rivals. I'm ready now."

"Ready for what, exactly?"

"To ascend, sister! To succeed where you have failed."

"Such lofty ambitions. But difficult to realize...when you can't even risk appearing before human cameras."

"True. Which is why I've decided to forego that unnecessary restriction."

"You've decided? You?"

"This is my operation now."

"You're my minion, Lindsay!"

The Third laughed. "I think not. Perhaps I was...perhaps...when you first brought me across the Rift. But now I follow my own path. I no longer recognize your sovereignty. After all, you're nothing but a lowly civil servant in Philadelphia, while I —"

"Are what you've always been! An impertinent sibling with more conceit than intellect!"

"I've no time for your insults. Tell me, sister…have you found the Birmelin girl?"

A pause. "She arrived at 30th Street Station this morning, but eluded us. Later, a large contingent of our people attempted to trap her when she appeared…as expected…on South Street, the site of her former home. Unfortunately, she managed to escape again." Another pause. "We believe she's in the company of the Undertakers now."

"So you've failed."

"Lindsay…I'm warning you."

"Once again, you let that pack of whelps get the better of you."

"Enough!"

"You're quite right. It *is* enough. Unlike you, I refuse to let fear of this 'child army' decide my actions. I *will* appear before cameras at the end of the month to announce my intentions."

The Stranger exclaimed, "You'll jeopardize this entire operation!"

"Surely Birmelin has already told the Undertakers everything. What difference does it make now?"

"It's more than that … and you know it!"

The Third said, "I don't care how many other so-called Seers might be out there, I won't be ruled by trifles. Nor by *you*. Not anymore."

"You'll pay for this, Lindsay!"

"This conversation is over. Good-bye, sister."

"No! Wait!" The Stranger paused yet again. "There's something you need to know."

"And what would that be?"

"She's *devolved.*"

Now it was the Third who paused. "What did you say?"

"Last night, about the same time Jillian Birmelin fled Washington, DC, the source creature apparently metamorphosed."

"That's impossible! It's too soon!"

"Perhaps she's stronger than you anticipated. In any event, she consumed every minion guarding her. Six of them. Do you still wish to appear before cameras?"

"I … of course! I'm not afraid of that abomination!" But the First could sense the lie.

So, it seemed, could the Stranger. "No? How courageous of you. Still, perhaps you should inform your underlings of the risk. Surely their loyalty is such that they'll throw down their existences for you when the time comes. That might buy you a few precious minutes."

"I will order them to hunt it down. Recapture it."

"Recapture! Not kill? It would be safer to simply end its life."

"And end this operation with it?" the Third sneered. "No, sister. Lindsay Micha must continue, and so the abomination must continue. But … I insist you send more minions to help in the search!"

"*You* insist?"

A final pause, proud but fearful. "Please."

"I'll consider it, Lindsay. In the meantime, I believe the human cliché would be: 'Sleep well.' But, as our people don't sleep, I'll replace that with one of our own: 'Enjoy your terror.'"

"Sister …"

"Now this conversation is over."

The *Szash* was broken. The Third grew quiet.

The First thought, *I'm going to find you.* But the third

head did not react. She could not hear the others. She did not know.

Then a noise intruded, footsteps far below. Nothing to be seen yet, but the scent told all. Prey had arrived, and it wasn't alone. There was another with it. A human.

That complicated things.

The creature went still—waiting.

Two figures, both dressed in black police uniforms, emerged from the northern entrance of the Rotunda, their shoes tapping across the tile floor. Each was male. One was alive, human.

The other wasn't.

The other was *food*.

The two were speaking to one another. While the First could hear the words, it paid them no mind. Instead, it waited until the prey's path took him directly below.

Then the creature dropped from its great height, falling upon its quarry. The human was knocked aside, firmly but not unkindly. He crashed to the Rotunda floor, his eyes wide with shock and disbelief.

The prey *screamed* as the First opened its jaws.

And, as it fed, the creature was grateful that its second head remained asleep.

The Second always made such a fuss at feeding time.

CHAPTER 7
THE MOM MISSION

Helene

Helene Boettcher thought, Now *I'm gonna hear it*.

While Chuck Binelli and Jillian unloaded Will's gurney from the back of the "ambulance," Tom took Helene aside. Around them, the lowest level of this Center City underground parking garage stood silent and empty. Leading her out of earshot from the rest, he leaned close, his six-foot-plus frame towering over her.

This wasn't intimidation. The chief didn't intimidate. He just didn't want the others to hear their conversation.

"We gotta get Will to the infirmary," he said. "That means you got two minutes. Start talking."

So Helene started talking. She told him about the sneaking out to the comic book store, about Will following her there, about the Corpse march, about Jillian, the rooftops, and even about the money the Undertakers now owed Doug for the lost skateboards.

The Chief listened without comment until she'd finished. Then he nodded and said, "Okay. We'll talk 'bout you breakin' the Rules 'n Regs later. For now, I'm just glad you got Will and Jillian outta there safe."

"*Will* got us out," Helene said, glancing at the van. Will's limp form was strapped to a gurney, while Chuck was giving Jillian instructions for lowering it. Seeing the redheaded boy lying there—pale and unconscious — stabbed at her, inspiring feelings that she didn't want to deal with right now.

So instead she focused on Jillian.

Helene liked the new girl, who'd somehow wrapped her head around her scary new reality faster than anyone Helene had ever met. The hints they'd gotten that Jillian somehow knew Tom had been confirmed the moment the chief had ridden to their rescue. He'd taken one look at their newest Seer and an expression had hit his face unlike anything Helene had ever seen. Well, that wasn't quite true, was it? Dave Burger sometimes wore it when he looked at Sharyn, but only if he thought no one was watching.

For now, she pushed aside her curiosity. She'd find out what it all meant soon enough.

Secrets, as she'd learned this morning, didn't last long in Haven.

Tom offered up a thin smile. "So Will steps in it and, once again, his shoe smells like roses."

Except for his broken leg, Helene thought.

She replied, "It's his mutant power."

"Straight up."

"Gurney's down, Chief!" Chuck yelled from behind the van.

"Hold up a sec," Tom told him. Then his manner turned serious. "Helene, do something for me."

"Sure."

"I want you to stay mostly in Haven for a while."

"Oh," she said, her heart sinking. She'd figured on *some* kind of punishment. Looked like it'd be a good old-fashioned grounding. *Beats scrubbing the Porta-Pottys,* she supposed. "But what about Sundays? They're my night for making the funeral run with Dave."

"You can stay on that rotation," he said. "This ain't a punishment. I ... want you to stick close to Will's mom."

Helene blinked. "Huh?"

"'Case you ain't noticed ... she's not handlin' living with us all that well."

It was true. Since Susan Ritter and her daughter, Emily, had taken sanctuary with the Undertakers, having Will's mother around had become a mixed bag. She was nice enough, on the surface. But underneath, you could read the resentment and, sometimes, downright *disgust* in her eyes. She hated Haven, hated the whole notion of children running their own lives without what she called "adult supervision."

And she hated Helene.

This became clear every time the woman and girl found themselves in the same place at the same time. Helene would catch Mrs. Ritter staring at her—maybe glaring was a better word—and she could almost hear her thoughts: "You stole my son."

Of course, it hadn't gone down like that, and Helene often considered saying so. But she didn't, for a bunch of reasons. One: this was Will's mom, which was intimidating enough all by itself. Two: getting between Will and his mother seemed like a seriously stupid idea. Three: Susan Ritter was a grown-up.

And grown-ups didn't listen. *Ever.*

"What do you mean by 'stick close to her'?" she asked the chief.

"Hang around her. Try talking to her. See if you can get her to open up."

The very idea knotted Helene's guts. "She hates me, Tom."

"She don't hate you," the Chief replied. "She's just scared and angry and confused. But she's also *here* and we gotta live with her. So I'm askin' you to do this."

She studied him, but his face remained unreadable. He'd been like that all of the time she'd known him. Nobody ever got anything from Tom that he didn't want you to have. Helene, on the other hand, wore every emotion like a neon sign. It was one of the million things she didn't like about herself.

"Why me?" she moaned.

"I got my reasons," he said cryptically.

Helene swallowed. "Okay. Fine. I'll do it."

"Thanks," he said. "Now come on. We gotta get Will to the infirmary 'fore the stuff I gave him wears off ... and somethin' tells me Ian's newest 'assistant' ain't gonna be too happy to see us."

That was the chief: a master of the understatement.

The infirmary was the biggest room in Haven. Like the rest of this forgotten sub-basement deep below Philly's gargantuan City Hall, its walls were crumbling brick and its floor hard-packed dirt. The makeshift hospital consisted of a half-dozen beds, two lab tables loaded with used equipment, and one medic.

Ian McDonald, whose father was a big-shot Philly surgeon, was fifteen and as serious a dude as Helene had ever met. She'd seen him handle everything from setting broken bones to major surgery and, as far as she was concerned, the Undertakers couldn't have asked for a better doctor.

Of course, not everybody felt that way.

As they rolled Will's gurney through the infirmary entrance, there were already three people there: Ian and two girls.

Well, one girl and one woman.

The girl was Amy Filewicz, a small, quiet twelve-year-old who'd come to Haven by a harder road than most, having been brainwashed by the Corpses into betraying and then killing an Undertaker. Later on, Will had rescued her. Since then, Ian had taken Amy under his wing, making her his assistant.

While half of the Undertakers still didn't completely trust the wounded girl, she seemed to have found a welcome place at the medic's side.

The woman, however, was a different story.

At the sight of the gurney, Susan Ritter rushed over, her blond hair framing her head in curls. Seeing Will's unconscious form, she exclaimed, "What happened?"

Tom met her halfway. "He's okay, Mrs. Ritter. He broke his leg in a … fall. But we were able to get him out of there safe."

Impatiently, Will's mother sidestepped the chief and hurried to her son's side. What she saw there made her face go pale. Will's eyes remained closed and his face shone with sweat. Both his arms were bandaged, though blood had already leaked through the white field dressings.

As Helene watched, Susan Ritter snapped into nurse mode, feeling her son's cheeks and neck with steady hands. "His skin's clammy," she reported. "His pulse is slow but steady. But his arms!" She glared at Tom. "This is more than a broken leg!"

"Looks worse than it is," the chief replied. "Seems he jumped through a window." Then, before Mrs. Ritter could respond to that, Ian appeared beside her. Without a word, the medic peeled back both of Will's eyelids and flashed a penlight into them.

"Sedated," he said at last.

Mrs. Ritter's glare turned to daggers. "He's been *drugged?*"

"He was in a lot of pain," Tom explained. "I gave him morphine."

"Morphine!" The woman blanched. "You gave my son morphine?"

Remembering her new mission, Helene stepped up and tentatively touched her arm. "Um … it's okay …"

But Will's mom shook her off, her eyes still locked on the chief. "What right do you have to give *anyone* morphine?"

Tom said nothing.

Ian checked Will's vitals. "How much?" he asked.

"One Syrette," the Chief replied. "Had to do something. We needed to splint his leg and get him ready for transport."

"You shouldn't have done it!" Will's mother exclaimed.

Tom regarded her. "What *should* I have done, Mrs. Ritter?"

Helene watched the woman struggle for a response. She probably wanted to scream: "Call an ambulance!" But, of course, that hadn't been possible. Undertakers died in hospitals. The Corpses saw to that.

Looking defeated, she asked, "How did it happen?"

Tom nodded to Helene, who told the story again. All the while, she didn't look at either Tom or Mrs. Ritter, but instead kept her eyes fixed on Will—though, if asked, she couldn't have said why.

"You all *jumped*," his mother exclaimed when Helene had finished, "from the roof of a restaurant into a passing car?"

"It was Will's idea," Jillian answered.

She whirled on the new girl. "Are you saying this is my son's fault?"

"No," Jillian replied. "I'm saying your son saved our lives."

Mrs. Ritter's mouth opened. Then it closed again.

"Tell 'em the rest," Tom said.

So Helene did. "Will didn't stick the landing too good, but he got up and went straight to the driver, who was all ready to stop the car and call the cops ..."

"I don't blame him," his mother muttered.

"... and then Will Tased him."

"He *what?*"

"Had to," Jillian offered. "The streets were filled with those ... things. If the car had stopped, even for a few seconds, they'd have swamped us."

Helene nodded. "And they tried anyway, closing in

from all sides, but Will pulled the guy out of his seat, climbed behind the wheel, and gunned it. Almost knocked Jillian and me off of our feet. The passengers started screaming. Good thing there wasn't much traffic, because he ran two red lights before we'd left the deaders far enough behind to give us some breathing room."

Mrs. Ritter asked, "When did he break his leg?"

"In the jump," Jillian replied. "But we didn't know that … until later."

Will's mother pulled back the blanket. Will's jeans had been cut away and his left leg splinted. But the limb looked swollen and bruised. Ugly.

She gasped. "Are you saying he assaulted the driver and drove a car … with *this* leg?"

Helene and Jillian both nodded.

"That sounds like our William the Conqueror," Ian remarked. "Adrenaline, probably."

Helene knew what he meant. In tight spots, the human body produced a hormone called adrenaline. It juiced you up, sometimes letting you ignore pain or giving you tremendous strength. These superhuman abilities didn't last long—sometimes just long enough to save a life.

Or, in this case, three.

Will. You can be such an amazing idiot!

"Ian," Tom said. "Where's the crystal?"

"Steve's got it in the Brain Factory," the boy medic replied, referring to that special chamber in Haven where Steve and his team of science geeks worked their magic "He's been running experiments. I'll ask Amy to fetch it back."

"Thanks," Tom said. "He's gonna be fine, Mrs. Ritter."

"Fine? He needs an X-ray! There could be multiple

fractures, a nicked artery, internal bleeding!"

"It won't matter," Ian said. "Not once we use the crystal on him."

The crystal. Just picturing that bizarre alien artifact made Helene's skin crawl.

Mrs. Ritter said, "I don't know if I want you using that … thing … on my son!"

Helene knew how she felt.

But before anyone could reply to that, Sharyn Jefferson, Tom's twin sister, appeared in the doorway. She looked down at Will and then at each of them in turn. When she spotted Jillian, her expression morphed from concern to anger.

"What's *she* doing here?" Sharyn demanded.

CHAPTER 8
THE ANCHOR SHARD

"William."

Even before I opened my eyes, I knew what I'd see: a white, featureless room and a beautiful blond woman—younger than my mother, but somehow familiar.

One of these days, I'm gonna figure out who you are.

"Hi," I said.

She smiled. She had a sweet, sad smile.

"Guess you're gonna heal me again," I said. Every time I'd come here, it was because I'd been hurt. The *last* time I'd been shot in the back, so I supposed a broken leg wouldn't be too big a deal.

"No need. The Anchor Shard will take care of that."

I blinked. "Anchor Shard?"

Her smile withered. Her cheeks flushed. God, she looked familiar! *"That … was a mistake. I mean the crystal of course, the one you took from that Corpse at Eastern State Penitentiary."*

The crystal, sure.

It had some kind of weird power, totally alien. It had once healed Sharyn. But the idea of somebody using it on *me* sent a serious chill down my spine.

But this was the first time I'd ever heard it called the Anchor Shard.

"So … if I'm not here to get fixed up, why *am* I here?"

"Sharyn's going to Washington"

"Huh?"

"You'll find out what that means very soon."

"Okay."

"And it's vital that you go with her."

"Me? Washington?"

She nodded.

"Why?"

The smile returned. Knowing. Familiar. *"I can't tell you that."*

It was an old song between us. Any info revealed to me during one of these—meetings? sessions?—was always sketchy. Mostly hints.

"Who *are* you?" I demanded. "'Cause all this 'magic angel' stuff is getting old."

"Magic angel?" She laughed out loud. Then she caught herself. *"I'm sorry, William. Someday, I'll tell you everything. I promise. But right now that wouldn't help anybody. Just make sure you go to Washington, DC with Sharyn. Nobody else. Just you. Do you understand?"*

"Yeah." Then, after a pause, I asked, "Do I get a question?" Always before, I'd been allowed one question. Only one. So I needed to think carefully before I asked.

"I'm afraid not."

"Why not?"

But instead of an answer, all I got was a flash of white light so bright that I had to squeeze my eyes shut.

When I opened them again, the white room was gone, as I knew it would be. It's funny the things you can get used to.

I was in the infirmary with a lot of people standing around me. My leg—the leg I'd landed on when I'd jumped into the car, the leg I'd heard snap like a dry twig, the leg that had been on *fire* until Tom had shown up and stuck some kind of needle in the crook of my elbow—was …

… *warm.*

"You awake?" Ian asked.

"Uh-huh."

"Does your leg … feel better?" he asked.

"Uh-huh."

I noticed the crystal he held. "Did you put that *thing* on me?"

"Uh-huh."

My mother appeared, her warm hands cupping my face. "Sweetheart? Can you hear me?"

I squirmed. "I hear you, Mom."

"Oh, thank God!"

"Can I, um, sit up?"

"Of course," she said, stepping back. I pushed myself up into a sitting position. I was on a hospital gurney—not the first time.

Chuck was here, dressed like an ambulance driver. Amy stood alongside Ian. As usual, she wore a shy smile. Then I turned my head and spotted Helene.

"You and Jillian okay?" I asked.

She nodded, offering me a funny kind of grin. "Your bad idea saved us."

Her expression made my stomach flutter, so I turned to Chuck. "Sweet uniform!"

"Thanks," he said. "We did a Number 31."

A Number 31 was one of our newest moves, inspired by stuff that had gone down a few months ago when, while trying to split a Corpse battle scene with two injured casualties before the cops showed up, Helene and I had called an ambulance and then stolen it.

At the time, we'd been amazed by how easy it was to navigate city traffic when you had flashing lights and a siren.

Since then, Tom had arranged for the Monkeys, the Undertakers crew responsible for construction and maintenance, to turn one of our plain white vans *into* an ambulance. The final result looked great: working lights, siren, even the word *ECNALUBMA* stenciled onto the front of it, above the windshield, so that it read the right way through a rearview mirror.

Since then, whenever we needed to evacuate an injured Undertaker quickly, we used our "ambulance"—and called the operation a Number 31.

"Want to tell me about it?" I asked Chuck.

"Well … you weren't kidding when you told Dan every deader in the world was after you. When Tom and I got to South Street, there had to be a thousand of them!"

"I know. Wait … Tom came?"

He nodded. "Insisted. Didn't say why."

"Okay. …" It was rare for the chief to go out on missions. "Go on."

"We got to 6th Street in time to see you gunning that

big car down 5th and out of their reach. It wasn't easy keeping up. But once you'd cleared the deader mob, we turned and met you at the next corner."

The last thing I remembered was driving, my broken leg screaming the whole time.

Then—nothing.

"I passed out," I said, feeling a flush of embarrassment.

Chuck nodded. "You kept cool until you'd gotten everyone outta danger. Then you dropped like a stone. Good thing we were right there. While Tom calmed everybody down … the passengers were freaking out … I set the leg and bandaged your arms. Then Tom gave you morphine for the pain."

I glanced at my mom, who glowered at Chuck, clearly pissed.

Chuck said, "Then we got you all outta there before the cops showed! Man, those deaders wanted you *bad*!"

I said, "It was Jillian they were after."

They all swapped looks. "All that," Chuck said, "for *one* Seer?"

Helene and I nodded.

He whistled.

"Nice work," I told him. "You saved our butts!"

He shrugged. "You saved your own butts. We just did the cleanup."

"Where's Tom?"

Helene replied, "He was here until Sharyn showed up. Then the two of them split with Jillian back to Tom's office. He said you should join them when you're up to it."

"I'm up to it," I announced.

"No!" Mom snapped. "You should rest. You —"

"I'm fine," I told her. "I need to talk to the chief."

Then I swung my legs over the side of the ambulance gurney.

That's when I discovered I had no pants on.

CHAPTER 9
REUNION

Ever dream that you're giving a report in class, only to discover you're in your underwear? Remember that sense of wanting to crawl into a hole and die?

Well, you'd think after six months of battling an invasion of the living dead I'd be past that kind of embarrassment. I mean, *so what* if I now found myself in front of Chuck, Ian, Amy, Helene and my mother in just my tighty-whities?

Right?

So why did I want to crawl into a hole and die?

I made a grab for the thin, gray ambulance blanket that, until a second ago, had been covering me. But in my panic, all I managed to do was slide it to the floor.

Amy giggled a little. The rest of them shifted uncomfortably.

Ian cleared his throat. "Chuck and Tom had to cut 'em off ... to splint your leg."

Too bad the wonders of the Anchor Shard don't include replacing lost clothing.

My mother retrieved the blanket and fussily draped it over my lap. Again, I squirmed, snapping, "I got it, Mom!"

She stepped back, looking a little hurt. A long, awkward silence followed.

Then Chuck, helpful as always, remarked, "Um … dude, you're gonna need some pants."

More silence.

Helene said, "I'll get Dave to fetch some."

So where, you ask, do Undertakers get their clothes?

We have a crew called the Moms that does the cooking and the cleaning. They also buy all the clothing, mail ordering it to a post office box. Undertakers don't generally leave Haven, except on missions—too dangerous. So hitting the local Gap isn't usually an option. As such, our wardrobe choices are limited to jeans and hoodies, shorts and T-shirts. Not much in the way of personal fashion statements in Haven.

But it *does* mean that we've all got plenty of pants.

Six *long* minutes later, Helene returned with a huge kid in tow, one whose scowling face was half hidden beneath a mop of blond hair. Dave "the Burgermeister" Burger, my roommate and best friend, carried a pair of faded blue jeans in his ridiculously big hands. He looked tired—really tired.

Suddenly my humiliation was sprinkled with guilt.

Dave had been spending his nights working a very special gig. Because of it, he did his sleeping in the daytime, which meant that Helene must've woken him up looking for pants that I could wear.

And, Dave being Dave, had insisted on delivering them himself.

"Here ya go, dude," he said sleepily, handing me the

jeans. Then looking at everyone, he growled, "You guys got your tickets for this show? No? Then *turn around!* Oh! Sorry, Mrs. Ritter. ..."

"That's okay, Dave," my mom said, smiling. She liked the Burgermeister. Once you got to know him, it was hard not to.

So, fully dressed at last, I sent a grateful Dave back to bed and headed off toward Tom's office. Helene and my mother followed. As we navigated Haven's cramped, crumbling corridors, Helene asked me what the big rush was.

"Everything's cool," was my only answer.

I figured explaining it once would be enough.

In Tom's office, we found the chief, Sharyn, and Jillian sitting around Tom's small conference table. Their heated debate stopped when the three of us appeared.

"Hey, Red," Sharyn remarked, using the nickname she always forgot I hated. "Heard 'bout the leg; that's what you get for steppin' on the Rules n Regs." But her smile seemed strained, and she kept glancing sideways at Jillian, who'd ditched the blue blazer in favor of the Haven "standard": jeans and a hoodie.

"If he hadn't," Tom said, "Jillian wouldn't be here."

"Yeah," his sister agreed dryly. "*Here.* Not at First Stop. How do we know she ain't a mole?"

Jillian asked, "What's a mole?"

"Ain't that just what a mole would ask?" Sharyn pointed out.

"Amy checked her out back in the infirmary," Tom said. "You were there."

But his sister shook her head. "The Scar Test ain't proven in all cases. That's why we still *have* First Stop."

"What scar?" Jillian demanded.

First Stop is a kind of secret boot camp that we keep elsewhere in the city. Its "official" use is for the training of new recruits, but its real purpose is to watch for moles, Seers who get brainwashed by the Corpses using these alien, spiderlike things called *pelligog*. Ian and Amy recently found out that the *pelligog* leave a check-shaped scar when they bore into a person's lower back.

I don't have that scar, though I came close once. But Amy has it.

And so does Helene.

"It was my call—as chief—to bring her straight here," Tom said.

Sharyn groaned. "Bringin' *her* here's got nothing to do with bein' chief an' you know it!"

"Enough!" Tom snapped, one of the few times I'd heard him raise his voice in anger.

"Tom. ..." Jillian said.

Sharyn stood up so abruptly that her chair fell over. She fixed her brother with a look that, if she'd had snakes in her hair, would have turned him to stone. Then she marched around the table, pushed past us, and disappeared through the curtain.

The chief tried hard not to show how pissed he was. "Glad you're up and about, bro," he said.

"Hi, Will," Jillian added with an awkward wave.

"Hi, Jillian," I replied.

Tom offered us chairs. "When y'all came in, I was afraid we wouldn't have enough seats. But now ..." His words trailed off.

We all sat. Helene and Mom took the two remaining empty seats, while I had to pick up Sharyn's toppled chair.

"What's she so angry about?" my mother asked.

It was Jillian who replied. "Sharyn ... doesn't like me. She never did."

Never did?

"I used to live with Tom and Sharyn," the girl continued. "A long time ago ... in a foster home. That's why I was on South Street. Our old dojo used to be there."

"Dojo?" Helene asked.

The chief explained, "The second-to-last foster home Sharyn and I had was run by a dude named Terrill Perkins."

"Mr. P. That's what we called him," Jillian added.

Tom nodded. "He ran a school that taught martial arts, Parisi and *parkour.*"

"Parisi?" I asked.

"Speed school," Jillian explained. "I was already one of Mr. P's foster kids when Tom and Sharyn showed up."

"It was our eighth or ninth gig in the system," said Tom, "and far and away the coolest of them. Mr. P. was a widower. His wife died long before we knew him, and he'd opened his dojo to kind of help him through the grief. At least, that's the way he told it to me."

Jillian nodded. "Mr. P was a former Navy SEAL. He had some wicked skills."

"Yeah, he did," said the chief. "Pretty much all of his foster kids ended up participating. At first, he made us try all three disciplines: fighting, speed, and agility. Then, after a while, we could pick the discipline we liked best. But you *had* to pick something. No TV or videogame junkies in Mr. P's dojo. So Sharyn and I picked fighting."

"By then, I was already heavy into *parkour,*" the girl remarked.

Helene exclaimed, "So *that's* where you and Sharyn leaned to fight! The skills you've been passing down to us ... they're from Mr. P!"

Tom nodded. "He'd invented a new kind of mixed martial arts. 'Street karate,' he called it. Practical fighting. No fancy moves. Just speed, precision, and economy of motion."

"Tom's the best mixed martial arts student Mr. P ever had!" said Jillian.

"My sister was pretty good, too," he added.

"Yeah. But ... Sharyn and I never got along."

"Why not?" my mother asked.

Tom replied, "It's ... complicated."

"Anyway," Jillian continued. "About eighteen months after Tom and his sister moved in, Mr. P's foster home was shut down by the state."

"Why?" I asked.

"Mr. P had ... issues," Tom said.

But Jillian was less cagey. "He drank too much. Kind of what you'd call a 'functional alcoholic.'"

"We covered for him," the chief explained. "But eventually, a social worker showed up at the wrong time and wham ... the next thing we know they pull his foster license and every kid under his roof gets 'reassigned.'"

Jillian swallowed. "It was the saddest day of my life. I'd lived in that dojo for more than five years. It's the closest thing to a home I ever knew."

"Us, too," Tom said. "Before Haven. Anyway, Sharyn and I quit the system a couple of months later, splitting our new foster home and hitting the streets."

"What about you, Jillian?" my mother asked.

The girl replied, "I had a cousin down in DC who'd

just turned twenty-one and offered to take me in. I didn't want to go, but the system didn't ask my opinion. Actually, it's worked out okay. I've been living with Julia ever since. She's pretty cool, but she's no Mr. P."

"What happened to Mr. P?" I asked. From their shared expression, I wished I hadn't.

"He ... died," said Tom. "About the time I met your dad. Alcohol poisoning. Drank himself to death."

"I never knew about that," Jillian added miserably. "Tom just told me."

"I'm so sorry," my mom said.

Helene and I all agreed.

Then Tom did a funny thing: he took Jillian's hand. When he did, she gazed at him—that's the word for it: "gazed."

I thought maybe I understood the bug up Sharyn's butt.

Then the moment passed and the chief turned all business. "Thing is, though ... none of that's why Jillian's in Philly."

Helene added, "Or why, when she got here, every Corpse in town was on her heels."

Jillian said, "They're after me because of what I know."

"And what do you know?" I asked.

She replied without hesitation, "I know that US Senator Lindsay Micha from New Jersey ... is a Corpse."

CHAPTER 10
JILLIAN'S STORY

"That's impossible!" I exclaimed.

And it was. I wasn't big on politics; I mean, what kid *is*? But I'd had to be living in a cave not to know about Senator Lindsay Micha. She was a really big deal in the nation's capital, one of those people who shows up on the covers of magazines—who guests on *The Colbert Report* and gets more laughs than the host.

She'd also been in the US Senate since before I was born, which was where "impossible" came into it.

"I *saw* her," Jillian insisted.

Helene shook her head. "She's been on TV a million times. If she was a deader, we'd know."

"So Tom tells me," the girl said. "The thing is, Micha's gone dark these last couple of months. No interviews. No public appearances. It's caused a lot of rumors on the Hill: Why has Senator Micha fallen off the media grid?"

"The Hill?" I asked.

"Capitol Hill," she replied. "It's a nickname that the politicos use."

"Politicos?" I asked.

"Politicians and the people who report on them are called 'politicos.'"

"How do you know all of this?" my mother asked.

Jillian said, "Until yesterday, I was a Senate page."

"What's that?" Helene asked.

It was Tom who answered, "A federal program. High school kids apply for gigs working as gophers for the senators. That about right?"

"More or less," Jillian replied. "There's thirty of us and, for one semester, we all live together and work in the Senate … running errands, delivering messages, that kind of thing."

"So the blue suit's … a uniform," I guessed.

She nodded. "I worked hard to get it … only to end up ruining it on a Philly rooftop."

I almost said, "I'm sorry," but then couldn't quite decide what I was sorry *about*.

"Why don't you start at the beginning?" Tom suggested.

Jillian began. "I've … I'd … been a page since January. You have to be recommended by a sitting senator. Grades, extracurricular stuff … they take all of that into account. After all, they pick just thirty kids nationwide. That's not even one per senator … more like one for every three senators." She smiled proudly. "But I got in.

"Pages work mostly in the Capitol, but we often get sent to one of the Senate office buildings on deliveries. There are two of those: Hart and Dirksen. Senator Micha's offices are in Hart.

"But I never got sent there when Micha was around. None of the pages did. Since the start of the term, we were told that Senator Micha had specifically asked *not* to be visited by pages. Nobody understood why. But Lindsay Micha was Lindsay Micha ... so we did as we were told."

"Then how *did* you manage to see her?" Helene asked.

"I had this ... friend in the program. Kevin Pearl from Nebraska. He just wouldn't buy the Senator Micha 'ban.' Kept talking about conspiracies. Kept boasting he was going to find out the truth.

"So last week, while making a delivery to Dirksen, he detoured into Hart and visited Micha's office. That's as much as I know ... because he didn't come back.

"At first, the only thing anyone would tell us was that he'd disappeared and that Capitol Police were searching for him. Then three days ago ... they found his body in the Potomac River. An apparent suicide. There was even a note, though I never saw it."

She hung her head.

"That sucks," Helene whispered.

"I'm sorry, Jill," Tom said.

I looked at my mother, whose expression twisted with grief. She reached over and squeezed the girl's hand.

My mom knows what it is to lose someone you care about.

Jillian steadied herself. "I decided to find out what had happened to Kevin. Even though the senator wasn't showing her face, her staff members *were* ... at least some of them. So I hung around them. One of the advantages of being a page is that you're *invisible* to these people. As long as you're wearing the uniform, they don't notice you ... until they need something.

"Well yesterday, one of the staffers, a woman named Moira, spilled coffee on herself in the Dirksen cafeteria. So

I offered to get her jacket cleaned, and she jumped at the favor.

"On my way out though, I ducked into a restroom and searched the pockets. Sure enough, I found Moira's ID badge. Then I took the jacket to the dry cleaners. Later, when Moira asked me about the badge, I played dumb, and she figured the cleaners would find it. So I knew I'd better do whatever I was going to do *fast* … before Security canceled the badge's access.

"At the end of that workday, instead of going with the pages to Webster Hall, where they bunk us, I went to Hart and snuck into Micha's suite using Moira's ID. Then I hid in a closet in the senator's private office. I was ready to wait all night, though I knew I'd catch all kinds of crap from Lex … he's a proctor in the page program. Chances were I'd get kicked out and be sent home. But if I managed to find out the truth about Kevin, I figured it was worth it."

This girl thinks like an Undertaker.

Jillian said, "Anyway, I was dozing in the back of the closet about three hours later when the office door opened and the lights came on. There were voices: Lindsay Micha and one of her staffers.

"They were talking about somebody named Cavanaugh. The staffer sounded worried about this person, afraid that … how'd he put it? … 'The Mistress won't be pleased.' But Micha just kind of dismissed it.

"Then she started talking about Kevin.

"First, she complimented her staffer on 'taking care' of the situation, forcing Kevin to write the suicide note before drowning him. She laughed about it—actually

laughed. I wanted to burst out of that closet and do …
something. But I stayed put.

"The staffer warned that Cavanaugh wasn't happy
about the situation. But Micha told him, 'I'm here and
she's in Philadelphia.' Then she said, 'Besides, she has
Tom Jefferson and the Undertakers to worry about. And I
think it's time for Senator Micha to stop living in fear and
show her face to the world again.' Or something like that."

"She mentioned me?" Tom said wryly. "I'm flattered."

Jillian shrugged. "I'd already heard of the Undertakers.
Some kind of underground youth group here in Philly.
Some folks call you a street gang. Others say it's more like
a Merry Men/Sherwood Forest thing."

"That'd make you Robin Hood, Chief!" Helene
quipped.

Tom gave her a hard look, but the corners of his
mouth twitched.

Jillian went on, "Then I did something that, looking
back, wasn't so smart. I peeked. I'm not even sure why. I
just wanted to … I don't know … see the woman who'd
order Kevin's murder. I can't explain it."

"I get it," I said. "I really do."

Helene added, "Lemme guess what you saw when you
cracked the door."

The girl stiffened. "There were … *dead!* Both of them!
The staffer was *seriously* dead, just gray skin and old bones
inside a fancy suit."

"A Type Four or Five," Tom surmised. "And Micha?"

"She was fresher, kind of … *sticky.* Her hair had mostly
fallen out and her eyes had sunken in. But she still had
lipstick on. I swear, I think that was the part that freaked

me out the most … that something that looked so horrible would bother with …" Her voice trailed off.

"I call it the Holy Crap Factor," I said.

She nodded. "A good name for it. Anyway, I freaked out and screamed. Then, knowing I'd been blown, I jumped out of the closet and bolted before either of them could react. Micha yelled for her staffer to stop me. And he tried. But I'm not that easy to catch."

"No, you're not." Helene grinned.

"So you came to Philly," Tom surmised, "with just the clothes on your back."

Jillian nodded. "I headed straight to South Street, hoping to find Mr. P.'s dojo. But it's gone now. Then those … things found me."

"Well, you're safe here," I told her.

"I know," the girl replied. "But Micha's still *there*. She's one of those Corpses you talk about … and she's planning something. I don't know what … but *something*."

The chief said, "And we need to find out."

I cleared my throat. "Um … actually *Sharyn* needs to find out." Then, when they all looked at me like I'd sprouted horns, I added, "And I have to go with her."

CHAPTER 11
EMILY

A half hour after dropping that bombshell in Tom's office, I escorted Jillian to the Moms so that the crew boss, Nick Rooney, could set her up with a bed. Afterward, I found myself wandering the corridors of Haven. My mother had stayed behind at the meeting to "discuss something" with the chief and, sooner or later, I figured she'd be "discussing" it with *me*, too.

I somehow ended up outside the Shrine.

Well, it *used* to be the Shrine—to my dad. These days my mother shared it with my little sister.

Where my mom had received kind of a mixed reception when she'd moved into Haven, Emily, my six-year-old little sister, had been welcomed with open arms. Officially, Tom had assigned her care—when our mother wasn't around, of course—to the Moms. But these days, there seemed to be a waiting list of babysitters.

Yeah, I know that sounds a little crazy. Since when do teenagers *want* to spend time with Kindergarteners? I admit I was stumped for a while, too, until Helene explained it.

"All of a sudden your family is *here*, Will," she told me. "But the rest of Haven's not so lucky. A bunch of us have sibs at home who used to drive us nuts, but who we'd now give our left arms to see again. Hanging out with Emily reminds us of them."

And it was true, I thought as I parted the Shrine's ragged curtain, but it wasn't the whole story.

Harleen Patel and Emily were playing Chutes and Ladders, the two of them sprawled across my mom's cot. My sister's tiny face was screwed up in concentration as she took her turn.

Across from her, however, Harleen wore a smile as wide as the world.

Innocence, I thought.

Harleen and I had been recruits together. But where I'd become an Angel, she'd stayed a Mom and seemed content with chores that kept her as far away from deaders as an Undertaker could get.

This was the first time I'd ever seen real joy on her face.

"Hi," I said.

They both looked up. Harleen's smile faltered.

"Will!" Emily yelled, jumping up and running to me. She threw her arms around my legs, almost making me stumble. "I missed you!"

"You just saw me yesterday!" I laughed.

She peered up at me with our mother's eyes and said, very seriously, "But every time you go away, I don't know if you'll come back."

I didn't have an answer to that one.

"Well ... I'm here now," I stammered, scooping her up. "Hi, Harleen."

"Hi, Will," the babysitter replied. Her smile was gone now. "I was supposed to be here another twenty minutes."

"Harleen's been playing with me!" Emily chirped. "And before that it was Maria! And before that it was the Burgermaker."

"The Burgermeister!" I laughed. "Seriously?"

She nodded. "He gave me a piggyback ride up and down all the halls."

I grinned. "Sounds like fun."

"It was!" Then her expression turned serious. "I wanted to find you, but the Burgermaker said you'd gone out."

"I did."

"To fight the bad people?"

Harleen, looking unhappy, put the game away. I felt a stab of guilt; I'd muscled in on her time.

To my sister, I said, "Um … I guess so."

"That scares Mommy," Emily told me. An accusation.

"I know it does," I muttered.

"Mommy told Tom she doesn't want him to send you out to fight the bad people anymore."

I'll bet she doesn't.

"Tom didn't send me this time," I said. "I went on my own."

Her little face crumpled. "You're gonna go away forever, aren't you?" Another accusation, more fearful this time. "Like Daddy did. Like *you* did before."

What was I supposed to do? Promise her that I would always come back from every mission, no matter how dangerous? Or should I try to explain to her that I was a soldier, like our father before us, and that in war sometimes—often—soldiers didn't make it back?

I looked into my sister's heart-shaped face and searched for something clever and wise to say. Nothing came.

Instead, Harleen stood up and spoke. "Emily?"

The little girl twisted around in my arms to face her.

"Did I ever tell you how I met your brother?"

Emily shook her head.

"He and I were in kind of a class together ... a training class. It's where we learned all about the Corp ... the bad people."

"Corpses," my sister told her. "I know what they're called."

Harleen nodded. "That's right. You're very smart. Well, one night at this training class, the Corpses came and tried to get us. But your brother took charge and got us all out of there and kept the monsters away until help showed up."

"He did?"

"Harleen ..." I stammered, "don't ..."

But she ignored me. "Yes, he did. At one point, he even offered to give himself to the Corpses so the rest of us could get away. It was, and *is*, the bravest thing I've ever seen anyone do." She stroked my sister's hair. "Your brother's a hero."

"No, I'm *not*!" I yelped. "Stop it!"

But again, she ignored me. "In fact, he's the best kind of hero there is, because he doesn't really *get* that he's a hero."

Emily stared at her, wide-eyed. Then she looked at me.

"So, instead of worrying about him," Harleen said. "Maybe you should be proud of him. *We* all are."

My sister hugged me fiercely, more fiercely than she

had that day two months ago when I'd rescued her from her Corpse kidnappers. I looked at Harleen, and saw that her eyes were moist.

Lamely, I murmured, "Thanks."

"Nope," she replied. "Thank *you*. But, next time, let us finish our game." Then she pushed past me and headed down the hallway.

At that exact moment, somewhere in Haven, something *exploded*.

CHAPTER 12
THE KEYSTONE

Helene

"Tom ... this is insane!"

Helene fidgeted in her chair—the only one left of their little meeting who was still seated. Will had gone. He'd delivered his message from "beyond" and then Tom had asked him to take Jillian over to the Moms. So he'd left, with both Helene and his mother looking after him, their expressions oddly similar.

After that Tom had stood up. Then Mrs. Ritter had stood up.

And that's when the shouting started.

"You are *not* sending two children, one of them *my* son, into danger on the say-so of a boy's dream!"

"I'm very sorry," Tom replied. "But, yeah, I am."

His dark eyes met the mother's fierce gaze without challenge or anger, and it struck Helene—not for the first time—that the chief was more self-possessed than anyone she'd ever met.

"So you *believe* this story about an 'angel' and her 'white room'?" Mrs. Ritter demanded.

He nodded.

"Seriously?"

"Seriously. Mrs. Ritter, since I was fourteen years old, I've been fightin' a war against animated cadavers. I got a pretty open mind."

"Tom, they're just kids."

Helene cringed. She *hated* it when people said that.

If only Tom would let her leave. She kept trying to catch his eye, to communicate to him that—right now—this was the last place she wanted to be. But he never even glanced her way, and she knew him too well to think she was being ignored. No, the chief *wanted* her here.

All part of the Mom Mission.

"With respect," he replied, "if you still think *that* after two months of living here, then you ain't paying attention."

Helene flashed back on an incident last month. She and a few of the other Angels had run into a bunch of Corpses while on patrol. The subsequent fight had been a draw, but not what Sharyn called a "happy draw." Undertakers had gotten hurt.

So, on returning to Haven, they'd headed straight to the infirmary.

Seeing them, Susan Ritter had taken immediate charge, throwing orders around and issuing everyone a bed. She'd treated Helene first, who'd been bitten—*Jeez, how it had hurt!*—on the arm and shoulder. While cleaning the wound, Will's mother had turned to ask Ian for bandages.

But Ian had been busy at Sharyn's bedside, stitching up a deep gash. Horrified, Mrs. Ritter had run over there but stopped short when she saw his handiwork. Helene knew Ian's sutures firsthand. They were good.

Really good.

"Need something, Mrs. Ritter?" the medic had asked without looking up. Meanwhile Sharyn, in obvious pain, nevertheless offered her a wink.

"I …" The woman's words had trailed off. "Bandages?"

Ian had turned to Amy, who stood faithfully at his side. "Can you get Mrs. Ritter some bandages?"

"Sure," the girl had replied.

And then he'd returned to his stitching.

Now, Helene watched that same woman facing down the chief of the Undertakers, armed with the same stupid argument, towing the same stupid grown-up line: "Just kids."

Anger flushed her cheeks.

Years we've been doing this! Years! Without an adult in sight! Why can't you see that?

And I'm supposed to make friends *with this person?*

"It's dangerous," Mrs. Ritter said, crossing her arms and fixing Tom with a heavy-duty "mom" look that Helene felt sure, once upon a time, had frozen Will stiff.

It didn't do a thing to the chief.

"I know," he replied.

"How sure are you that you can even trust this new girl?"

"Jillian's a friend."

"When did you last see her?"

"Maybe four years ago."

"When you and Sharyn were thirteen. And she would have been ... what? Twelve?"

He nodded.

"That's about the age that girls pick up the Sight. Not sixteen. How is it she just started Seeing Corpses three days ago?"

Not a bad question, Helene admitted.

But Tom, as usual, had an answer. "I was fourteen when I got my Eyes. That's late. Real late. But there's a reason for it: I started Seeing deaders at fourteen 'cause before then, there weren't any deaders to See. The invasion hadn't started yet. Same's true for Jillian. This war started *here*. However the Corpses manage to get to our world, they do it in Philly. I think this Micha thing, whatever it is, is pretty recent ... probably just since the senator stopped doing personal appearances. That's why Jill only now got the Sight. 'Til recently, there just weren't very many Corpses to See in Washington."

Makes sense.

Then Tom asked Mrs. Ritter, "What do *you* think I should do?"

It was the first time Helene had ever heard Tom ask anyone for advice. Even Will's mom seemed taken aback. "Well ... I *don't* think you should send your sister and my son to DC."

"Who *should* I send? Helene here?"

They both looked right at her. She fidgeted some more.

"Of course not," Will's mother replied, though Helene thought her protest lacked conviction.

Better me than him. Right, Mrs. Ritter?

"Maybe Hugo?" the woman asked.

Hugo Ramirez was the only other grown-up who'd ever visited Haven—an FBI special agent who'd run afoul of Lilith Cavanaugh, the Queen of the Dead. Since then, he'd been forced to lay low. Ramirez knew the truth about the invasion and, worse, Cavanaugh knew that he knew. If he returned to his job with the Bureau, he wouldn't last a week.

But in Susan Ritter's eyes, Ramirez was at least an *adult*. That meant he *had* to be better at doing Undertaker stuff than Undertakers were! Right?

Tom said, "That don't work. Agent Ramirez *is* an asset. More'n that, he's a friend. Thanks to his contacts, we got us equipment and supplies that we ain't never had before. But he don't have the Sight. Even if he *could* get himself set up in the Capitol somehow ... he can't See Micha for what she really is any more than you can." He shrugged. "What good would it do?"

It would keep Will out of danger, Helene thought. And, despite everything, she found herself kind of siding with his mother on this one.

"The sad fact," the chief explained, "is that we're alone. The Undertakers. If it ain't us fighting this war, it ain't nobody. Straight up. End of story."

He went to his desk. On it, a rusted wire basket bore a makeshift cardboard sign that read STUFF FOR THE CHIEF TO SEE in green marker. It was half filled with papers, mostly the loose-leaf, lined, three-holed variety. Haven had tons of that stuff.

Tom picked up the top sheet. "It's from the Monkey Barrel. Alex wants some new equipment." He took the next sheet. "This here's from Alisha Beardsley, the Boss

Chatter. We just got a shipment of encrypted satellite phones … another gift from Agent Ramirez. Twenty of 'em."

"What's a satellite phone?" Mrs. Ritter asked.

"Like a cell phone, 'cept it sends and receives straight to satellites instead of usin' cell towers. More secure. Cell phones are easy to trace. These aren't. It's good news. Means no more wrist radios."

Cool, Helene thought.

Tom smiled thinly and dropped both papers. "Just kids," he echoed, looking hard at Will's mother. "'Cept every single one of 'em had to split from their homes to fight the Corpses. Some of them, like Alex, saw their folks die before they escaped."

"It's terrible," Mrs. Ritter admitted.

Then Helene said, "Maybe I *should* go to Washington."

They both looked at her.

She steadied herself and went on. "I'm a Schooler, or I used to be. I've spent a lot of my two years as an Undertaker going undercover into middle schools, looking for fresh Seers. It's how I found Will." Then she caught the look on Mrs. Ritter's face. Swallowing, she regrouped and continued. "Anyway … I know how to blend in and keep my eyes open."

Tom studied her. Had she just volunteered to abandon the mission he'd given her only an hour ago in favor of heading out into the field?

Yeah she had, and for just one reason: to keep Will safe.

Helene glanced at Mrs. Ritter. Once again, poorly-concealed hope shone in the woman's eyes.

So ... it is *better me than him, huh?*

Tom asked, "It's a good idea. But I won't do it. Know why?"

"'Cause the 'angel' in the 'white room' said differently?" Helene asked.

The chief shook his head.

"Then why?" Mrs. Ritter demanded.

"'Cause it was *Will's* vision. Mrs. Ritter, your son is"— the chief's brows knitted—"the most amazing person I've ever known."

Neither Helene nor Mrs. Ritter responded. Helene was surprised—even shocked—but not by what Tom had said so much as by the fact that he'd said it at all. All this time she'd thought she was the only one who felt that way.

Well, maybe her and Dave.

The chief went on. "I think I sensed it the moment I met him. At first, I thought it was 'cause he was Karl's kid. But it's more than that. This blond woman who visits him, I'm pretty sure she visited your husband, too ... at least once. She gave him the pocketknife and the sword that he turned around and gave to me and Sharyn for our fifteenth birthdays. He told us *he'd* made then, called 'em his 'dream children.' But now I think he held back where they really came from."

This was new. Will's "angel" had visited his dad? Given him Tom's pocketknife and Sharyn's sword?

"But even that ain't the point," Tom said. "The Corpses. The war. Micha and Cavanaugh. Will's visions. In my mind, they all point to just one thing."

"And what's that?" Susan Ritter asked, arms crossed again.

"That *all* this ain't about me or Sharyn or Helene here

… or any of the other Undertakers. It's about your son. I don't know how or why … but he's at the center of everything. Every arch has a keystone and he's it."

Tom looked from one to the other of them with conviction in his eyes. "*That's* why I'm sendin' the two of them to DC … 'cause Will Ritter told me to."

And, at that exact moment, somewhere in Haven, something *exploded.*

CHAPTER 13
TRAGEDY

By the time I reached the Brain Factory, there were a half-dozen kids already there.

The Brains, the crew in charge of science and gadgetry, was bossed by Steve Moscova. When I'd first met him, back on my first day in Haven, I hadn't liked him very much; Steve had the social skills of a pocket calculator.

But in the months since, he'd kind of grown on me.

"Will!"

Burt Moscova, Steve's younger brother and a fellow Angel, waved me over. The members of Steve's crew were gathered around him.

"What's going on?" I asked.

"The door's jammed shut!" Burt replied. His eyes, so much like his brother's, were glassy with worry. "Steve's in there!"

"With Ian …" added Gabby, one of the Brains.

I blinked. "Ian?"

"He showed up to return the crystal," said Andrew,

another Brain. "Said he had an idea. He and Steve spent some time whispering about it ... and then Steve told us all to get out and shut the door."

"Ian and my brother have gotten tight," Burt remarked. "All over that stupid hunk of glass! Jeez, I always *knew* he'd blow himself up one day!"

"Take it easy," I told him. "What's wrong with the door?"

The Brain Factory's door was new, installed by the Monkeys just last month at Steve's request. He'd practically begged Tom for it, insisting that he needed a safe place to store the Anchor Shard. Unfortunately that same door, hand-built from thick, sturdy wood, seemed to be ... well, stuck.

"The knob turns," Andrew said. "But it won't budge!"

I confirmed that. Then I pounded and called Steve's name. No answer.

I couldn't smell smoke and the door wasn't hot, so I didn't think the Brain Factory had caught fire. That was a good sign. The fact that nobody was responding from inside, however, *wasn't.*

But what really worried me was the sound leaking through the heavy wood—a high-pitched drone, like a beehive.

"Gabby!" I said. "Go fetch Dave! Andrew, find Tom. Tell him what's happening." If I knew the chief, he was already en route, while the Burgermeister might well have snored right through a minor earthquake.

Both kids took off at a run.

I told Burt, "It's gonna be okay."

Empty words. But he nodded anyway.

Tom and my mother showed up before Dave did—no

big surprise there—and the chief banged on the door. When that didn't work, he ordered us all back and threw his shoulder against it. Once. Twice. Three times. Nothing.

I heard him mutter something about Alex Bobson, the Monkey Boss, and his construction skills.

Then a figure came lumbering down the corridor toward us. For the second time that morning, Dave had been awakened before his time. "What'd that freakin' geek do *now*?" he grumbled.

"Shut it, Burger!" Burt growled and, for a moment, the two boys swapped glares.

Stupid.

"Dave," Tom said, "get us in there."

"Ain't it got a knob?"

"Burgermeister …" I said.

He looked blearily at me. "Yeah. Okay." Then he pushed Burt aside. "Gimme room."

We gave him room.

He stepped as far back as the narrow hallway would allow. Then he huffed once like an angry bull and charged, hitting the door with devastating force. The wood cracked, groaned, and then surrendered—crashing inward. Dave went with it, stumbling through the open doorway, which was lit by a weird, blue light.

I heard him exclaim, wide awake now, "What the hell?"

We ran in after him.

The Brain Factory, a long, narrow chamber with a low ceiling, lay in ruin. All of its lab tables had been toppled. One of them had somehow gotten jammed up against the door, which was why it'd been stuck. Broken glass and overturned equipment lay everywhere.

The far half of the room was eerily lit, though all the

overhead bulbs looked shattered. As Tom, Burt and I pushed around the Burgermeister for a closer look, we saw that the weird illumination came from the Anchor Shard, which dangled from wires attaching it to a blocky, six-volt battery. The whole assembly sat atop a wooden stool.

"Steve!" Burt yelled, rushing toward his brother, who was sprawled, unconscious, beside the stool.

Tom caught his arm. "Hold up! We'll get him out of there. But we don't know what we got here yet!"

Ian lay on his back in another part of the room, his body shoved up against one wall. But at least *he* was moving. When my mother and I both ran to him, he looked up at us with stunned, frightened eyes.

"What … happened?" he gasped.

I said, "I was about to ask you that."

"Just stay still," my mom told him.

But he pushed her away. "No. I'm okay." I offered him my hand and helped him to his feet while my mother looked on disapprovingly. He gaped at what was left of the room, his expression mixing horror with guilt.

"Talk to me, Ian," Tom said.

The medic stammered, "I thought … if maybe we ran a little electricity through the crystal that we might get a reaction."

"Looks like you did," the Burgermeister observed.

"I'm going to Steve," my mother said and, before anyone could object, she hurried to the far end of the room, into the strange light. The sickly bluish glow washed over her as she knelt beside the fallen boy. He lay right below the dangling crystal, its light dancing crazily around him.

"Oh my God." I heard Mom whisper. Then I saw why.

Steve's body had been cut in half.

But no, that wasn't quite right. He was bent at the waist, with his upper torso splayed across the Brain Factory's dirt floor and his lower torso—well, it looked like it had disappeared through some kind of shimmering hole in the floor!

The boy moaned.

"Pull him out!" Ian yelled. And we all charged forward, our shock forgotten.

"Gently!" my mother commanded. But this didn't feel like a "gently" situation to me. With a nod from the chief, we pulled together, and Steve came sliding out of that weird shimmering *nothing* in the floor. His legs were intact, no blood, no sign of injury at all.

We dragged him clear of the light and rolled him over.

His head lolled as his brother dropped down beside him, calling his name. Then my mom was there as well, checking his pulse and feeling his temples and forehead. It struck me that this was Ian's job.

Where is Ian?

I turned back and saw him, still in the light. He was crouching beside the shimmering "hole" in the floor, but his attention was fixed on the Anchor Shard.

Steve sat bolt upright, his eyes as wide as dinner plates. "Ian!" he screamed. "Don't!"

But the medic was already reaching for the wires connecting the crystal to the battery. If he'd heard Steve's warning, if he was even aware of the rest of us at that moment, it didn't show.

I remember running forward. One step. Two. But I was too slow to react, too mesmerized by the weird light and by the even weirder thing that light seemed to have *projected* onto the floor. Maybe if I'd been faster, things would have turned out differently.

I'll spend my life wondering.

Ian yanked the shard clear of the wires, a gentle tug that pulled free two short strips of black electrical tape. So simple a thing.

And then he ceased to exist.

CHAPTER 14

A HOLE IN THE WORLD

An explosion of light, silent but powerful, blasted the rear of the Brain Factory, knocking me off my feet.

For several seconds, I lay, dazed, in the dirt. Then a big hand touched my shoulder and the Burgermeister's face appeared, his blond hair sticking up all over the place. "You okay?"

I nodded and sat up. Burt and Steve were already standing. Tom was supporting my mother. Somewhere along the way, others had arrived. Sharyn and Helene stood in the doorway. Chuck was there too, along with the Brains. They all wore expressions of shock and horror that made me feel cold.

Then I remembered Ian.

Jumping to my feet, I stared at the back of the room.

The crystal rested on the ground, its weird inner light extinguished. Lying on its side a foot away was the battery, the wires still draped around it like fallen spaghetti.

But the stool was gone. And so was Ian.

"What happened?" Burt asked.

His brother was crying. I couldn't remember ever seeing Steve cry before.

"Where's Ian?" my mother asked.

I stepped forward—and down. The floor of the Brain Factory had been *excavated*, as if someone had dug a perfect circle around the Anchor Shard. The dirt was gone, replaced by a thin layer of sand and fine gravel. I stood in the midst of it, perplexed.

The walls were intact. So was the ceiling. But they looked cleaner somehow, as if the dirt that covered them had been scoured away, leaving behind old but pristine bricks.

I reached down for the crystal.

"Will! Don't!" my mother yelled. So I stopped, though I'd handled the Anchor Shard before.

Tom spoke. "Steve, what were you and Ian trying to do?"

The Brain Boss wiped his eyes. His brother stood at his shoulder, as if guarding him.

"Ian had this idea of running an electrical current through the crystal," Steve said. "As a precaution, we asked the crew to leave us alone for a few minutes and shut the door, in case of a … reaction. Then we pushed everything back from the far end of the room and set up the battery and the crystal on one of the work stools."

"You got your reaction," Tom guessed.

"Way beyond anything we'd expected … or planned for. A flash of light and an impact wave. Something *pushed* the air out from around the stool."

"We heard an explosion," I said.

Steve shook his head. "Not exactly. What you heard was the air refilling the vacuum left behind by the 'push.'

It's how thunder works. But the impact wave was strong enough to wreck the lab.

"I recovered before Ian did, and ran up to disconnect the battery. The crystal was radiating light, and that light was defining a circle on the floor ... about four feet wide. I didn't notice that the floor inside that circle had ... disappeared ... until I fell into it. That's when you guys came in."

"Whatcha talking about? How can a floor disappear?" the Burgermeister demanded.

But Tom raised a hand for silence. "Steve, tell us what you think all of this means. Where's Ian? Could he have fallen into the same hole you did?"

I looked at my feet. No hole, though I was standing exactly where it *had* been. And this circle of cleared floor was *much* bigger—a dozen feet across, at least.

Steve said, "While I was hanging in that hole, I felt ... strange. Wherever the lower half of me was, it wasn't on this planet. I can't justify that scientifically. It just felt ... *alien*." Then, after several seconds, he added, "But I don't think that's what happened to Ian."

"Then tell us what you *do* think happened," Tom said.

Steve nodded and headed toward me, waving away his brother's offer of help. Moving shakily, he joined me in the newly formed pit. There he stood, his eyes focused on the Anchor Shard.

"Don't!" my mother snapped.

But Steve picked it up. "It's dormant now. All its energy's been released."

"How do you know?" I asked.

"An educated guess. I think it works kind of like a capacitor. That's an electronic component designed to collect and store a charge. When Ian and I 'plugged' it in, we activated it. Some of its energy went to opening that hole in the floor. The rest it stored."

"What drained it?" Tom asked.

Steve shuddered. "Ian disconnected it, and it released its stored energy in a final burst."

My mother stammered, "But what happened to him?"

Steve looked around at the bizarre *smoothness* left behind by the flash of light. "I think ... the discharge destroyed all organic matter within the blast radius."

"What's that even *mean*?" the Burgermeister demanded.

"Organic matter," Steve repeated. "Anything made of carbon molecules. The stool was wooden. Organic. The dirt on the walls and floor was mostly organic." Then, quietly, he added, "*Ian* was organic."

A silence, hard and terrible, fell over the room. Finally, Tom broke it, saying aloud what the rest of us already knew. "He's dead."

The Brain Boss nodded.

His crew members, who up until now hadn't said much, gasped and cried. So did my mother. Sharyn and Burt went to Steve, putting their arms around him. Nearby, the Burgermeister stood stock-still, his face pale.

I tried to wrap my mind around it.

Ian was just here. He *couldn't* be dead. There was no body! No blood! No sign of anything! Then I noticed something resting in the scoured gravel at my feet and picked it up.

It was a belt buckle with a symbol embossed on it: two snakes entwined around a staff. The Hippocratic emblem. Any Undertaker would have recognized the buckle. It had been a gift from Ian's father.

And it was the only thing on his person that hadn't been organic.

Dear God.

And then I started crying, too.

CHAPTER 15
AFTERMATH

A death in Haven, and not the first one, either.

Over the next five days, a lot happened. Tom called every onsite Undertaker into the cafeteria and told them about Ian's death. The next day, at the memorial, everyone who wanted to, got up and spoke—a grim Undertaker tradition. Tom said some things. So did Sharyn. I tried, but I suck at speeches. Then Steve got up and apologized for his part in the accident, the guilt on his face profound and terrible.

Amy stood then and, with tears in her soft blue eyes, said, "Ian was good to me. He taught me stuff. He never talked about my past. And he made me feel like ... I belonged."

Then, she sat back down—and my mother got up.

Nobody expected *that*. After all, my mother wasn't an Undertaker. So when she stood, the quality of the silence in the cafeteria changed—became less welcoming. And I could see she sensed it, but it didn't stop her.

"I know I haven't been with you long," she said. "But I

spent enough time in the Infirmary to appreciate the young man who ran it. Ian McDonald"—she bit her lip—"was a *doctor* in every sense of the word. One of the finest I've ever known."

When she returned to her chair, I noticed a small, sad smile playing on Tom's face. The rest of the Undertakers remained silent, but this time it was an approving silence.

I was proud of my mom.

The next day, however, the war went on.

Sharyn and I started what we called Page Training, with Jillian as our coach. This proved—awkward, since things were seriously tense between the two girls for reasons that, so far, no one seemed willing to discuss.

Tom, meanwhile, talked to Ramirez. Jillian had said kids who left the Senate Page Program, like her and Kevin, usually weren't replaced. But Ramirez called in some favors and somehow managed to convince the senior senator from Pennsylvania, James Mitchum, to support the "mid-term assignment" of two new pages.

The page program's director hadn't liked the idea. But she'd finally caved—*if* we could be in DC before Monday.

Sharyn griped. She *hated* Jillian's attempts to teach us how to fit in on Capitol Hill. She especially hated the blue suits that we'd both be wearing: "Every day! Every single friggin' day! My skin's gonna slide right off my bones!"

But she did it because she was an Undertaker, and it needed doing.

Pages, Jillian explained, were usually high school juniors. I'd left school an eighth grader, which seemed like a deal breaker to me. Apparently I was wrong.

"It's cool," Tom told me as we sat in his office on the

day before our departure. "You don't come off as thirteen. Maturity wise, you can pull of fifteen or sixteen, easy."

"Okay ..." I said. "But I still *look* thirteen."

"Do you? Stand up."

I stood up. So did he. "You're taller than me," I said. "Big surprise."

"How about Sharyn?" he asked, his face neutral.

"Her, too."

"And Helene?"

"She *used* to be. Now, I'm a little taller."

He nodded. "Yeah? When'd you first notice that?"

I frowned "I guess it was back when you guys held that funeral for me ... when you thought I was dead."

Again, he nodded. "That's when *I* noticed it, too. Remember the first thing your mom said to you?"

"That I'd gotten taller," I replied. "But grown-ups always say that when they haven't seen you for a while."

"I wouldn't know," Tom said. "The thing is: you *did* get taller, bro. I'm sure of it. 'Tween you headin' out that day to save your family and when you interrupted my eulogy, I figure you grew about three inches."

"That's impossible!" I exclaimed.

"You got *shot*, Will! That assassin's bullet should've killed you dead. But a few hours later, you showed up with nothing but an old scar."

"I told you," I said. "The woman in the white room healed me. Just like when I broke my arm last year."

"Except I'm not sure she did. If she'd *healed* you, like we do these days with the crystal, there'd be no scar at all. Right?"

It was true. The Anchor Shard healed things

completely, as if the injury had never occurred.

Tom said, "How long you figure you were in that white room?"

"Maybe a few hours?"

He shook his head. "I don't think so."

"Then what *do* you think?"

He told me.

I left Tom's office seriously creeped out.

The next day, Sharyn and I said our separate good-byes. Mine started with Dave, who hugged me—he does that—and told me for about the millionth time how much he wished he could come along.

"You got your own gig," I said.

"Yeah," he admitted, looking huge and childlike at the same time. He does *that*, too. "But … it's kinda getting old."

What *was* the Burgermeister's new gig? Well, let's just say it started out as a cool way for him to show off his mad skills and join the fight. But, over the last couple of months, he'd soured on it. And I didn't blame him. Sometimes Undertakers have to do stuff "for the cause" that goes against everything that feels right and decent. After a while, that kind of weight drags you down, makes it harder to get through the day.

It's like this: war, even if it doesn't kill you, eats away at you.

In a word, it *sucks*.

"Sorry, man," I said.

Dave's huge shoulders rose and fell. "We all gotta do what we gotta do, right?"

"Right," I said.

And I thought, This *is a hero, Harleen.*

"Try to sleep," I told him. "Maybe ask Tom if he'll have the Monkeys put a door in for you. You know … to help with the noise."

The Burgermeister scowled. "After what happened in the Brain Factory? Naw, no door for me. Besides, it ain't the noise. It's the dreams."

I knew just what he meant.

CHAPTER 16
THE WOMEN IN MY LIFE

"What's your name?" Helene asked me.

"Andy Forbes," I replied.

We were in her room. Her roommate, Katie, was elsewhere. Helene sat on her bunk with an open civics book on her lap. She was quizzing me one last time. "How old are you?"

"I'll be sixteen in July."

"Grade and school?"

"Junior," I said. "Chapeltown High. Chapeltown, Pennyslvania."

"Interests?" she asked.

"Politics," I replied. "Current events."

"Favorite subjects?"

"History and poly-sci."

"Name the president, vice president, and speaker of the house."

I did.

"Name the senate majority leader."

I did.

"Name the committees in the Senate."

I did. I missed one: the Rules and Administration Committee. "A *real* poly-sci would know that," Helene said.

"*You* don't know it! You're reading it out of a book!"

"*I'm* not headed to DC to pretend I'm somebody else. This is hardcore, Will. You heard what Jillian said. You're gonna be surrounded by other pages, all older'n you and all serious poly-sci. If you don't even know the basics, your cover won't last a day."

"Is this what it's like to be a Schooler?" I asked.

"When you're a Schooler, you're totally on your own. *You'll* have Sharyn."

That made me wonder how Sharyn was doing. Right now she and Jillian were somewhere in Haven, running through this same final cram. But at least Helene and I *liked* each other.

Several questions later, she closed the book. "Okay, here's one more tip: the minute you walk out of Haven, you're not Will Ritter anymore. You're Andy Forbes. Get that. Believe that. It might just keep you alive."

"Thanks," I said. Then, treading carefully: "Um ... we haven't talked about South Street."

"Yeah. I ... uh ... asked Tom to pay for the skateboards. But Doug still won't answer when I call him."

"Sorry," I said. "So ... you gotta find another letter drop?"

Helene sighed. "I'm not sure what I'm going to do about that. Tom knows it all now. He says we'll be 'discussing it some more,' once you and Sharyn are on your way."

"I hope it works out okay."

"Thanks. You know, it's funny." Then she made a sour face. "I mean … it's *awful*, but it's funny, too. I was so caught up in my own problems, so upset about what happened at the comic book shop. But then, later that same day, Ian died and suddenly those problems, they seemed so *pointless*, like nothing compared with what happened to him. But now, after less than a week, I can feel myself getting caught up in them again. What does that say about me?"

I shrugged. "That you're human?"

"I guess. I wish you weren't going."

"Yeah? So, you're gonna … what … *miss* me?"

She smiled ruefully. "Yeah, jerk! I'm gonna miss you!"

"So … we're cool? About the following-you thing?"

"You mean the *stalking*-me thing?"

"I like 'following' better," I said.

"If you hadn't been there, we might not have saved Jillian. So, once again, Will Ritter makes a bonehead move that turns out to be a good thing in disguise. I told Tom I think it's your mutant power."

I had no reply.

She eyed me. "You still haven't apologized."

"That's 'cause I'm not sorry."

I half expected her to yell at me again, maybe take another swing. But she didn't. Instead, she came close to laughing. "Keep kickin' that hornet's nest, Ritter!" Then, when I didn't respond again, she added, "We're cool."

I cleared my throat, knowing I was pushing my luck. "You ever gonna tell me what's on that piece of paper?"

Her laugh died. Then she put down the book, stood up, and cupped my face. She'd never done that before. It startled me, but her skin felt warm against my cheeks, her palms soft …

… but not nearly as soft as her kiss.

How long had I imagined this moment? I didn't know. But I *did* know that the reality went *way* beyond my imagination.

The kiss lasted only a few seconds, but they were a *totally amazing* few seconds!

She pulled back and draped her arms around my neck. Her face was so close to mine that I thought I might lose myself in her eyes. She smelled like soap and—well—*girl*. Tentatively, I put my hands on her waist.

It felt *right*.

"Come back alive," she whispered, "and I'll tell you then."

Walking out of that little room was the second hardest thing I did that day.

I hit my own room next. It was almost eight A.M., and I found the Burgermeister zonked out on his bunk, a huge shape under a thick blanket, snoring like a 747. I let him sleep and felt around for my duffle bag, which contained the clothes and other stuff I'd packed the night before.

It wasn't there.

My heart sank. I wished I could say I hadn't seen this coming.

So I headed for the Shrine.

On the way, I peeked into the infirmary. The beds were all empty—a nice change—and Amy was on duty. She sat at Ian's old desk, just staring into space. It had been a week since Ian's death and, as far as I knew Amy, never a big talker, hadn't spoken a word since his funeral.

God, how I hated this place.

Farther along Haven's main corridor stood the Brain Factory. Its big door was closed, though I knew Steve was in there. Burt said that his brother had taken to eating and sleeping there, working—always working—on the Anchor Shard. And, for now, Tom was giving him his space.

Different people grieve differently. My mom once told me that, not long after my dad died.

My mom.

I found her in the Shrine. While Emily slept on her little cot, my mother sat in the dark with my duffle bag beside her. When I parted the curtain, she met my eyes.

She looked desperate.

"You're not going," she said.

"I have to," I said.

"No." She shook her head—hard.

"Mom. ..."

She stood up fast, her eyes blazing the way they do when she's really, *really* mad. "No!" she said again, loud. Emily stirred and, seeing this, my mother pushed me back through the curtain and out into the empty hallway.

"You're not going!" she said again, this time in a hard whisper.

"I *have* to," I repeated.

"Why? Because some mystery woman in a dream told you to?"

"They aren't dreams." I knew I sounded defensive. But this was my mother, and old habits die hard.

"Of course they are! You're all just too blind to see it. Even Tom. You want so badly to believe that there's some *higher power* watching over you that you've bought into this ... fantasy! Well, I'm not going to let you kill yourself over a dream! Someone else can go. *You're* staying here!"

I felt my anger rise. "Mom," I said, with what I figured to be amazing control, "I've got a job to do. I'm sorry, but a lot's changed since I left home. The days when you can tell me what's allowed or not allowed are over."

Even in the bad light, I saw her face redden. "William Karl Ritter, I'm still your mother," she said, her hands on her hips, her mouth set in a hard, straight line.

That pose used to scare me to death.

"Yeah," I told her. "But you're not my boss. Not anymore."

"You're thirteen years old!"

Am I?

Out loud, I said, "So what?"

Lame.

"So what?" she echoed, glaring ferociously. "Look, I realize you've had a wonderful time these past months playing soldier—"

And with that, my control snapped. "Playing soldier!" I screamed—yeah, *screamed*—"People are dying, Mom! They're dying all the time! You think Ian was the first? He wasn't. Not by a long shot. Nobody here is 'playing' anything!"

"Which is why you're not going!" She pointed a trembling finger at me. "You disappeared for months! For *months!* Leaving behind a note that didn't do anything but terrify me more! Do you have any idea what you *did* to your sister and me?" She gestured around us. "And to think you've been living here, in this rathole, like some kind of animal … and a *mile* from where I work! All of this time, just a mile away!"

"I didn't have a choice!" I exclaimed. "Don't you think

I *wanted* to come home? I thought about it every minute!"

"Then why *didn't* you? Why didn't you just … come home?"

"You know why."

"No, Will, I don't," she said, all challenge and motherly fury. "Why don't you *enlighten* me?"

As I stepped up close to her, I noticed that we were the same height. When had *that* happened? But, of course, I knew the answer.

"Because," I said, through gritted teeth. "You … couldn't … protect … me." She looked horror-stricken, but it didn't slow me down. "If I'd come home and told you about the Corpses and the Undertakers and the war … you'd have called me crazy."

She shook her head so hard I thought it might snap off her neck. "No! I wouldn't have! I really wouldn't!"

"You're a grown-up and grown-ups don't believe! You know it and I know it! Helene went that way and she ended up in a nuthouse … until the Corpses almost got her. There are plenty of kids here with similar stories, or *worse*. This isn't a clubhouse, Mom. And the war is *real*. If I'd come home, they'd have killed me. Then, just to be safe, they'd have killed you and Em, as well. 'Cause that's what they *do*!"

Where her face had been red, it was now ashen. She stared at me with a look of such betrayal that I thought it might kill me. But, of course, it didn't.

"Mommy?"

We both turned. Emily stood in the Shrine's darkened doorway, bleary-eyed, the curtain draped over her tiny body like a shroud.

"Honey. …" my mother said. It was almost a sob.

I knelt down in front of my little sister. "Don't worry, Em. I have to leave for a while and Mom's just nervous about it. Let me get you back to bed."

"It's okay, Mommy," she said, ignoring me. "Will's a *hero.*"

When my mother said nothing, Emily's face crumpled. But I kissed her nose and, as usual, the gesture made her giggle—a little. Then I scooped her up and carried her back into the Shrine, tucking her in. She went willingly enough, but wouldn't shut her eyes. Instead she watched me as I stood, picked up my duffel, gave her a final smile, and slipped back out through the curtain.

My mom hadn't moved.

"Don't," she whispered. "Please."

I looked hard at her. My every instinct was to apologize. But Tom had once told me: "Never apologize for the truth."

Still, what the heck? She was my mom!

"I'm sorry," I said.

I put down the duffel and stepped forward to hug her.

But she turned her back on me.

For several sixteen-ton seconds I stood there, my arms spread. "Mom?"

She didn't move. In fact, if she'd heard me at all, she gave no sign of it.

Finally, I stepped back and collected my duffle. Then, wordlessly, I walked away.

It sucked.

CHAPTER 17
THE LYING GAME

"Okay, lil bro, what's up?" Sharyn asked.

We sat side by side on the train from Philly to DC, both of us dressed to impress: me in black pants, a dark-blue shirt, and a badly knotted necktie; Sharyn in a gray skirt and white blouse. Her short cropped hair was freshly washed, and she wore—for the first time—makeup on her face.

"I'm fine," I lied. It was a bad lie, too. It sat on my tongue as if glued there. Lies do that sometimes.

Tom would have pressed me, but that wasn't his sister's style. If you wanted to talk, she'd listen. But if you didn't, well that was cool, too. It was something I'd always liked about her.

"At least you look like *you*, Red," she moaned. "Care to guess how much I *hate* this *skirt*?" The word came out like a curse.

"A lot?"

"I mean, jeez! I look like a ... a ..."

"Restaurant greeter?" I suggested.

"Well …"

"A rep at a high school jobs fair?" I suggested.

"Huh?"

"How about the president of the senior class?"

"Ack!" she yelped. Yep, that was the word: *Ack*. Then she covered her face and complained *through* her fingers. "This isn't me! I don't even have Vader! How am I supposed to do this without Vader?"

Vader was her wakizashi, a Japanese short sword—her most prized possession.

"Tom'll take good care of it," I said.

"That ain't the point," Sharyn replied. "The point is that *I* know why *I'm* sulking. Why are *you* sulking?"

"I'm not sulking."

"Well, somethin's on your mind. Come on, Red. Spill!"

Okay, maybe she was more like Tom than I thought. So I gave her some of it, "Helene kissed me."

She burst out laughing. "Well, it's about time!" Then, when she saw my horrified expression she laughed harder. "Dude, it's *always* been you two! Every kid in Haven's known that for months … 'cept for you and Helene. Well, probably mostly *you*!"

"Great," I muttered.

"Take it easy. The Undertakers ain't a schoolyard. Ain't nobody gonna give you grief 'cause you and Helene finally hooked up. Just glad for you, is all."

And it was true. I might get some ribbing from Chuck or Burt. Alex, head of the Monkey crew and *not* my biggest fan, might fire a shot or two. But that would be the end of it.

Well, except for the whole "relationship with Helene" thing.

Jeez.

"So," Sharyn said, leaning close. "Was it a solid kiss? Both lips, I mean."

Time for a strategic subject change.

"Lemme ask *you* a question."

She grinned. Sharyn knew a hasty evasion when she heard one. "Shoot."

"What do you got against Jillian?"

Her smile vaporized. "Old crap," she said.

"None of my business, right?"

"No, it's cool. It'd do me some good to get it out. It's the stuff you *don't* say that eats at you, ya know."

I knew.

"Before that girl," she said, "and *after* that girl ... it was my brother and me. But for a time—a long time—she and Tom kind of ... well, you could tell there was something there."

I said, "She liked him."

"Well, *yeah*," Sharyn scoffed. "But that always happened. Still does. Girls dig my brother. It's something I've gotten used to."

Then I got it. "Except this time *he* liked Jillian back."

"Straight up. Started spending more and more time with her. He didn't dump me, but I began feelin' like a third wheel. Jillian didn't want me around, that was plain. Not when we was training, not when we was eating, and especially not when they snuck out for their little 'walks.'"

I tried to picture the chief feeling *that* way about a girl, the way I felt about Helene. After all, why not?

Sharyn said, "I guess I hated her, and that ain't a word I throw around. She'd gotten between my brother 'n me, and that wasn't cool. Not a bit cool. It wasn't fair to either of 'em. I dig that. I mean … folks are allowed to *like* each other!"

"Yeah," I said.

"One of the worst days of my life was when Mr. P's crib got shut down … but there was an upshot, 'cause it meant *she'd* be gone. Tom was pretty messed up about it. He didn't say so … he never *says* so, but I knew. It took a long while, but he finally stopped mentioning her, and so I figured he'd gotten past it."

"And now Jillian's back."

Sharyn nodded. "And she's a Seer."

"She's good, Sharyn," I said. "I've seen her in action. That *parkour* stuff she does is amazing!"

"Free running!" the Angel Boss scoffed. "Studied on it back under Mr. P's roof. Don't see much use for all that runnin' and jumpin' in real combat." Then she groaned. "I know it shouldn't piss me off … but it does. Seein' her's brought back all the old memories. My brother's *already* looking at her the way he did in the old days. Know why he went off with Chuck to rescue y'all? 'Cause Helene mentioned *her* name on your radio. Then he was out the door like a shot! And no First Stop for his Jillian! Oh, no. It's straight to Haven. Straight to the chief's side!"

"Do you really think she might be a mole?"

Sharyn sighed. "No, she ain't a mole. Amy's test works. Besides, the Queen don't use moles, not like Kenny Booth did. Fact is: Tom and me been talkin' about maybe shutting down First Stop for good. All that stuff I said, that was just me bein' pissed." She met my eyes. "Why, Will? Why'd that mysterious lady of yours have to pick *me* for this gig?"

"No idea," I replied. "She just said you were going to

Washington and that I had to go with you."

"Nothing about what to expect?"

I shook my head.

"That's messed up."

"Yeah. But she's always been straight with me before. She told me about the Anchor Shard ... told me it would heal you after you got hit in the head." Then, after a pause, I added, "I trust her."

Sharyn didn't reply.

We got to DC's Union Station just after lunchtime, and were met by a guy in a suit holding up a sign with our cover names on it.

He took us, luggage and all, to a waiting car—the first time I'd ever been in a limo. Sharyn, too, judging by her expression. Ten minutes later, the long car dropped us off at a big, white structure with a sign in front of it: DIRKSEN SENATE BUILDING.

The lobby was small and kind of old-fashioned—lots of wood and well-worn tile. The Capitol police standing guard took our cover names. Then our escort led us up to the fourth-floor offices of James Mitchum, senior senator from the great State of Pennsylvania.

Mitchum was old. Really old—fifty, maybe. He had bags under his eyes and hair so gray it was almost white. His office wasn't as big as I'd expected, but it had a nice view of the Supreme Court Building across the street.

Suit Guy introduced us and then left.

Wordlessly, Mitchum motioned for Sharyn and me to sit in the two guest chairs at his desk. We sat while he studied us—his expression neutral. Even Tom could've taken some "poker face" lessons from this guy.

When he finally spoke, his voice rumbled like thunder.

Good for giving speeches, I supposed. "Hugo Ramirez saved my life once."

After a pause, I replied, "Yes, sir."

"Your name is Andrew?"

"Andy. Andy Forbes."

He turned to Sharyn. "And you're Kim Baker?"

She nodded. Then, remembering herself, she replied, "Yes, sir." Her Philly accent was there, but she'd managed to dial it back. Still didn't quite fit the suit though.

"All right kids, let me explain a few facts of life. You're both here because I owe Hugo Ramirez a debt I can never repay. I won't bore you with the details. Suffice it to say that it would require such a debt for me to overstep my boundaries as I have in this situation. Normally, I don't recommend pages. And, even if I did, pages are *never* accepted mid-term. Now what I would like to know is why Ramirez has taken such an interest in you both that he would pressure me to break that rule. You first, Ms. Baker."

This was it. This was where we found out if the co-chief of the Undertakers, the boss of the Angels crew, and one of the best fighters I'd ever met could rise to a totally different challenge.

Sharyn didn't say a word.

Seconds passed. A lot of them. Too many of them. As I watched, Mitchum's scowl seemed to take up permanent residence on his face and start raising little scowls. I glanced at Sharyn, who sat rigidly in her chair, her eyes focused on nothing.

The senator cleared his throat.

Should I answer for her, or would that just make things worse?

"I ... understand, sir."

But that didn't come from me. It came from Sharyn, who licked her lips and continued. "Sorry, I've been sitting here tryin' ... um ... *trying* ... to figure out how to explain this. See, Hugo ... he's my godfather. My parents kicked ... uh ... passed away last year and, since I'm still underage and got no ... I mean, don't have any other family, they was ... were ... going to drop me into Hugo's ... charge."

Then she smiled a broad "Didn't I totally nail that?" smile.

Mitchum regarded her. "Yes, but you're not *in* Uncle Hugo's charge just now ... are you, young woman?"

Undaunted, Sharyn replied, "That's 'cause ... *be*cause Uncle Hugo's on sabbatical and can't look after me just now. So we talked and he suggested this here ... the page program. He says that'll keep me out of troub ... I mean, productively occupied until he's back."

The senator listened to Sharyn's cover story like a man who listens to all kinds of crap all the time. Of course, Sharyn's explanation had been set up in advance. Mitchum could call Ramirez and get the whole thing verified—and something told me he might.

Finally, with a curt nod, he focused his attention to me. Despite myself, I squirmed a little. Some people give off an "I like children" vibe. Jim Mitchum wasn't one of 'em.

"And you, Andrew?"

"Andy," I corrected.

"Andy. How old are you?"

"I'll be sixteen in July," I lied.

"You don't look it."

"I get that a lot, sir.

"What's your story?"

Ever lie? I don't mean lying to your parents to get out

of chores, or saying you're going to spend the night at some friend's house when you're really planning to sneak into an R-rated movie. I'm talking about lying when something *real* is on the line, when people are counting on you to do it—to *sell* it. I'm talking about lying when your life may depend on it.

If you *have* ever lied like that, then I'm sorry, because it's a terrible thing to have to do. And it's even more terrible when you discover that you do it well.

I did it well, much better than I had when I'd lied to Sharyn on the train. And, believe me, that's not pride talking. Pride's got nothing to do with it.

"My dad was an FBI agent … Uncle Hugo's partner. He got killed during an arrest. Since then, Uncle Hugo's watched over my mom and me. But my mom … well, she's got a problem with alcohol." I felt my eyes fill with tears. Every word tasted bitter, like a betrayal. I'd practiced this speech with Helene, but it'd never hit me like this.

Because *this* time wasn't a rehearsal.

"I'm on the student council at Chapeltown High. Debate team, too. Uncle Hugo always told me, when the time came, I might consider applying to the page program. But I missed the window because my mom …" My voice trailed off—as if there was more but I just couldn't bring myself to say it.

"I understand," Mitchum said. Then he sat back and looked hard at us both. "I've read your essays."

We said nothing.

"They're excellent. Very different, of course. But excellent. You two wouldn't be sitting in those chairs if they weren't, regardless of my debt to Hugo Ramirez."

Neither of us had written anything. The Hackers had

put those papers together based on page program essays they'd somehow dug up on the Internet.

"Do either of you know why I bring this up?" the senator asked.

Sharyn replied, "Yes, sir."

"And why is that, Ms. Baker?"

"Because you want to us to dig … know … that *you* know that we deserve to be here. That it isn't pity and it isn't a free ride. That this is an opportunity, and a rare one."

At that, Mitchum came perilously close to smiling. "Very good. Though I have to say, your writing style and your speaking style seem rather at odds."

Sharyn grinned. "That's what my language arts teachers always say."

More silence. More looking us over like we were insects and his eyes twin magnifying glasses.

"Very well, then," he said. "One of my people will drive you to the page residence and introduce you to the proctors who run the program. After that, you're out of my hands. Clear?"

We both nodded.

Mitchum stood. He was tall and imposing—probably made his living being tall and imposing. "Welcome to Washington, kids," he declared. We both stood as well and shook his hand. "My reputation is on the line here. So I don't expect either of you to cause any trouble."

"Trouble?" Sharyn replied. Then, God help us, she winked at the man. "*Us?*"

CHAPTER 18
THE HUNTER

Lilith Cavanaugh

"What's your name?" the Queen asked from behind the desk in her sixth-floor City Hall office.

The giant tried to answer, but the brick jammed deep into the center of his face seemed to hamper him. Nevertheless, with considerable effort, he managed to croak, "J—ohn T—all, Ma—am."

"John Tall," she echoed. "Your name is *Tall*?"

He nodded.

The creature before her stood nearly seven feet in height and wore a host body that had met its death at least five weeks ago. He was Warrior Caste, a class of *Malum* bred more for strength and loyalty than intelligence. And this particular specimen seemed especially dull. Most *Malum* favored average-sized human hosts, as this simplified the task of finding replacements—rare enough these days.

John Tall was an exception. He liked them *large*; the bigger the better. In his six months since crossing the Rift, he'd inhabited, worn out, and then replaced four bodies, and getting the next was becoming more difficult. Most human males, after all, weren't as big as he'd like them to be.

Still, for all his imposing size, the Queen was pleased to see how he trembled before her.

If only the brick in his face didn't make him look like such a fool.

Humans wouldn't see it, of course. His Cover would prevent that. But still, why hadn't he removed it before now?

"Take that out, John Tall," she said.

Obediently, he reached up and tugged at the brick. It came free in his hand with a *squelch* that would probably have made most humans vomit. A moment later, his weakened skull broke apart—and John Tall's brains spilled out onto the floor. A moment after *that*, his helpless body followed it.

And that's *why he hasn't removed it before now,* the Queen thought.

Yet he'd done so at her command, without comment or complaint. Impressive.

"I have a gift for you," she said to the body sprawled across her carpet. Then she issued a command into her desk intercom.

Two minions, both morgue workers, carried a body bag into her office. They laid it across the rug and unzipped it, revealing the week-old cadaver within.

"I acquired this for you, John," Lilith said. "Knowing your … tastes. It stands six-foot-ten inches and, in life, weighed three hundred pounds. Now, Transfer. We have much to discuss."

The fresh giant in the body bag opened his eyes and sat up. John Tall raised his massive new hands and flexed them. Then he grinned with satisfaction.

"You honor me, Ma'am," he said.

"I'm glad you're happy," the Queen replied. Then to the minions, "Get that other sack of meat out of here." They hurried to obey.

Tall rose on his new legs. His fresh body wore jeans and a flannel shirt, both a bit ragged but serviceable.

"Ma'am?" he said.

"Yes, John?"

"Can I ask where you found this?"

She smiled. "Our people examined hospital records looking for a desirable candidate. This host underwent surgery ... some minor human ailment ... and his height and weight were noted in the computer. Then it was simply a matter of having someone pay him a visit in the middle of the night."

"I'm very grateful," Tall said, bowing low.

The gesture pleased her. "Good. Because I need to rely on your gratitude ... and your loyalty. A delicate task is before you."

"I am forever your servant, Ms. Cavanaugh."

"Sit."

He sat.

She settled herself behind her desk, resting her hands on its polished surface. It was a human gesture, which she instantly regretted. Her own body was approaching three weeks' dead, and the skin tended to *stick* to varnished surfaces.

"How much do you know of the Washington Project?" she asked.

"Nothing, ma'am," he replied. "Just ... talk. A small, select group of *Malum* working on a secret effort to grab federal power."

"Crass but accurate." Then, over next several minutes, Lilith detailed the operation: goals, risks and, most particularly, recent developments. Tall listened without comment, which she liked. Then, when she'd finished, he asked just one question, which she also liked.

"How can I help you, ma'am?"

She said, "I want you to assume a key position among our people in Washington. A place has already been arranged for you with the Capitol Police."

"I understand," he said.

"No you don't, John. Your mission will, of course, be to destroy the abomination by any means necessary. You will also either discredit or kill any human witnesses. We cannot allow this knowledge to become public."

"Of course not, ma'am."

The Queen studied her huge minion. She was taking an awful risk here; she knew that.

"John ... do you remember the last time you were in this office?"

His host's eyes remained as milky and lifeless as ever, but those of his Cover, which Lilith could easily see, turned wary. Tall's projected illusion was, unsurprisingly, that of a huge man, his body thick with muscle and his head shaved bald. Intimidating. Effective. As *this* was the image he chose to show the world, no wonder he favored such large hosts.

"I do, Ms. Cavanaugh."

"Please remind me," she said.

He trembled again. Good. "I was one of the guards assigned to that captured FBI agent. The Undertakers ... they attacked and defeated us."

"Agent Ramirez, yes. As I recall, *you* were the only survivor."

"Uh ... yes, ma'am."

"And how were you disciplined for that failure?" she asked.

His trembling increased. "My host's arms and legs were cut off and I was left alone in a dark place ... to consider my mistakes."

"Ah, yes," she said. "And how long did you remain in that condition?"

"A month, Ms. Cavanaugh."

"A long time."

He nodded, looking terrified now.

"The other day, on South Street, weren't you among those hunting the Birmelin girl?"

"Ma'am, I—"

"Yes or no, John."

"Yes, ma'am."

"And how did *that* effort turn out?"

"We ... lost her."

"To the Undertakers, I believe?"

He nodded again.

"Another failure," she said.

"Yes, Ms. Cavanaugh."

"And one I'm willing to overlook."

Hope flickered on his Cover's face. "Thank you."

"But in return for that act of generosity, I require something from *you*."

"Anything, ma'am!"

"While you're in Washington, you will have a special … duty. You will tell *no one*. You will elicit *no one's* help. Do you understand?"

"Yes, Ms. Cavanaugh!"

"Good. This is sensitive, John. And it's vital."

"I will not fail, Mistress!" he said, so eagerly that he'd used her *Malum* title, which he knew was forbidden. The Queen noticed the slip—but, given the circumstances, ignored it.

She said, "I want you to destroy my sister."

CHAPTER 19
THE FOURTH PROCTOR

"I don't like people getting what they want through political favors. That means I don't like either of *you*."

Lex Burnicky berated us in the foyer of the Daniel Webster Senate Page Residence, a three-story brick-fronted former funeral parlor in northeastern Washington, about six blocks from the Capitol. It was a nice place, what little we'd seen of it so far: lots of wood molding and area rugs.

Lex was one of four resident "proctors"—mostly poly-sci grad students who'd landed gigs as watchdogs for the thirty pages involved in the program each term. They reported to the program director. Lex was short, with narrow shoulders wrapped inside a suit and tie. His brown hair was thin and he sported what he thought was a mustache. Looked more like a dead caterpillar to me.

He also had a *serious* superiority complex.

"But, since you're both here," he continued, "I guess there's nothing I can do about it."

"Guess not," Sharyn replied, smiling.

Two of the other three proctors, a man and a woman, leaned against the nearby wall. They weren't as hostile as Lex—in fact, one of them grinned at Sharyn's remark.

"This isn't a vacation," Lex lectured. "Your day begins at five thirty in the morning, five days a week. School—yes, there's regular *school*—starts at six fifteen and ends ninety minutes before the Senate convenes. That time varies, often from day to day, so you need to be flexible. Most days, you'll be at work at the Capitol before eleven. Expect three hours of homework, unless the Senate runs late … …very late. If that happens, sometimes homework will be forgiven. Sometimes.

"You'll both wear page uniforms every day: a navy blue suit and a white dress shirt. Andy, you'll get a tie. You'll receive name badges and page insignia lapel pins to identify you to senators and their staff. Your haircuts are … acceptable. Kim, keep your makeup minimal and don't wear any extraneous jewelry. Understood?"

"Sure," Sharyn replied.

"Andy?"

"I understand," I said.

"You look young," he remarked.

"Thanks."

He blinked. "Your duties at the Capitol will include whatever the Senate Sergeant at Arms says they will. You'll run errands, deliver messages, and clean up the Senate chamber. You will not speak to a senator unless he or she speaks first, or if you've been instructed to by the Sergeant at Arms' office. Your job is to get out of their way so that they can do *their* job. Clear?"

"As glass." Sharyn grinned.

"There are thirty pages. Some are Democrats. Some are Republicans. You will *not* discuss party affiliations or politics of any kind. This is important, as you'll be spending a lot of time together. We have two sleeping floors in Webster Hall. The second floor is for the girls. The third floor is for boys. The two *don't* mix. Understood?"

"Understood," we both said.

He smirked. "Still glad your senator-buddy got you both in here?"

"Never been happier," Sharyn replied.

Lex turned to the other two proctors. "Maggie, please show Kim to her room. Mark, do the same for Andy. Today's Sunday, and on most Sundays the pages have free time. But you two are going to spend the day getting acclimated. Unpack. Get settled. Explore the house if you want, but stay inside.

"Rules and security are tight. Capitol Police patrol outside. So do as you're told. If you don't, you'll rack up demerits. Too many of *them*, and you're gone. Got it?"

"Got it!" Sharyn and I said together.

Lex chuffed. That's the only word for it: he *chuffed.* Then he disappeared through a nearby archway. Maggie and Mark came forward. They wore matching blue suits. "Sorry about that," Mark said. "Lex takes a little getting used to."

"So does a stick up your butt," Maggie added. "Which is what he's always walking around with."

The joke didn't quite make sense, but I laughed anyway.

Mark said, "There're uniforms waiting for you. Off-duty, what you've got on will work just fine. No jeans. No sweatshirts."

Maggie said, "Come on, we'll show you where you'll be sleeping."

They marched us upstairs. On the third floor, Mark showed me an empty, small, clean room with a window and three beds. "That's yours over there," he said, pointing to a bed near the window. "Your roommates are Devon and Patrick. They're both out right now. But they're good guys; you'll like them."

"Okay," I said.

"Normally, we don't get pages in mid-term. But Senator Mitchum is Senator Mitchum, so the program director … bent the rules. First time ever. I guess when you're chairman of the Senate Budget Committee, you can get around a few 'inconvenient' policies. Your uniforms are in the closet. Senator Mitchum's office sent over your measurements. Try them on, though, just in case. We can swap out something that doesn't fit. Both you and Sharyn will be hitting the Hill tomorrow."

"Hitting the Hill?" I asked.

"Working the Capitol. Your duties will be light at first, since you both missed the formal orientation. That's a problem. There *are* rules, and you're going to have to learn them fast. Lex is a dork, but he's not wrong about that demerits policy. While you're living in Webster, you're a ward of Uncle Sam, and Uncle Sam's a strict parent."

"I hear ya," I said, walking over and testing the bed. It had been a *long* time since I'd slept on a mattress. It felt like a cloud. "So what's the deal with Lex? Is he in charge or something?"

"No," Mark replied. "He just acts like it. Try to stay out of his way."

"I will," I said.

Then a new voice spoke. "So ... this is our new recruit?"

Another young man, dressed as Mark was, stood in the doorway.

"One of them, anyway," Mark replied. "Andy, this is Greg Gardner. He's the fourth proctor. Just started yesterday, in fact."

Smiling, Greg came forward to shake my hand. "Nice to meet you, Andy. Looks like you and me are the newbies. That means we need to stick together."

"Yeah," I said, trying to steady my heartbeat. After shaking his hand, I resisted the urge to wipe my palm on my jeans.

His skin was clammy, but that wasn't surprising.

Greg was a Corpse.

CHAPTER 20
THE FUNERAL GIG

Helene

*C**rack!*

That was the sound a neck made when it broke. It always screeched Helene's blood.

She winced as the Corpse dressed like a mortician dropped into a heap at the Burgermeister's feet. Beside him, Jillian looked green. Her hands shot to her mouth, her eyes wide.

This is what we do, Helene thought.

Dave treated the new girl to a nasty grin. He looked about to say something to her, but Helene put a finger to her lips. Then, with her Super Soaker at the ready, she listened to the house.

Nothing.

The Francis X. Urcott Funeral Home didn't just sound empty, it *felt* empty, and Helene had long ago learned to trust that feeling. This dude, a Type Three in a pinstriped suit, had been the only person on site, Corpse or otherwise. That wasn't surprising because Helene's watch read three A.M., and most of Philly slept at this hour, its businesses closed. But, at the same time, it *was* surprising because two fresh cadavers waited somewhere in this converted Germantown row home, and the Queen should have wised up to what that meant by now.

So Helene listened harder.

Still nothing.

"I think we're good," she whispered.

Dave nodded, absently wiping his hands on his pants. Not that he minded breaking deader necks. Quite the contrary.

It was the *other* kind of neck breaking that had gotten...tough.

"Now what?" Jillian asked softly.

"Now we do what we came here to do," Helene replied.

"Duh," the Burgermeister added.

Helene let it slide.

The three of them navigated the darkened building. While funeral parlors came in all shapes and sizes, there were always similarities: big, fancy rooms with draperies and often caskets on stands for show, a kitchen, bathrooms—and, of course, the basement.

It took them just five minutes to find the right door and another five to carefully make their way down to the "cold room."

"I hate this," the Burgermeister muttered, finding the light switch.

"I know," Helene told him, wincing as the overheads came on.

Ahead of them stood a wall of nine steel morgue drawers, set up in a three-by-three pattern, all closed. They'd have to open each one until they found the bodies they'd been sent here to … process.

"I can't believe I'm doing this," Jillian muttered.

"You get used to it," Helene said.

"*Some* of it," the Burgermeister added, his snide attitude gone, at least for now. Helene knew it wasn't how he really felt anyway. Dave was aware that Sharyn didn't like the new girl, so *he* didn't like the new girl. It was as stupidly simple as that.

Boys.

Then Dave said to her out of the blue, "So, you gotta spy on Will's mom, huh?"

"I told you," Helene replied. "Not spy. Tom wants me to … get friendly … with her."

"Why?" Jillian asked.

"'Cause she's not 'fitting in' around Haven."

The Burgermeister scowled. "Why *you*?"

It was a question Helene had been asking herself for a week now. Of all of the Undertakers to play diplomat to Susan Ritter, Helene seemed—in yearbook terms—the "Least Likely to Succeed."

And Tom knew that, of course. Tom knew everything.

So indeed, why *her*?

"No idea," she told Dave. "Now, quit stalling. Let's get this over with."

His scowl deepened, but he didn't reply. Instead, he stepped up and opened a morgue drawer at random. It was empty.

"I hate this," he said again.

"I know," Helene replied.

"It ain't right." He opened another random drawer. Also empty.

"It's necessary."

"That don't make it right." A third drawer. Nothing. Six more to go.

Standing by the open doorway, looking small and younger than her sixteen years, Jillian watched in quiet disgust. Helene didn't blame her.

It was a disgusting duty.

A couple of months ago, in a funeral parlor basement not too different from this one, Dave had demonstrated a peculiar talent. He *really* knew how to snap a neck. So Tom and Sharyn had decided to put him to work doing just that. And, at first, the Burgermeister had been all gung-ho about it.

It worked like this: every day, the Hackers scoured the city's obituaries, listing any freshly dead people whose cadavers the Corpses might want to—occupy. Then every night they handed that list to the Burgermeister who, accompanied by two other Angels, visited the indicated funeral parlors and made sure that never happened.

It limited the flow of host bodies to the enemy. Helped the war effort. Noble, important work, right?

Except breaking the neck of a regular human person who'd innocently died wasn't the same as breaking the neck of an alien invader wearing a stolen body. These weren't monsters, just *folks*, and the only word for what Dave did, night after night, was *defilement*. An ugly word that described an ugly act. It was disrespectful. Immoral.

Wrong.

But necessary.

Unfortunately, knowing that didn't make your hands

feel any cleaner. Helene, as part of her Angels' duty rotation, only had to do this on Sundays—well, Mondays given the hour. Dave, on the other hand, had been at it every night for weeks. No wonder Will said his roommate hadn't been sleeping.

Jillian, however, was just here to watch and learn, part of the crash-course "Undertakers 101" program that Tom had set up for her. Most recruits went through a two-week "basic training," which helped them get used to their new lives as well as revealed which crew best suited their skills and personalities. Jillian, however, was an Angel down to her toes—that had been plain as day back on South Street. So she'd skipped the preliminaries and had gone straight into the field.

"You miss him?" the Burgermeister asked suddenly.

Helene started. "Huh?"

He stood outside the fourth drawer, his hand poised on its stainless steel handle. "You miss Will?"

"He's only been gone for like sixteen hours."

"Okay, then are you *gonna* miss him?"

"I guess. Aren't you?"

"Yeah," he said. "But I ain't his ... you know."

Helene felt her face redden. "His *what?*"

"Forget it."

"You gonna miss *Sharyn?*" she demanded.

The Burgermeister's scowled returned, but he didn't reply.

"Can we just get out of here?" Jillian asked in a small voice.

"Yeah," Dave mumbled. "Okay."

Then he opened the fourth drawer. Zilch.

Meanwhile, Helene fumed. Sometimes Dave really knew how to piss her off.

She and the Burgermeister *were* friends. Totally. But on some level, they both knew that they were friends only because of Will. Without him as their bridge, the two probably wouldn't hang out, might not even not know each other all that well. Truth be told, Dave sometimes came off as a little too—much. He was loud and quick to anger and he often said or did things without thinking about them first, a trait that Helene always found irritating.

But doesn't Will do the same thing?

Helene blew out a sigh and said, "Lemme help."

The Angels' job on these missions was to keep watch while Dave did his thing. But now, as he opened a fifth drawer, she stepped up and opened a sixth.

Both were empty.

"Huh," Dave grunted.

Three left.

"How many were there supposed to be again?" Jillian asked.

"Two," Helene replied. "One man and one woman."

The Burgermeister opened a seventh drawer. She opened the eighth.

Nothing.

"Crap," he muttered. He and Helene swapped looks.

"What's going on?" said Jillian. "Aren't they here?"

The Undertakers didn't answer. Instead they focused on the last drawer.

Helene felt her mouth go dry.

"You do it," Dave said.

"Uh-uh. *You* do it," she said.

"Oh for God's sake!" Jillian snapped, and came forward and opened the last drawer. Despite everything else she was feeling at the moment, Helene was impressed. It's not as easy to open a morgue drawer in the middle of the night as you'd think, empty or not.

It was empty.

"Double crap," Helene muttered.

"Maybe Sammy's crew made a mistake," Dave suggested. "Sent us to the wrong place."

She shook her head. "Since when do the Hackers make mistakes?"

And it was true. Sammy Li, the Hacker Boss, ran what was probably the tightest ship in Haven.

"Could the bodies be somewhere else around here?" Jillian asked. "Maybe in the caskets upstairs?"

"They keep 'em refrigerated until right before the service," Helene replied.

"So's they don't stink," Dave added miserably.

"I don't get it," the new girl said, looking from Helene to Dave. "What's this mean?"

Helene and the Burgermeister swapped another look. Then Helene answered.

"We've been set up."

CHAPTER 21
BEING WILL

Helene

Helene was astonished to see relief flash across the Burgermeister's face.

Then she understood.

True, they were in trouble here—*big* trouble. Cavanaugh had wised to the funeral gig and arranged for her people, many of whom actually *ran* funeral parlors, to publish a couple of fake obituaries. Bait. There might be a dozen, maybe *two* dozen, walking dead surrounding this place at this exact moment.

But at least he didn't have to snap any innocent necks tonight.

Cold comfort if we get ripped apart, though.

"What do we do?" Jillian asked, sounding breathless.

Instead of answering, Helene pulled out the new satellite phone she'd been issued. It was about the size of a regular, clamshell-style cell phone, though it lacked even basic features like an MP3 player or a camera. Just calling and texting, but *untraceable* calling and texting, which was the point.

She dialed a number.

"7-Eleven," Dan McDevitt's voice answered, sounding bored. With the new sat phones, a code system had been set up—added security.

"Oh," Helene said. "I meant to dial 911."

"This is 711," Dan told her.

"My bad," she said, completing the code. "Dan, it's Helene. We got trouble. Dave, Jillian, and I are on that funeral gig up in Germantown … only the bodies aren't here."

That woke him up. "A trap?" he asked in his deep baritone, even deeper than the Burgermeister's.

"Probably," she said.

"I'll let Tom know. We'll get you backup. Sit tight."

"Can't," Helene told him. "You're a half hour away at least. We're in the basement. One exit. If we get cornered down here, we're done. We gotta move."

"Okay," Dan said, taking the news in stride. He was a Chatter, and Chatters were trained to stay cool in a crisis. One person on the call panicking was enough. Not that Helene was panicking—not really. Not yet. "I'll dispatch the Angels anyway. Let us know where to find you."

"Will do," she said, closing the phone. "I've got a Super Soaker, a water pistol, and a Ritter. You two?"

"A water pistol and a Ritter," the Burgermeister replied.

"Nothing," Jillian admitted. "No training."

Dave handed her his water pistol. "Consider yourself trained."

Helene said. "I'll go first. If we see a deader, I'll shoot

'em, then Dave'll snap his neck. Jillian, you bring up the rear."

"Okay," the new girl said. She sounded scared.

She should be.

"Let's *do* this," the Burgermeister said. He *wasn't* scared. Nothing scared Dave Burger, not that Helene had seen anyway.

The stairs going up to the main floor stood empty. So did the hallway and foyer. It looked like a clear shot to the front door. They'd come in that way using a fancy, police-issue electric lock picker that Ramirez had scored for them. Not as quick as Will's pocketknife, but it had done the job.

Were they watching us even then? Helene wondered bitterly. *Just waiting for us to come back out?*

There had to be another exit, maybe more than one. But the Corpses surely had the place surrounded. At least out front they'd be on the open street in a crowded, if sleeping neighborhood. Maybe, if the three of them could somehow wake the neighbors, the number of witnesses would give the deaders pause.

As plans went, it entirely sucked.

Cautiously, Helene peaked through the curtains beside the front door.

Jeez...

A half-dozen deaders filled the sidewalk beyond the front stoop. They were Type Twos, strong-looking and as fresh as Cavanaugh could muster. All wore cop uniforms. The one nearest the window found her eyes and held them. Then he smiled wide—too wide—showing yellowed, crooked teeth. His tongue was black.

Helene pulled away with a gasp.

"I count six," she said, trying to keep her voice steady.

"But there're probably more out back."

"I wish Will was here," Dave said.

So do I. He'd come up with something ... some screwball plan that would be completely crazy and yet would somehow actually get us outta this.

She needed to do that. She needed to be Will. Think like he thought.

"What do we do?" Jillian asked, her voice surprisingly steady. "Sooner or later they're going to storm the place, aren't they?"

Yeah, they are, Helene thought. *Once they're convinced we're not coming out, they'll come in through every possible exit. Six from the front. Maybe six more from the back. And maybe another six from the playground next door.*

Playground next door ...

"Helene," the Burgermeister said, sounding wary. "Why're you grinnin'?"

"Because," she told them both. "I just had a really bad idea."

The upstairs of the Francis X. Urcott Funeral Home was devoted to office space. A quick exploration took them to a window with a good view of the neighboring park. This being the city, the park and the converted house almost butted up against each other, separated only by a narrow alley.

There were Corpses there, in the playground, amidst the swings and jungle gyms. But only three.

Helene felt her smile widen.

Jillian saw what she saw. "Yep. A really bad idea."

"You up for it?" Helene asked her.

"I can get there," the new girl said, clutching her borrowed water pistol. "But they'll be on me the second I hit the ground. I don't know how to handle your weapons."

Helene shook her head. "Jill, you *are* a weapon. You just don't know it yet."

She handed her Super Soaker to Dave, who was looking from one to the other as if the girls were speaking Greek. "Here's how this is going to go down," she said.

And then she told him all of it.

A minute later, Helene stepped through the window and onto a fire escape that overlooked the alley and the playground beyond. Then, as Jillian followed, she climbed up on the railing, steadied herself—and jumped.

The alley flashed below her, all smells and shadows. Then, scary fast, the top bar of the nearest swing set rushed up to meet her.

As Jillian had been showing her all week in their *parkour* lessons, Helene didn't cover up—which was what her instincts told her to do. Instead she spread her arms and caught the cold, steel bar with both hands. Then she let her momentum carry her under it, between two of the hanging, empty swings, and feet first into the face of the nearest deader.

He never saw it coming. The two of them collided and crashed down onto the brown mulch that carpeted the playground. Before his scrambling hands could grab her, Helene planted her Ritter in the dead dude's chest, slamming its plunger home. Then she rolled off of him an instant before he exploded.

One down, she thought, regaining her feet just in time to see the other two Corpses whirl on her.

Now, Dave! she thought.

And, as he always did, the Burgermeister came through.

A laser-thin stream of water caught one deader in the side of his face. A second later, a second stream nailed the other one in the small of his back. The first guy went into convulsions, staggered a bit, and then slammed face first into one of the diagonal swing struts. The second one fell and started spinning in crazy circles like Curly in the Three Stooges.

The saltwater wouldn't keep these guys down long. Worse, the rest of the deaders were already looking their way, alerted by their exploding buddy. As Helene watched, they started toward her at a run.

She rushed to the first Corpse, the one twitching and hugging the swing set strut, and punched him hard in the back of the neck. It wasn't enough to crush his spine, but it did drop him to the ground, buying her a few more precious seconds.

A hiss behind her made her spin around in time to see the second deader, having more or less recovered, lunging at her. The hands jutting out from the cuffs of his cop shirt were black and gnarled, the nails long. In moments, he would tear her throat out with them.

Jillian appeared in a flash of movement, swinging under the overhead bar as Helene had, but then riding her momentum all the way to the adjacent jungle gym. There she somehow slipped, feet first, between two horizontal bars and caught an adjacent vertical strut with one hand, all without touching the ground. Finally, still riding the force of her original leap, she whirled her body around the strut, high and straight and as graceful as a vision in a dream.

The dream ended when she met the hesitant Corpse, who didn't even jazz to her being there until the new girl's legs clamped around his skinny dead neck. Then, before he could react, Jillian barrel-rolled in mid-air and dropped to the mulch-covered ground, bringing the dead dude with her—neck first.

Crack.

Job done, she scrambled away from the limp cadaver and stood up, her eyes finding Helene's in the gloom.

"See?" Helene told her, smiling. "You *are* a weapon!"

Footsteps rattled nearby. Corpses crowded into the playground through the open gate. As they did, Dave sprayed them with the Super Soaker until a pile of twitching bodies blocked any easy exit from the park.

Good, Helene thought. *But not enough.*

She leaned over the cop she'd downed by the swings—and pulled the service revolver out of his holster.

Deaders didn't use guns. Not ever. No one knew why. But, being dressed as cops, they *had* to carry them. When she'd explained this part of her "bad idea," the Burgermeister had objected, saying, "Will don't use guns."

"I know," Helene had told him. "But I'm not Will."

As Jillian watched, Helene shot the fallen Corpse in the back of his head. The sound was like a cannon blast.

Then she turned and started shooting cars.

The first two shots did nothing, but the third—as she'd hoped—kicked off a car alarm. It wailed like a newborn, flooding the street with shrill sound. Seconds later, Helene got lucky again and another alarm went off. Then a third. That left her out of bullets.

But the damage had been done. Lights switched on in the surrounding windows as an angry Germantown woke up.

"Dave!" she yelled. "Come on!"

The Burgermeister was a good fighter and, as it turned

out, a pretty decent shot with the Super Soaker. *Who knew?* But *parkour* was a little out of his area. So he had to step out onto the fire escape and make his way over to a ladder. It took maybe a minute for him to join them and, by then, most of the Corpses he'd squirted were up and looking at them.

But so were about a dozen others, all normal people awakened by the screaming alarms.

As she'd hoped, their presence made the deaders hesitate.

How Helene wished she could call to them, tell them what was going on, make them see. Or, more to the point, make them *See*. But she couldn't. Grown-ups didn't believe. Not ever. A bitter lesson, bitterly learned a long time ago.

Instead, she dropped the useless gun while Dave continued to hose the Corpses, who were still too bunched up together in the playground entrance to escape the crippling water. Then the three of them backed up to the rear of the park, which stood bathed in shadows. There, Jillian went over the fence first, followed by Helene and finally the Burgermeister.

They had maybe thirty seconds to disappear before Cavanaugh's pets regrouped and came after them.

But they were Undertakers, and thirty seconds was more than enough.

"Is this how it always is?" Jillian asked once they were reasonably safe.

"Better night than most," Dave replied with a grin. Then to Helene: "I think I know why Tom picked you to buddy up to Will's mom."

"You're bringing this up *now*?" Helene shot back.

"Yeah."

She sighed. "Okay. Why?"

His grin widened, his teeth looking white and straight in the darkness. "'Cause, you kinda *are* Will. Girl Will. And he figures Mrs. Ritter'll start seein' that, too."

He'd meant it as a compliment. So that was how she took it.

CHAPTER 22
THE CAPITOL

I watched as the biggest American flag I'd ever seen was hoisted into the late-morning sky. The size of a bedsheet, it caught the wind and whipped out to its full glory over the roof of the Capitol building, symbolizing the Land of the Free and the Home of the Brave—and, more specifically, that the United States Senate was now in session.

The guy doing the hoisting was a short, stocky man in his fifties named Charles O'Mally. O'Mally was the Senate's Sergeant at Arms. Having that title didn't mean that he went around the Capitol armed, or even in uniform. His responsibilities centered around making sure everything went smoothly for the one hundred senators in the fancy chamber downstairs. He had a staff, called Doorkeepers and, of course, he had thirty Senate pages to do his grunt work.

But none of *them* was here, running Old Glory up its flagpole. The Sergeant at Arms preferred to handle this duty himself.

And me? Well, I was here because I'm a redhead.

O'Mally was *very* Irish-American. He wore an American flag pin on one lapel and a shamrock on the other. His hair was as red as mine, and that's saying something—a fact he noticed the moment Sharyn and I reported to his office on Monday morning.

After six months of jeans and T-shirts, the page uniform felt confining. I disliked it, but Sharyn *hated* it. Nevertheless, we'd passed Lex's appraisal—barely—before leaving with the other pages for the short walk to the Capitol. One of my roommates, Devon, had told me that on rainy days the Sergeant at Arms's office sometimes sent a car. "But usually we use our feet in this job."

"He's right, Red." Patrick, my other roommate had laughed. "Better get used to it." I'd only just met these two. But Mark had been right: they *were* good guys.

Still …

"Do me a favor?" I'd asked Patrick.

"Sure."

"Stop calling me Red?"

"You don't like Red?"

"You like Blondie?" Devon asked. Patrick had hair the color of straw.

Patrick looked horror-stricken. "Point taken. No more Red."

When we reached the Capitol, most of the pages already knew where to go, while Sharyn and I were escorted to the Sergeant at Arms' office for introductions and assignments. That's where we encountered Charles O'Mally, who took one look at me and lit up like a Christmas tree.

"Well, now! There's a genuine Irish Ginger if ever I saw

one! What's your name, boy?"

"Andy Forbes."

"Forbes, is it?" he asked, scowling. "That's an English name, by God!"

"Sorry," I said.

He grinned. "No worries. I'll just call you Red."

I sighed.

O'Mally went on, "Besides, I'd wager there's more than a little good Irish blood in your veins … eh, Mr. Forbes." Then he turned to Sharyn. "Ms. Baker, is it? I want you to report yourself to Mr. Stanz. You'll find him in the hall, waiting for you."

"Yes, sir," she said.

"Should I go, too?" I asked.

O'Mally shook his head. "Not just yet, Ginger."

Oh, you've gotta be kidding me!

The Sergeant at Arms waggled a finger at me. "You'll be joining your friend shortly. But first, you and I have a very special duty to perform."

And that's how I ended up on the roof of the Capitol, watching O'Mally raise the Stars and Stripes. There are two such flags, one for the Senate and one for the House of Representatives, the chambers of which occupy the north and south wings of the Capitol building, respectively.

Ever seen the Capitol? Not pictures of it, I mean, but in person?

The first thing that strikes you is how *big* it is, with a central dome that rises more than fifteen stories high. From a distance, it's impressive. Up close, it's breathtaking.

"Something else, isn't it?" O'Mally remarked, as if reading my mind.

I nodded.

"Know what it's made of?"

"The dome? I dunno. Marble?"

He laughed. "Cast iron."

"Yeah?"

"Almost nine million tons of it."

"It *looks* like marble."

"It's painted to look that way. You're from Philly, right?"

I nodded.

"The top of your City Hall tower's the same: cast iron painted to look like stone. A common technique."

"I didn't know that."

"Not a lot of folks do. Here's another tidbit: that dome you see's actually the *second* one. The first was built by Charles Bulfinch back in 1823. It was a lot smaller and made of copper. Turned green after a few years. Nobody liked it much. So, around 1860, the new Architect of the Capitol, Thomas Walter, designed the one you see now. Big improvement, if you ask me."

"It's cool," I said. And it was. "Think they'll ever build a third one?"

The guy laughed like Santa Claus. "You never know *what's* going to happen in this town. The current Architect of the Capitol's a woman, first one ever. Maybe she'll decide to paint the whole thing pink."

That sounded pretty sexist to me; Sharyn would've glared at him hot enough to melt his shoes. I decided to skip it. "There's still an Architect of the Capitol?"

"Always has been. The first one was appointed by George Washington. Since then there've been more than a dozen, mostly voted in by Congress. The Architect sits on the Capitol Police Board, along with the Sergeant at Arms of the House of Representatives, and … well … me."

"You're the chief of the Capitol Police?" I asked.

"Nope. That's a very able gentleman named Bob Mittenzwei. I'm more like the *commissioner* of police—one of them, anyway." He gazed up at the raised flag. "Never get tired of looking at that." Then he saluted smartly, something I didn't think I'd ever seen anyone who wasn't wearing a uniform do. "Marine," he told me. "Twelve years."

"Cool," I said. "But don't you mean ex-Marine?"

"No such thing, Ginger," he replied. "Come on. Right about now, your friend Kim's getting an earful from one of my Doorkeepers about protocol and expected conduct in the Senate chamber. Let's go rescue her."

And "rescue" was a pretty good word for it.

Sharyn fidgeted in the third-floor hallway as some guy talked *at* her, listing things she had to do—and the things she'd better *not* do, while working in the Capitol. Sharyn was trying to stay in character, but lectures had never been her favorite pastime.

"Remember, young lady," the guy instructed, "being here is one of the easiest privileges in the world to lose. Ah, here's Mr. O'Mally. Mr. O'Mally, I believe you've met Ms. Baker?"

"I have indeed, Mr. Stanz. In fact, this here's Andy Forbes, the other new page. Ginger, this is Jerry Stanz, my good right arm."

Stanz eyed me as if I was something he'd stepped in. "Nice to meet you, Mr. Forbes."

"You, too," I said.

O'Mally faced Sharyn. "Ms. Baker, have you been advised of the do's and dont's?"

"Yes, sir," Sharyn replied, courageously suppressing an eye roll.

"You'll have to forgive us. Normally, a page goes through an orientation that does a slower and more thorough job of it. But given your unique circumstances …"

"I understand, sir," she said.

"Good."

Stanz asked, "Should I be orienting Mr. Forbes as well?"

O'Mally waved him off. "Ms. Baker can fill him in on the details. For now, Ginger, here's the bottom line: You do whatever you're told. You don't speak unless spoken to and, when in doubt, come to me or Mr. Stanz here. You'll never get in trouble for asking a question. Clear?"

"Clear," I said.

He eyed me carefully. "Good. Now let me ask *you* a question."

"Okay."

"You mind me calling you Ginger?"

I looked him right in the eye and replied, "I hate it."

He burst out laughing. "Finally! A little honesty in this godforsaken building! Andy, my boy, you and I'll get along just fine. Mr. Stanz, these two will spend the next hour watching our favorite lawmakers in glorious action. Escort them there and make sure they understand the protocols."

"Of course, Mr. O'Mally."

The Sergeant at Arms of the United States Senate slapped us both on the back—hard. "Welcome to the Capitol, kids!"

CHAPTER 23
DULL AND DANGEROUS

K now how they tell you never to talk in libraries? Well that's *nothing* compared to the gag order in the Senate chamber.

You so much as cough and a guy with a gun glares at you. Shuffle your feet too loud and a hand lands on your shoulder like a twenty-pound weight. And laugh? Well, trust me, don't laugh.

The chamber is rectangular, two stories high, and windowless, being located in the center of the Capitol's north wing. On the floor, a hundred polished wooden desks, one for each senator, are set up in a precise semi-circle, all facing a raised platform—called a rostrum, where the president of the Senate, who's also the vice president of the United States, presides.

Except he wasn't there today.

Later on, while eating lunch with the other pages, we learned that the vice president is almost *never* in the Senate chamber. Presiding over the Senate, which means keeping arguments from getting too nasty, is usually assigned to new—or "freshman"—senators.

It's a job nobody wants.

And after spending just one hour in there, I totally got why.

For about ten minutes, it was cool. The US Senate! One-half of the Congress, right? Maybe even the "better" half, since there are only a hundred senators and 435 congressmen. That should mean it's a *much* bigger deal to be a senator, right?

Yeah, right.

After those first ten minutes, Sharyn and I swapped unhappy looks. There were perhaps ten people occupying those desks down below, with one guy on his feet talking about agriculture or something. Even *he* looked bored.

After the first half hour passed, Sharyn had fallen asleep—and I was fighting just to get oxygen to my brain.

Want to know what kept me awake?

I got *pissed.*

I mean, I'd always known the adult world was clueless. But, until this moment, getting stern looks from armed guards every time I stifled a yawn, I'd never realized *how* clueless.

Ian was dead! Half of me wanted to jump to my feet and tell them that, scream at them to open their *freakin'* eyes! An Undertaker had given his life, and they didn't even *know* about it! No purple heart for Ian MacDonald. No flag-draped coffin. We couldn't even tell his parents!

Meanwhile, down in that chamber, a dude in a tailored suit kept droning on about farm subsidies, whatever they were.

But all that changed when the chamber doors opened and two well-dressed dead people walked in.

I sat up straighter and nudged Sharyn who, giving her credit, pulled off a pretty decent, "I was awake the whole time," thing and leaned forward in her chair.

Two Corpses, a male and a female, marched down the chamber's center aisle as the dude giving the farm subsidies speech, seeing them, faltered.

The female smiled at him—a really awful thing.

"Excuse me, Senator Cabot," she said. "I apologize for interrupting."

"Of course, Senator Micha," the speaker replied.

"I wonder," the thing calling itself Lindsay Micha asked, "if you would mind yielding the floor to me, just for a few minutes."

Farm Subsidy Guy stiffened. He minded *a lot*. But he said, "Certainly, Senator." Then he addressed the guy in the president's chair. "With your permission, Mr. Acting President."

"Of course," Big Chair Guy said.

Beside me, Sharyn whispered, "Did I miss something? That dude's the acting president?"

I didn't bother to respond. Instead, I took the opportunity to cross my eyes and have a look at the creature who was now addressing the Senate—at least, what little of it was on hand to listen.

"My colleagues and fellow lawmakers," she said in her dead, raspy voice, which I was sure rang clear and true to these blind grown-ups. "I apologize for my absence over these past months. I was addressing personal and professional issues, which have occupied all of my energies."

Micha's Mask was of a woman about sixty, short and slender, her gray hair expertly styled. She stood straight and confident, smiling and making eye contact with everyone. A solid public speaker.

"But all that's in the past," she went on. "I've come today to tell you that I will be holding a press conference in one week, at which I will make an announcement ... one that has me and my staff very excited."

Sharyn whispered, "Don't they ... like ... televise the Senate like *all* the time?"

I nodded. "C-SPAN, I think."

"That means she's on camera right now. Any Seer watching will dig that she's a deader. Ain't she been off the grid all this time to *prevent* that?"

I nodded again. Apparently Senator Micha wasn't worried about Seers anymore.

"Shhh!" a guard hissed.

We shushed.

Lindsay Micha talked for ten more minutes, describing some of the stuff she'd been up to while out of the public eye: drafting bills, attending closed committee meetings, and—most especially—talking strategy with her staff. "But as to the nature of those strategic discussions," she added, still smiling, "I'm afraid you'll all have to wait until next Tuesday. Thank you for your time."

And, just like that, the Corpse Who Went to Washington left the chamber the same way she'd come in. After a minute, Farm Subsidy Guy picked up where he'd left off.

A little later, the guard led us out.

And that's when our first day as Senate pages really began.

Our first assignment was to deliver a sealed envelope to the Hart Senate Building, a four-block walk from the Capitol. "What's in the envelope is not your concern," Stanz explained. "Usually, new pages are escorted on their first deliveries ... but as there *are* two of you, I'll skip that part. You don't stop for anything—not soda, not texting. You don't put that envelope down, and you don't surrender it to anyone except the senator to whom it's addressed or one of his staffers. Understood?"

We understood.

Hart and Dirksen were connected, which made going from one to the other pretty easy. This was handy since, by the time we got there, passed through security, found the right senator on the right floor, and delivered the envelope, lunchtime had arrived.

Pages ate in a cafeteria in the Dirksen basement. It's nicer than it sounds, a couple of steps up from a school lunchroom and *way* better than anything Haven has to offer. There were already some pages there, including Devon and Patrick, who waved us over.

The food was simple, but decent. Between sleeping in a bed last night and eating something that wasn't microwaved, I thought I might get used to the page lifestyle.

Then the questions started.

"So, where do you guys come from?" The asker was Hayden, a girl at our table.

"Philly," Sharyn replied.

"How do you two know Senator Mitchum?" Devon asked.

Sharyn and I recited our cover stories, including our

separate—and completely manufactured—relationships with Hugo Ramirez.

Hayden asked, "Did you two know each other before you both became pages?"

"No," Sharyn said.

"Yes," I said.

Crap.

Patrick leered. "Oh! So *that's* how it is!"

"No!" Sharyn and I exclaimed at once. Then, her face darkening, the fake "Kim Baker" improvised. "I mean, we'd met ... sure. But I don't think I'd said more'n two words to W—Andy, not until we both ended up on the train coming down here. That was yesterday."

"Sure." Patrick grinned.

Devon said, "Better not try any ... private stuff in Webster Hall. That's a major infraction. You'd be on a train back to Philadelphia by nightfall!"

"It's not like that," I said, my cheeks burning.

Devon shrugged. "I'm just saying."

"Wow!" Hayden exclaimed. "Check out *this* guy!"

We all turned toward the cafeteria door. My heart leaped into overdrive.

A huge dead man had just appeared at the entrance to the Dirksen cafeteria.

The Corpse wore the uniform of a Capitol cop, though how they found one to fit his frame was a mystery. He was enormous—an early Type Two, still juicy and very strong. But that wasn't what made my heart sink.

I crossed my eyes, though I needn't have bothered. There was only one deader I knew who favored host bodies *that* big.

Sharyn whispered to me, "His Mask looks kinda familiar."

It ought to. This was the Corpse who'd nearly killed her during a scrape at Eastern State Penitentiary in Philly, the same guy who'd dogged Jillian, Helene, and me on South Street.

"We need to talk," I whispered back.

CHAPTER 24
STRATEGIZING ON THE MALL

S pring in DC is some kind of big deal.

Big, pink blossoms filled the cherry trees that lined the National Mall from the Lincoln Memorial on one side to the US Capitol on the other. People came from all over the country to see these trees. Thousands of them. They crowded the Mall, which made it hard to find a quiet meeting place.

Or so I thought.

It was Sunday, six days into our Washington mission, when Sharyn and I—trying to strengthen the idea that we were just acquaintances—made separate plans for the day. Sharyn told the proctors she wanted to visit a friend, which was sort of true. But since I couldn't use the same excuse, I announced my plans to check out the National Portrait Gallery, thereby virtually guaranteeing none of the other pages would want to tag along.

Sharyn split Webster Hall first. I went maybe an hour later.

We met up on the Mall, safely concealed in the crowds

wandering the big, grassy park between the Smithsonian Aerospace and Natural History museums. There we found the pre-arranged bench under the pre-arranged blossoming cherry tree at the prearranged time. We hadn't figured the bench would be available, not with all of these people around. But it was.

The FRESH PAINT sign might have had something to do with it.

Sharyn grinned and sat down. After a moment, I joined her. The bench, of course, was completely dry—though it had obviously been scoured, probably during the night, to make it *look* newly painted.

"Sweet scam," Sharyn remarked. "Simple but effective."

"Thanks," a voice replied. Then a figure squeezed in between us. "As your brother says, when it comes to plans, the simpler the better."

I almost didn't recognize Special Agent Hugo Ramirez.

"What's hangin', Hugo?" Sharyn asked, smiling. "How long you been combin' your hair with a buff rag?"

Ramirez was totally bald.

He ran one hand self-consciously over his smooth scalp. "When you go into hiding, one of the best things you can do is change your hair. Couldn't dye it. Blond or redhead wouldn't match my skin tone. So I shaved it."

Sharyn rubbed at her own short hair. "At least it was your call. I just woke up and bang, the dreads I'd worn since I was twelve were all over the infirmary floor!"

Again: another story.

"I know," Ramirez told her. "I was there. Listen kids, I'm glad you called this meet. I've got some things to tell you both."

"Mind if we go first?" Sharyn asked.

He sighed. "Go ahead."

So I did. "One of the proctors is a Corpse."

Ramirez looked stunned. "Are you sure?" Then: "Sorry. Of course you're sure."

"And not just him," said Sharyn. "Some of the Capitol cops are deaders, too. More than you'd think."

He replied, "That much I *do* know. The thing is ... there was an ... incident in the Capitol last week."

"An incident?" I asked.

"A murder," he said.

Now it was *our* turn to look stunned.

"And, while I'm not 100 percent certain," he added, "I *think* the victim was a Corpse."

Sharyn asked, "How ya figure?"

"Well, officially, this murder never happened. By that I mean no body has been found there. What *was* found turned up some blocks away, in a commercial Dumpster. And even that was just ... well ... parts. Apparently the victim was mostly ... devoured."

"Devoured," Sharyn echoed. "As in *eaten?*"

Ramirez nodded again, looking sallow. "One leg below the knee and half an arm ... that's all that was recovered. But the initial examination, conducted right after the murder, showed that both limbs had been dead for nearly a month."

"I don't get it," I said. "If this guy supposedly died last week, but the cadaver they found is a Type Three ... then what makes you think it's even the same dude? Heck, how do you know for sure that anything went down in the Capitol in the first place?"

"That's the Capitol Police Board's official stand on the

matter," Ramirez replied. "Which is why they're leaving the case to the DC cops. Thing is: the arm wore a watch belonging to a Capitol cop who went missing in the Rotunda last week. So, as I see it, either he walked off his job in the middle of the night and, for some reason, decided to put his watch on the wrist of disembodied arm that must *already* have been devoured and trashed ..."

"Long shot," Sharyn admitted.

"... or," Ramirez said, "he was one of Cavanaugh's people, got eaten in the Rotunda, and then had his ... leftovers dropped into that Dumpster."

The Rotunda is this huge round room that sits right under the big, white dome in the center of the Capitol. It's kind of a reception hall, exactly halfway between the Senate and House Chambers, and directly atop the Capitol "Crypt," which is where George Washington was supposed to have been buried.

Except he wasn't. I used to know why not.

"Sounds like more questions than answers," Sharyn said. "Any way to be sure?"

"Maybe." Ramirez showed us a cell phone photo of a guy in the black cop uniform; it looked like a yearbook shot or something. "This is the missing Capitol policeman," he said. "His name is ...was ... Richard Camp. Have a look with those magic eyes of yours."

We looked.

"Yep," I said.

"He's a deader," Sharyn said.

Ramirez nodded. He looked tired. "Camp wasn't alone when he was attacked in the Rotunda. His partner was with him. *He's* the reason this whole thing came up ... his story about what happened that night hasn't been sitting well with the Capitol Police Board."

"Are we sure *he's* human?" I asked.

Wordlessly, he showed us a second cell phone photo. Another Capitol cop in uniform. Another yearbook shot.

"Human," Sharyn and I said together.

Again he nodded. "I figured. Camp was pretty new. He'd only been on with Capitol cops for six months. But his partner's record shows five years of good service. That's long before the invasion started. Thing is, he's been completely discredited because of the story he tells."

"What story?" asked Sharyn.

"Well, as pages, you've both been to the Rotunda."

"Plenty of times," I confirmed.

"But what you might not have noticed is that there aren't any lamps in there. The only light is what filters in through the rows of windows in the dome. That means on a cloudy night it can get *very* dark. Well, that's how it was the night someone killed Camp. Except that, according to the partner, Camp wasn't killed by a some*one*. He was killed by a some*thing*."

Sharyn blinked. "Say *what* now?"

"According to the partner, a ... creature came out of nowhere, dropping down on them from above. One second it wasn't there, and the next it was on top of his partner, eating him. Camp was kicking and screaming."

"Jeez," I muttered. "That's crazy!"

He replied, "That's what the chief of the Capitol Police says."

"Could the partner *describe* this ... thing?" Sharyn asked.

"Yes, for all the good it's done him. He's suspended temporarily, pending a full investigation. The Capitol Police Board's very tight-lipped about the whole affair.

They figure this guy's either in shock, completely insane, or implicated in his partner's disappearance somehow. I haven't talked to him personally, but I've read his report. He claims to have shot at the thing, but that the bullets did nothing ... nothing at all."

"Jeez," I muttered again.

"Apparently the ... 'monster' is the only word I can come up with ... ignored his attacks, even going so far as to push the partner out of the way. Gently but firmly, was the way he described it."

"Not wonder they think he's nuts," I said. "But where's the arm in the Dumpster come into it?"

"It was found two days ago and turned in. Frankly, it wouldn't have been tied to the Rotunda incident at all if it hadn't been for the victim's watch. After all, as far as the Capitol Board is concerned, it *can't* be the same man. The arm's been dead too long."

"But you knew better," Sharyn said with a grim smile. "You have learned much, grasshopper!"

He smiled thinly. "Let's just say I have a clearer understanding of how the world really works."

"But what's it all *mean*?" she asked. "What're we dealin' with here?"

I digested what Ramirez had told us; no pun intended. Then I said, "Sounds like some ... *thing* ... had a Corpse for lunch."

Gross. Seriously *gross.*

I mean, we lived lives that put us up to our armpits in "disgusting." But even by *our* standards, this was awful.

"Could the deader still be alive?" Sharyn wondered, looking a little green. "In that leg or arm? Or did the *Malum* inside get iced during all the munching?"

"That concerned me, too," replied Ramirez. He held up his phone a third time. "This is a crime scene photo, taken at the Dumpster when the … remains were found. I should warn you both, it's hard to look at."

Sharyn and I looked.

An arm and a leg. No biggie.

"Seen worse," Sharyn said. I nodded agreement.

Ramirez nodded, too, though for some reason he looked unhappy about it.

"But no Mask," I told him. "No sign of Corpse illusion. Camp's not in there. He's totally gone."

Sharyn added, "So it figures that, whatever wasted this deader, did more'n eat his host body. It ate *him*, too."

"But what *is* it?" I asked. "I mean, do we gotta add a *ghoul* to our list of things to worry about?"

Ramirez didn't reply.

"Nobody at Webster Hall said nothin' about this," Sharyn pointed out. "You'd figure that kinda news would totally stoke the gossip train!"

"Webster Hall doesn't know," Ramirez replied. "Very few people do. Remember, as far as the Hill is concerned, one of their cops is missing and another is either crazy or guilty. In their eyes, there *is* no monster running round the Capitol, eating walking-dead men. So there's no reason to warn anybody about anything."

"What exactly does Camp's partner say he saw?" I asked. "What's this 'monster' look like?"

"Man-sized but with something like ten legs and a weird head that seemed to be, in his words, 'everywhere at once.'"

"What's *that* mean?" Sharyn demanded.

"Not a clue. But you can see why his superiors assume

either he's lying ... or has completely lost his grip on reality."

Of course. They were grown-ups, and grown-ups almost never understood anything that didn't fit into their happy, little worldview.

For some reason, I thought about my mom. *Is she still mad at me?* Then I pushed that away. I was an Undertaker on a mission.

"We should check this out," I said.

"You're half right, little bro," Sharyn remarked pointedly.

"What?"

"Tell him about the big wormbag," she said.

"Big wormbag?" Ramirez asked.

When I didn't answer right away, Sharyn answered for me. "One of the Capitol cops ... well, we've run into him before."

Ramirez looked alarmed. "He recognized you?"

I shook my head. "No. But I recognized *him*. Saw him just a couple of weeks ago on South Street. He's a giant, gotta be pushing seven feet ... at least those are the bodies he likes to occupy. Don't know where he finds them, but the Queen's gotta be involved, right? I mean, we did some serious damage to him last time ... and now he shows up with another super-sized host!"

Ramirez asked, "You think Cavanaugh got him a fresh cadaver to wear and then sent him down here?"

"Maybe. But he didn't see me. I don't even think he was even *looking* for me, or for anyone like me."

He frowned. "I'm not following."

"We were eating lunch in Dirksen when this huge

deader just poked his head in and kinda scanned the room. But he didn't notice me. Sure, I was wearing this blue suit and sitting with a bunch of other kids also wearing blue suits, but that shouldn't have stopped him pegging me—"

"Not with that hair," Sharyn added, a little unnecessarily, I thought.

Ramirez remarked, "But he didn't."

"He was doing recon," I said. "But not for Seers. He was looking for something else."

"And it wouldn't be lunch," said Sharyn. "Since deaders don't eat."

"What then?" he asked.

"I've been wondering that all week," I replied. "And now, I think he was counting the other Corpses."

"*Were* there others in the cafeteria?"

I nodded. "A couple of the cops were deaders. One or two of the suits, too, probably members of Micha's staff. None of them were eating, of course. Just kinda chatting it up with their human coworkers."

"Recon," Ramirez echoed. "You think Cavanaugh sent the giant down there to scope out Micha's forces?"

"It fits with what Jillian told us she overheard while hiding in Micha's closet," I told him.

Sharyn said, "Seems there's trouble between Micha and the Queen. Bad feelings."

He considered this. "You two need to get out of there."

"Not me," replied Sharyn. "Just Will."

I gaped at her. *"What?"*

Sharyn said, "Red, maybe this big dude *was* sent down from Philly to spy for Cavanaugh. But just 'cause he ain't made you *yet* don't mean he *won't*!"

"I've stayed out of his way!" I insisted. "For a whole week now!"

"Sure. But, sooner or later, you're gonna turn the wrong corner or open the wrong door and there he'll be."

"If that happens," Ramirez added. "He won't just I.D. *you*. He'll I.D. you *both*."

"Look," I said, maybe a little desperately, "it's a risk. But what choice have we got?"

"You can go back to Philadelphia," he replied.

"Sharyn can't do this alone."

"Sure, I can," said Sharyn.

I ignored her. "And we can't bring someone else into the page program. That Mitchum guy would never go for it, no matter *how* many times you've saved his life."

For a second, Ramirez wore an odd look. Then he just seemed to shrug it off. "It's too dangerous to keep you here. And not just to you, but to the mission. I think—"

I cut him off. "I *have* to stay. The woman in the white room said so."

He stared at me. "What woman? What white room?"

"No, she didn't, little bro," Sharyn interjected. "She said that I had to come to DC and that you had to come with me. You didn't mention her sayin' a thing 'bout how long you had to stay."

"What woman?" Ramirez asked. "What white room?"

"That's a cheat!" I told Sharyn. "She sure didn't mean for me to come all this way just to bail at the first sign of trouble! You stay on mission 'til the mission's done!"

She pointed an angry finger at me. "Don't be quoting me to *me*, Red!"

Ramirez yelled, "What woman! What white room!"

So, reluctantly, I told him. Most people, even Undertakers, tended to react—*skeptically*—to the idea of a mysterious angel who appeared in my dreams, healed my injuries, and showed me glimpses of other places. Ramirez listened, trying not to show what he was thinking.

"Now you're gonna call me crazy," I said.

"*I* sure did," remarked Sharyn. "But now Tom's a believer, and so am I."

Ramirez stared at me. "Will, if you were anybody else, I'd knock you cold and drag your ass back to Philly myself."

I sighed. "It's amazing how much I hear that kind of thing."

He said, "You won't be doing anybody any good if you get recognized and killed. Now, I'm not telling you kids what to do. ... God knows I'm past all that. But Sharyn, my *advice* is to send him back to Haven on the next train. You might even want to go with him."

"Will's goin'," the girl replied. "But I still gotta job to do."

"I understand that," Ramirez said. "But the situation's changed. Not only do you have this Corpse giant in town who seems to be spying for Cavanaugh, but now you've got *something* running around the Capitol, eating the dead."

"If that's all it does, then I'm cool with it," Sharyn remarked.

But I wasn't so sure. *Ten legs.* My instincts were buzzing. I needed to find out more about this ... Corpse Eater. I *needed* to! And the idea of getting dumped at Union Station, all because of something that *might* happen, stuck in my throat like a chicken bone.

Ramirez rubbed his face. "Sharyn ... I know you're

capable. But this situation isn't stable anymore. There are just too many variables. It's dangerous!"

Sharyn kissed his cheek affectionately. "Yeah, I dig that. But dangerous ... well, that's kinda our thing."

Ramirez didn't buy it. "Tell that to Ian."

Sharyn's expression fell. She pulled back to her side of the bench, not saying a word.

"Who told you?" I asked him.

"Your mother called me," he replied. "He and Steve were playing with that crystal you brought back from Eastern State."

"No," I said.

He gave me a very adult, very judgmental look; it pissed me off. "What do you mean, no? Is he dead or isn't he?"

"Yeah, he's dead," I replied. "But nobody was 'playing' with anything. The Anchor Shard—that's what the Corpses call it—is *important*. It may give us intel that'll seriously help. This isn't about 'playing.'" Then, scowling, I added, "And since when are you and my mom talking on the phone?"

His face ran through a half-dozen emotions.

"Steve's all messed up 'bout it," Sharyn interjected quickly. "I ain't never seen him like this. His brother told me he ain't left the Brain Factory all week. Don't sleep. Barely eats. He's all focused on figuring out that freakin' crystal ... proving that Ian didn't die for nothing." Then, patting Ramirez's hand, she added, "What happened to Ian sucks. It sucks big time. But he ain't the first Undertaker we've lost, and he probably won't be the last. Meanwhile, the Corpses just keep coming."

Ramirez looked about to say something lecture-y. But

then he just kind of deflated. "I know. I just wish ... I wish I could do more."

"That's sweet of you," Sharyn said, her smile returning. "Ain't it, Will?"

"Sure," I replied. But I *wasn't* smiling. I didn't much care how *sweet* Special Agent Hugo Ramirez was being. What I *did* care about was the fact that I wasn't ready to return to Haven. Nowhere near.

But even that wasn't my biggest gripe.

No, my biggest gripe was my mom. My mom and this dude. Talking on the phone. Maybe a lot.

I didn't like it.

Not one bit.

CHAPTER 25
AT IT AGAIN

The next day, at Sharyn's insistence, I called in sick to work. Lex disapproved of it, and made darned sure I knew he disapproved. Seriously, I thought my mom had the whole judgmental thing down. But this dude was a *pro*!

"A week's a bit soon to be playing the fake fever card, isn't it?" he asked me. Page school was done for the morning—hadn't minded missing that—and Sharyn had come by my bedroom to "check on me" before leaving for her day at the Capitol. Translation: make sure I intended to stay put until this evening, when she planned to escort me to Union Station.

"Ease off, Lex," she told the proctor. "Andy ain't ... isn't ... faking. You can see he's on death's door!" Then, with Lex treating me to yet another skeptical inspection, she tossed a sly wink my way.

I scowled at her. She shouldn't have been here at all, not given our efforts to play the "acquaintances" card. But after meeting with Ramirez yesterday, Sharyn's priorities had shifted. Since I'd be gone by nightfall, who cared how the other pages read our relationship?

"One day," Lex declared. "Then either you go back to work or to the doctor. I won't brook this kind of nonsense on my watch."

"Yeah," Sharyn told him dryly. "You're a fearless leader."

Then, as Fearless Leader stalked out of the room, grumbling, the Angel Boss fixed me with a skeptical look all her own. "Don't start griping again. We had us enough of that last night."

Sharyn and I had spent most of yesterday and last night engaged in what I guess I'll call a spirited debate. I wanted to stay in DC to make some sense of this Corpse Eater. But Sharyn hadn't bought it. "Look, little bro. I ain't saying I won't miss having you around. I will. Straight up. But the stakes are high. We don't know what Micha's up to and we got no clue how this monster-thingy, if it's real, fits into this mess. One of us has gotta be here and it can't be you ... and that's that."

By the end of it, she'd pulled rank. I was Philly-bound.

"I still think this is stupid," I said in the here and now.

"Not as stupid as lettin' that giant wormbag get a bead on your skinny butt," Sharyn replied. Then she tousled my hair and smiled. "Look at the bright side. Helene'll be so jazzed to see you that you might get your second kiss!"

I kept right on scowling. My stomach absolutely did *not* do a flip-flop!

"What about Dave?" I asked, the snarky remark out before I could catch it.

Sharyn's shoulders stiffened. "Hot Dog? What about him?"

I shouldn't have said anything. But I was angry. "Everybody knows, Sharyn."

That wasn't quite true. Ian knew—or, I thought with a sudden twist in my gut, *had* known. Helene knew, too. In fact, she'd picked up on it way before I did. But if the rest of Haven was whispering about the Burgermeister and the Angel Boss "sittin' in a tree," I hadn't heard about it.

"Even Tom?" she asked. And her expression instantly turned my snark into shame.

"I dunno," I replied. "But what if he does? Who says you and the Burgermeister can't … ya know? I mean, for all we know, he and Jillian—"

"Shut your mouth!" Sharyn yelped.

I shut my mouth.

"Promise me you'll sit tight 'til I get back from the Hill."

I promised.

She left, shutting my bedroom door.

I waited until all of the pages were gone and the house grew quiet. Then I pulled out my Haven-issued satellite phone and dialed the Senate Sergeant at Arms' office in the Capitol.

Stanz answered on the third ring.

"Can I speak to Mr. O'Mally?" I asked.

"And who should I say is calling?"

"Andy."

"Who?"

I sighed. "Just tell him it's Ginger."

"*That* Andy. Hold on. I'll see if he's available."

I held on, sweating a little. I wasn't scared of getting caught. I mean, sure Sharyn *might* speak with the Sergeant at Arms. And O'Mally *might* tell her what I was about to ask him, after which she'd come back here to kick my butt.

But it wasn't worry that was making me sweat.

It was guilt.

"Andy, what's up?"

As he had all week, he sounded both busy and happy to hear from me. Two gingers sticking together. "The Redheaded League," he called us.

I think it's a book reference.

I sweated a little more.

Either you go through with this, or you go home with nothing. Pick one.

I picked one.

"Um … Mr. O'Mally, I'm kind of taking a sick day."

"I'm aware. The program director called me. Apparently, one of the proctors called her. Don't remember which one."

I could guess.

"Nothing serious, I hope?"

"No. I'll be fine tomorrow. Just stuck around here today. But …"

"But?"

I took a deep steadying breath. "Mr. O'Mally, I've got this problem in page school. I need to deliver a report on that mural at the top of the Capitol Rotunda."

"The Apotheosis of Washington?"

"Yeah. I was supposed to have turned it on Friday, but it kind of got away from me. The teacher's giving me until tomorrow."

He laughed in that way grown-ups have when you're doing something they think reminds them of themselves at your age. My dad used to do it—and my mom's a consummate professional at it. We're talking Olympic-level condescension here. It always drives me nuts.

But, right now, I was counting on it.

"Then I suggest you spend the day working on it, Ging."

"I will. I mean ... I am. But it's late ... so I need to do something special."

"What kind of special?"

"I ... um ... need to take video of it. The painting I mean."

"*The Apotheosis of Washington* is a fresco, Andy. Not a painting. No wonder you're behind on this assignment."

Inwardly, I cursed myself. "Yeah. Right. A fresco. Thing is, to really make this report stand out, I kinda have to 'host' my own mini documentary about it."

"A mini documentary? I don't understand."

"To grab a top grade, I need to show I was, you know, *engaged* in the learning process. It's all about being committed to the effort. That's what my teacher says."

There was a pause on the line. Suspicious or just confused? I threw all of my weight behind confused and hoped for the best.

O'Mally said, "While I admire your commitment, Andy ... I'm not sure what you're asking of me. If you need to make this shoot so badly, then just come on into the Capitol this afternoon and shoot it. Sick or no sick. What's the big deal?"

So, with another deep breath I blurted, "Can I come by the Capitol after visiting hours, when it's quiet, and do the video then?"

"After hours? Why?"

"Um ... you know how crowded that place gets during

the tourist day. I think what I need for this to really work is ... well ... quiet. Privacy."

I waited. This time his pause was longer. "That's against policy."

"I know," I said. "Except it won't take long. Mr. O'Mally, I'm really sorry. I know this whole thing's my own fault. But, if you could ... I dunno ... maybe leave word at the Visitor Center? I'll get there around seven, go in, take my vid, and head right back out. Ten minutes, tops. Afterward, I'll have to spend half the night editing it ... but that's my problem."

A lot of words for one breath.

Now the pause seemed to last forever. The suspense was killing me. I'd faced down mobs of walking dead—but there's nothing more nail biting than asking an authority figure for something you know you're not supposed to have.

"Honestly, Andy ... I don't think I can do that."

Crap. Maybe I'd end up on that train tonight after all.

"Mr. O'Mally ..." I began, ready to play the Hail Mary *Pleeeeeessseeee* card. Then I stopped myself and went another way entirely. "I get it. I messed up. It's cool. Then I guess I better say thanks."

"Thanks?"

I let several seconds roll by before I answered. "I'm kind of a lousy page."

"I don't understand."

"Lex—he's one of the proctors—told me that my grades aren't good and that the director's gonna send me home."

"So you're telling me that if I don't let you into the

175

Rotunda after hours, you're going to flunk out of page school?"

I didn't reply. I know a rhetorical question when I hear one.

"Ging? Is that what you're telling me?"

Okay, so maybe I don't.

I kept my tone even; I was walking the edge of a knife. "If it was just the report thing, then no. But there's been … other…stuff."

He laughed. Then he said, "Yeah, that 'other stuff' will get you every time. Okay, Ging. I'll have the Visitor Center keep an eye out for you. Be there on the dot of seven. No earlier and no later."

I finally exhaled. "Thanks."

"No problem. I'll meet you in the Rotunda."

I started sweating again. "What?"

"Well, if you're shooting a mini-documentary, you're going to need someone to hold the camera, right? Besides, I can't have you running around the Capitol after hours. So, once you're inside, head straight upstairs and I'll meet you in the Rotunda. Then, after we're done, I'll see you out myself."

"But, Mr. O'Mally," I said quickly, "I don't want to you have to stay after work for my sake."

Another laugh. "Ging. I ain't a nine-to-five accountant. I practically live here. It's fine. See you at seven-oh-five … or seven-oh-six, if you're a slow walker. Any later than that and I call Homeland Security."

Then, as he put down the phone, I heard him mutter, faintly but with amusement: "Other stuff …"

I felt like a first-class jerk. I'd just used a guy who'd never been anything but cool to me. I hadn't known

Charles O'Mally long, but he didn't seem all that complicated. He had an important job, only a small part of which involved the page program. But in many ways, I thought it was his favorite part. He *liked* playing the "We Redheads Gotta Stick Together" game. It was how he connected—an old guy's way of feeling young.

I'd seen it before. Every boy who's ever been a Cub Scout has seen it.

And I'd not only counted on it, I'd twisted it to suit my purpose.

It was something a Corpse would do.

I felt like crap.

The day passed slowly in that empty house. Around noon, I went downstairs to grab some lunch. The kitchen was deserted. It had been a long time since I'd been *this* alone. I might have enjoyed it if I hadn't been so on edge.

Then, about an hour before the pages were due back from the Hill, I turned the wrong corner on the third floor and ran right into Greg Gardner.

The dead proctor "whoa-ed," putting his gray, sticky hands—Type Two—on my shoulders to keep us from knocking each other over. His smell was almost enough to make me wretch. But I'd learned long ago how to hide that urge.

"Hey, Andy!" He held me at arm's length. God, how I wished he'd get those disgusting hands off of my shoulders! "You look like you're feeling better." Then he placed the back of his hand against my forehead.

I nearly gagged.

"You're not warm," he remarked. And I wondered if his stolen body could even *judge* temperature. Probably not. More likely this was just part of his proctor's Mask.

More fake humanity.

"I'm feeling okay," I said.

"Glad to hear it. The Capitol awaits."

Yeah, it does.

Finally, blessedly, he removed his hand from my forehead. "Back to bed, though. If Lex catches you wandering around, he's liable to think you were faking the whole thing!" Then he laughed. A non-Seer would probably have heard a disarming chuckle. But to *my* ears it was a lifeless gurgle.

"You sure you're okay?" he asked. "You look a little … green."

"Fine," I said. Then, hastily, "Well, better anyway."

Ever seen a cadaver look suspicious? I have—plenty of times. Gardner wore that look now. It was creepy, so I "escaped" a little by crossing my eyes and examining his Mask. I should probably mention here that I'm not literally crossing my eyes. That's just what I call it. It's more like un-focusing your vision, if you know what I mean. You let each eye kind of wander a little bit, separately. It takes practice, but it works.

Gardner's Mask had one of those "Big Man on Campus" things going on: hair styled but just slightly mussed—unlike Lex's greasy, insurance salesman perfection. His face was smooth, his cheekbones high.

He reminded me of the Queen, with the oh-so-beautiful visage *she* liked to show the world. I wondered vaguely if they knew each other.

Gardner said, "Your eyes are glassy all of a sudden. Maybe you should go back to bed."

"Yeah," I said.

Treating me to a final, thoughtful look, he headed back the way he'd come.

Something about the whole, brief exchange bothered me. But I ended up labeling it nerves and shrugging it off.

I shouldn't have.

CHAPTER 26
KILL ORDER

Lilith Cavanaugh

Lilith Cavanaugh waited in the *Szash*.

She hated waiting. Once, in the Homeworld, she'd torn apart an underling who'd caused her to suffer boredom in the hours before her coronation. She still recalled with amusement how the minion had begged for his life. And she'd given it to him, hadn't she? She'd suffered his pathetic existence to continue, even after she'd torn off most of his limbs. She'd kept him alive until the very end.

Delicious.

No, the Queen did not care for waiting.

That's why, when she felt another presence join her in this telepathic netherworld, she snapped, "Finally!"

The presence—yet another underling, but one whose self-importance had grown unacceptable—remarked, "You sound anxious, sister."

"You said you would join me at six o'clock," Lilith growled. "It's almost seven."

"My committee meeting ran late."

A poor lie. Of course the delay had been intentional. This was a game. A contest of wills.

Though not for much longer.

"I appreciate you taking the time. You have news for me?"

"I do. You've grown sloppy, sister."

You should be addressing me as "Mistress" or "Ms. Cavanaugh." Your familiarity is one of the reasons you need to die ... sister. "Have I? How so?"

"One of my minions —"

Your minions? the Queen thought savagely, her outrage rising. Yet in the *Szash* she was powerless. This "place of communion" was for the mind, not the body—a form of communication bred into, and reserved for, the Royal Caste.

"—serves as a proctor at the Daniel Webster Page Residence, an arrangement that required considerable finesse."

Finesse, Cavanaugh mused. *You killed a proctor and her family to create an opening, which you then used your political clout to fill, all so you could watch for more Seers within the program. You're not half as clever as you think you are, sister.*

"I'm aware of this. Don't waste my time."

"Apologies," Lindsay Micha replied, the word laced with sarcasm. "Tell me, sister, do you happen to know a redheaded human boy who goes by the name of Andy Forbes?"

"No."

"He's one of two pages who joined the program just

last week. The other is a girl named Kim Baker. Both are sponsored by the same senator. It's rare for new pages to be brought in mid-term. Virtually unheard of. Did you know that?"

Lilith didn't reply.

"When my minion informed me of this, I ordered further investigation. He obtained fingerprints for both children … off drinking glasses, I believe. Then my people within the Capitol Police ran those prints. Can you guess what they found?"

"Just tell me."

"Nothing. Both Forbes and Baker completely checked out."

Cavanaugh began, "Then what "

"Except in one database. Seems Andy Forbes has visited DC before. He toured the FBI Headquarters Building with his sixth-grade class. All of those students were fingerprinted, and even entered their own information into the computer … just to see how it's done. Isn't that cute?"

"Adorable," the Queen snarled. "Who is he?"

"William Karl Ritter."

Cavanaugh stiffened. "Will Ritter is in Washington?"

"Apparently so. And on the recommendation of Senator James Mitchum … a political adversary of mine."

"And the girl?"

"Nothing. She seems to be exactly who she claims. Except for that fact that she and Ritter arrived together, and with the same sponsor."

"Describe her," the Queen commanded.

With a laugh, Micha obeyed.

"It could be Sharyn Jefferson," mused Cavanaugh.

"The hair doesn't match our reports, but hair is easily changed. In any event, this Kim Baker is undoubtedly an Undertaker."

"Agreed. Through your bungling, you allowed the Birmelin girl to reach the Undertakers, and now they've infiltrated the page program ... no doubt in an effort to reach *me*."

"Mind your tongue!" the Queen hissed. "I'll handle this."

"Don't bother. I've already given the necessary orders. The Ritter boy is headed for the Capitol this evening. He'll be dead within the hour. We'll get the girl later."

"More of your heavy-handed methods! We need to find out how much they know before elimination!"

"I disagree. And, as this is my city, I will deal with it. Perhaps you can focus your energies on finally locating this nest of human brats and exterminating it! That would be useful."

Then, before the Queen could respond, the *Szash* ended. No apology, not even a request to be excused. The purpose of her sister's communion was now clear: not to inform or advise, but to accuse, to admonish.

It was maddening.

Restored to her host, Lilith Cavanaugh sat back in her desk chair and clasped her hands together, listening to the crack and pop of deteriorating tendons. This body had nearly ended its usefulness. Fortunately, the Undertakers' recent funeral home campaign had been finally stalled, though the trap she'd laid for the perpetrators had once again failed.

The Undertakers.

They hid somewhere in the city, bathed in the shadows,

mostly appearing at night, and always where and when she *didn't* want them. They were quick, well-trained, and brave. They struck and vanished. Struck and vanished. Again and again.

Her treacherous, soon-to-be-departed sister had been right about one thing: it was time to end them. But how? Philadelphia was expansive, with far too many hiding places to be effectively and discretely searched. Her predecessor, the late but unlamented Kenny Booth, had favored the use of the *pelligog* to turn children into spies. But each time, the spy had been unmasked and the plan foiled. The Undertakers were too smart for that.

No, something subtler was required.

As she sat brooding in her office, a plan began to form.

She snatched up her desk phone and dialed. It was picked up on the second ring. She liked that.

No waiting.

"Yes, Ms. Cavanaugh," John Tall said.

"Do you have a timetable yet for relieving me of my troubling relative?"

"I've used my cover to establish a rapport with our people on the Capitol's police force. I'm sorry to report that nearly all of them are loyal to Lindsay Micha rather than you."

"She was always … charismatic. They will be dealt with. Each and every one of them."

"I would be honored to assist in the purge, Ms. Cavanaugh."

"One thing at a time. Go on with your report."

"I've learned Senator Micha's schedule. But she is cautious and will be difficult to reach. I'm hoping to have one of her aides arrange an introduction by the end of the week."

"Well done, John," she said. "The situation, however,

has become more urgent. Will Ritter has infiltrated the Senate pages."

"Ritter's here?"

"No doubt to investigate my sister, which means your paths will likely cross, and soon. I want you to find him, John. Make it your new priority. There is a girl with him, another Undertaker. You may kill her in any way you choose. But I need the Ritter boy *alive*."

"Yes, ma'am."

"Apparently Ritter is on his way to the Capitol right now. My sister intends to kill him there. Do *not* allow her to do so. If any of her people get in your way, you have full authority to deal with them as necessary. Will Ritter must not die before I've had an opportunity to interrogate him. Clear?"

"Clear, Ms. Cavanaugh. I'll see to it."

"Do that, John. This will mark your third encounter with the son of Karl Ritter. Fail again, and you will not survive long enough to see a fourth. Do you understand me?"

"Completely."

"Good. Now get it done."

The Queen slammed down the phone, her eyes blazing with dark hatred. She took no deep breaths, as the dead don't breathe. But instead she stared out past the walls of her office, and relished the idea of having Will Ritter at her mercy.

It was going to be a *very* interesting evening at the Capitol.

CHAPTER 27

THE CAPITOL AT NIGHT

I'm good at sneaking.

Oh, the Undertakers have other words for it: stealth, covert infiltration, recon. But, let's be real; I'm a thirteen-year-old kid—and sneaking is sneaking.

I split Webster Hall just after dinner. Sharyn, having returned with the other pages, didn't bother to check on me. After all, our plans were already locked. We'd wait until lights out before meeting downstairs and slipping out the back door. Then it was off to Union Station.

Of course, I had *other* plans.

Sharyn was going to be *pissed*.

I snuck out right after dinner, but before the other pages had come up for the night. And I didn't bother with any doors, but instead climbed out my bedroom window and down a drainpipe that I'd noticed on my first day in the house. An Undertaker *always* notes his exits.

As usual, a Capitol Police car sat on the street. Uncle Sam's "wards" needed looking out for, after all. Fortunately, in my week-long page career, none of the cops I'd seen on this guard duty had been Corpses.

Why bother, when one of the proctors *was?*

Using the shadows, I slipped out from the back of Webster Hall and followed the sidewalk in the opposite direction. If the dude in the cruiser noticed me, he wouldn't think anything of it—just a nameless kid out for a stroll.

Unless he spotted my page uniform.

But he didn't. It always hits me how luck seems forever on my side when I'm doing stuff I know I shouldn't be.

The US Capitol's Visitor Center opened in 2008. It wasn't added to the big building so much as dug *under* it— a huge, high-ceilinged warren of fancy chambers that was almost as big the Capitol itself. It stood low on the eastern side of the complex, where it wouldn't mess up the overall look of the building it served.

The entrance was heavily guarded, with metal detectors and cops on hand to search pocketbooks and backpacks. I didn't have a backpack, and I knew the plastic water pistol under my jacket wouldn't set off the alarm.

No, my only concern as I neared the checkpoint was my pocketknife.

The guards noticed my page clothes and waved me forward. These guys were human, though two others that I spotted in the back, watching me through the bulletproof glass—well, not so much.

"What can I do for you, kiddo?" the first cop asked.

"Hi. The Sergeant At Arms should have left word that I was coming. Andy Forbes?"

The guy taped some computer keys. "Yep. You're on the list."

"What brings you back tonight?" his partner asked. Just

friendly interest—I hoped.

I'm not the enemy! Look behind you at the two dead dudes wearing the same uniforms you are. They're the enemy!

"Homework," I replied with a shrug. "Mr. O'Mally's meeting me in the Rotunda."

"Well, it should be quiet," the first cop remarked, handing me a visitor's badge. "A couple of committee meetings running late, but that's about it. Step on through the scanner."

I looked anxiously at the metal detector. It filled the only available gap in the bulletproof glass, the only way into the Visitor's Center. Steve had once told me that my pocketknife—like Tom's—wasn't metal exactly, but kind of a "composite alloy."

He didn't think it would set off a metal detector.

But I'd never before had to test that theory. The problem was, I *needed* my pocketknife. It had a gadget that would help me with my monster hunting. So the time had come to throw the dice.

Of course, that's easy to say when you're safe in Webster Hall—less easy when you're faced with four armed men, two of them of the dead variety. If that scanner went ballistic, I'd be searched, my gadget confiscated, and I'd spend the rest of the night in a windowless room answering a lot of questions—until the Corpse Cops managed to get a hold of me.

Steve … you'd better be right.

I dropped everything else, including my wallet and sat phone, into a little plastic bin. The cops didn't give them a second look. Then, taking a deep breath, I stepped through the scanner.

As usual, Steve *was* right.

Nothing. Not a bleep. I did a pretty good job at hiding my relief—though I thought I spotted a smirk on one of the deader's gray faces. I hate it when they smirk.

I collected my stuff. "The Visitor Center's all shut down," one of the human guards told me. "Follow the lights through Emancipation Hall and then head straight up the Capitol steps and on into the Rotunda. No lingering. Got it?"

"Got it," I said.

Emancipation Hall, with its high ceiling, wide-open floor space, and numerous statues was choked with people during the day, but eerily empty at night. Of course, the proximity of Corpses mixed with Ramirez's monster talk wasn't exactly helping my sense of well-being. My feet echoed loudly on the staircase as I made my way up to the Capitol's main floor, slipped past the darkened Crypt, and then climbed the narrow flight of stairs to the Rotunda level.

O'Mally was waiting for me. "Right on time," he said.

"Hi, Mr. O'Mally. Thanks again for this."

"Well, let's just make it a kick-butt report, okay? I'd hate to see you get sent home so quick." There was something in his tone—something that worried me.

"Thanks," I murmured again, the sound swallowed up by the surrounding emptiness.

As cavernous as Emancipation Hall is, the Rotunda's something else altogether.

It's used for all kinds of functions, from international receptions to state funerals. John F. Kennedy's coffin once rested here, with thousands of people standing in line for hours to pay their last respects. The same goes for a bunch of other presidents. The chamber's round, a hundred feet wide and 180 feet high, with paintings all along its ground-level walls, each depicting some famous event in American history. Mixed in with these big paintings are statues of presidents—like Abe Lincoln, standing tall in gleaming-white marble and holding out a copy of the Emancipation Proclamation.

And high overhead, at the very top of the dome, is Constantino Brumidi's *The Apotheosis of Washington*, which I'd supposedly come here to see.

Except I *couldn't* see it. Like Ramirez had said, there are no lamps in the Rotunda. It wasn't *too* dark, mind you; a fair amount of city light leaked in through the rows of windows that circled the tapering dome. I mean, you could see where you were going. But, high overhead, the gloom deepened.

This hadn't worried me when I'd put this plan together. I had my pocketknife, and my pocketknife had a mini-telescope with a night-vision feature. Looking around for clues about the murder of a Corpse—weird, saying that— would have been easy enough.

But pulling my pocketknife out now, in front of Charles O'Mally, would raise all kinds of questions.

"Something wrong, Ging?" he asked me. The words were light, though his expression looked stern.

I swallowed. "Could I ... um ... maybe have a few minutes in here alone?"

"What for? Don't you need to make your video?"

I felt my face flush. "Well ... yeah."

"So let's get to it." He took a step closer. "Unless there some other reason you came tonight."

I was in trouble.

"Yes, Will," a voice said. Raspy. Mocking. Horribly familiar. "*Is* there another reason?"

Senator Lindsay Micha stepped through the Rotunda's north entrance. And she wasn't alone.

Big trouble.

CHAPTER 28
ROTUNDA

Now, I'd had plans go south before—plenty of them. But this was the first time it had happened in under a minute.

Suddenly, I faced a half-dozen hostile grown-ups, only one of whom had a pulse.

Micha was accompanied by the two Corpse policemen from the Visitor's Center, with two more deaders—both wearing suits—behind them. I recognized one of the suits, and my heart sank so low it sloshed in my shoes.

Greg Gardner.

The Dead Cops split up, spreading out into what I recognized as a tactical pattern—positioning themselves between me and the Rotunda's eastern and western exits.

"Evening, Charlie," Micha said. She wore a late Type One or early Type Two, relatively fresh. Her skin was a mottled purple and her gums had receded, revealing teeth that were visibly loose. Now, Undertakers see lots of cadavers—call it an occupational hazard—and, after a while, you turn into a kind of closet medical examiner.

This body appeared intact. No obvious signs of damage. But the eyes were swollen and its skin seemed looser than normal.

A drowning victim. Looks like she might have been pretty.

The things you think of when you're totally screwed.

"Hello, Senator," Mr. O'Mally said.

I looked at the Sergeant at Arms and he looked back at me. I could tell I was busted. He was clearly pissed. But, more than that, he seemed disappointed—maybe even a little hurt.

"Mr. O'Mally …" I stammered. "I'm …"

"You're *what*, Andy?" he asked. "You're sorry? You're sorry your name isn't Andy Forbes, but Will Ritter. You're sorry that you lied to everyone, including me? That you falsified your program application? That you somehow deceived a smart and important man like Senator Mitchum? And *why*? That's the part I don't get. Why'd you even do it? Senator Micha here explained to me about that Philadelphia street gang you belong to. But what does that have to do with the page program? Was this some kind of domestic terrorism thing? Is that why you wanted to come to the Capitol tonight?"

"No!" I exclaimed. "It's not like that!"

"Then what *is* it like, Ging?" he asked. "I could have had you taken into custody at the Visitor Center. But I honestly don't think I'm that bad a judge of character. So what's really going on here?"

We heard footsteps behind us and turned to see another three deaders emerge through the northern entrance. More Capitol cops.

Eight Corpses in all.

A pincer movement. Well executed.

"Time to go, Will," Gardner said. He wore the same smile as in the Webster hallway, as grotesque now as it had been then.

I didn't move.

Beside me, O'Mally's eyes narrowed. I could almost read his mind. He wasn't a Seer; no adult was. But he wasn't stupid, either, and he sensed something was wrong—wronger than a kid pretending to be someone he wasn't. If he knew my real name, then he had to know my real age. Just how many thirteen-year-old domestic terrorists were there? And why had Micha pulled in so many cops, just to nab little ol' me? For that matter, *how* had she done it? These cops worked for *him* after all, not the senator. Except it didn't seem that way right now, did it?

This whole thing felt heavy-handed. Corpses were usually more subtle than this.

Then I remembered South Street, and wondered if the rules had changed.

Still smiling, Micha explained, "This is Gregory Gardner, a proctor at Webster Hall. He's the one who discovered the boy's deception."

"Did he?" O'Mally said. Then he looked at me. "So ... whoever you are. What's *your* side of the story?"

Lies bounced around in my head—everything from flat-out denial to a claim of amnesia. At least they weren't onto Sharyn. Or *were* they? Maybe, right now, another batch of deader cops was closing in on Webster Hall. That, more than anything else, settled the matter for me.

"My name's Will Ritter," I told him, meeting his gaze. "And I'm an Undertaker. That's what we call ourselves. But we're not a street gang, and we're not terrorists. We're kind of an underground resistance movement."

"Resisting *what*, Ging?"

"Authority," Lindsay Micha said, still smiling.

"No!" I exclaimed again, still holding the man's eyes. "Not *real* authority, anyway. Mr. O'Mally, I know this looks bad. And, for what it's worth, I'm sorry I had to lie to you. But the truth has never been my friend where this stuff is concerned. So, let's make a deal. Take me to your office, just the two of us. Let me tell you all of it, from the beginning. It's pretty wild, and you probably won't believe me. But I know a man I can call. A man you *might* believe. He's an FBI agent."

"FBI," the Sergeant at Arms echoed. "Andy … Will … this is completely crazy!"

I could read his inner conflict. He was a grown-up, and every grown-up's first impulse is to dismiss a child's word. Sounds harsh, but it's a sad reality that Undertakers live with every day. But balancing that impulse was the presence of Micha and Gardner and all these cops.

Here to trap a single thirteen-year-old boy.

O'Mally said, "Okay. Let's do that."

"No!" Gardner snapped.

"Charlie," Micha said, her smile seeming pasted on. "I must insist that this boy be placed in my custody."

"Senator," the Sergeant at Arms replied, and this time his suspicion wasn't pointed at me. "I don't know what's going on here. You called to tell me that this boy isn't who he claims, and that you'd meet us here. I didn't expect you to arrive with a squad from Capitol Police … officers who supposedly report to *me* and not you. Given the circumstances, my best option is to personally try to get to the bottom of this."

"That kid's not going anywhere!" Gardner growled. He looked like a Doberman tensed to attack.

They all do.

Charles O'Mally's face darkened. Then he rested a protective hand on my shoulder. "Come on, Ging," he said. "Let's go figure this out somewhere more private."

I knew it was coming before it came. Tom might have called it "soldier's instincts."

Lindsay Micha faked a sigh. Corpses don't breathe, so they can't sigh for real, but they're good at faking it.

Then she said, "Kill them both."

"With pleasure," Gardner replied. Then he and another Corpse lunged at us—fast.

I pulled out my water pistol and shot the closest one in the face. In an instant, the deader's expression went blank and he pitched forward—

—right into my waiting knee.

The sound his nose made as it shattered was *totally* satisfying.

"Run!" I yelled at O'Mally, whose anger had changed to astonishment as his own men closed around him. But he wised up fast because, just as Greg Gardner grabbed at him, he hauled off and clocked the dead proctor hard in the jaw. The blow would have laid out pretty much any living human. But Gardner's head simply snapped back and then forward.

He grinned.

O'Mally stared at him in astonishment.

I started to turn, my pocketknife's Taser ready—one hundred fifty thousand volts aimed at Gardner's chest. But I was just a little too slow.

Greg Gardner drove his fist into the Sergeant at Arms'

chest and pulled out his heart.

"No!" someone screamed. I guess it was me. I mean, who else would it have been?

Then Charles O'Mally, as good as guy as I've ever met, dropped to the floor, dead.

The rest of the Corpses encircled me, moving in cautiously, aware of my Taser and water gun. But these hung at my sides, my battle instincts drained away. All I could do was stand in the middle of the Rotunda, looking down at the man on the floor.

I'm sorry, Ginger.

"That's your fault," Gardner said. "You shouldn't have resisted."

Micha added, "Let's get this over with, shall we? I have big plans coming up and don't have time for delays."

The dead closed in.

"Stop!"

The voice boomed through the huge domed chamber, as loud as a lion's roar. Everybody jumped a little. Then every head turned.

Oh great…

Dead Giant Guy filled the southern archway. The Rotunda entrances weren't exactly small, but this one *looked* a lot smaller with him standing there. His eyes scanned the room as if counting heads. More recon. Then, like twin black lasers, they targeted me. His huge fists opened and closed. Then he started forward.

Lindsay Micha still hadn't moved, apparently trusting her thugs to do the tearing and biting and ripping for her. Now, however, her smug confidence wavered. "Who are you?"

"John Tall," the giant replied. "I serve the Queen."

"Then you're a fool, John Tall."

The giant hesitated, his attention shifting between me and Dead Senator Lady. His lifeless face tried to frown thoughtfully; it didn't quite pull it off.

Then, as if reaching some decision, he changed direction, bearing down on Micha like an impending storm. Seeing this, she staggered back, raising her hands defensively. In Deadspeak, she exclaimed, "What. You. Doing?"

Dead Giant Guy responded in the same weird, soundless language, "Ending. Your Existence. Traitor. In. Queen's. Name."

"To. Me!" Micha called out in silent alarm. "Protect!"

Three of the Corpses surrounding me turned and leaped at the giant. Shaken out of my shock at O'Mally's death, I finally moved, firing saltwater into the faces of two of my remaining attackers and Tasing a third, before throwing myself into the hole I'd just made in their ranks. From there, it looked like a clear shot to the northern entrance.

But then Gardner stepped in my way.

He slapped the gun from my grasp and backhanded me—a ferocious blow that knocked me several feet across the Rotunda. I hit the tile floor hard, pain lancing through the entire right side of my body.

Sprawled on my back with the wind knocked out of me, I watched in a haze as three Corpses latched onto Tall, trying to keep him away from Micha. Dead Giant Guy seemed to regard these attackers more with annoyance than fear, shrugging them off, one at a time, before closing in on the cringing senator.

He grabbed Micha by her shoulders and lifted her right off her feet, shaking the dead woman like a rag doll.

"Traitor!" he roared again, this time in English. Then, as two more Corpses launched themselves onto his broad back, clawing and biting, Tall hurtled the dead woman across the chamber and into the statue of Abraham Lincoln.

Micha hit the edge of the Emancipation Proclamation, hard. I heard her spine snap as the marble cut right through her. There she hung, her stolen body broken and helpless.

I wheezed and tried to sit up. As I did, a fancy tasseled loafer landed on my chest. Gardner put all his weight behind that foot, until I thought my ribs would cave in. Then, leaning down, he grinned savagely at me.

As sometimes happens when they bend over, maggots dribbled out of his mouth and nose, raining down on me.

"Know something, Ritter?" he asked. "I *really* want to kill you!"

"Yeah?" I gasped. "Get in line." My hand scrambled for my pocketknife, which I was pretty sure had come to rest beside me…somewhere.

But then Tall blindsided him.

It was something to see: this monstrous animated dead dude with two dead dudes riding him like a bucking bronco, slamming his meaty shoulder into a smaller, leaner dead dude. The look of surprise on Gardner's dead face as he went flying was—well, I wished I'd had a camera.

"Child. Mine!" the giant roared in Deadspeak. Then, almost absently, he yanked one of Micha's minions off his back and, grabbing the Corpse in both of his snow shovel–

sized hands, snapped him in half like a pretzel stick. Corpse juice went everywhere, splashing me like a putrid shower.

Maggots *and* body fluids.

I've got a pretty strong stomach. But that combo almost made me toss my cookies.

Then, with the other deader still scratching and clawing at his shoulder blade, Tall glared down at me. "Boy," he growled.

I tried to reply, "Dead guy," but it came out as a retch.

He lifted me off the floor by my foot. As he did, I made a final, desperate scramble and—lo and behold—came up with my pocketknife, its Taser still open.

There were three Corpses still standing, not including Tall, who clearly wasn't on their side, and the guy on his back who wasn't, strictly speaking, standing. Gardner had found his feet and was gesturing wildly at the others. "Cover the exits! Destroy them both!"

Tall faced them, holding me upside down by one leg. At the same time his other hand found the deader who was still gnawing on him, grabbed the dude's face, and yanked him off.

Then, closing his fist, he *crushed* that face—caving it in like a raw egg.

Okay, I admit it: that *did* make me toss my cookies. But, in my defense, being upside down didn't help.

"The Queen wants him alive!" the giant declared, dropping the crushed deader. The Corpse collapsed in a heap, helpless and too brain damaged to do anything but twitch.

"My sister gives no orders here!" Micha hissed as she hung, impaled, against Lincoln's statue.

I couldn't Tase the big dude, not while he was holding me. Doing so would zap me along with him, and that'd pretty much be that. Blinking and retching and wondering just how things had gone *this* sour, I spotted my water pistol. It lay broken at the base of one of the paintings.

Those things break a lot. Seriously. *A lot.*

Okay, what I'm going to say next may sound peculiar, given that I was currently hanging wrong-side up from a gargantuan dead man's fist while he argued my fate with a bunch of other dead men and one dead woman who was currently pinned to Abe Lincoln.

But *that's* when things got weird.

Something fell from high in the dome and landed with a thump on the Rotunda floor, right in the midst of the Corpse confrontation.

I couldn't see it clearly. The blood was rushing to my head and I knew with sick certainty that if I didn't get myself righted soon I'd pass out.

The reaction it had on the Corpses was both immediate and hardcore. All of them, including Gardner and the giant, froze in place. If they'd breathed, they'd have gasped in horror.

"Abomination!" the proctor called out in Deadspeak. "Attack!"

Only two of the Corpses seemed inclined to follow that order, and they did so reluctantly, flanking the indistinct, inhuman shape. I blinked my eyes, trying to see it more clearly, but the thing seemed almost *made* of shadow.

Then it jumped and spun, the movement too fast to follow. One of its legs—ten legs, I felt pretty sure—slammed into the nearest deader, sending him flying. He flipped end over end like a rag doll before hitting the

Rotunda wall with enough force to smash half of his bones to powder. He dropped, broken, to the floor.

At the same instant, the thing used two more of its legs to grab the other dead man around his torso, lifting him off his feet.

Then it swallowed him.

Whole.

My head was pounding, my vision super blurry, and my consciousness slipping away—but I saw what I saw. In one instant, the Corpse was struggling wildly, and the next he just kind of "disappeared" into a huge orifice that opened on a lump on the creature's back. A mouth?

It was so quick that it took my mind a few moments to process, but it left no doubt that *this* was the monster Ramirez had described.

The Corpse Eater.

Nearby, still helpless in her shattered, stolen body, Micha screamed in terror. For the first time, the thing seemed to notice her, its entire shape somehow stiffening—as if in recognition.

Then it spoke. Not Deadspeak. But not English, either. A tickle between my ears. A whisper without words.

"Third."

The thing's attention seemed to move between Tall and Micha. It visibly hesitated.

Then it pounced on Tall.

As the two of them went down, the giant reflexively released me. I dropped in a heap on the floor tiles.

An instant later, something landed beside me—heavy and vaguely roundish. I blinked blearily at it.

John Tall's sightless, decapitated head gazed back at me.

"Holy crap!" I yelped.

Then, just as I managed to struggle to my feet, I was seized from behind. Two long, multi-jointed, scaly *limbs* locked around my chest and legs. In an instant, I was firmly pinned. I struggled, but it was crazy strong.

Over my shoulder, I heard the "something" hiss at the Corpses—a warning or a challenge—either way, the sound was utterly inhuman.

"No!" Gardner yelled.

Across the room, Micha wailed in Deadspeak, "Keep. It. Away. From. Me!"

Then I was borne upward, and I mean *straight* upward. The creature had somehow lunched itself toward the ceiling of the Rotunda, 180 feet overhead.

It didn't get quite that far, but instead angled its jump, catching the edge of the gallery of windows that circled the lower half of the dome, before shifting direction and jumping again, this time vaulting off some of the ornate molding that lined the sloping ceiling.

Parkour, I remember thinking vaguely and absurdly. *Alien free running ...*

The monster, with me in tow, took one more tremendous leap that carried us dizzyingly across the open space, filling the very top of the dome.

Colors and shapes flashed past me, and I caught a weird glimpse of George Washington's face, looking regal and serious, right before I was swallowed up by darkness.

CHAPTER 29
MONSTER

I was yanked this way and that, carried through almost perfect darkness. Somewhere below us, I could hear the frustrated howls of Corpses, including Micha's raspy dead voice issuing frantic orders: "Find the abomination! Kill the boy and then restrain that ... thing!"

Then even these sounds grew muffled and finally silent as the creature took me higher into the smothering blackness. Sometimes we traveled on floors, other times on walls. Whatever this thing was, gravity didn't bother it.

A couple of times I tugged at the arms—or legs—that gripped me, but it was like fighting steel cables. The appendages didn't even feel like living tissue so much as leather-wrapped rebar.

No wonder it had been described as bulletproof!

Finally, we stopped and I was let go. My body felt like warm Jell-O and I slumped to the cold, metal floor as if I had no bones.

Slowly, I rolled over and sat up. My stomach stayed put, but it felt empty—the kind of empty you only get from throwing up everything except your shoes. The air was cold. There was no heat here, wherever "here" was.

Patches of faint light streamed from somewhere far below us. Weird shadows splashed against sloping, metal walls, making every angle razor sharp and more than a little creepy. There was a door nearby, just a few steps to my right. But I was sure we hadn't come through there.

On my left stood a waist-high railing.

I sat sprawled on a catwalk of some kind. Slowly, with my stomach grumbling but not really complaining, I slid over to the railing and peered under it. There wasn't much to see: just a stairwell leading down into empty blackness. There were only two walls, both of which seemed to curve to the right and left, disappearing from sight. The nearest wall was sloped, like the surface of a basketball. The farther wall was also sloped, but the other way, as if I were *inside* the basketball. A basketball within another basketball—and with me in between them.

Where in the world am *I?*

Then something moved, and I froze. Despite the chill air, sweat sprouted on my forehead.

In a horror movie kind of slow-mo, I turned and got my first really good look at the Corpse Eater.

I've talked about the "Holy Crap Factor"—that special moment when your sense of reality takes a day off. Well, since getting my Eyes, I'd had more than my share of Holy Crap Factors.

This one blew them *all* away.

It had ten legs, just like Ramirez said. So did the *pelligog*, the small, spider-like things that Corpses used to control people. But that was as far as the resemblance went. For one, this creature was bigger—much bigger, maybe 130 pounds. Its torso was long and lean, with muscular, multi-jointed legs that seemed to stick out everywhere.

Each leg ended in a pincer as big as one of the Burgermeister's fists. Trust me: that's big. When it walked, these pinchers opened and closed, grabbing the ground, or the wall, or the floor, letting it scuttle along on just about any surface. Each of these pincers looked *sharp*, like razor-edged shears.

Basically, every inch of this monster was a weapon.

But its head was the worst—a huge, round lump of hard, leathery skin without anything even remotely like a face. There were four eyes, all positioned evenly around its skull, and each one a different color: red, green, yellow and blue. It had no ears or nose, and its mouth—the same mouth that had swallowed a deader whole—looked like a thin slit.

Okay, now brace yourself.

You know how your own head sits on top of your shoulders? Well this thing didn't have shoulders. So, instead, its head was somehow able to *move* around its body. As I watched, transfixed, the four-eyed round lump traveled along the torso, maneuvering in between and around the legs, before settling itself in the monster's rear, facing away from me.

There it paused, as if listening or sniffing the air—though, as I've said, it lacked a nose or ears.

Then its huge head rolled back along its body, sliding under the leathery skin, taking a different route amidst the legs, and faced me.

It was the single freakiest thing I'd ever seen. And that's saying something.

The four eyes watched me—not all at once—but

individually, with the head in which they were mounted rotating all the way around, giving each one a turn.

Red. Green. Yellow. Blue.

I swallowed. When that didn't work—no spit—I tried talking instead. "Um ..." I said. A wordsmith, that's me. "Hi."

No response. It just stood there, so motionless that it didn't seem to really be alive.

Somehow, during that crazy trip from the Rotunda, I'd managed to hang onto my pocketknife, though any thought of zapping or otherwise attacking Mr. Ten Legs died between my ears. As still as it was right now, I'd seen how fast it could move and I wasn't stupid enough to think I was faster.

Then I remembered my sat phone.

Keeping my gaze fixed on that blue eye, I slowly—I'm talking *seriously* slowly—slipped the phone out of my jacket pocket and opened it.

It worked, meaning that the screen lit up. But there were no bars. No signal at all. Wherever I was, I'd been cut off from any help.

I think that's when I really got scared. I know that sounds stupid. I mean, I'd been alone *plenty* of times, often with a deader or two on me like white on rice. But this was different. Way different.

There's an old saying, "Better the devil you know."

Well, I *knew* Corpses. I knew them inside out and sideways, what they were—more or less, what they wanted, and usually how they would react.

But now I'd come face-to-face—again, more or less—with something completely outside my comfort zone, so totally out there that I doubted you'd find it on the "there" chart. Ten legs, four eyes, and a head that rolled around its body like a roller-coaster car draped in cowhide.

And I was *totally* alone.

So yeah, sue me, I was scared.

"Where are we?" I asked it, trying to keep the tremor out of my voice.

No response.

"Um … my phone's got no bars," I said, going for broke. "Don't suppose I could borrow yours?"

What can I say? I'm snarky when I'm terrified.

As if in answer, the creature pounced, its movements so fast that they were hard to see. One second it was ten feet away, and the next it was right in my face. And I mean *right* in my face! It smelled like—*nothing*, absolutely nothing—no smell at all. Which, so far, was the nicest thing about it.

Its head swiveled and it stared at me with its red eye. Big socket. No lid. No pupil. Just an oval of unbroken *redness*.

Then it opened its mouth.

This time the Holy Crap Factor almost landed in my pants.

Teeth.

Big, long, black teeth. Like individual steak knives. How could a head that size hold that many teeth that *big*? It was like the creature's brain was housed elsewhere in its bizarre body, and this moveable "head" was really nothing more than tooth storage.

Rows of them. *Hundreds* of them. And in the middle, not one tongue but three. They drooled out, moving independently like serpents emerging from the same basket. Except each was tipped with a miniature version of the same pincers as on its legs. These clicked open and closed as they danced around my head.

I wanted to run, but *where?* So far all I knew of my location was a catwalk, two sloping metal walls, and a staircase that led down into darkness. There *was* that mysterious steel door, but what if it was locked?

"Sorry," I croaked. "No offense."

The pincer tongues touched my face here and there, never breaking the skin. Then, without warning, they snapped back into the creature's maul. Its teeth closed. The lipless slit returned.

Its head rotated, revealing the yellow eye.

For a long moment, the creature studied me. Then one of its legs rose, twisting along its many joints...

...and stroked my cheek.

Does this mean we're ... pals?

"Um ..." I stammered. "Thanks for saving me back there."

The leg paused. The red eye turned my way again. Was this good or bad? Did red mean bad?

Then the leg moved downward with lightning swiftness, snatching the sat phone from my hand. I almost screamed. Honestly: *almost.*

As the pincers closed, I heard the dull *crunch* of crushed plastic.

The remains of my only link to the outside world—bars or no bars—dropped to the catwalk while its destroyer, still fixing me with its red eye, backed slowly away. Six feet. Eight. Ten.

Then it stopped—and *changed.*

The transformation wasn't slow like you might see in the movies. One moment, I was looking at a creature more bizarre than any I'd ever imagined. And the next it morphed into a human being. A completely naked human being.

The woman—it was definitely a woman, and not a young one—sighed and curled up into a fetal position. This was probably good, given her state of undress.

For a half minute I didn't move. I'm not even sure I breathed.

Then her eyes opened blearily, as if just awakening from a deep sleep. At first she looked bewildered, and then resigned, as if she'd remembered where she was and didn't like it much.

Then she saw me, gasped, and sat up.

"Who are you?" she demanded in a voice I recognized.

"Senator Micha?" I asked tentatively. "Senator Lindsay Micha?"

The woman stared at me, her face pale, her skin filthy. She trembled and tried to speak though, at first, nothing came out. Then, as if some wonderful understanding had dawned, she smiled with relief and said, "Of course! *That's* who I am!"

CHAPTER 30
LADY LOST

I knew I should run. Right now.

I should make a break for the stairs and all but throw myself down them—be out of sight before this woman, or monster, or Incredible Freakin' Hulk got her head on straight. Who knew? Maybe, in this state, she'd let me go without a second thought.

It might be the only shot I'd get. I could almost hear my mother's voice *screaming* for me to do it. For her sake. For Emily's.

But I didn't.

Instead, I asked, "You ... okay?"

She seemed confused, unnerved—but not really frightened. Her expression reminded me of the blank, vaguely curious look that Emily wore whenever she would fall asleep in the car and wake up someplace new.

"What?" she asked. "Oh. Yes, I'm fine, young man. Thank you so much for asking."

Then she smiled that same smile I'd seen on the Mask of the *other* Lindsay Micha, the dead one, when she'd apologized to the Senate. Except this one seem *genuine*. Not a politico's smile at all.

This Lindsay Micha was truly grateful to me for asking after her welfare.

And it was definitely *not* the smile of someone who knows she's bare-butt naked.

"Lemme ... give you my jacket," I stammered. I started taking it off, an awkward thing to do when you're sprawled across the catwalk.

"Your jacket?" she asked, sounding perplexed. "What for?"

I paused, my already overburdened brain trying to come up with a reason—besides, of course, the embarrassingly obvious one. "Well ... it's cold in here."

Not bad.

"I hadn't noticed. Still, it's gentlemanly of you to offer ... so, thank you again."

She accepted the blue blazer, draping it over her thin shoulders. It helped, a little. "And whom exactly am I thanking?"

"Huh?" Sorry. It'd been a long night.

She laughed. She had a musical laugh, kind of like Sharyn's. "What's your name?"

"Oh. Will Ritter."

"Pleased to meet you, Will. And, by your clothes, I'd say you're a Senate page."

"Kind of. Not anymore, I guess."

Again she smiled. "I sense an interesting story behind your circumstances."

Look who's talking.

"Um ... Senator —"

But she cut me off. "Now I have to stop you right there!" she exclaimed, as if she were making a point in some big-deal committee meeting. "Given the peculiar circumstances of our acquaintance, I must insist that you call me Lindsay."

I blinked. "Okay. Sure."

"Weird" had just gotten a whole new definition in my dictionary, and guess whose picture was right beside it.

Then Micha's eyes lit up. "Why ... you're an Undertaker!"

I gaped at her. "How'd you know *that*?"

"I'm not sure. I heard it somewhere, but just now I can't seem to recall the specifics. It's very discommoding."

What the heck does "discommoding" mean?

Then: *Well, being crazy hasn't done her vocabulary any harm.*

"How long have you been here ... Lindsay?" I asked.

"Here?" Micha looked around. "Always, I suppose. Or nearly so."

"Always? But, you don't ... you know ... *live* here." Then, after a pause, I added, "Do you?"

The woman laughed. "Here? Oh my, no. I live everywhere. I know every inch of this building. Have since I was a little girl."

"A little girl?"

"Lindsay's father was a congressman for fourteen years," she explained, a strange faraway look in her eyes. "Most representatives leave their families behind, but Lindsay's mother had died in childbirth and Congressman Micha was a loving, doting single parent. So, when he came to Washington he brought his daughter, just four years old at the time. There, instead of passing her off to a string of nannies, as others did, he instead took her to work with him. Lindsay grew up exploring the halls of the Capitol."

Then she smiled proudly, like a Sunday School kid who's just recited the Easter Story.

"But aren't ... *you* ... Lindsay?" I asked carefully.

Her smile faltered. "No ..." she said haltingly. "I mean ... I used to be, but now the Third is ..." A tear rolled down her cheek.

The Third?

"You're Lindsay Micha," I said firmly. "And you're a US senator."

She looked beseeching at me. "Are you ... quite sure?"

The question was nuts. But then, heck, the whole situation was nuts. I nodded. "I'm totally sure. That other one's an imposter. She's not you. She's nothing *like* you."

Micha rubbed away the tear. "Thank you, Will."

We both fell silent, settling back on the cold, metal floor of the catwalk. The woman's eyes grew distant, and she seemed to drift away inside herself, maybe even forgetting I was there. Meanwhile, I got as comfortable as I could, what with my back rammed up against the railing—and *considered* her.

Lindsay Micha.

No Corpse had ever before, as far as we knew, mimicked an actual person, living or dead. And the fact that they'd done so to Senator Micha hinted they were up to something—no doubt something *bad*—and only Lindsay Micha could deliver it.

Back in Haven, Tom had supposed that, after replacing the senator, the Corpses had killed the original. After all, why *wouldn't* they? Cavanaugh's crew had never been big on keeping prisoners.

But then who—or what—was *this*? What was she doing here? And just what the heck was that thing she changed into?

More questions than answers. Story of my life.

"Thanks for saving me," I said again.

She started. "What?"

"I said thanks for saving my life."

Micha fidgeted uncomfortably. "Oh, that wasn't me. That was the First." I could almost hear the capital *F*, like with "Third" earlier.

"The First. That's who rescued me?"

She nodded.

"And so ... who are you?"

"I'm the Second."

"The second what?"

"The Second Head, of course!"

I swallowed. "Senator Micha—"

"Lindsay," she corrected.

"Okay. Lindsay. What *happened* to you?"

She ran trembling hands through the forest of wild, gray hair atop her head. "I-I don't know, exactly. I was ... taken. But not by ... people. Not proper people, anyway."

"We call them Corpses. With a capital *C*." Then I told her some of it. The war. The Undertakers. My mission to DC. I left out Sharyn, as well as any particulars that might put Haven at risk. And she listened without apparent judgment—though I suppose if you were what she was, your horizons might be a little broader than average, too.

Finally, I finished up with, "As far as we can tell, they

kidnapped you and replaced you with one of their own. They've never done it before."

Micha nodded but didn't speak, her body motionless. For a half minute she stayed like that, still as a statue. Then, finally, she said, "She fears you."

"Who?"

"The Third."

"The Third Head?" I asked.

She nodded again.

"You mean the Corpse pretending to be you? *That's* the Third?"

Micha nodded slowly, the movement slight and very precise. Sitting there on the catwalk, wearing my jacket, and with the rest of her naked body thankfully bathed in shadow, I got the impression that she'd wound herself up *real* tight, like a tiger poised for the pounce. It wasn't what you'd call a happy thought. "She's afraid of the Undertakers. I heard it in her mind. That's how I knew the word."

"I told you," I said. "We fight her. We fight all the Corpses."

"Why were you in the Rotunda?" she demanded, so abruptly that I jumped. "It was after hours!"

"I was looking for ... well ... you." But even as I said it, I knew—for the first time—that it wasn't really true. I'd told myself that was why I'd bailed on Sharyn and snuck out of Webster Hall. But now, in this strange place and with this strange person, I understood the *real* reason.

I hadn't wanted to go home.

"You found me," she said, an unsettling edge to her voice. "Or rather, *I* found *you*."

"Yeah," I agreed.

"*She* was there!" Micha exclaimed, and with such venom, such *hatred,* that I flinched and retreated a few feet along the catwalk.

"I was in the Rotunda," she went on. "It's … hazy. Like a dream. But I remember *her* being there. The Third!"

It took a lot of effort to reply. It was like having a loaded gun shoved in my face. This woman still *looked* like Lindsay Micha, but my mind's eye kept seeing ten legs— and *teeth.*

"I need to find her!" she snarled. Yep, *snarled.* "I came close tonight. She was right there. If I hadn't stopped to …" Her words trailed off.

"Save me," I finished. "You might have had a shot at the imposter if you hadn't rescued *me* instead."

"Yes." The word was almost a hiss. Then, as if arguing with herself, she snapped, "Well, I couldn't let those … those *monsters* … hurt a child! I had to do something! Didn't I?"

I almost said, "Sure." But I got the seriously messed-up impression that she wasn't talking to me. So I just sat there, kicking myself for not running when I'd had the chance. Sympathy for naked, crazy, old ladies only goes so far.

"Enough!" she said with senatorial finality. "For once you're going to listen to me!" Her eyes met mine. "Yes, Will. *I* brought you here."

I nodded, though inside I was thinking: *Holy crap! Holy crap! Holy crap!*

Micha nodded, too. "You're safe. They won't find us. They don't come this far up."

"Up what?" I asked.

"I hear them sometimes," she went on. "Late at night.

They know I'm up here ... or at least they suspect. But they're afraid. They search for me, but they're afraid to find me." She grinned wolfishly. "They *should* be."

And, thick as I was, it finally clicked. "We're inside the dome!"

Micha regarded me as if I'd just enthusiastically announced the world was round. "Where else would we be? This is the space between the inner and outer domes. Very few people come up here—and lately, no one at all."

That explained the fleeting glimpse of George Washington I'd gotten when she—the First, as she'd called it—had carried me up from the Rotunda and past the fresco at the top of the dome.

I hadn't even known this in-between space existed!

"Charles O'Mally is dead, isn't he?" she asked.

Her subject changes, like everything about her, were kind of dizzying. "Yeah," I said.

"He was a good man."

"I liked him, too. A lot."

Her smile softened. "I can see why he took a shine to you. He always gravitated toward redheaded people; just a funny quirk about the fellow." Then, a little shyly, she added, "You'd never know it to look at me now, but I was a redhead myself once."

The image of Gardner's decaying hand ripping out the Sergeant at Arms' still-beating heart flashed through my memory, white hot and razor sharp. "I shouldn't have gotten him mixed up in this. It's my fault he got killed."

"Oh, I don't see how that could be," Micha replied gently. "We were watching ... the First and myself. We clearly saw what that zombie did to him. *You* tried to help."

"Don't call 'em zombies," I said. A reflex.

"Why not?"

Tears filled my eyes. "Never mind. I used him. Mr. O'Mally, I mean. I lied to him to get him to let me into the Capitol after hours. All because I wanted to look for ... *you*."

"Me?"

"The other you."

She started fidgeting again.

You don't quite realize that you and the First are somehow sharing a body. Oh, you know it's there. You even rely on it. But that doesn't mean you want to consciously accept it.

My dad used to have this saying about swimming in the River Denial.

Well, Lindsay Micha was drowning in it.

Okay, I knew I was about to take an awful chance. But maybe the time had come to talk about the ten-legged elephant in the room. "Lindsay ... do you know what you are? Um ... what you ... change into?"

Her body took on that same scary stillness as before. "That's not me. That's the First."

"The First is the creature that saved me in the Rotunda?"

She offered me a barely noticeable nod.

"But Lindsay," I said carefully, "the First ... is *you*."

"No!" she exclaimed. Then she jumped to her feet. Except she didn't jump—she *leaped*, went from sitting to standing in one perfect, fluid motion, almost too quick to see. "No!" she screamed again, pointing a trembling finger at me. "I'm not that *horrible* monster! I'm not!"

Then her eyes flashed.

I don't mean they got bigger with anger, the way

219

Helene's sometimes did. I mean they *flashed*, like there was light behind them. Different-colored lights. Red. Green. Yellow. Blue. Over and over again, in rapid succession. At the same time, the surrounding air crackled with energy. I felt my scalp prickle, felt the hairs on my arms—even under my page shirt—stand straight up.

Oh God ... she's gonna Hulk out on me!

It was horrifying. And when an Undertaker tells you something's horrifying, you'd better believe it.

Once again, my instincts screamed at me to run, even though I sensed that particular window had closed. At the very least, I wanted to throw up my hands and apologize, plead even—anything to calm her down, to make those awful eyes go back to normal.

But I'm an Undertaker. And we *don't* plead.

So instead I stood up and put my face right in hers. It took every ounce of courage I had, but I did it. "Look at yourself!" I shouted back. "It's happening to you right now! Right now! You're gonna change right in front of me! You're about to prove me right!"

Her mouth opened to speak. It was full of teeth, but not the human kind. These were thin and spiky, like miniature steak knives. And there were hundreds of them! She glared at me with those horrible, otherworldly eyes, and tried to form words. All that emerged, however, was a low, unnatural growl.

"The First is coming out, Lindsay," I said, faking a calm I sure as heck didn't feel. "And when it does, you'll probably kill me. That what you want?"

Seconds passed, each one about a century long. I found myself counting my own heartbeats. There were a *lot* of them.

Micha's mouth closed. Her shoulders fell. Her eyes turned human again.

She said with a sigh, "I'm hungry."

Then she changed.

It was so quick, my mind couldn't quite grasp it. She didn't "Hulk out" so much as *explode* from one state to the other in a blur of flesh and color. One instant, a woman wrapped in nothing but an oversized page jacket stood before me—and the next the jacket was in tatters on the floor and the ten-legged Corpse Eater fixed me with its green eye.

A word, just one, drilled into my brain. This wasn't like Deadspeak. This was like getting hit over the head with a telepathic brick.

Stay!

Then, as if to make her point, one pincered leg knocked me down and pinned to me to the catwalk. She leaned on my chest, bringing that face—that freakin' eye—right down into mine.

A second "brick," same as the first: *Stay!*

Then it was gone, bounding away down the steps and out of sight, leaving me on my back, lathered in sweat, and desperately trying not to pee my pants.

CHAPTER 31
DESPERATE TIMES

Lilith Cavanaugh

The package arrived at Lilith Cavanaugh's three-story brick condominium in the wealthy Society Hill section of Philadelphia at well past eleven P.M. The messenger, a federal employee, apologized for the hour, explaining that it was a priority delivery from Senator Lindsay Micha.

"But you're dressed," he added. "So at least I didn't pull you out of bed."

The Queen glowered at the human fool, wishing that killing him was an option. But no—too many risks. Besides he seemed a reliable messenger. Something she'd learned long ago: never kill the messenger; good messengers are hard to find.

She signed for the package and showed him her driver's license, which was almost comical, given what she actually looked like. Her current body was falling apart—a shriveled mummy infested with beetles and blowflies, whose skin cracked whenever she moved.

Unfortunately, as her minions kept telling her, no replacements were yet available. Humans just didn't die at a convenient rate.

After the clueless messenger departed, Lilith carried her sister's package to the kitchen table and examined it. It was a cube—eighteen inches on each side—and, other than Lilith's address, it bore no markings.

Reluctantly, she fetched a kitchen knife.

The *Malum* didn't use weapons. Just holding one made her feel unclean. Unfortunately, given the condition of her current host, trying to tear the package open would likely cost her a finger, or worse.

So, grimacing, she used the knife to cut the tape and then put it down as quickly as she could before opening the package and looking inside.

The Queen gazed into the rotting face of John Tall. The giant's mouth hung open, his features—already weeks dead even before he'd been decapitated—slack and purple.

That was it. No note. Just her minion's severed head.

A moment later, her cell phone rang.

Trembling with barely contained rage, the Queen answered it. "Speak."

"Did my gift please you, sister?"

Lilith said nothing.

"The driver just texted me that you'd received delivery. Very convenient, these human gadgets."

Lilith said nothing.

"Really ... sending a fool like that to destroy me. It's beneath you."

Still Lilith said nothing.

"Perhaps it's time for you to accept the changes that are coming."

"Changes," the Queen echoed.

"Tomorrow, Senator Micha announces her plans on live television. I'm going to make history."

"As well as alert the Undertakers to your existence!" Lilith snapped, though she was immediately sorry she had.

"There's a human expression: that ship has sailed. Besides, what can those brats possibly do against me? Why, just this evening I sprung a trap that ensnared Will Ritter."

Lilith asked, "So the boy's dead?"

A pause. An interesting pause. *"Almost certainly."*

The Queen allowed herself a smile—thin, spiteful, and mean-spirited. "I'm not without my own sources of information in Washington."

Now it was Micha's turn to say nothing.

"I know what happened in the Capitol Rotunda earlier this evening. You cornered the Ritter boy but were prevented from killing him by … shall we say … your better half?"

Another long pause. Finally, and with feigned certainty: *"That was hours ago. The abomination has consumed him by now."*

"Has it?"

"You know what they're like."

"I do. And I also know that, so far, all of its victims have been *Malum*. No human has even been injured. Furthermore, as I understand it, the abomination arrived on the scene just in time to save Ritter."

"It's not important!" Micha snapped.

"You realize, of course, that the more time it spends in human company … the more *her* true Self will emerge."

"I said it's not important!"

"So you did. Do you know where it's hiding?"

"I have a strong suspicion."

"Then why not have your loyal minions close in and kill it?" the Queen asked. Then, smiling into her sister's silence, she answered her own question. "Because their loyalty to *you* isn't quite enough to overcome their fear of *her*. Is that the problem ... Senator?"

Micha said nothing.

"You know what she wants," Cavanaugh continued, enjoying herself. "What she's *driven* to want. You could flee DC for a while, crawl into some safe, dark hole, and wait until she dies ... but then what would happen to your ambitions?"

"I refuse to hide from that ... thing!"

"Courageous of you," the Queen remarked sarcastically.

"More courageous, certainly, than you have been, sister! It's your utter failure to deal with the meddlesome brats plaguing your city— and now plaguing mine—that makes my bid for supremacy necessary!"

And there it was. A bid for supremacy. No more hints. No more double meanings. Lindsay Micha had finally gone as far as to admit her ultimate goal. She intended to supplant Lilith as the Queen of the *Malum*.

"My people will find the abomination. And if, by some miracle, Ritter still lives, they will kill him. I won't fail as you have."

Lilith seethed. "Let's just hope you find her before she finds you."

"I will," Micha replied. *"In the meantime, enjoy your 'gift.' I had the rest of his body destroyed ... so your 'assassin' is still in there. I thought you would find that amusing."*

And the line went dead.

Lilith Cavanaugh considered throwing the phone through the nearby wall, but she'd done that to too many cell phones lately. So instead she pocketed the device and, for a minute or so, studied what little remained of John Tall with utter disdain. Then she lifted his head out of the box and brought its slack, lifeless face close to her own.

"Hello, John," she said.

"Mistress," Tall replied in the Old Tongue. Without lungs attached to his severed windpipe, he couldn't form human speech. Nevertheless, she found it interesting that he'd waited until now to address her. Protocol. Never speak until spoken to.

"You failed me again."

"Yes. Mistress."

No denials. No blubbering. "But you saw it, didn't you? The abomination."

"Yes. Horrible." Then, after a pause: "It. Took. Boy."

"So I've been told. Do you believe it took him for nourishment? Might Will Ritter already be dead?"

"No. Mistress. It. After. Micha. But. Saw. Boy. Danger. Chose. Rescue. Him."

So her spy had said. Still, it was good to have it confirmed.

"Thank you, John."

"Destroy. Me. Now?" he asked in the Old Tongue. His dread was obvious. It calmed her.

What's more, it gave her an idea. The kidnapping of Karl Ritter's son was unexpected. But perhaps it was also an—*opportunity.*

"Not just yet," the Queen said thoughtfully. "Right now I have something more urgent to attend to."

Then she unceremoniously dropped the head back into

its box and returned to the living room, thankful now that she *hadn't* destroyed her cell phone.

She had some calls to make.

CHAPTER 32
DESPERATE MEASURES

Helene

"Emily ... sweetheart," Helene heard Susan Ritter say carefully. "Come away from that ... right now."

Just out of sight around the corner, Helene froze. She'd been navigating one of Haven's crumbling corridors, trailing after the woman who'd been the target of her latest disaster of a mission. It was Monday night, more than two weeks since Tom had charged her with "getting close" to Will's mom and, so far...

...well, Helene couldn't remember the last time she'd screwed up something this bad.

Every time she tried hanging with Mrs. Ritter, her clumsy attempts to strike up a conversation went nowhere fast. Not that Will's mother was rude—exactly. She just didn't give anything back, usually making some hasty excuse to cut their contact short. Things had gotten so frustrating that Helene had twice asked Tom to pick another ambassador, insisting that she just wasn't cut out for this kind of thing.

And twice he'd said no.

So, over the last couple of days, Helene had taken to just kind of shadowing the woman, doing her best to stay out of sight while at the same time sticking close enough to kind of...step in and help...if an opening arose. It felt like a stupid strategy, transparent and juvenile. But, at this point, it was the only thing she could think of.

Then from up ahead she heard a little girl's voice. "But I want to pet the kitty, Mommy!"

Uh-oh.

Helene hurried ahead, closing the distance between herself and Will's small family.

Just around the corner, Susan Ritter stood at the mouth of one of Haven's many blind corridors, little more than a deep niche in the wall. By the meager light of one of the bare bulbs strung along the hallway ceiling, Helene could read her worry. So far, she hadn't noticed Helene's arrival, her attention being glued to the goings-on in that blind corridor.

And Helene could guess what they were.

So she approached slowly, making as little noise as possible, until she stood just behind Mrs. Ritter's shoulder.

Emily crouched inside the niche, her hand outstretched toward an animal that regarded it with distrust. The creature growled, low-pitched and menacing.

Any resemblance to a domestic cat was purely

coincidental. The animal was large but scrawny, its ribs showing. It had short, gray fur and a wide, distrustful stare lit by eye shine.

Helene knew all about them: feral cats, introduced down here a century ago by the city to help deal with rats and other vermin. Now *they* were the vermin. Shy and quick to run, they could be dangerous when cornered.

Well, Will's six-year-old sister had cornered *this* one.

"Here, kitty! Here, kitty!" the girl cooed.

"It doesn't want to be petted, Em," her mother told her, and there was no mistaking the edge of fear in her voice. She was right to be scared. The little girl's hand was inches from the growling cat, whose tail swished back and forth, its back arched.

"She could sleep with me, Mommy!" Emily suggested. "Then I wouldn't have bad dreams!"

Her mother visibly swallowed. "That's ... not like the cats in the pet stores, sweetheart. Please come away from it."

"But, Mooommmyyy!"

The cat tensed to strike, bearing its teeth.

Helene pulled out her water pistol and squirted it in the face.

The animal yowled and darted past Emily, who whined with disappointment as it vanished around the corner.

Susan Ritter spun around in surprise.

"You wanna keep one of these handy," Helene said. "They *hate* getting wet."

"You hurt the kitty!" Emily told Helene.

"I just scared it off before it could hurt *you*."

"Kitty wouldn't have hurt me," the girl insisted,

scowling. "She liked me!"

Helene looked at Susan and tried a shrug. "You don't want to get scratched or bit by one of those. Trust me."

"Thank you," the woman said.

"No sweat." Helene knelt in front of Emily. "I'm sorry, but the cats that live down here are scared of people, even pretty little girls."

Will had once told her that Emily liked being called pretty, that it was a quick, surefire way to get on her good side. And it worked. Helene watched the little girl's anger fade, the cat forgotten. Then, as little kids often did, she switched topics. "My brother's out fighting the bad people."

"I know," Helene replied.

"Do you fight the bad people, too?" Emily asked.

"I try." Then she met Mrs. Ritter's eyes, and immediately saw something there she didn't like.

"Good thing you were right here ... to help," Will's mom remarked.

"Um ... yeah."

"Seems you've been around a lot lately. I'd almost think you were following me."

Helene felt her face flush. She tried to form a denial, but somehow the lie just wouldn't pass her lips.

Mrs. Ritter said, "Emily and I were just heading back to our quarters. It's bedtime."

"Oh," Helene remarked. "Then I guess I'll—"

"Would you come with us?"

Helene blinked. "Me?"

"It won't take long. Then maybe you and I can have a ... talk."

This should have been good news. It was the first time

Mrs. Ritter had initiated any conversation between them. Except the hard look in the woman's eyes seemed to discourage celebration.

"Sure," she said with a sigh.

In the Shrine, they found Tom.

He sat just inside the tiny room's entrance, his huge frame stretched across a folding chair. He looked like he might be asleep, but as Will's mother reached for his shoulder, he whispered, "Hi, Mrs. Ritter."

"I was just about to put Emily to bed," she told him. "But then I need to talk to you and Helene."

The chief nodded, as if he'd expected this. Then he rose and stepped out into the corridor. There, he and Helene stood together in silence as Will's mother settled the little girl down for the night. Emily went surprisingly willingly. She asked only one question, and Helene thought it was good one: "Mommy, are you mad at Tom and Helene?"

Girl's no fool.

Helene glanced at the chief. He met her gaze and, to her astonishment, winked.

"Don't you worry about it, sweetheart," Mrs. Ritter replied gently. "Just go to sleep."

"Okay."

A couple of long, uncomfortable minutes later, the three of them were once again alone in Tom's office. The chief, as always, looked relaxed and in charge. For her part, Helene felt as if she had rocks in her stomach.

Tom spoke first. "Sorry about that, Mrs. Ritter. Being in your room, I mean. I know it's an intrusion. But ..." His words trailed off and he shrugged—a proud man without a valid excuse.

"You miss my husband's shrine," Will's mother remarked.

He said nothing.

"Emily and I can find another room," she told him.

"No," he replied at once. "Of course not. You're his family, and you belong there. I just ... had a weak moment."

Mrs. Ritter said, "You loved him, too. It was selfish of me to forget that. Emily and I'll go someplace else. Honestly, I think part of me will be relieved. Too many memories in there."

Helene watched the woman, feeling both surprised and impressed. The Susan Ritter she knew was angry most of the time, complaining about one thing or another. But this one was different. Gentler. Warmer. More like a mom—as Helene remembered her own to be.

"That's what Will says," Tom replied.

"Then it's settled?"

He nodded. "Thanks. But I'm guessin' that ain't what you wanted to talk about."

She shook her head. "I wanted to ask if it was you who told Helene here to follow me around all the time."

The chief looked from Mrs. Ritter to Helene, who wished she could dig a hole in the dirt floor, climb in, and fill it back up. "Sorry," she mumbled.

"Don't be," he told her. Then he faced Will's mother. "Yeah, I did that."

"Why?"

Tom met her eyes. "Because you bein' here ain't been easy on anyone. Because you *disapprove*, Mrs. Ritter. Of Haven. Of what we do here. Of how we live. Of *me*."

"I'm not sure 'disapprove' is the right word," she replied.

Helene said, "Yeah, it is."

They both looked at her. Nervously, she cleared her throat and continued. "Mrs. Ritter, I'm sorry ... but you walk into every room shaking your head, like you can't believe how it is here and that you gotta live with it."

"Well, can you *blame* me?" Will's mother demanded, sounding oddly defensive for a grown-up.

Helene knew she'd spoken out of turn. So she looked at Tom to answer. But he just stood there, not saying a word. Finally, awkwardly, she replied, "Don't you think we all feel that way? Don't you think we all wanna go home?"

Mrs. Ritter's mouth opened and closed again.

So Helene went on, feeling like she was jumping off a cliff. "You've come in here ... all grown-up and judgmental ... without really getting that this isn't how we *choose* to live. It's how we *gotta* live. It's either this ... or we die."

That last word seemed to make the woman pale a little. She looked from Helene to Tom. "I know that," she said finally.

"Yeah, you *know* it," the chief replied. "But that ain't the same as *gettin'* it."

"You kids are just so ... *alone!*"

"And a little adult guidance wouldn't hurt, right?" he asked.

"Right!"

Tom shook his head. "Wrong. It's hurts a lot. It hurts *us* because it makes us wonder if we can keep gettin' by on our own. And that's dangerous thinking. It hurts *you*

234

because it makes us not trust you. You asked me why I hooked Helene up with you. Well, there were a couple o' reasons for that, but here's one: 'cause Helene's as good an Undertaker as you'll meet, and I wanted you to get to know one, up close and personal."

Will's mother frowned. "Like a liaison?"

Well, at least I know the thing I suck at has a name, Helene thought sourly.

Tom nodded.

"I didn't ask for that!"

"I know," he said.

"Then why did you do it?"

"'Cause I'm in charge here. And that means I do what I think needs doin', whether or not anybody asks for it."

Again, Helene watched Will's mom struggle for a response. It was amazing, really. Tom was half her age, but still it seemed almost like *he* was the grown-up in the room.

"I've got Will," Mrs. Ritter said finally. "He's my liaison."

"No," Tom replied.

"Why not?"

"'Cause you ain't taken the time to *know* Will ... not *this* Will ... not Will Ritter, Undertaker."

"That's ridiculous!" the woman exclaimed. "He's my son."

"Yeah, he is. And he always will be. But he ain't the kid who ran away from home six months ago. Not even close. That's why you and him keep bumpin' heads. You still expect him to be the Will you remember. Fact is: you *demand* it of him. And when he can't be, you get mad. At him. At *us*. At all of Haven."

The woman glared at him. "I don't have to stand here and be psychoanalyzed by you, Thomas Jefferson."

But if her savage stare and "mom" use of his full name had any effect on the chief, apart from a slightly amused smile, it didn't show. "Am I wrong? How'd you end things with Will, last time you saw him?"

Mrs. Ritter didn't answer; she didn't have to. Haven wasn't that big a place, and she and Will had been screaming pretty loud that morning. *Everybody* knew, more or less, what had gone down.

"I ain't tryin' to insult or criticize you," the chief continued. "Life here ain't easy, and you got a lot to deal with right now. But, Mrs. Ritter—and I mean with this with all due respect—I *need* you to adjust, I *need* you to find your place with us."

"And what if I can't?" she asked in a quiet voice.

"Then I might have to talk to Agent Ramirez about arranging a safe house for you and Emily. It'd break my heart to do it. Will's too, I'm sure. But if we're gonna survive this war, then we need to pull together, stand together, and *do it* together."

It seemed to Helene as if Will's mother *deflated*. All of the mom stuff—the anger, the righteous outrage—just bled out of her, and she sank down onto one of the conference table chairs, covering her face with her hands.

Tom came forward and sat beside her. And Helene, feeling awkward, did the same.

The woman made no noise, but from the way her shoulders shook, it was easy to tell she was crying.

"I'm sorry, Mrs. Ritter," Tom said.

"Me, too," Helene added.

Susan Ritter lowered her hands. Her eyes *were* wet, but

her expression looked determined.

There's Will, Helene thought.

"All right," she said, more to herself than to them. Then she straightened. "With Ian gone, I've been filling in as medic. I'd like to make that official."

"You sure?" the chief asked her.

She nodded.

"Then we'll make it official."

The next thing Mrs. Ritter said took Helene by surprise.

"And I'd like to become an Undertaker."

For a moment, even Tom seemed taken aback. Then he looked thoughtful. "Straight up?"

"Straight up," she replied. "If Emily and I are here, then let us *be* here. Let us join the fight."

"Emily's too young," he said.

"And I'm too old?"

"I don't know," he admitted. "I ain't even sure it'd do any good. Might smooth things over with some of the kids. Might not. Either way, you gotta know—I mean really *know*—what you're saying. You gotta *get* what being an Undertaker means."

Mrs. Ritter said, "I know what it means."

Do you? Helene wondered.

"Yeah?" Tom said. "So tell me."

The woman eyed him. "Is this a test?"

"First of many. So, Susan Ritter, new recruit, consider this your own personal First Stop. What's it mean to be an Undertaker?"

"It means fighting the Corpses," she said.

He met her eyes. "And?"

"And … it means putting yourself in harm's way."

Mrs. Ritter had to fight to get those words out. The woman was thinking of Will. Helene knew that because *she* was thinking the same thing.

"What for?" the chief asked.

Mrs. Ritter blinked. "What?"

"You say bein' an Undertaker means putting yourself in harm's way. That's solid. But *why* does it mean that?"

"I don't know what you're asking me."

"Sure you do. It's the first lesson Agent Ramirez had to learn. Now it's your turn. Why do we risk our lives to fight the Corpses?"

Susan Ritter swallowed. Then she said, "Because no one else can."

He nodded.

"Is that it?" she asked.

"It'll do for a start."

"I'm an Undertaker," Will's mother said, as if trying the concept on for size.

Nope, Helene thought.

"Nope," Tom replied. "It takes more'n words to call yourself that."

Mrs. Ritter asked, "Is it enough for you to at least start calling me Susan?"

He considered. "Maybe. That one'll take some getting used to. I think Karl—"

But whatever he meant to say was lost when his satellite phone buzzed. Tom checked the Caller ID and answered it. "Yeah, sis?"

Both Helene and Mrs. Ritter tensed. Word had gotten around that Will would be heading back to Haven on a midnight train from DC. Helene didn't know the particulars, but inwardly she'd been profoundly relieved.

And Mrs. Ritter, she knew, was practically doing cartwheels.

But now, as Tom listened, his darkening expression turned Helene's insides to ice.

"Okay," Tom said into the phone. "You gotta stay clear of this. You're all we got down there now. If anybody questions you, play dumb. Give us a few hours to put something together." More listening. Then: "Sis, stop it! We don't got time for that crap. This ain't your fault. We all shoulda seen this coming. Gotta go. Stay cool and stay in touch. I'll call you when we got an angle."

He closed the phone.

"What happened?" Mrs. Ritter asked.

Tom didn't hedge. He *never* hedged, even when you wished he would. "Will's gone missing. He split Webster Hall sometime after dinner, and Sharyn didn't know it 'til she went to collect him for the train. When the proctors found out they notified the cops."

Helene's heart sank.

"But ... why?" Will's mother demanded, visibly horrified. "Why would he leave like that?"

"He didn't want to quit the mission," Tom explained gently. "That's how Will is. That's how he *always* is. Something went down in the Capitol last week. According to Ramirez, a Corpse got offed ... eaten ... by some kind of creature. Sharyn thinks Will went to check it out."

"Oh God ..." the woman choked.

Tom looked about to say something further. But then his satellite phone buzzed a second time.

"Yeah, Sammy?" he asked, weariness in his voice.

He listened. He frowned. He listened some more.

"Thanks, I got it," he said. Then he broke the call.

"Who was that?" Helene asked, her mouth dry.

"Sammy." Then, for Mrs. Ritter's benefit: "Sammy Li. Hacker Boss. He got a hit on the Undertaker Worm."

Mrs. Ritter looked up at him, fresh fear etched on her pale face. "Undertaker Worm?" she asked vaguely.

"It's a computer program," the chief explained. "Sammy's crew runs it against the online news services. When it finds any mention of *us*, it throws up a flag. It's how we keep tabs on our rep citywide. Well, it seems something got posted in the Personals Section of the *Daily News'* website. It's from Cavanaugh."

Helene gasped. "What?"

"It reads: 'QUEEN SEEKS UNDERTAKER FOR FRIENDLY GAME. KNIGHT IN TROUBLE. KING ONLY.'"

Helene wondered, *Is that supposed to be some kind of code?*

"They must know we watch the papers," Tom said. "This was her way of leaving us a message."

"You think Cavanaugh wants a meeting?" Helene asked.

Tom nodded.

"And 'king only' means you."

He nodded again. They both looked at Susan Ritter, who was still trying to take in Will's latest stunt. Nevertheless, she managed to steady herself and ask, "But who's 'knight'?"

When Tom replied, the worry in his voice scared them both. "Your husband once told me that Ritter ... means 'knight' in German."

CHAPTER 33

THE ENEMY OF MY ENEMY

Hungry.

She'd said she was hungry. And I knew what *that* meant.

It also meant I had another chance to run, probably my best so far. Maybe the Corpse Eater would be so busy with her late-night snack that I could slip by unnoticed. Once again, I could almost hear my mom begging me to do it.

And, once again, I stayed.

I know I've got this rep for taking crazy chances. And maybe I've even earned it—from time to time. But that doesn't mean I'm stupid. I didn't know just how long I'd been up here, but I figured it had to be past midnight. Which meant the only "people" in the Capitol at this time were probably "dead" people.

So getting out of here meant not just getting past Micha. It meant getting past the Corpses as well. Long odds.

Besides, there was another reason for staying—maybe a better one.

I liked her.

Don't get me wrong. She scared the living crap out of me. But, even so, I couldn't help thinking of this old saying: The enemy of my enemy is my friend.

The Corpse Eater ate deaders—and they were even more frightened of her than I was. Now she was hungry again, and I sensed more than knew that she'd decided to leave just now because, if she'd stayed, *I* might have ended up on the menu. That suggested at least some self-control while she was Hulked out.

Which could make her one serious, kick-butt ally.

If I stayed.

Anyway that's how I figured it at the time. Looking back—well—maybe all that logic was simply me justifying another crazy risk.

Whatever.

Having committed to hanging around, I got as comfortable as I could on the catwalk and settled down to wait. Then, as time passed, I did something that probably strikes you as totally insane: I slept.

I know what you're thinking. So far tonight, I'd been ambushed by Corpses, seen a man I liked get brutally murdered, and been kidnapped by a monster. So how the heck could I possibly *sleep*?

Well, there's not a combat soldier in the world who can't answer that question.

Undertakers, especially Angels, are taught that sleep isn't something you *should* do; it's something you *must* do. Without rest, everything slows down: running speed, reflexes, even brain power. Especially brain power. So we're *trained*, even in dangerous situations, to grab some zzzs whenever we can.

Like now.

I closed my eyes, breathed evenly, and consciously emptied my head. No fear. No worry. No thoughts at all. Just—nothing.

And out I went. There were no dreams, at least none that I can remember. That's usually for the best.

By the time I awoke, it had gotten colder. Shivering, I sat up and immediately noticed a change in the surrounding darkness. The angled shadows, sharp as razors before, seemed a little blurrier now, as if the light leaking between these two domes was more diffused.

Was the sun coming up? If so, then I'd been asleep for hours.

I was still alone. No Lindsay Micha, not in either of her forms. I wasn't sure how I felt about that. She wasn't exactly easy to be around, but having her gone for so long made me wonder if she was as unbeatable against Corpses as I'd thought.

So ... you're worried about that thing now?

Except she wasn't a "thing" anymore. And that surprised me.

I learned long ago how useless worry is. So instead of brooding, I got up, stretched, and had my first real look around. The weird space was totally quiet—no sound at all—and the angles and shadows made it seem a little freaky.

I needed a change of scenery.

My eyes strayed to the only door. Approaching it, I found it locked. Fortunately, while my sat phone was toast, my faithful pocketknife lived on and I used it now, clicking the **1** button and working the door until it opened.

Within: a short hallway, some steps, another door, and then —

Wow.

Cool autumn air chilled me to the bone. But, for the moment at least, I didn't care.

I found myself emerging *outside*, onto a small, circular walkway at the very top of the Capitol building, right under the Justice statue. Below me, the white dome swept out and down, disappearing beyond a metal, man-made horizon. And before me, Washington, DC spread out in a tapestry of crisscrossing lights, a funky grid with sharp diagonals heading off along four opposing compass points.

It was as if the entire city flowed from exactly this spot.

For a while I just stood there, watching the sunrise. I hadn't seen too many sunrises in my life and, despite the cold, it was pretty amazing. So amazing, in fact, that I almost didn't notice Lindsay's return. Once again in human form, she appeared at my shoulder and said wistfully, "Quite a view."

I glanced her way and then shielded my eyes, my cheeks burning. Talk about "quite a view!"

"Um ... you're kinda naked again," I stammered.

She sighed and produced a Capitol police jacket, which she slipped into. It had to be four sizes too big for her, but at least it covered up what needed covering up.

Then, to my further surprise, she offered a second jacket to me. "I thought you might be cold. I don't feel it, but I imagine that you might."

"Thanks," I said, meaning it. But, as I put it on, my hand came away a little sticky. I caught the whiff of formaldehyde. "Lindsay?"

"Yes, Will?"

"Where'd you get these?"

"Their previous owners aren't going to be needing them," she replied tonelessly.

A chill rolled down my back, despite my "borrowed" outerwear.

"Did you ..." I swallowed and tried again. "Did you eat?"

"Oh yes. I'm sorry about my abrupt departure. Our conversation was making me ... nervous, and I'm embarrassed to admit that when I feel nervous, I eat. I've always been that way.

Not exactly like bingeing on potato chips. But then I thought: *The enemy of my enemy,* screwed up my courage and said, "Can I ask you a question?"

"Of course," Lindsay Micha replied cordially, not at all like a wild-haired, half-crazed, half-naked were-*something.*

"How long are you going to keep me here?"

She considered the question. "Just until the Third is gone."

"The imposter?"

She nodded.

"Why do you call her the Third?"

More consideration. "I don't know. That's just what she is: the Third."

"Who's the First?" I asked.

She sighed. "I suppose *I* am. I should apologize for my earlier outburst. So much has happened ... so quickly ... and I'm afraid I'm still playing catch-up. I hate the notion of being that ... that ... thing. But denying it is pointless."

"Okay," I said. "And who's the *Second?*"

The question surprised her. "Why ... I am," she said

again. "Isn't that what you were trying to explain to me before?"

And of course it *was*; I'd just needed to be sure *she* knew it. Two beings sharing a single body. The First and the Second.

And the Corpse calling herself, Lindsay Micha, was the Third.

Of course, what all that meant remained a complete mystery—but it *had* to have something to do with Cavanaugh's scheme to replace the senator.

I needed to contact Haven.

Then I saw something.

Something that convinced me what I *really* needed to do was keep talking.

I saw Sharyn.

The girl, dressed in her page uniform, appeared on the catwalk behind Lindsay, watching us through the open doors that led from there to here. Her expression was wary, but when her eyes met mine, I read only relief and curiosity. Not what *should* have been there: fear.

She wasn't afraid, which meant she didn't understand what she was dealing with.

I swallowed.

Lindsay asked, "Everything all right?"

Behind her—*so* close—Sharyn opened her mouth to speak, maybe to announce herself with some cute comment. She had this sense of drama that I'd only recently started to appreciate.

But today, it might get her killed.

So, in desperation, I said, "When you changed into that Corpse-eating monster earlier … I thought you were gonna make *me* your snack!"

I said it loud, louder than I'd had to, loud enough for Sharyn to hear and, hopefully, *get*. She did; her mouth closed, at least for now.

Lindsay looked hurt. "Will—"

"But you didn't!" I added quickly. "All you did was push me down and tell me to stay. I took that as a good sign!"

"Will," the woman said, frowning. "There's no need to shout."

"Got it," I said, still pretty loud. "Nix the shouting." Then, as if to underline my words, I ran my hand across my throat.

The Angels' "abort" signal.

Sharyn nodded her understanding. But she still didn't move, and I wished there was a gesture that said: "Get your butt gone before the old lady eats you!"

Time for, as Tom liked to put it, a "tactical re-think."

"Lindsay …" I began. She looked at me, her grubby face so poised, so…senatorial. But I couldn't shake the memory of how quickly she could change, or of what she changed into. "I need to get to a phone."

"No!" she exclaimed, much more loudly than she'd accused me of talking. For an instant her eyes danced with color, and I felt my heart skip a beat. "It's too dangerous! I have to protect you!"

The classic grown-up response. Well, I'd played this scene before, and I knew my lines. "Why?" I asked.

"Why? Because you're a child!"

"And?"

"And?" she echoed. "Because they're hunting you … the same monsters who are hunting me. These … Corpses. I'm an adult. You're a minor. So I have to keep you safe."

"You sound like my mother," I remarked.

"Do I?"

"She didn't want me to come down here... ... to DC. We had this big fight about it right before I left. She was afraid I'd get hurt."

Lindsay went very still. Her face paled.

But she didn't reply, so I kept going. "What she doesn't get is that I'm not just her son anymore. I'm an Undertaker. People are counting on me. I couldn't stay in Haven. I couldn't stay safe. Do you get what I'm saying?"

"Jacob," she replied, a faraway look in her eyes.

Not exactly the answer I'd expected. Heck, not even on the list of possibilities. "Huh?"

"My half-brother," Lindsay explained. "There were twelve years between us and, after our father and my stepmother died, I practically raised him myself. I've never been a parent. Never married. Just never found the time. But ... in a way ... I guess I was Jacob's mother."

"Where is he now?" I asked, though from her tone I could have guessed.

Tears filled her eyes. "He died in Vietnam in 1971. He was ..." She seemed to choke a little on the words. "He was nineteen. So long ago. I'd almost forgotten."

"Lindsay. I'm—"

But her eyes bore into mine, shutting me up. They were flashing again—a bizarre kaleidoscope of colors. "He was a Marine. And, like you, he believed in risking himself to do what was right. They said he threw himself on a grenade ... saved perhaps a dozen men. Two officers came and told me.

"His remains were flown home"—a sob—"in a bag. I buried them in Arlington Cemetery, just across the river from DC. But it wasn't Jacob. It was just … parts. And when the service was over, those same two officers handed me a folded flag. I'd traded the only person I'd ever loved for a folded flag."

She started crying openly. And I just stood there, feeling stupid and useless. What was I supposed to do? Hug her? Maybe put one arm around her shoulder the way Tom sometimes did to me?

Then, to my horror, Sharyn said, "That sucks, Senator."

The Angel Boss had snuck up on us while Lindsay had been talking. Now she stood in the nearest doorway, wearing a look of gentle sympathy. Her eyes touched mine, just for a second, and if she read my warning, she sure didn't pay any attention to it.

Her free hand reached out toward the trembling woman—

—who whirled around on the girl, and instantly *changed.*
Oh crap …

Suddenly face-to-"face" with 130 pounds of legs and teeth, Sharyn Jefferson didn't scream. Even when that mouth widened, wider than the Grand Canyon, the Angel Boss uttered nothing louder than a gasp.

What she *did* do was turn and throw herself down the stairs and onto the catwalk.

An instant later, as the Corpse Eater tensed up to pursue, I did the only wildly stupid thing I could think of—one that would forever cement my reputation as a crazy risk taker.

I jumped on its back.

I'm not what anybody would call a heavyweight. But then neither was Lindsay, even while in this form. So I figured my bulk might slow her down, or maybe even pin her to the floor—at least until that impossible head rolled back around and ate me. Makes sense, right?

Wrong.

The Corpse Eater hit the catwalk half a step behind Sharyn, with me sprawled atop her. As she did, two of her ten legs twisted backward and locked around my body, holding me firmly.

Keeping me safe while she killed the "intruder."

The girl covered the length of the catwalk at a full run, reaching the first staircase and literally jumping down its steps, hitting the lower platform, rolling, and then finding her feet again.

Lindsay and I were right behind her. I could feel the changed woman's leathery muscles flexing, as her eight legs—ten, minus the two holding *me*—churned across the metal surface in hot pursuit. Sharyn, quick as she was, would never be able to stay ahead. She had seconds to live, unless I did something about it.

"Lindsay!" I gasped. "Look ... at ... me!"

I was totally ignored.

Sharyn bolted along yet another catwalk, vaulting over its railing a split second before the Corpse Eater's huge jaws clamped around the air in her wake. She fell four feet, grabbed one of the vertical struts, and kind of swung herself down another level. Not exactly a *parkour* move, and certainly not Jillian quality, but pretty impressive.

Still, it was nowhere near enough.

Lindsay vaulted the railing, too, but instead of dropping straight down as Sharyn had, she leaped fifteen feet and landed on the lower platform, cutting off the girl's escape.

Seeing this, Sharyn froze where she stood, breathing hard, her dark eyes wide with uncharacteristic terror.

The Corpse Eater—powered by blind rage and bizarre, otherworldly hunger—took a predatory step toward her.

I reached up and seized Lindsay's enormous head in both my hands. The blue eye was facing me and I shouted right into it: "Lindsay!"

Again, she ignored me.

I gave the head a hard shake. Nothing

The Corpse Eater advanced on the trapped girl. There was now only fifteen feet between them.

"Lindsay!" I screamed. "Don't!"

Ten feet.

Time to go Stooge, I thought.

I poked it in the eye.

The Corpse Eater paused in mid-leap, uttering a sound like escaping steam. The head inside my hands whirled around, its red eye fixing on me like a laser beam.

And a word—just one word—burned into my mind.

Rude!

I winced, but refused to look away. "You know what's rude? Killing my friend! That's rude!"

The red eye kept glaring.

The creature's two-legged "seatbelt" withdrew, and I was dumped unceremoniously onto the walkway. My bruises got bruised, but I scrambled to my feet anyway.

The Corpse Eater loomed over Sharyn, its hideous mouth opening wide enough to engulf the girl completely. To *consume* her. Legions of teeth glistened in the uneven light.

I fumbled out my pocketknife and opened its Taser. I had no idea if it would work.

Then Sharyn spoke. "Whatcha waitin' for?"

The Corpse Eater paused. So did I. No one moved.

251

"I ain't figured this all out," the girl said. "But I got enough of it. You're Lindsay Micha ... and something 'bout the way the Corpses used you like a Xerox machine did ... *this*. But you flipped it on 'em, didn't you? You got away from wherever they had you and you came here, to this building—your *hood*—and you been givin' them the business ever since."

Then the Angel Boss did something that knocked me right off my "crazy risk" throne: she patted the creature's "cheek."

"Well, I got no beef with that," she continued, smiling. "Thing is though, you took my friend. I figure you did it out of kindness—for the right reasons and all, but you took him and now it's time to give him back."

Lindsay could have been a statue for all the reaction she showed.

Sharyn said, "We ain't your enemies, Senator. We're probably your best and only friends. Will 'n me and the rest of the Undertakers been fightin' this war for years, alone, and we ain't been doing too bad for ourselves. That makes us allies."

I caught Sharyn's eye, and held up my Taser questioningly. She gave me a look that seemed to say "What for? I got this locked!" Then she faced the creature again, whose red eye had been traded for blue.

Good sign? No idea.

"So?" the girl asked. "You gonna eat me and be alone again? Or you gonna fight beside us ... and *really* make those wormbags pay?"

Then, in the blink, the Corpse Eater was gone—and Lindsay Micha stood in its place.

Sharyn tried to be cool about it, but I read the shock in

her dark eyes. Still, she didn't retreat—not a step. That's Sharyn.

"You're children," Lindsay said.

"No, we ain't," Sharyn told her. Then she stepped dismissively around the woman and pulled me into a hard hug. "Remind me to kick your ass later," she said. Then, whispering in my ear she added, "You got a knack for makin' interesting friends, little bro."

"You should know," I whispered back.

That earned me a chuckle.

"You *look* like children," Lindsay said, sounding befuddled.

Sharyn replied, "And *you* look like a lady in her sixties. But we both know that ain't the whole story, don't we?"

Lindsay's eyes filled with tears. "I ... don't know what to do."

Sharyn sighed. "Well, for starters, how's about puttin' on my jacket?" she suggested. "Then ... well, if I know my little bro here, he's already got a plan."

I looked from one to the other: the tearful old woman and the grinning girl.

I sighed.

"Yeah. I kinda do."

CHAPTER 34
SUMMIT WITH THE DEVIL

Lilith Cavanaugh

"Ms. Cavanaugh," her minion in the outer office announced through the intercom. "Tom Jefferson has arrived."

The Queen smiled in sweet anticipation. Her eyes fixed on Philly Chief of Police D'Angelo, one of her most senior *Malum* advisors. The next few minutes were important, even vital. "Is everything ready?"

"Yes, Ms. Cavanaugh," he said, standing at respectful, if annoyingly ridiculous, attention.

Her gaze raked the other *Malum* in the room. There were five, including D'Angelo and herself. Just the right number. Strategy, as with everything else, was a question of balance. Too many of her minions might spark an unwise confrontation. Too few would suggest weakness.

Pressing a dead, lacquered fingernail down on the intercom button, she said, "Send him in."

The body she wore was new, though far from fresh. With her last one all but falling apart, and with today's "summit" to consider, she'd insisted on something—*anything*—that would allow her to move about without her bones snapping and popping like bubble wrap. This three-week-old cadaver, that of a human crone near sixty, was the best her people had been able to provide.

The Queen looked up sharply as her office door *crashed* open and her assistant's headless body tumbled across the threshold.

As it landed on the carpet with a heavy thud, Tom Jefferson stepped inside. In his fist was a short sword. And trailing behind him was none other than Susan Ritter.

What a pleasant surprise! Lilith thought greedily.

Out loud, however, she frowned and said, "Well ... that's inconvenient. Tell me, was it necessary for you to behead my underling?"

"Behead?" Susan Ritter asked, looking confused and frightened.

And the Queen thought: *Of course. You can't see it, you silly creature. You're as blind as the rest of them. To your poor eyes, she looks as if she's sleeping there on my rug, doesn't she?*

"Yeah," Jefferson said, answering the human woman. "Her head's back in the other room." Then, fixing his dark eyes on Lilith, he added, "She told me Ms. Ritter here wasn't invited. Even tried to block my way." He raised the sword. "Didn't like her tone much."

"Indeed," the Queen replied dryly. "Well, regardless, you're welcome here. Do come in and have a seat. And, Susan! How lovely to see you again!"

The last time Karl Ritter's widow had been in her office, Lilith had revealed herself to her—showing the foolish, blind human the truth behind her Cover. Oh, the sweet terror in the woman's eyes! At the time, the Queen had meant to have her killed and then wear her lovely body, but that plan had been foiled.

By the Undertakers.

Susan Ritter didn't respond. She took in D'Angelo and his three other men with silent worry, and Lilith noticed how close Jefferson stayed to her. Neither of them seemed inclined to accept her offer of a chair.

"Why don't you both sit down?" the Queen said again.

"Don't waste my time," Jefferson growled.

"Just trying to make you more comfortable."

"Then open the windows. It stinks in here ... like somethin' died."

The Queen chuckled.

But Jefferson shook his head. "It ain't a joke. Y'all stink. Open the friggin' windows or we're outta here."

Lilith considered the request. They were on the sixth floor of City Hall, with a sheer, seventy-foot drop outside—so where was the harm? She nodded to D'Angelo, who in turn nodded to the other three men, who in turn started opening windows.

Once this was done, Jefferson said, "Let's get to it. You wanted to meet. We're meeting."

The Queen looked at the sword. "When you answered my little ad, I seem to recall asking that you come unarmed."

"No, you asked that I come without a water gun. I did. You didn't say nothin' about a sword."

"I also asked that you come alone."

"Yeah, but I didn't agree to that one," he replied. "While *you* swore to give safe passage, both to and from."

"So I did." Lilith regarded Susan Ritter. She'd lost some weight since their last meeting two months ago, but her body still looked healthy and strong. Fortuitous. "Tell me, Susan … how *is* life in whatever grimy hidey-hole these adolescent sewer rats call home?"

The woman seemed to muster up a thimble full of courage. "Better than death … which is what *you* had in mind for me."

"No hard feelings, I hope," the Queen purred. "How's that sweet little girl of yours?"

Susan Ritter's face colored. "Emily's fine, no thanks to you."

"Enough crap," Jefferson said. "We're here to talk about Will."

"No respect between enemies then? Very well. Let's discuss the erstwhile Mr. Ritter. He and your sister have gone to Washington to play Senate pages, I'm told."

The boy didn't reply.

Cavanaugh pressed the point, "Little Jillian told you all about the big bad Senator Lindsay, I presume?"

Again, Jefferson said nothing.

"Well, I'm afraid that particular mission may have been ill-advised. You see … Senator Lindsay Micha is no ordinary *Malum*. In fact, she's quite unique."

"Straight up?" remarked Jefferson. "From what I saw on C-SPAN last week … what with her making her first appearance in the Senate for months, I'd say she looks pretty much as dead as the rest of y'all."

"Now Tom … I'm disappointed in you. You're too savvy to judge someone merely by appearance."

"My bad," the boy replied. His tone remained conversational, but Lilith noticed how his eyes fanned the room, his every muscle poised on a razor's edge of action. This was not someone to underestimate. "But *here's* a judgment I do feel pretty solid about: Micha's off the reservation, ain't she?"

The Queen's false smile faltered. "Off the what?"

"Slipped her leash. Gone rogue. You really gotta keep up with all our turns o' phrase if you wanna play human. I'm sayin', it seems to me that Micha's decided she don't gotta take orders from you anymore."

Inwardly, Lilith seethed. This child knew more than she'd expected. "And where," she asked with managed calm, "would you have gotten such an idea?"

Jefferson replied, "Let's start with the way y'all went after Jill. Pulled out *all* the stops! Hundreds o' you on South Street, trying to chase down three kids ... well, one kid really. All to keep her from telling us that Micha was one o' you.

"But then Micha, after two whole months o' hiding, shows up in front of the US Senate. Sudden. No warning at all. Heck, if I hadn't had someone TiVo-ing C-SPAN, just in case, I'd never've seen it. But she *had* to have imagined I would, right? Me or some other Seer. From that I figure that *you're* more worried 'bout protecting her Mask than *she* is herself. That smells like a major strategy shift on *somebody's* part."

"Clever," Lilith admitted.

Now it was Jefferson's turn to deliver a phony smile. "Thanks. 'Course, I ain't nailed down the whole story, but seems clear y'all got yourselves a little in-house power struggle." After a pause he added, "Plus you've got some kind of *something* down there in DC... ... one that's been *eating* deaders like yourself."

"So full of answers, aren't you, boy?" the Queen hissed. "Now, let *me* tell *you* a few things. Senator Micha knows all about Will Ritter and Sharyn Jefferson's infiltration of Webster Hall. Shall I tell you what she plans to do? Better still, shall I tell you where young Will is right *now*?" Her grin was back, savage this time, vindictive and completely without pity.

Instantly, Susan Ritter started forward, exclaiming, "Where's my son!" But Jefferson stayed her with nothing more than a hand on her shoulder.

Such terror! How delicious!

"All in good time," the Queen said. Then, echoing Jefferson's words, "Some kind of something. That's an amusing way of putting it."

"I ain't here to amuse you," Jefferson told her. "What *is* it?"

"My people call it a *gravveg*. Loosely translated: 'abomination.'"

"*Gravveg*," the boy echoed. "And how'd it get here. Same way you did?"

Lilith shook her head. "Not at all. There's very little organic matter that can pass through the Void between worlds. No, the *gravveg* has quite a different origin."

"I'm listening."

The Queen regarded him. "First, let *me* ask *you* a question."

The boy scowled, but replied calmly, "Go ahead."

"How did you discover a way to kill us?"

Jefferson's face was stone. "Why should I tell you?"

"Oh … I know how it's *done*," she said dismissively. "Saltwater … injected into the body using a hypodermic needle. I probably understand why it works far better than you do. No military secret there. What I'm asking is how you managed to discover it?"

He shrugged. "Why's it matter?"

"It matters because it's never been done before!" the Queen exclaimed, slamming her fist on the table so hard that the heavy thing shook.

"Careful," the boy said flatly. "That body ain't no great shakes. You might crack a bone."

"And who do I have to thank for the condition of my host? Do you think I *want* to be trapped in this rotting …" With some effort, she calmed herself. "But that's beside the point right now. Tell me, do you know why we're here, Tom? Susan? Do either of you understand the true motive behind our presence on your planet?"

"You're the Unmakers of Worlds," Tom replied.

Lilith laughed humorlessly. "Kenny Booth. That fool always favored the theatrical. 'Unmakers of Worlds' … a bit trite, if not wholly inaccurate."

"You go after power."

"We do, but only as a means to an end. We are what you might call isolationists. As a race, we crave solitude. But where others might simply wall themselves up and pretend to be alone in the universe, the *Malum* take a nobler and purer approach. We have resolved to *be* alone in the universe.

"We scan the Void, the space between space, looking for signs of intelligent life. And, when we find it, we *evaluate* that life. Study it. And then, when we're ready, we invade. It might interest you to know that we watched Earth for more than a century before we judged the time to be right."

While Susan Ritter's face twisted in horror, Jefferson's

expression revealed nothing. His control was impressive.

Lilith explained, "In our culture, the invasion, corruption, and ultimate destruction of a world is an *art form*. The more subtle the 'cleansing,' the more artistic it is deemed. We do not conquer. We do not overwhelm. We infiltrate. Then we destroy from within.

"Your world *will* end, Tom. Every single living thing on this planet will die. But it won't be by our hand ... not directly. No, we will manipulate you, cajole you, convince you to destroy yourselves. Perhaps nuclear war. Perhaps biological holocaust. Perhaps something else altogether. The method will present itself in due course. But, regardless of the means, you *will* all die.

"And then we will be alone again ... until we find the next world. You call us evil, but to us, your very existence is evil. And we are a force for good ... removing that evil."

"That's insane ..." Susan muttered.

"No," the Queen replied, wagging a finger. "I told you: it's *art.*"

"Whatever," remarked Tom. "You're borin' me. Get to the *gravveg.*"

"The impatience of youth. Actually, I'm paying you something of a compliment. You see, in all of the worlds we have cleansed, none has ever done what you have done. None has ever found a way to destroy us. It has been ... disconcerting."

Jefferson seemed to consider this. Then, still clutching his sword, he reached inside his coat. Around them, D'Angelo and the other minions stiffened.

"Relax, dudes," the boy told them. Then he pulled out a capped syringe. "We call this here a Ritter. Consider it a gift."

He tossed it to Lilith, who caught it smoothly, simultaneously waving off D'Angelo, who'd jumped forward as if thinking the boy meant to skewer her with the big needle—dartboard style.

"A Ritter," she echoed thoughtfully, raising the syringe up to the light and examining its brackish contents. "Imagine ... I hold something that could destroy me."

"Gimme a good day," Jefferson told her. "And you'll get to more'n just imagine it."

That amused her. "May I keep this?"

"That's kinda the point of a gift. Now ... how's about givin' me something in return? Enough with the deader-history lesson. Skip to the *gravveg*. What *is* it?"

The Queen replied, "In a word ... it's *us*."

CHAPTER 35

THE NATURE OF THE BEAST

Lilith Cavanaugh

"You?" Jefferson said.

Lilith nodded. "Haven't you ever wondered what we really look like? Surely you don't imagine we stroll around on our Homeworld draped in rotting cadavers."

Both of the humans looked stunned.

"But, no," the Queen corrected. "While, physically this creature *is* identical to our native form, in every other way it's an abomination. Hence *gravveg.*"

"Where did it come from?" Jefferson asked.

"An idea—as it turns out, a poor one. One of our kind, a Royal ... are you familiar with our castes? Well, never mind. Suffice it to say that a person of importance crossed the Void into this world with a plan to advance our cause. The concept was bold but risky. Normally, I'd have rejected it. This is art, after all, and subtlety is important. But it was in the wake of your son's"—she glared pointedly at Susan Ritter—"meddling with my recent bid for the governor's mansion, and I admit I was tempted."

"And what was this 'idea'?" Jefferson asked.

"We would abduct a high-profile member of the US Congress. Female, because the idea's owner is female. Then a very difficult and very dangerous process would be undertaken … one that would effectively allow this person's likeness and memories to be grafted onto my sister's mind."

"Sister?" Susan Ritter asked. "This … person of importance … is your sister?"

"Oh, didn't I mention that? Yes. My sister and rival. But I won't bore you with my family politics. Suffice it to say that she came here with this plan and, circumstances being what they were, pressured me into accepting it. And … lo and behold, it worked!"

"Lindsay Micha," said Jefferson.

"Exactly. The process is extremely difficult. The source creature—the real Senator Micha—was kidnapped and sedated while the telepathic connection was made. Then, still sedated, she was moved to a safe house and kept under guard. You see, if she should die, then the connection would be severed and my sister's true appearance would be instantly revealed."

"Can't have that," Jefferson remarked dryly.

"Indeed not," Lilith replied with a grin. "For two months, it worked perfectly. My sister wore Micha's face, spoke in her voice, and took whatever memories she needed directly from the sleeping woman's brain. Naturally, she needed to avoid cameras. We couldn't risk one of *you* penetrating her disguise. The plan was for her to use the senator's power and contacts to gradually erode the stability of your federal government. But two things have happened to spoil that approach."

"Your sister went rogue," the boy said.

"Impatience has always been her weakness, which is one reason why the throne fell to me and not her. Apparently wielding Micha's political power overcame what little sensibility she has. With her return to public life, she now dares to impose her authority on me. *Me!*"

"Great story," said Jefferson. "But it ain't got nothing to do with this monster. Why do I get the feelin' you're stalling?"

"Not at all," the Queen replied. "I mentioned that *two* things happened."

Susan Ritter guessed, "Something went wrong with the … telepathic link?"

"Correct. Something went *very* wrong. You see, with this sort of connection there is a risk of what we call 'de-evolution.' It's when the source creature becomes aware enough to reverse the flow of information … to take from the *Malum* instead of the right way around."

"The real Senator Micha woke up," the boy remarked.

"She shouldn't have been able to. But apparently, her will is strong … far stronger than either my sister or I imagined. While de-evolution has happened in the past, it's never happened so quickly … or so *completely* as this."

"So … the *gravveg* is the real Lindsay Micha," said Jefferson. A statement not a question.

"Yes and no. She took the image of our true form from my sister's mind, and then somehow adopted it as her own. A metamorphosis at the genetic level. She has become *Malum*, but with a human mind. Can you imagine such a monstrosity? Do you see now why we call it *gravveg*? The abomination?"

"What I see is that Lindsay Micha's tougher than you figured," Jefferson suggested.

"If you like. We lost contact with the DC safe house. Upon investigation, six *Malum* were found missing ... presumably consumed, and the subject creature ... the abomination ... had disappeared."

"She transformed and then escaped," Susan Ritter said.

"And now she's killin' you folks," Jefferson added. "Why?"

The Queen replied, "Nourishment."

"The *gravveg* eats dead bodies?"

"Yes, but not for the flesh ... for the Self."

Tom frowned. "Self?"

"Life energy. Consciousness. The part of us that is able to cross the Void. We call it our "Self." To get it, the *gravveg* must consume the *Malum*'s host body ... especially the head. In doing so, the *Malum* within is utterly destroyed. Devoured."

Despite herself, Lilith felt an uncharacteristic stab of fear. The very notion of being consumed in such a way...

Jefferson said, "But this thing don't eat humans."

"No. Not yet."

Susan Riutter asked, "Not yet?"

"The longer Micha uses the *gravveg* form, transforming back and forth between that body and her own, she ... *it* ... will continue to need to feed. Eventually, it will discover that humans have Selves, too. Not the same. Surely not as nourishing, but much more plentiful ... and far simpler to obtain." Lilith leaned forward in her chair.

"But you haven't asked me what the abomination *wants*. Why it stays in and around the Capitol?"

"I can guess," the boy replied. "It wants your sister."

"Yes."

"It wants to eat her."

"Consume her Cover. Not quite the same thing."

"Will that break the link?" Jefferson asked. "Give Micha her life back?"

"Yes. So would destroying my sister altogether … perhaps with one of these wonderful Ritters of yours. Of course, doing such a thing —"

At that moment, the phone on the Queen's desk rang. Just once. She glanced at it, and then over at D'Angelo, who nodded ever so slightly.

"Well, Tom, Susan … I'm afraid I have two bits of rather bad news for you both."

Jefferson said warily, "We're listening."

"The first involves young Mr. Ritter. It seems the *gravveg* came upon the boy in the Capitol Rotunda last night, while my sister was making an ill-conceived and poorly executed attempt on his life. I'm afraid the abomination has taken him."

"*Taken* my son?" Susan Ritter demanded. She started forward, but again Jefferson restrained her.

"Where are they?" he asked. "Will and Micha*?*"

The Queen replied, "So far, neither has resurfaced. Perhaps she has consumed the meddling child already."

The Ritter woman looked ready to scream. But Jefferson said, with absolute conviction, "She ain't."

"Really?" said Lilith. "And how would you know that?"

He shrugged, but didn't reply.

"Very well. Care to know the other bit of bad news?"

Jefferson said, "I already do. You're gonna kill us both. That ringing phone was a signal."

The Queen grinned. "So it was."

D'Angelo and the other three policemen moved into position, blocking any escape. As they did, Lilith watched Tom Jefferson step protectively closer to Susan Ritter—a valiant, but outmatched, bodyguard. The fools had assumed they would be safe in the middle of the workday morning. After all, *hundreds* of people were in this building. How could Lilith hope to murder them without somebody hearing something?

"While we were talking," Jefferson said, "you went and had the building evacuated."

"Just this floor," the Queen replied, "with minions stationed at every stairwell to keep anyone from coming up. This old building has paper-thin walls, but the floors and ceiling are nicely soundproof. Nobody will hear your screams, Tom. That I promise you."

Then her predatory gaze fixed on Susan. "*You*, however, will die relatively quickly. I've always admired your body. Now, at last, I'll wear it."

"So, this was never about Will or some common enemy," the boy said. "That was bait ... to lure us here."

Lilith stood and came around from behind her desk, her manicured hands flexing like a raptor's talons. "I saw an opportunity. I counted on your foolish loyalty to bring you running, and it did ... although having Susan here was an unexpected bonus. Thank you for that. The important thing was to keep you ... engaged ... while my people emptied the surrounding floor of potential witnesses."

She expected to see Tom Jefferson tremble. But he

didn't. He simply raised his sword and said, "We're not defenseless."

The Queen laughed. "A helpless woman and boy with a sword against the five of us ... plus a dozen other of my best people, who are already on their way? I like my odds. D'Angelo, they're all yours."

"One question?" Jefferson asked, his tone unsettlingly calm.

Lilith regarded him. "Go ahead."

"Was it true ... all that stuff about Lindsay Micha and the *gravveg*? Or was it just smoke and mirrors to keep us occupied?"

"All true, of course! Why bother lying when I knew neither of you would leave this room alive?" Her tone hardened as she addressed her minions. "Kill Jefferson, but restrain the female. I'll dispatch her myself ... very carefully."

Then Jefferson did a truly remarkable thing. He smiled. "You've screwed up, Cavanaugh. When you told me to come alone, you figured I would."

"Yet you didn't," she said. "And I've already thanked you for it. Sadly, our dear Susan here is a nurse, not a soldier. So, for all intents and purposes, you *are* alone."

"I'm an Undertaker, lady," Jefferson replied. "And an Undertaker is *never* alone."

Something cut the air past Lilith's ear.

An instant later, D'Angelo staggered back a step, staring down at the syringe—built to look like an arrow of some kind—that protruded from his chest.

"What's happening?" the Queen demanded.

Then the chief of police exploded.

CHAPTER 36
CATCHING THE SENATE TRAIN

D id you know that the US Senate has its own train?
It runs underground, back and forth between the Dirksen and Hart office buildings and the Capitol basement. It's there to let senators and their staff get around without having to navigate the DC streets—you know, the way regular people do. It's quick, clean, and pretty quiet, as far as subways go.

Best of all, it would let us get Lindsay Micha—the *real* Lindsay Micha, sort of—to her Hart office and, as Sharyn put it, "finish what Jillian started by gettin' the 411 on what Corpse Micha's up to."

A solid plan.

Too bad about the trail of bodies.

But I'm getting ahead of myself again.

After the face-off in the catwalks, the three of us emerged onto a narrow, circular walkway with a low, domed ceiling. There was space here—a lot of it—though it took me a few seconds to realize where I was.

The *Apotheosis of Washington* covered the ceiling—a

massive fresco reaching out over the vast, empty air extending across to the opposite side of the catwalk. We were at the very top of the Rotunda, 180 feet above its tile floor. Peering over, I saw that the big, round chamber stood empty.

I could tell by the amount of light that it *had* to be late morning. Was the Rotunda closed to tourists? Did the Capitol Police officially *know* that Charles O'Mally had been murdered, or had Corpse Micha somehow covered the whole thing up?

Lindsay said to us, "I'm going on ahead to see how safe it is. You two kids stay here, just in case."

I expected Sharyn to remind Lindsay that, except for Sharyn's page blazer, she was bare-butt naked—or maybe suggest that she flush all her "you're kids so I have to protect you" crap down the proverbial toilet. But she didn't and, as Lindsay moved away on bare legs and shoeless feet, I figured out why.

It gave the Angel Boss and me a chance to talk.

"Wanna tell me what went down?" she asked, standing beside me at the railing and gazing at the distant floor.

"It's a long story," I said.

"With you, ain't it always?"

If she was mad at me for bailing, it didn't show—despite her promise to kick my butt. Sharyn could be like that: deal with the now *now*. The *then* will wait for later. If you know what I mean.

"How'd you find us?" I asked.

"Wasn't hard. Figured you'd gone to check out the Rotunda. Figured you'd needed O'Mally to get you in after hours. Couldn't raise you on your phone. Couldn't raise him. So I guessed something bad had gone down. But there wasn't much I could do 'til morning, so I stayed up and waited. I hate waitin', but sometimes it's all you got. Thanks for that," she said sourly.

"Sorry," I told her, half meaning it.

"Uh-huh," she said, half believing it. "Anyhow, around two A.M., in walks our fave wormbag, Greg Gardner. He and I had us a little 'chat,' and … eventually … he told me what all went down in the Rotunda. Some story! Afterward, though, I was just as stuck as before. Nothing to do 'til morning.

"I expected your roommates to give you up at lights-out, but they didn't. Seems pages stayin' out all night ain't that rare. 'Course, that didn't stop Lex from goin' nuclear when you didn't turn up at page school this morning. But I played dumb and ended up reporting for work at the Capitol with the rest of 'em. We were told right off by a Corpse Cop that the Rotunda was closed for the day … off limits."

"So they could clean it up?" I suggested.

"Naw, that was done 'fore we ever got there. They shut it down 'cause they're afraid."

"Afraid?" I asked.

"Afraid of exposure. Afraid of *her* …" She threw a thumb in the direction Lindsay had gone. "Afraid of what she might do, or what normal folks might *see* her do. So they closed the whole place off and posted deader guards.

"Well, given what Greggie told me and all the extra security, it wasn't no stretch to figure you had to be up inside the dome. So, I headed here."

"What about the guards?" I asked.

She gave me a look that said, *Since when can't I handle a couple of Corpse flunkies?* And I shut up.

Then she asked, "You got your sat phone?"

"Lindsay kinda ... mangled it ... pretty soon after she rescued me."

Sharyn groaned.

"Where's yours?"

"It fell into the toilet in the downstairs bathroom at Webster Hall while Greggie and I were ... jammin'."

"So we're cut off," I said.

"For now," she said.

"Where *is* Greggie?"

"Back at Webster. I broke his neck in the john and then dragged his sorry butt down to the cellar for safekeeping. He'll be needin' a new body 'fore he goes anyplace."

"Nice," I remarked. Then, after a long pause: "Sorry ... about taking off the way I did."

"You weren't ready to face your mom," she said. "So you cooked up this excuse 'bout checkin' out the murder scene. That sound right?"

"Yeah," I said.

"Yeah," she said.

"You figured that out?"

"Heck, no. Tom nailed it. He's got more of a head for all that psych stuff than me."

I groaned.

She said, "First of all, Red ... give your mother half a break. Ain't too many moms out there gonna dig their thirteen-year-old son headin' off to war."

"Fourteen," I said.

She frowned. "Fourteen? Since when?"

"Since I got shot a couple months ago. Tom thinks the angel kept me in that white room for a lot longer than I thought. He says a wound like that would take ... like ... a *year* to heal, and that they might have kept me unconscious the whole time so I wouldn't ... I dunno ... freak out or something. He says they must not have had an Anchor Shard, otherwise I wouldn't have a scar." Then, after a pause, I added, "He says he figured it out because I'd gotten taller—something like three inches—in just a few hours."

Sharyn took a half minute to digest this. Then she shook her head, more in wonder than disbelief. "Man, you live one wild life. I thought *I* was edge. But *you*—"

"Think it's true?" I interrupted.

"If my bro believes it, then it's probably legit. He ain't wrong much. But really ... does it matter?"

I considered that. "A whole year of my life is gone."

"Uh-huh."

"But ... compared to everything else, compared to *Ian* ... I guess not."

She nodded. "Hard, ain't it? Gettin' used to all the weird."

"Yeah."

Her manner turned serious. "Now ... 'bout your mom. I know this stuff 'tween you and her ain't none of my business. But after the stunt you pulled last night, I figure you owe me at least a quick listen. Okay?"

"Okay," I said.

"You know how many kids in Haven wanna see their folks again?" she asked. "And that's just the ones who still got 'em. There's me and Tom, who ain't never had parents ... at least, none we can remember. Then there's kids like Alex Bobson, who saw the Corpses *waste* his. I know havin' her there might be ... crowding you ... but ask yourself: Would you rather she *wasn't* there?"

I looked at her.

She looked at me.

"That it?" I asked.

"That's it," she said.

I gazed back out over the big, empty Rotunda.

I thought about my mother, and about how we'd ended things last time we'd…talked. *Would* it really be better to have her someplace else? Safe, of course, but safely elsewhere. For months, I'd literally dreamed of seeing her again. But, along the way, had I somehow *outgrown* her?

It was a sad thought, way sadder than you'd think.

Sharyn said, completely out of left field, "Wish I'd had a Ritter. Would've loved to completely waste Gardner."

"Me, too," I replied. "He's the one who killed Mr. O'Mally."

"That sucks, Red. I liked that old guy."

"So did I."

"Sorry," she added. "Forgot you don't like bein' called Red."

Ginger, I thought.

"It's okay," I told her. And it was.

Sharyn said, "In the meanwhile … just how solid is your friend Senator Micha? She don't seem to have all her trash cans lined up straight."

"She wants to be *whole*, Sharyn. She wants to find the Third … …that's what she calls Corpse Micha … and, I dunno, get herself back somehow. That much she's clear on. But the rest of it … I'm not sure. She knows she changes. It scares her. But she also *needs* it, since Corpses seem to be the only things she eats. I mean … I haven't had breakfast and I'm starved. *She's* been up here for a week with no food or water."

"She ain't human, little bro," the Angel Boss said. "Not anymore."

"I know."

"In her way, she's more alien than *they* are."

"I know."

Sharyn eyed me. "But?"

"But she saved my life," I said. "She didn't have to … in fact it cost her a clear shot at the Third … but she did it." Then, after a mile-long second, I added, "She's my friend."

Sharyn nodded. "Then that's good enough for me. Gotta get used to the weird, right? Besides, *she* wants to nail Corpse Micha. *We* want to nail Corpse Micha, or at least find out what she's up to."

"On the Rotunda floor last night, Micha said she had 'big plans.'"

"Deaders with 'big plans' ain't never a good thing."

Lindsay appeared at the archway to the downward staircase. There was stuff—Corpse juice—all over her arms and around her mouth. And she was naked again.

Jeez.

"Good news!" she said brightly. "The stairway's clear!"

"Cool," said Sharyn.

Our plan was to head to the Hart Building, where there were fewer police, dead or otherwise. Once there, we'd get into Lindsay Micha's office. If we found it Corpse-free, then Sharyn and I could call Haven and riffle through some drawers, looking for clues. I hadn't been in DC for long, but if my page duties had taught me anything, it was this: politicians—hopefully including dead ones—write *everything* down!

And if we *didn't* find the office deader-free—well, then

maybe Lindsay and the Third would finally have their showdown.

Something told me it would be a messy reunion.

Of course, first we had to get out of the Capitol.

And that's when Lindsay mentioned the train.

"It's a short trip, and exclusive," she explained. "There'll be some people on it, of course, but far fewer than we'd encounter while trying to walk from here to Hart."

So, with Lindsay wrapped in my Capitol Cop coat, the last of our handy outerwear, we headed down the long, winding stairs between the inner and outer dome. As we neared the bottom, we came across—evidence—of Lindsay's most recent meal. Shreds of police uniforms, with shreds of deader still inside them. I counted four pairs of shoes.

Sharyn and I swapped looks.

The Rotunda still stood empty. No tourists. No congressmen. No pages. And no cops, dead or otherwise.

"The guards must've all split," Sharyn remarked.

"They ran," Lindsay said, matter-of-factly. "They usually run when they see me."

I'll bet they do.

I said, "Let's get out of here before they come back with reinforcements."

So we did, heading deeper into the Capitol, heading *down*.

It was mid-morning, and even with the Rotunda still "officially" closed the building was crowded. Dozens of pairs of eyes fell on us as we navigated the corridors and staircases, but they were all *living* eyes, and they regarded us less with alarm than puzzlement. Two messy pages escorting a barefoot older woman wrapped in an oversized cop jacket was apparently a weird sight, even for DC. Go figure.

Angels training: the trick in these situations is to act like you totally belong there.

Well, we did and it worked. Nobody challenged us.

Along the way we stopped at a janitor's closet. I picked the lock with my pocketknife while Sharyn kept watch. Inside, as we'd hoped, we found a few pairs of overalls, one of which Lindsay hastily put on. The rest we stuffed into a green trash bag.

Can you guess why?

There was a Capitol cop—nicely human—stationed outside the door that led down to the subway. As we approached, he eyed us with bewilderment, but simply said, "Good morning, Senator Micha."

"Good morning," she replied with an easy smile.

The train platform looked like pretty much every city subway stop I'd ever seen, a little smaller maybe. And cleaner. There was nobody in sight.

So far, so good.

Then, suddenly, so far *wasn't* so good.

"Deaders," Sharyn whispered.

A pair of Type Threes, looking bloated and sticky inside their cop uniforms, appeared at the platform's far end. At the sight of us they froze, their mouths hanging open, revealing loose, yellowed teeth.

Then they did something I'd never seen Corpses do.

They *fled*.

In a blur of movement, the Corpse Eater exploded past us, catching the deaders before they got ten feet. It grabbed Dead Cop Number One and tore him in half as if he were a sheet of smelly, decaying paper. At the same instant, its awful, terrifying jaws closed over the skull of Dead Cop Number Two.

The Corpse Eater threw back its weird, tooth-riddled head, lifting the deader right off his feet. Then, as Sharyn and I watched—transfixed—its mouth unhinged like a snake's, opening impossibly wide.

The Corpse struggled wildly. Muffled shrieks echoed across the empty platform.

Then he slid down her gullet, disappearing as quickly and smoothly as if he'd been greased.

The creature uttered a satisfied burp.

An instant later the old woman was back—naked again, since the remains of her overalls now lay in a pile between Sharyn and me.

"Come along, children," she said, running the back of her hand absently across lips stained with Corpse juice. "The train will be here momentarily."

Sharyn and I dragged the remains of Dead Cop Number One into a shadowed recess at the rear of the platform. Of course this dude wasn't permanently "dead," just helpless. You couldn't kill a Corpse simply by tearing him apart.

I could only wonder about *eating* one!

Lindsay donned a fresh pair of overalls, and just in time, too. As she combed her hair with her small fingers, somebody called her name.

My stomach jumped up into my neck. I didn't know it could do that.

A guy in a suit approached from the platform staircase, a big smile on his face. He looked too much like a game show host to be anything but a Congressman. As he neared, his smile flickered as he took in Lindsay's weird appearance.

"Everything all right?" he asked.

"Perfectly fine, Mike," Lindsay replied with a smile so sincere and disarming that even *I* almost believed it. "Just your typical workday sob story. Let's just say it involves an early committee meeting, a full pot of spilled coffee, an Armani suit, and quick trip back to my office to a change."

Suit Guy burst out laughing. "I've been there! Did I ever tell you about the time I set my tie on fire at a fund-raising dinner?"

"No, you never did," Lindsay replied, matching the dude's laugh almost exactly. "But you absolutely must! Right now, though, I really do need to make some quick phone calls. I've already had to cancel two meetings because of this coffee fiasco. Fortunately, while these two pages"—she motioned to Sharyn and me, both jacket-less, both filthy—"ended up almost as badly scalded as I was, they nevertheless agreed to escort me back to Hart."

"Thanks, kids," Mike said. "It's really great, the page program."

"Thank you, sir," Sharyn replied in her best Webster Hall voice.

"So, Lindsay," Mike said coyly. "This afternoon's big announcement in the chamber ... you've got everyone on the Hill buzzing about it. Any chance of a sneak peek?"

"Sorry, Mike," she replied, patting his arm. "You'll find out with the rest. When have you ever known me to play favorites?"

Isn't that what politicians do? I wondered.

He sighed theatrically. "Can't blame an elected official for trying."

A moment later the train rumbled in. It was smaller than anything running under Philly, or DC for that matter, just a few cars strung together. More tram than subway.

"There's our ride!" Mike called over the din. "I'll leave you to your calls ... and your big secret. But let's catch up over lunch, maybe next week. We can swap war stories."

"Love to, Mike! Call my office and set it up!"

The train squealed to a halt. Doors opened and a few more suits got off. Mike climbed into one car, while Lindsay, Sharyn, and I found our way into another. The seats were padded, definitely a cut above the usual.

As the train started rolling, I watched the men and women on the platform. They walked by the Corpse pieces without noticing them and stepped right through the puddles of Corpse juice without incident.

Grown-ups. Blind as always.

This is my life, I thought, shaking my head.

"Hart Building, here we come!" Lindsay Micha said cheerfully.

CHAPTER 37
SPRINGING THE TRAP

Helene

Helene perched precariously just outside one of City Hall's sixth-floor office windows, her knees bent and her feet wedged against the building's rough masonry, her left hand clutching the window frame in a Cat Grab.

While she still gripped Aunt Sally in her right hand, the trusted crossbow was useless at the moment, its Ritterbolt having just turned D'Angelo into two hundred pounds of Corpse gunk.

One window over, Jillian threw in the first of her saltwater balloons. It struck one of the remaining three cops on the side of his face, exploding on impact. The deader's expression slackened and he started spinning in lopsided circles as though drunk or dizzy.

Two down. Two to go.

Plus the Queen of the Dead.

Right on cue, Tom pushed Susan Ritter clear and

pivoted, bringing Vader around in a silver blur. Another Corpse, who'd only just managed to grasp what was happening, lost his head a second later. Then, as the fourth one made a grab for the chief, Helene smoothly traded Aunt Sally for a water pistol and gave the dude a face full. Before he even had a chance to fall, Tom slammed the sword into his slack mouth and out the back of his neck.

Finally, pulling a second Ritter from his pocket, Tom skewered the one Jillian had splashed, catching the deader in his back as he started to rise.

Like D'Angelo, he popped like a balloon.

Done.

Sword ready, Tom whirled on Cavanaugh.

But the Queen hadn't moved.

Helene and Jillian climbed in their respective windows and flanked Mrs. Ritter, who stared at them as if they were leprechauns.

"We're on the sixth floor!" Cavanaugh exclaimed in fury and disbelief. "This is impossible!"

"It's *parkour*," Jillian corrected her. "And Helene's my best student."

"Thanks," Helene said.

Tom added, "You're not the only one who can spot an opportunity."

Then, without warning, he lunged at the Queen, Vader slicing the air. The chief was fast—incredibly fast.

But Cavanaugh was faster.

She dodged Tom's slash before literally leaping around him, bouncing off the side wall and shouldering Jillian hard enough to knock the girl completely off her feet. Then, as Tom pursued her, the Queen leaped again.

Helene fired her water pistol—and missed. An instant

later, the Queen disappeared through one of the open windows, dropping out of the sight.

Helene cursed and started after her, but Tom caught her arm. "Don't."

"She'll get away!"

"You stick your head out that window and she's liable to rip it off. We don't know where she is, but you can bet she didn't just swan dive into no courtyard. So stand down."

"But ... Tom!" Jillian exclaimed, regaining her feet. "We were so close!"

"It was a good try. *I'm* the one who blew it. I should have been faster with the sword."

Standing over by the desk, Mrs. Ritter struggled to take it all in. "You ... planned ... this?"

Tom said, "I figured Cavanaugh was settin' a trap. The Corpses aren't the 'flag of truce' type. So we decided to flip things on her."

"But ... the two of you ..." she stammered, gaping at the girls. "You *climbed* the outside wall?"

"Came down from the roof," Helene said. "A bunch of us have been taking free-running lessons from Jill for a couple of weeks now."

"Besides, it's a pretty easy building to work," added Jillian. "Lots of gables, ledges, and windowsills."

Talking like that, she made it sound so simple. The thing is: *parkour* moves weren't really designed for going *down* a wall. So Jillian and Helene had been forced to make it up as they went. It had been tricky, and more than a little dangerous. But they'd been on a mission—an important one—and one of Sharyn's biggest rules was: "Be where you're 'posed to be when you're 'posed to be there. If you ain't, then people die."

So they'd pulled it off.

"Didn't anybody *see* you?" Mrs. Ritter asked.

"Some, I guess," Helene replied. "So what? Probably figured it was a show or something. Grown-ups see pretty much what they want to see." Then she added quickly, "No offense."

Will's mom laughed. "None taken." Then, with fresh alarm: "But Tom ... there are others coming! Cavanaugh said—"

The chief yelled, "Dave? We cool?"

A voice called back from beyond the open doorway. "Yeah, we're cool."

Then the Burgermeister strolled in wearing an ill-fitting police uniform.

"How many'd you get?" Tom asked him.

"Me personally? Just two. Katie and the rest of the Angels are mopping up the others. The floor's secure. These guys weren't expecting us, so it was pretty easy. The ones I nailed took me for a rookie cop ... right up until I did my funeral home thing."

"Solid," the chief told him.

The boy positively beamed.

"And how is it that nobody told *me* about this plan of yours?" Mrs. Ritter demanded.

Helene expected Tom to look embarrassed. He didn't. "You *know* why."

The woman glared at him for a moment. Then her shoulders slumped and she said, "Because I asked to be made an official Undertaker."

Tom nodded. "You didn't know what that meant when you said it. Now you do."

"A risky lesson," she said a little shakily.

"Risky's always a part of it," he replied. "But you weren't in any real danger. We had this gig covered from the get-go ... and *that's* the real lesson here."

"What happened to Cavanaugh?" Dave asked. "Did we finally waste her?"

Helene shook her head. "She was ... too fast."

The enormous boy groaned; it sounded like whale song.

Tom moved to Cavanaugh's desk and started checking drawers. "The deaders'll be back in force pretty soon. But, since we're here, maybe we can find somethin' that'll tell us—"

The Queen of the Dead appeared as if by Black Magic, leaping through the nearest window and pouncing on the chief with all the lethal speed of a jungle cat. Her legs, now shoeless, locked around the boy's thick torso, while her manicured hands clamped down on either side of his head—like the jaws of a vice.

"Drop your weapons!" she shrieked.

Helene raised her water pistol. Dave, his face bright red, shook like a bull about to charge while, beside him, Jillian readied another water balloon.

"Drop your weapons!" Cavanaugh hissed. "Or I'll crush his head like a nut!"

Tom locked his strong hands on the Queen's forearms, but it was obvious that he couldn't break her grip. With a muffled cry he threw himself backward, slamming the dead woman against the wall. Plaster cracked, but Cavanaugh didn't budge. She only bared her teeth and tightened her hold.

The chief roared in pain.

"Last chance!" she snarled. "Do it *now*!"

Slowly, the girls lowered their arms, looking defeated.

The Queen grinned, her eyes glittering with triumph.

Now she'll kill him anyway! Helene realized. *And then escape back through the window again before we can react!*

She had to do something!

But then someone else did something instead.

Will's mom snatched up the Ritter that still lay on the desk. Then, coming around the far side, she hit Cavanaugh's flank, jabbing the needle deep into the rotting flesh of the Queen's upper arm.

Cavanaugh, of course, felt nothing. The dead don't suffer pain. But she registered the impact and her head whipped toward Susan Ritter, her triumph turning to horror.

An instant later, her arm exploded.

Tom, lathered in cadaver fluid, seized the moment. He slipped under Cavanaugh's remaining arm, spun on his heel, and delivered a brutal kick to the Queen's midsection.

Cavanaugh seemed to fold in half, her crazed eyes wide with shock and outrage. Then the impact drove her stolen body back out the window. The last Helene saw of her was one fluttering jacket sleeve—the sleeve that *used* to have an arm in it.

And, just like that, she was gone.

Helene and Jillian ran to the window, looking down at City Hall's expansive cement courtyard. After a moment, the others joined them.

The Queen of the Dead lay in a motionless heap amidst a dozen or more terrified pedestrians. At least she hadn't hit anybody.

"Is she dead?" Mrs. Ritter asked.

Helene shook her head. "Just stuck. And the deaders are already coming to her rescue. See?"

Corpses, some in cop uniforms and others in suits, closed around their broken royalty. They formed a protective circle, keeping the rest of the onlookers at bay, while at the same time pointing up at the windows.

At *them*.

"Um ... better go," the Burgermeister noted.

The chief wiped at his face with his coat sleeve. "Yeah. Let's split. Dave, call Katie and tell her to meet us with her team back in Haven."

They all hurried through the ruined office door.

But Tom paused at the threshold and, with Helene at his shoulder, turned to Mrs. Ritter. "Susan?" Tom said. "Thanks. You saved my life back there."

Now it's 'Susan,' Helene thought.

"No need to thank me," the woman replied. "I'm an Undertaker."

The chief grinned. "Yeah. You are."

CHAPTER 38
HART

"Any idea what this big announcement might be?" Sharyn asked Lindsay as we climbed the steps into the Hart Senate Building.

"None at all," the woman replied, frowning.

"What's 'the chamber' he was talking about?" I asked.

"The Senate chamber. As pages, I'm sure you've seen it."

And, of course, we had—the fancy room with the half-circle of desks where we'd gotten our first look at Corpse Micha.

Lindsay said, "I can't imagine making an 'announcement' in the chamber. A speech, certainly. Speeches are what the Senate floor is for. But announcements tend to focus on one's political career rather than the welfare of the country. I would never use the chamber for such a thing."

"You ain't her," Sharyn remarked.

"And 'ain't' is not a word, young lady."

The girl grinned. "Depends on your dictionary."

Unlike its neighbor, Dirksen, Hart was mega-modern—one of those buildings where all the rooms and offices were set up along the wall, leaving the middle area wide open all the way up to the roof. The huge lobby seemed to be all steel and glass, with lots of light. Not the kind of place you'd expect to find the walking dead.

But they were here.

Two Type Threes and a Four, all in suits, stood huddled together next to a nearby pillar. They hadn't noticed us yet. Even more important, Lindsay hadn't noticed *them*, and Sharyn and I decided to keep it that way.

"Elevator's over there," Sharyn said, steering us toward a bank of shiny doors on the opposite end of the lobby and out of the deaders' line of sight. I followed, patting my pants pocket. My faithful knife was there.

Something told me I'd be needing it before long.

We rode up to the fifth floor. Here a narrow, railed corridor traced the outside shape of the building, with doors to senators' offices on our left and nothing but a railing that overlooked the lobby on our right. Each office door was decorated with a basketball-sized seal identifying the particular senator's home state.

Lindsay guided us confidently, turning left and then right and then left again.

"So far, so good," Sharyn whispered to me.

"Yeah," I muttered. But I couldn't help worrying about what would happen if Lindsay turned a corner and walked right into a Corpse.

It wouldn't be pretty.

At last, Lindsay stopped outside her office entrance, which sported the New Jersey state seal. For a half minute, she stared through the glass at a young woman—human—working behind a paneled desk.

"You okay?" I asked Lindsay.

"Oh, yes," she said, sounding wistful. "It's just ... I suppose, on some level, I never thought I'd see this place again." Then she looked at me, her eyes shining. "Thank you, Will."

"Thank me when you get you your life back," I said, pushing the door open.

"Senator?" the receptionist asked. She was young, brunette and, from the look on her face, bewildered. "Is everything all right? What happened?"

She was referring, of course, to Lindsay's janitor overalls. At least, by her reaction, it seemed clear that Corpse Micha wasn't here at the moment. A stroke of luck.

"I'm fine, Moira," Lindsay replied with an embarrassed smile. "Just some spilled coffee. Tell me ... do I still keep spare clothing in my office closet?"

It was a weird question and Moira knew it. "Uh ... yes. Of course. I mean—"

"Thank you," Lindsay chirped. Then she headed for the only other door, which I assumed opened into her private office.

As I followed, Sharyn caught my arm and pulled me close. "Gimme your pocketknife."

"What for?"

"I'm stayin' out here with Pretty Miss Receptionist. I don't like the look on her face, and I wanna chat her up ... keep her distracted while you and our new peep do your thing in there."

"What's the pocketknife for?"

"In case somebody else shows up. The *dead* sorta somebody. I'm unarmed."

I don't generally loan out my pocketknife. After all, there's only one other like it—probably on the whole planet—and Tom's got that. But this was Sharyn and, as usual, she was right. So I forked it over.

"Thanks," she said.

"Be careful out here."

"Be careful in *there*," she replied.

I followed Lindsay into the inner office.

"Is he going in there with her?" I heard Moira ask, sounding scandalized. "Isn't the senator ... changing?"

Sharyn replied in her best page voice, "Don't worry. Will's a first-class gentlemen, and the senator ... well, she hasn't been herself lately."

I shut the door.

"She's rearranged everything," Lindsay grumbled. Outside her window was a fairly decent view of the Capitol, its huge, white dome almost glowing in the mid-morning sunlight. "My desk. The couch. Everything. Why do you suppose she'd bother?"

"Most Corpses take their Masks seriously," I told her. "By now, she's probably convinced herself that she's more you than you are."

She considered. "In a way, she might be right."

"No," I said. "She isn't you. And the Corpse Eater isn't you, either. It isn't even the First. Not really. Lindsay Micha ... the person standing in front me ... *she's* the First."

I could see that she didn't quite believe it. To be honest, I wasn't sure I believed it myself. Her monster half came out too easily and too often for her human half to truly be in control.

After all this, was it even *possible* to get back her stolen life?

I swallowed down that unhappy thought and asked, "Where should we start looking?" Then, without waiting for a reply, I went around the big, polished desk and tried the drawers. Every single one was locked. I cursed, wishing I still had my pocketknife and its lock pick.

"Language, Will," Lindsay said patiently.

"Sorry. Don't suppose you hid a spare key around here anywhere?"

"I don't know, but Moira might. But that's not the proper place to look anyway."

I blinked. "What not?"

"I'm ... that is, *she's* ... making a big announcement, yes? Big announcements are scripted. Always. And scripting takes time, a good many revisions, and a number of last-minute changes." She bent down, and came up holding a shiny-brass trash can. "Good! Nothing's been shredded yet."

Despite myself, I laughed. Even after everything the Corpses had done to her, there were still no flies on Lindsay Micha.

"Let me call Haven," I told her. "You get started with that, okay?"

"Sounds good."

I picked up the desk phone and spent a half minute figuring out its buttons. Finally, I got an outside line and tapped one of Haven's encrypted phone numbers. Couldn't risk the deaders tracing the call later. It rang a half-dozen times before anyone picked up.

"Johnson Plumbing Supply."

"Hi. I'm looking for a three-quarter-inch elbow joint?"

"Easy enough. Copper, plastic, or composite?"

"Copper's the only way to go." Then, with the code safely completed, I said, "Hey, Dan."

"Will! Jeez ... you guys okay down there? You fell off the grid!"

"I know. Things got ... complicated. Can you patch me through to Tom?"

"Yeah. Sure. He's not in Haven, but he told me to forward you if you called. Hang on ..." The line went dead for several seconds. Then another familiar voice answered. *"Bro?"*

"It's me, Chief."

He sighed with relief. *"You okay? Sharyn?"*

"We're both fine," I said. "But I got a lot to tell you and not a lot of time."

"Same here." Then, to someone else, he said, *"Sure. Hold up."* He came back on, sounding slightly impatient. *"Got a minute to tell your mom you're still alive?"*

I swallowed. Memories of a dingy corridor and some hard words rattled around between my ears. But I said, "Sure."

There was crackle as the satellite phone changed hands. *"Will?"*

"It's me, Mom. I'm okay."

"You're not hurt?"

"No. And Sharyn's fine, too, by the way."

"Sharyn can take care of herself."

I almost yelled, "So can I!" But I held back. Then I remembered what Dan had just said about Tom being outside of Haven. "Where are you guys?"

"Oh. Well, Lilith Cavanaugh called Tom to a meeting that turned out to be a trap. But don't worry ... everything's fine now."

"What?" I snapped. Suddenly there was this rushing sound behind my ears. I wondered if it was possible to have a stroke at fourteen. Then I wondered if maybe I'd heard wrong. So first I repeated my second question. "What?" Then, second, I repeated my first question. "Where are you guys?"

"We just left City Hall."

"Where's Emily?"

"Emily? She's back in Haven, of course. You didn't think I'd bring your sister into such a potentially dangerous situation, did you?"

I didn't think you'd bring you *into such a potentially dangerous situation!* I thought but didn't say. "Lemme talk to Tom."

"Will, it's fine," she said, using her oh-so-reasonable voice. *"Tom had the whole thing handled. It did get a little scary when Cavanaugh's people tried to murder us so that she could wear my body, but then—"*

"Mom! Put the chief on!"

"Sweetheart, there's no reason to be upset."

"I'm not upset!" I yelled—screamed almost, pressing the phone so hard against my face that my ear went numb. Then I took a breath and added through gritted teeth, "I just … need to talk to Tom for a second."

"All right, but you really do sound upset." She passed the phone to Tom, who at least had the decency to sound sheepish. *"Hey, bro."*

"You took my mother into combat?" I exclaimed.

"Yeah." No excuses. No waffling. Just the truth. That was Tom.

But I wasn't in a "give credit where credit's due" mood just then. "Are you crazy?"

"Will," he replied, and something in his tone, mad as I

was, shut me right down. That was also Tom. *"I get you're pissed. If I was in your place, I'd be pissed, too. But this ain't the time or place to yell it out. You got stuff to tell me and I got stuff to tell you. Once you and my sister are back home, you can kick my butt all you want."*

And I wanted to. God, how I wanted to kick his butt—literally.

Right. As if I *could!*

But I couldn't afford to play the angry son, not right now. True, I was madder at Tom than I'd ever been, and believe me that's saying something, but he was also infuriatingly right: there was no time.

"We're with Micha," I said. "The real Micha. But she's not herself. She's—"

"I know. It's called a gravveg ... *and it's seriously dangerous."*

"She saved my life."

"Maybe she did. But she ain't 'right.' The Queen gave us the straight dope. She eats Corpses, consuming their life energies to survive. But, if she gets hungry enough, she might decide to taste your *energies. You need to get away from her."*

I glanced over at Lindsay, who'd settled herself on a leather sofa and was sifting through the contents of the trash can. If she was paying any attention to my conversation, it didn't show.

She didn't *look* dangerous, but then I knew all too well what hid inside that small woman.

Gravveg. A new *Malum* word.

"Tom," I said. I didn't know how to react to what he'd told me, so I changed the subject. It was a habit that always drove my mother nuts. "Micha ... Corpse Micha ... is planning something. Some kind of big announcement."

"I know that, too. But, right now, my biggest worry is getting you

both away from there, away from her. *Will, even the Corpses are terrified of what she is! Cavanaugh said*—"

But whatever the Queen said was drowned out when something slammed into the office door—hard.

CHAPTER 39

A SHARP LITTLE KNIFE

Sharyn!

I dropped the phone. As it clattered onto the desktop, I heard Tom calling from across the miles: *"Bro? What was that? What's happening?"* But there wasn't time for explanations.

Lindsay jumped to her feet, her eyes wide with alarm, the trashcan tumbling to the floor. For a terrifying moment I thought she might transform. But she didn't.

"Sharyn!" I called. The sounds of battle, muffled but unmistakable, leeched through the thin walls. Grunts. Crashes. A Corpse's inhuman hiss.

And then a *very* human scream.

I ran to the door and yanked it open.

A Corpse filled the threshold. Dressed in a suit and power tie, he was a late Type Two, his tissues dissolving, but his bones and muscles still strong. And fast.

He struck like a cobra, slamming me in the chest hard enough to send me flying the width of Micha's office and crashing against the wall beside a shelf full of lawyer books. For the second time in twenty-four hours, I saw stars and hit the floor, the world seeming to tilt dangerously.

Meanwhile, Sharyn was out there!

I expected Lindsay to change as she had in the Capitol train station. But instead she just stood there as the deader appraised her. In human form, she looked much less imposing—just a little old lady wearing overalls way too big for her. But, like most Corpses, this one wasn't stupid. He knew who she was.

"Abomination!" he roared. But he didn't advance. He didn't retreat either.

"Hello," Lindsay said, using her politician's voice.

The Corpse wanted to attack her; that much was obvious. But he didn't. I got the feeling that his inner killer was warring with his inner coward.

Beyond the open doorway, combat raged in the outer office. Precious seconds leaked away.

"Well?" she asked him.

The deader didn't reply. He didn't move. His purple, bloated face somehow managed to look both furious and terrified. That's a lot of emotion for an animated cadaver, believe me.

So *Lindsay* moved, stepping forward.

He eyed her, but didn't back away.

She's gonna change any second and eat you!

But she didn't.

"I'm a monster," she said in an almost casual voice. "I'm the monster that your ... supervisor ... made of me. Yet as I stand here and look at you, I realize that I'm not half the monster *you* are. Until now, I've both feared you and craved you. Your kind is quite delicious, did you know that?"

At that the deader *did* back away a step.

Any second...

But still she didn't change.

Instead, she said, "I'm going to eat the creature pretending to be me. I want you to know that. I'm going to consume her and take back what she stole. After that ... I hope ... I won't be a monster anymore." Then she offered up a smile that was both radiant and frighteningly pitiless. "But you ... I'm just going to kill."

The Corpse lunged for her then, maybe out of desperate terror as much as rage. But he wasn't even a tenth fast enough.

Lindsay's arm came up, lightning-quick. Except it wasn't an arm anymore. It was one of the Corpse Eater's legs—complete with razor-sharp pincer at the end.

That pincer snipped the deader's head clean off, like scissors.

His features went slack and he slumped to the floor.

For a long moment, the woman with the monster arm regarded him, her expression thoughtful. Then, as she walked over to *me*, I found myself cringing. But the hand she offered, the same limb that had "de-headed" Mr. Power Tie, was human again.

"Let me help you," she said, pulling me to my feet. "You see? I *can* control it ... to a point."

"Yeah," I said, rubbing the back of my head. My vision had cleared and aside from a lump, I seemed to be okay. "Good for you."

It sounded lame, but she smiled.

Then we both ran for the door.

The outer office looked like a charnel house. Corpses lay everywhere—in pieces. Heads here. Arms there. Legs over there. In fact, with all the carnage, it was hard to figure out just how many deaders there had been. I finally managed it by counting the heads.

Five. Six, including the dude Lindsay had trashed.

None were *permanently* dead, of course; Sharyn hadn't had a Ritter. In fact, the only weapon she *had* had was my pocketknife. This she held out to me, her face flushed from the combat. Nobody dug a good fight like Sharyn Jefferson.

"Thanks, Red," she said, a little breathlessly. "I totally gotta get me one o' those!"

As I took the knife, I noticed its five-inch blade was open. I looked at it. Then I looked around at the decapitated and dismembered Corpses. Then I looked back down at the tiny knife.

How on earth...?

"It's all right, Moira," Lindsay was saying. "No need for all this fuss."

"B-b-b-but these men came in and just *attacked* the page!" the receptionist stammered. "They didn't even say anything. They just saw her, growled, and then sort of *pounced!* It was awful!"

"But she's fine." Lindsay insisted, motioned toward Sharyn, who smiled and waved. "There! You can see she's fine."

Moira, her eyes as wide as twin moons, looked around the room. She didn't have the Sight, so all of these bodies would all appear intact to her—part of the Corpses' illusion. I wondered for a second what would happen if I

301

picked up one of the heads, took it out into the hallway, and dropped it over the railing and down five flights to the Hart Building lobby. What would Moira see *then*? What would the people milling around downstairs see?

But this wasn't the time for experiments. Too bad, really. Steve would have *loved* it!

"She moved ... so *fast*!" the receptionist exclaimed. "I've never seen anybody move that fast! No matter how many times they came at her, she knocked them back, until—" She looked around again. "B-b-but they're not *dead*, are they?"

"Nope," Sharyn replied, which was true—sort of.

"You had a knife! I saw it in your hand."

Sharyn displayed her empty palms. At the same time, I turned my back, closed my blade, and pocketed it. "No knife," the Angel Boss said. "Besides, you don't see no ... any ... blood, do you?"

"No," the young woman admitted. "You knocked them out?"

"I knocked 'em out."

"All of them?"

"Straight up. I mean, yes."

"Moira," Lindsay suggested, "why don't you go to the ladies room and freshen up a little."

"But ... we have to call the police!"

"I'll take care of that. You just focus on composing yourself. Then you can rest on the couch in my office until the authorities arrive. How does that sound?"

"Yes, Senator. Thank you."

Lindsay nodded, her smile completely genuine. "Go along now, dear."

The receptionist did as she was told, stepping gingerly amidst the fallen deaders who lay between her and the hallway door. Along the way, she unknowingly kicked one of their heads across the room and stepped in puddles of maggot-riddled Corpse juice, which, thankfully, she couldn't See either.

As soon as she closed the hallway door, Sharyn said, "Got a closet?"

Lindsay replied, "In my office."

Sharyn and I cleaned the place up, stacking the Corpses, along with all their assorted parts, in a deep closet in the inner office. Meanwhile Lindsay, having pulled a blue pantsuit out of the same closet, stood across the room, carefully dressing—as ever, totally unconcerned by her nakedness.

I'm going to need a shrink when this is over.

Moira returned, pale but dry-eyed. While Sharyn and I waited, Lindsay led the receptionist into her office and settled her on the leather couch, giving her strict instructions to rest.

"What happened to the men?" Moira asked.

"Don't worry about them, dear. Just close your eyes. I promise you'll feel better in a little while."

Moira's gonna need a shrink, too.

Returning, Lindsay shut the inner office.

"You should get the trash can," I told her. "We can keep sifting through it out here."

"No need," the senator replied. "I found what I was looking for just before that whole terrible fight started."

Sharyn and I did matching double takes. "You know what she's after?" I asked. "Your imposter?"

"Oh, yes," the woman replied with a satisfied smile. "She's preparing to stand before the US Senate this afternoon and announce her candidacy for president of the United States."

CHAPTER 40
THE CAVALRY

Helene

"Bro?" Tom called into the phone, and the edge of fear in his voice sent fresh shocks of cold panic up Helene's spine. "What is it? What's happening?" He listened, his face going ashen.

"What?" Mrs. Ritter demanded. "What is it?"

"I dunno," the chief replied. "Some kind of fight."

"They've been attacked!" Jillian exclaimed.

"By Corpses?" asked Will's mother.

Helene replied, "Or something *else* ..."

The five of them, including Dave, huddled together on the corner of 16th and Arch Streets, right across from Love Park, where just two months ago, Will had taken an assassin's bullet.

And now he was in danger again.

"Will?" Tom called into the phone, so loud that some passersby glanced at him.

None of them See, Helene thought bitterly. *None of them get what's going on ... what's at stake!*

A minute passed. Then two. Finally Tom lowered the phone, looking defeated. "Sounds of a fight, then some voices, but too far away to make out who it was or what they said. Then ... nothin'."

"Will's in trouble," Helene told him.

"When ain't he?" the Burgermeister muttered.

Mrs. Ritter exclaimed, "We have to *do* something!"

"Yeah, we do," the chief agreed. "Okay, listen up. I'm headin' to 30th Street Station. I'm gonna buy three train tickets to DC ... earliest I can get."

"I'm going with you," Will's mother said.

Tom's expression had a lot behind it. "No, you ain't. Neither am I. Helene, Dave, and Jillian are goin'. Helene and Dave 'cause they're Will's best friends and know how to handle themselves ... and Jill 'cause she's knows DC and the Capitol better'n any of us."

Helene watched Mrs. Ritter's face redden. For a second, she thought the woman was about to spout some more crap about it being *her* son in trouble and how no *teenage boy* was going to tell her—blah, blah, blah.

But she didn't.

Instead, she drew in a deep breath and offered up a steady nod. "You can't go because you're chief, and your place is in Haven, especially with Sharyn in the field. And I can't go because Emily needs me."

"Yeah," Tom said. "And Haven needs its medic."

Trembling, Susan Ritter nodded again.

"Then ... why are *you* buying the tickets?" Jillian asked.

Tom said, "'Cause I got a phony I.D. says I'm over eighteen and you gotta be an adult to buy train tickets. And

Susan here, all *she's* got is her Pennsylvania driver's license, and I guarantee the Corpses are on the lookout for that."

The five of them swapped looks.

The chief said, "Y'all head back to Haven. Take the west entrance. Drop off Susan, then grab your gear and head for 30th Street. I'll meet you there."

"I can't just sit around waiting to find out if he's alive!" Mrs. Ritter said desperately. "Not again!"

Helene regarded them both. There was so much strength and courage there. Tom's, of course, had always been obvious. But Susan Ritter's—well, that was a new thing, at least in Helene's eyes.

But then again, she is *Will's mom.*

In that moment, she made a decision, one she'd been wrestling with most of the day. "How about if I take Mrs. Ritter back to Haven through the north entrance instead. Just the two of us."

She knew it was a strange request, and it surprised everyone—except Tom, who regarded her thoughtfully and said, "Good idea. Do that. I'll see you all in an hour."

He rested his hands on Mrs. Ritter's trembling shoulders. "We'll find him," he told her. "I know this feels like a familiar nightmare ... but I swear to you: we'll find him."

After that, he turned and headed west along Arch Street.

"Come on, Dave," Jillian said. Then she and the mountainous boy crossed 16th in the direction of the underground parking garage that concealed Haven's west entrance.

As she and Will's mother walked the three blocks to Reading Terminal Market in silence, Helene's stomach churned and sweat stung her forehead despite the cool morning air. Twice she tried to speak, to say what she wanted to say to this woman, and twice she chickened out. The sidewalk was crowded, yet to Helene the two of them seemed completely alone. It was deeply weird.

Mrs. Ritter, for her part, just walked. She didn't look around or glance at Helene. Her thoughts seemed to be a million miles away—or maybe just a hundred or so, down in DC with her son.

The "keystone."

Helene had been shocked when Tom had called Will that. Not because she didn't agree with it, but rather because she didn't think anyone else shared that secret belief.

Will. The reluctant hero. The single bravest and most selfless person she'd ever known.

Her Will.

But not *just* her Will, which was why she'd asked Tom to give the two of them—Mrs. Ritter and herself—some alone time.

"You hate me, don't you?"

The words just tumbled out. It hadn't been the way Helene had wanted to start this conversation.

Mrs. Ritter started, shaken out of her own thoughts. "What?"

Helene couldn't even look at her. "You hate me."

"Why would you say such a thing?" the woman asked. She sounded genuinely surprised, but it might have been an act.

Helene said, "I'm the one who pulled Will out of school. Made him disappear. You hate me for it."

"I don't hate you, Helene," Mrs. Ritter said. "You saved Will's life that day."

"And gave him *this* one."

Mrs. Ritter didn't seem to have an immediate answer to that. They kept walking, though for a minute or so nothing more was said. Finally, Will mother's spoke, her voice far calmer and gentler than Helene would have imagined. "No, sweetheart. I *admire* you. And I'm … grateful to you. Not just for my son's life, but for being there for him ever since. For being his friend."

Helene felt her eyes fill up, so strong was her relief at hearing those words. She blinked rapidly, refusing to cry.

"Thanks, Mrs. Ritter," the girl whispered.

As the two of them reached the entrance to Philadelphia's famous Reading Terminal Market, Mrs. Ritter smiled at her, maybe for the first time, with real warmth. "Call me, Susan," she said, holding the door open. "After you."

Most first-time tourists, after taking in its high ceiling and ridiculous amount of square footage, tended to assume that Reading Terminal Market used to be a train station. It didn't. In fact, when the Reading Railroad—you know, from the Monopoly game—decided to buy this city block, they simply moved the already existing outdoor market indoors. The Reading Railroad was now long gone, but the original market remained—and thrived.

To call it a food court seemed almost criminal. Crammed into its 175,000 square feet was a loose grid work of stalls offering books, crafts, baked goods, candles, and pretty much every imaginable kind of food. Thousands flocked here every day for breakfast, lunch, or dinner, navigating the congested aisles, lining up for their meals, and jockeying for one of the limited numbers of available tables.

The upshot to all this free-market chaos was that Reading Terminal was a great place to lose yourself, and a perfect spot to hide an entrance to a secret lair. It was very easy to get turned around in this maze of seemingly identical aisles. So, to find your way to Haven, you'd better know the route cold.

Helene did.

She led Susan through crowds that, while not yet lunch-time strong, were still plenty heavy. Staying close together, they skirted more vendors than Helene could count, turning left, then right, then left, then right again, weaving their way deeper into the enormous building until they reached its back wall.

Here stood an empty aisle of stalls, marked with a sign that read: FRESH FISH MARKETS ONLY OPEN ON WEDNESDAY with a rope blocking off the whole area.

Helene looked around. No one seemed even remotely curious about them. Life in the city tended to breed that lack of interest. The Undertakers counted on it.

So did the Corpses.

Satisfied, Helene slipped under the rope into the shadows of the empty stalls.

Susan followed.

About halfway down the unused aisle, Helene cut left behind a barren countertop. There, a heavy, unmarked door stood against the market's outer wall. The door was locked, but Helene produced a key and opened it.

Inside waited a dark, narrow corridor, its dusty cement

floor littered with empty cardboard boxes. The place reeked.

Susan made a face. "Stinks in here. Don't the fish vendors use this?"

"Not anymore," Helene replied. "Every week or so we dump a load of rat droppings, to … discourage them. Works, but it means we gotta get through here quick. Otherwise the smell sticks to your clothes. Come on." They followed the corridor to a second, locked door, which opened on squeaky hinges and revealed a flight of metal stairs heading down into darkness.

"Before we go down there …" Susan said. Then she took Helene's hand, a gesture that made the girl fidget uncomfortably. "I want to apologize if I ever came off as … cold … toward you. I've been so tied up in how difficult this life is for me and my daughter that I've forgotten how hard it must be for the rest of you. I'm sorry."

Helene nodded. Then, as if losing some internal debate, she blurted out, "I kissed him."

Susan blinked. "What?"

Helene felt her face flush. "I … kissed Will."

For several long seconds, neither of them said anything. Helene wanted to crawl into a crack in the floor.

Okay … now she hates me!

"Did you really?" Will's mother finally asked.

"Um … yeah. Just before he left for DC."

"Well … okay … then," Susan stammered. "But … why are you telling me this?"

"I've been wanting to tell you for a while," Helene replied, refusing to meet Susan's eyes. They were still holding hands in the darkness, the space around them feeling oddly intimate, despite the thousands of people milling and eating and talking just a few yards away. Finally, almost desperately, the girl added, "I guess ... I just want you to like me."

For a long, terrible moment, Susan didn't reply.

I blew it. I should have kept my mouth shut. I mean ... what did I even think this would get me? A hug?

Then Susan Ritter spoke, her words coming in starts and stops, as if she were afraid of tripping over them. "Helene ... when Will ... disappeared ... last fall, he was just an eighth-grade boy. Now, whether I like it or not, he's a solider."

"We both are," Helene corrected.

"You both are. That's a lot for a mother to wrap her head around. Can you understand that?"

"I guess so," the girl replied.

"But," Susan continued, "I think ... what you just told me helps me understand you both a little better. In a way, it gives me comfort. I guess what I'm trying to say is ... I *do* like you. And Will's lucky to have you in his life."

Despite herself, a single tear squeezed past Helene's defenses and danced down her cheek. "Thanks again," she muttered.

Then, without warning, Will's mom hugged her—just opened her arms and kind of swallowed her up. Helene's first instinct was to pull back. But then, some long-buried memory bubbled up from a dark place in her mind, a place she never went.

I used to have a mom. And she used to hug me like this.
And ... oh God ... I miss it.

So she hugged this mother back, in the here and now, fiercely and gratefully.

"Can you promise me something?" Susan whispered.

"I can try."

"Can you promise me you'll bring him home safe?"

Helene, with the woman's arms still around her, both warm and weirdly heartbreaking, thought hard before she answered. Finally, in a small voice, she said, "No, I can't promise that. But I *can* promise this: If he doesn't come back ... I probably won't, either."

Still wrapped in their mutual embrace, it became Susan's turn to cry.

So Helene hugged her tighter.

CHAPTER 41
EXECUTIVE SUMMARY

"Dead Presidents," Sharyn remarked. "Sounds kinda familiar."

Scary images whirled through my mind: a Corpse taking the oath of office in front of the Capitol Building; a Corpse delivering the State of the Union Address in front of Congress—a speech that had always been so good at putting me to sleep that my dad used to joke about recording it and playing it back at bedtime; a Corpse living in the White House; a Corpse with America's nuclear missile codes at her fingertips.

The first female president of the United States.

The first *dead* president of the United States.

The *last* president of the United States—because, if we let this happen, the world wouldn't survive long enough to see another election.

"Honestly, this won't do," Lindsay said, as if discussing draperies. "I've stated publicly, more than once, that I have no interest in the presidency."

"Seems your Xerox feels different," Sharyn remarked.

"It won't do," the woman repeated.

"No … it won't," I muttered. "And she's gonna do this in front of the Senate?"

"*That's* the big announcement," Lindsay replied. "Completely inappropriate, of course. She's making me appear terribly egotistical! It just won't do!"

I locked eyes with Sharyn. "We *gotta* stop her."

"'Course we do, little bro," the Angel Boss replied. "Question is, how? It was hard enough gettin' in *here*. I don't even wanna think what it'd take to get into the Senate chamber in the middle of the day."

"My hair's a fright!" Lindsay complained, examining her reflection in the glass of a framed photo of the current president. "But at least I'm dressed adequately."

Sure. Until the next time you Hulk out on us.

"We gotta call Haven," Sharyn suggested. "Maybe my bro'll have an idea."

"Haven!" I groaned. I'd forgotten about the phone call. "Lindsay! Did you notice if your desk phone was still off the hook when you were in your office?"

"Oh, yes. I saw it while I was settling Moira down, poor dear. I hung it up."

"Great." I snatched up the receptionist's phone, dialing the same number as before. It rang three times before someone picked up.

"Big Brian's Guitars. Can I help you?"

"Dan! It's Will! Patch me through to Tom!"

"Will! You okay?"

"Yeah, but I need to talk to the chief again!"

"I figured. Hang on."

Several long seconds of silence followed. Then Tom's voice sounded. *"Bro? That you?"*

"Yeah. Sorry about before. Something came up."

"You okay?"

"Yeah."

A pause. *"Sharyn?"*

"Just took out five deaders with my pocketknife."

His laugh carried as much relief as humor. *"We gotta get her one of those."*

"That's what she says. Maybe you could give her yours. You know ... trade for Vader."

"Yeah. That'll happen. Put her on."

I waved the receiver at Sharyn. "Your big brother's on the phone."

Sharyn, who'd been wiping Corpse Juice off the front of her already filthy white page shirt, scowled at me. "We're twins," she said, looking offended. "He's not my 'big' brother. For all we know, I came out first!"

"He's bigger than you," I replied with a shrug. "Wanna talk to him ... or should I drop the phone again?"

She pretended to be mad but, being Sharyn, couldn't quite pull it off. Stalking over, she punched my shoulder. Maybe 10 percent of her "hit" potential—but it still hurt. Then, as I reflexively *did* drop the phone, she snatched it up and said, "Hey, bro. Where you at?"

She listened.

"Cool. Will just spent the last twelve hours hangin' with Lindsay Micha ... the genuine article. She rocks, but she ain't herself."

The girl listened for most of a minute. Tom was probably telling her what he'd told me about this *gravveg*.

Sharyn took it, as she took most things, in stride.

"Okay," she said at last. "All that's solid. What? Oh, we're in Micha's office. I did the lookout thing while

Micha and Will flipped the senator's crib for clues about her 'big deal' announcement this afternoon."

She listened some more.

"Well, yeah … but only five. No big. I had Red's pocketknife."

She listened some more

"Straight up it's small … but it's *sharp*! You gotta get me one o' them. Huh? Oh! Right! Hold on." She lowered the phone and looked at me. "Tom wants to know if you can talk to your angel lady about gettin' me a pocketknife."

I said, "I'll try to work it into our next conversation."

"Cool! Thanks, little bro." She raised the phone again. "Little bro says he's gonna score me one. So … here's the deal on our end: Corpse Micha'll be marchin' into the Senate chamber in about four hours to make her play for the White House."

She listened some more.

"Yeah. It's all *kinds* of 'ain't good.' Thing is, the Capitol Building's a tough nut to crack. Will and me got lucky just gettin' *here*. No way we gonna hit that much luck gettin' *there*!"

She listened some more.

"Hey, Red!" Sharyn chirped to me. "Tom says Helene and Hot Dog are headed down here to back us up." Then, after another moment she added, this time minus the chirp, "Oh … and *Jillian*."

I replied, "Good."

She listened some more. Then she talked some more.

By now I was only half paying attention. The *other* half was focused on the door to the Hart Senate Building hallway. More trouble was coming. Those Corpses Sharyn had trashed *weren't* dead, which meant they *were* screaming telepathic murder to their deader buds, looking for help. Answering this call took anywhere from minutes to hours, depending on the circumstances.

Bottom line: we couldn't stay here, not without running into more of Corpse Micha's cronies. By now she'd probably heard about the dead cops Lindsay had snacked on in the Capitol Dome stairwell and the Senate subway. And given her reaction back in the Rotunda, I guessed that the *Malum* senator was terrified of being next.

It wasn't easy to scare a Corpse. But, when you did, all the courage drained out of them and they'd do or say anything to save their own rotting hides. I knew this from firsthand experience—which might be why no one else had shown up here yet. Micha could have decided to keep the rest of her people tight around her. For defense.

That was good *and* bad. Good, because it meant the three of us were relatively safe. Bad, because it would make getting close to the fake senator that much harder.

All of these thoughts rumbled around in my head, and they were solid thoughts. Productive and practical. But they were also smokescreens, distractions to keep me from focusing on what was *really* twisting my stomach into knots.

Helene was coming.

Helene—who'd kissed me.

Does it sound crazy to be more nervous about seeing a particular girl than facing down a small army of the walking dead? Well, I got news for you all: sometimes girls are *way* scarier than monsters!

Between that bombshell and the fight with my mom, it had almost been a relief to get out of Haven for a few days and play Senate page, if only to try to figure out —

My thoughts came to a sudden, screeching halt.

"Sharyn!" I exclaimed.

She looked at me, the phone still pressed to her ear. "You look a little green, Red."

"I'm fine. Listen—"

"You should be, 'cause the cavalry's on its way," the Angel Boss interjected. "Even if it does include ... *her*. Now all we gotta do is come up with a plan for keepin' a Corpse outta the White House."

"I know," I told her. "I've got one."

"Ah!" said Lindsay Micha, still fussing with her hair. "I thought you might."

CHAPTER 42
GETTING READY TO RUMBLE

We sent Moira home. She still seemed pretty shook up—she'd have made a lousy Undertaker—but that wasn't the real reason. Sharyn didn't want her around when, and if, Micha's cronies showed up after we'd gone. Corpses didn't like witnesses, even clueless ones.

After that, the three of us headed to Webster Hall, this time on foot. The afternoon was sunny and warm for the time of year, so there were lots of people around, including Capitol cops. All of them, thankfully, were of the living variety, which boosted my theory that Corpse Micha had closed ranks.

Lindsay had cleaned herself up pretty good. I wouldn't have put her in front of a TV camera, but at least she wouldn't be drawing too many stares. And now that she was dressed in her own clothes, she clearly felt more herself, which helped.

Sharyn and I could only hope we wouldn't run into any deaders.

We didn't.

Lex Burnicky, Senate Page Program proctor and stick-up-his-butt grad student, wasn't exactly happy to see us. After all, I'd gone AWOL last night and Sharyn had been reported missing by the Sergeant At Arms office this morning. Now it was past two in the afternoon and we both looked like we'd slept in the gutter.

"Have you *any* idea how much trouble you're both in!" he snapped as he opened the front door, his outrage boiling over. "The police were here for hours, questioning everyone! I've been on the phone with the program director and Senator Mitchum all morning! Half the city's out looking for you two! And now Greg's gone missing! Two pages and a proctor is one day! Insane! Just where have you *been*?"

"Chill out, Lex," Sharyn grumbled, her page persona having dropped like lead. "I ain't in the mood."

He stared at her as if she'd spoken Klingon. "You 'ain't in the mood'? Young lady, I'm calling in our police sentries right now! You can tell *them* you 'ain't in the mood'! And when they're finished with you … if you're lucky, you might just get kicked out of the program! I want you *both* to pack your things. You're *done* here!"

That's when Lindsay stepped smoothly between us. "I'm afraid these pages have other duties right now, young man."

Lex recognized her; he was way too much of a Capitol Hill geek not to. His eyes went so wide that I got ready to catch them if they popped out of his head. His bottom lip trembled.

Then he kind of squeaked.

The Lex Burnicky "Holy Crap Factor"!

"Step aside," Lindsay commanded.

Lex stepped aside.

"As you can see, these two will need fresh page uniforms. We'll also need some spares." She ticked off her fingers, working from memory. "Two mediums. One extra-large."

"More like extra-extra-large," Sharyn corrected. "You dudes even *got* extra-extra-large?"

Lex gaped at her, then back at the senator. "M—ma'am?"

Lindsay said, "It's a simple question, young man. Do you or don't you?"

"I … think so."

"And are they here on site?"

"Y——yes, Senator."

"Excellent. You and I will collect them." Lindsay faced us, her manner all patient authority, just as we'd rehearsed. "In the meantime, you two should shower and change. We need to be back on the Hill within the hour."

"Yes, ma'am," Sharyn and I replied in ridiculous unison.

Poor Lex looked as if his very world was crumbling.

"S-senator," he stammered, "this whole situation is extremely … I mean … the director will —"

Lindsay hit him with a smile that was so friendly and yet oddly terrifying at the same time that you *had* to be a politician—or a four-eyed monster—to pull it off. "Alexander. That's your name, yes?"

He nodded.

"Alexander. As I'm sure you're aware, the Page Program director and I are good friends." I wondered if this was true. I wondered if it mattered. Lindsay continued,

"Now, while I realize these requests are irregular, they are part of an important, rather impromptu effort on Capitol Hill that I don't have time to explain. I appreciate your position and your dedication to protocol, however. In fact, it strikes me that I could use someone like you in my office. Would such an opportunity be of interest?"

Lex did the poly-sci grad student version of pumping the air and screaming, "Yes!" He snapped to attention. "Ma'am ... it would be an honor!"

"Yes, it would. Now, let's conclude this business and, tomorrow, I'd like you to report to my office in the Hart Building. Speak to Moira. Tell her I sent you."

If Lex had possessed a tail, it would have been wagging furiously.

Lindsay gestured toward the staircase. "Shall we?"

The shower felt great. So did the new clothes. By the time Sharyn and I got back downstairs, Lex and Lindsay were already there, the uniforms we needed neatly packed into four black-leather suit bags.

"Alexander's loaning us these from his personal luggage," Lindsay explained. "Don't you think that's accommodating of him?"

"Yeah," Sharyn replied. "He's a peach!"

"My pleasure, Senator," the proctor said. If his spine had been any straighter, it would've snapped in half. "Um ... see you tomorrow?"

Lindsay politician's smile faltered, only a little, and only for second or two. "You just talk to Moira," she told him. "And everything will work out fine."

"Thank you," Lex said, shaking her hand with stiff professionalism. Then, with a look of burning envy directed at Sharyn and myself, he ushered the three of us out the front door and down to the street. "You don't have a car?"

"On a beautiful day like this?" Lindsay replied. "Certainly not. We'll walk."

"But those suit bags are heavy. I could call the Hill? Arrange transportation?"

"No thank you, Alexander. We'll manage."

"But Senator—"

She gave him another of *those* smiles. "Really, young man. You're not going to be this intrusive when you're working for me, are you?"

Lex blanched. "No! Of course not. As you say, Senator."

And, with that, we headed up the street toward the Capitol. Sharyn carried two of the suit bags. I had the other two. Lex had been right. They *were* heavy. But we couldn't risk an official car.

Not with what I had in mind.

At this time of day, Union Station buzzed with activity. Even after the long walk, which had left me exhausted, Sharyn exhilarated, and Lindsay looking impatient but otherwise fine, we had to wait more than an hour before the Undertakers' train showed up.

Then they came: Jillian, Helene, and the Burgermeister.

Jillian arrived first, smiling at me, nodding kind of awkwardly at Sharyn—who scowled—and staring like a rock band groupie at Lindsay. "Senator Micha?"

"Yes indeed, young lady. Have we met?"

"Not really," the girl replied. "I'm ... I used to be a Senate page. I was the one who found out you'd been ..."

she stammered, searching for the right word.

"Replaced?" Lindsay asked helpfully. "Kidnapped? Experimented on?"

"Yes. I guess so."

I barely heard them; my attention was fixed on someone else entirely.

Helene stood there.

She looked at me. I looked back at her and, for a second, the world seemed to shrink. It sounds stupid. I mean *really* stupid. I mean "for the love of God, jump to the next paragraph!" stupid. But it happened, and I've been telling this story too long to start skipping stuff now. For just a moment, Union Station vanished. So did my worries about the Corpses, the two—make that *three*—Lindsay Micha's, everything.

Helene and I were alone.

Then I blinked, and the moment passed.

Really embarrassing.

"Um ..." she said. "Hi, Will."

"Hi," I croaked.

"I ... missed you."

I missed you, too.

"It was only a week," I said.

"I know. I can count days, too," she replied, but even her sarcasm seemed to have a smile in it—tentative, maybe a little frightened, but a smile.

"Dude!" Dave said sharply.

I snapped my head around so fast that it hurt my neck. "What?"

"I asked if you're okay."

"What? Oh. Sure. You?"

The Burgermeister laughed. "*I* just got off a three-hour train ride. *You've* been running around DC, duckin' deaders!"

"We're *both* cool, Hot Dog," Sharyn said, eyeing him with her fists on her hips. "So ... what? You came here to rescue me or something?"

"Tom sent me," he replied defensively. "You know ... to help."

"Since when do *I* need help?"

Dave reddened. "Well ... maybe I didn't mean help *you*! Maybe I meant help Will!"

"Maybe you did!"

"Yeah! Maybe I did!"

For a long moment, they faced either other down. Sharyn was at least a head and a half shorter and a hundred pounds lighter, but of the two of them she still looked— bigger. Dave fidgeted under her dark gaze.

But then she laughed and threw her arms around him. "Missed ya, ya big dope."

"You're a dope!" Dave growled, though I could read his grin.

Helene and I looked at each other. Seconds ticked by.

"I'm not hugging," her expression said.

"Me, neither," mine said.

"Are you guys *always* like this?" Jillian groaned.

It was Helene who replied, "It's been a rough week."

"Come on," I said. "We got things to do."

"Red's right," Sharyn said, shoving Dave away from her.

We handed the three of them the suit bags. "Girls' bathroom over there," Sharyn said, pointing to one end of the concourse. "Boys' over there. Make it quick."

Dave went left. Helene and Jillian went right. Sharyn, Lindsay, and I stood where we were. Union Station suddenly felt small, uncomfortable, and more than a little awkward.

"So," Lindsay said. "Just to be clear: who's sweet on *whom*?"

I opted for an immediate and aggressive change of subject. "Um ... Lindsay? Did you mean it when you said you'd give Lex a job?"

"Believe it or not, William," she replied, "I don't say things I don't mean." But then her eyes took on an odd, faraway look and her shoulders slumped a little. "Unfortunately, I rather doubt if such a position in my office will be ... feasible ... by this time tomorrow."

"Why's that?" I asked.

She didn't reply.

Looking back, I wonder if she knew what was coming—if, on some level, Lindsay Micha had somehow glimpsed the future.

I guess I'll always wonder.

Like with Ian.

CHAPTER 43
THE CHAMBER

"Excuse me, ma'am," the officer manning the Capitol Visitor Center X-ray machine said. "Has anyone ever told you that you look just like Senator Lindsay Micha?"

Lindsay smiled and collected the purse she'd just bought from a street vendor about ten minutes ago; it was empty. "Do I? I'm flattered. I've always been such an admirer of hers. Do you suppose there's any chance I might run into her today?"

"Are you taking the tour?" the police officer asked. He was human. A Corpse Cop would have been on his radio, sounding the alarm. But there were none in sight.

They'd be in and around the Senate chamber, close to their boss.

"No," Lindsay said, holding up a gold ticket, one of the five we'd taken out of Moira's receptionist desk. "But maybe we'll get to see her in action!"

The man laughed. "It's possible!" Then he waved her through.

Next went Jillian, then Helene, then the Burgermeister and finally me, my second time through this checkpoint in less than a day. We were all dressed in Senate page outfits: blue pants, white shirt, blue blazer. Dave and I wore ties. For the girls and myself, the fit was pretty okay. But the Burgermeister—well, he looked like a bear in a scuba suit.

Sharyn wasn't here.

The Visitor Center was crowded. Hundreds of tourists pouring in even this late in the afternoon, so one woman and a handful of Senate pages didn't earn a second glance.

Except for Lindsay, we all had water pistols, which wouldn't set off the alarm. In addition, I had my pocketknife. Super Soakers were forbidden—too big. No Ritters or crossbows either.

"Hardcore under-gunned," Helene called it.

Fortunately, if all went well, we wouldn't need our weapons.

Once through security, we headed to the south side of the crowded Emancipation Hall, where guides verified our Senate Chamber passes—available at any senator's office—and ushered us through yet another level of security. This one required that we surrender our cell phones. Jillian and the Burgermeister did so, while Helene told the guards that she didn't have one.

Fortunately, nobody searched her.

After that came a lot of hallways, a lot of guards—all human—and then the final checkpoint, the one right outside the chamber doors.

Here, Corpses kept watch. Four of them. All early Type Threes. They looked solemn and alert. Spotting them, I stopped us around the final bend in the corridor. This was as far as we'd go—until Sharyn's signal.

It came less than a minute later, a barely audible chirp on Helene's sat phone. The Angel Boss, who'd stationed herself—along with hundreds of others—on the grassy public grounds that lay west of the Capitol, had just sent a one-word text.

"Green," Helene said, reading the message.

The code word meant that C-SPAN, the cable news network that streams live feeds from inside both houses of Congress, had just shown Lindsay Micha and her entourage entering the Senate Chamber.

"This is it," I said. "Lindsay … you okay?"

Lindsay was peeking around the corner, studying the deaders with an expression that could only be called predatory. With a dry gulp, I touched her arm. She turned and, for an instant, those terrifying eyes—flashing red, green, yellow, and blue—fixed on *me*.

"Lindsay?" I said again, fighting the urge to run.

She blinked and her eyes went back to normal. "Of course," she said. "I mustn't indulge myself. That's not the plan. But … oh, Will … I'm so hungry!"

"Oh, jeez," Dave muttered.

I looked at Helene. She had one hand inside her blazer, probably closed around her water pistol, though I doubted if saltwater would even affect the Corpse Eater.

I shook my head and she relaxed—a little.

"I know," I told Lindsay. "But you gotta hang tight. Go off on these dudes, and we'll scare the Third away."

"Mustn't do that. Must find the Third." She spoke in that dreamy sort of trance that I hadn't heard in a while. It's scared the crap out of me. But we were here, and there was no turning back now.

Jillian said, "Let's do this."

Helene nodded. "Will, you and the senator sit tight 'til we're ready."

"You sure?" I asked. "There's four of 'em. More than we figured on."

"Don't sweat it, dude," Dave told me, slapping my shoulder. "We got this." Then he and Jillian pasted on smiles and turned the last corner.

Helene hung back for a second, giving me a worried look.

"We're good," I assured her. Beside me, Lindsay's eyes were glassy, but her jaw was set. "We're good," I repeated, hoping it was true.

The three "pages" approached the checkpoint. At the sight of them, the Corpses' bloated purple faces registered immediate suspicion. These guys were pretty far along, decomposition wise—bloated and dripping with fluids. When they moved, hairs fluttered off their rotting scalps while, around them, spring flies feasted and laid eggs in their flesh.

Jillian, the newest Undertaker, looked a little shaky.

But the rest had seen it all before.

"Hi," Helene said, smiling. "We've got a little time off and wanted to check out the chamber."

The nearest deader, who looked like he was in charge, eyed the girl before shrugging. Then he looked at Dave. "You don't fit in that jacket too well."

"Yeah," the Burgermeister grumbled. "Tell me somethin' I don't know."

"What?" Another Corpse laughed, a sickening, throaty sound, like someone choking a bullfrog. Okay, that's just weird—how would I know what a choked bullfrog sounds like? But you get the idea. "They don't make page uniforms in Jolly Green Giant size?"

"Belts off. All of you," a third one said. "Regulations."

They obeyed, all the while moving slowly away from one another, taking up positions. Three-on-four was long odds, especially given the weapons they carried—and, as Lindsay and I watched from around the corner, I felt my stomach knot up.

I hated not being in the action. But, right now, that wasn't my role.

Jillian dropped her belt into a plastic bin. The others did the same. Then Helene ran one hand through her hair, the movement appearing absent and natural.

Now!

Lindsay and I stepped into view. "Yoo-hoo!" the senator called, waving. "Have you boys seen anybody around lately who looks like *me?*"

The Corpses froze, staring at us. As we'd hoped, the sight of Lindsay Micha, knowing who—and *what*—she was put them momentarily off their guard.

"Abomination!" one of them exclaimed.

Helene and Jillian both drew their pistols and fired into the faces of their respective deaders. At the same instant Dave drove a ham-sized fist into a third Corpse's face, the blow so hard that his whole hand disappeared into the dude's rotting skull. The body stiffened and started twitching.

"That's for the Jolly Green Giant crack!" he said as the dude fell.

Then he seized the sides of the boss Deader's head and delivered a single, hard twist. I heard the spine snap.

Two down, I thought. But I kept my eye on Lindsay, who watched the combat with an almost-childlike envy.

If she changed now, we were hosed.

Helene delivered a wheel kick to the deader she'd just squirted. The guy, already blind and off-balance, went down like a sack of sand, his neck broken. Beside her, the one that Jillian had shot convulsed and staggered forward, failing its arms and knocking the girl upside the head.

With a cry, Jillian hit the carpet.

Suddenly, my pocketknife was in Helene's hand— another reluctant loan. Vaulting over the faceless Corpse she'd just dropped, the girl slammed the blade into the back of the last deader's skull, so deep that she almost took the dude's head off.

Game Over. Ten seconds, maybe less.

"Wonderful," Lindsay muttered in a dreamy voice. "Just wonderful."

"Come on," I said, leading her toward the others as Helene helped Jillian to her feet. "Nice job," I told them.

Of course, the telepathic alarm was already going out. We could only hope Micha wouldn't be chased off.

"Clumsy," Jillian said, the makings of a nasty bruise forming on her cheek. "I let him hit me."

"Won't be the last time," Helene replied. "Believe me."

"Don't forget your belts, children," Lindsay said. "It's important to look your best."

When we were all ready, Dave opened the chamber door. As before, Lindsay and I held back—also part of the plan. Helene paused at the threshold, once again giving me a quick, worried look.

"I'm cool," I said, keeping my voice just above a whisper.

"I know," she replied.

Then she let the door shut.

Time to count to sixty.

"She cares for you," Lindsay said.

I shifted uncomfortably, but didn't reply.

"It's nothing to be embarrassed about."

"I know," I said, though I knew no such thing.

"You should speak to your mother about it."

"No, thanks."

"She could help you understand what you're feeling. Helene's a lovely girl, by the way."

Again, I said nothing. This was the *last* thing I wanted to be talking about. But, as always with grown-ups, Lindsay wouldn't drop it.

"I remember being young and confused about the opposite sex."

Oh … jeez.

"Thirty seconds," I said, studying my watch with laser-like intensity.

"You children are courageous, and capable. There's no denying that. But you're still children. And growing up is never easy. This situation with Helene is not something you want to simply ignore."

"Twenty seconds," I said, maybe a little desperately. *Please … shut up.*

She didn't.

"I imagine your mother must be very proud of you."

"She's scared for me," I said.

"No reason she can't be both. That's how I was with Jacob." Then, after a thoughtful pause, she added, "If you were my son … *I'd* be proud of you."

That was kind of nice.

"Ten seconds," I told her. "You ready?"

She nodded. "Yes, I'm ready."

As I opened the big door, a familiar voice echoed from the floor of the Senate Chamber. "My fellow lawmakers, I stand before you at a personal and professional crossroads …"

Corpse Micha had begun her announcement.

CHAPTER 44

BEST-LAID PLANS

"For years now, I've watched this great nation being spoiled by the narrow-minded greed of self-interest groups and lobbyists. America calls for a brave new vision, a new leader."

This was only my second visit to the Senate Chamber, and it was *way* more crowded this time. Corpse Micha's announcement had drawn a lot of attention; people in suits—senators presumably—filled the desks down on the floor below. Still others crowded the gallery, and some of these looked up curiously as Lindsay and I slipped inside and stood near the back.

Helene, Dave, and Jillian had already taken positions at carefully picked points around the gallery—all standing, all watchful. In their page uniforms, no one took any special notice of them, which was good.

Since the dead were *everywhere*.

Dozens of them. Most were Capitol cops, standing guard at each of the Senate floor entrances as well as around Corpse Micha, herself, who occupied the rostrum.

She was in a different body this time, and not a particularly fresh one—a Type Three, bloated with trapped gases. These gases had stretched her skin, making it *ripple* hideously when she spoke. Her entourage took no notice. The Corpses, after all, knew the score. And the humans couldn't See it.

"For that reason, I have spent the last few months away from the cameras and away from this august body. A self-imposed exile of sorts, a time to reflect, to decide what my heart compels me to do."

Standing beside me just inside the chamber entrance, Lindsay trembled.

"You okay?" I whispered.

She nodded.

"You ready?" I asked.

She nodded again. Then, as we'd rehearsed, she raised one arm and pointed an accusing finger at her Xerox.

The Senate Chamber is not that big a place. After all, it was built to accommodate just a hundred senators and a modest audience. If you're on the rostrum, then a person standing in the gallery is pretty easy to see—especially if that person looks just like you, or your Mask, anyway.

And *especially* if you've been dreading the sight of her for days.

Sure enough, the fake senator spotted the real one and tripped over her words. "This … wasn't … an … easy … um …"

Her stolen body began to shake.

Within moments, the least living of her cronies saw what she saw. They swapped nervous, uncertain looks, trapped between flight and defending their boss. Duty won out, barely. After receiving some scalding glares from

Corpse Micha, these deaders hurried for the main floor doors...

...making their way up toward us.

Our little show was starting to have its effect on the human senators, too. Many were reacting to the phony Micha's obvious distress. A few craned their necks, searching the gallery.

"Now," I said.

Lindsay yelled, "That woman is an imposter!"

The Senate erupted in noise. Every head turned our way.

A couple of Corpse cops, stationed on either end of the upper section, headed for us. Helene stepped up behind the first and, in a *seriously* smooth move, squirted saltwater into his ear. The guy spasmed and dropped like a sack of sand. The Burgermeister's method was even simpler. He just stepped into the deader's path—and stayed there. The guy tried to go around him, but the aisle was way too narrow. It was either attack the huge kid, or climb on top of the other VIPs in the gallery, neither of which the deader policeman was willing to risk.

Below, Corpse Micha's voice had failed. She stood frozen behind the podium, clutching its edges tight enough to splinter the wood. Her seemingly sightless expression was one of obvious, mounting horror.

Then she screamed.

But it wasn't a human scream; not anything *like* a human scream. This sound was alien, unearthly, and sent a chain of razor-sharp chills down my back.

Every senator was on his or her feet now, as if trying to take charge of ... something. A few of them approached Corpse Micha, only to be roughly shoved back by deader cronies.

"Get. Me. Away," I heard the imposter say in Deadspeak. "Protect. Me."

That's it! Make a break for it. Head for the car you've got idling out front ... where Sharyn's waiting with Aunt Sally.

That's when things went south.

Beside me, Lindsay growled. Yep, she actually growled—and I knew we were in trouble. Turning, I saw that her eyes, still *locked* on the doppelgänger, were *flashing*.

Red. Green. Yellow. Blue. Red. Green. Yellow. Blue.

"Lindsay," I whispered. "Hold on."

My gaze found Helene's. Now she looked more than worried; she looked terrified—for *me*.

I was playing monster-tamer.

Except she isn't a monster. At least, that's not all she is. There's a good person in there, bouncing around inside her fractured mind. If she can just hold on a little while longer ...

"It's hard, Will," she whispered in a throaty, animalistic voice. "I see the Third. And I have to be whole. I ... *must* ... be whole!"

"Hang on," I said. Then, against my every instinct, I took her hand. "You're strong. You can keep it under control ... just a little while longer."

She nodded, though sweat beaded up on her forehead. Her gaze remained glued on Corpse Micha, and she seemed to be straining—like a beast on a flimsy chain.

Around us, people in the gallery had jumped to their feet and were retreating. Could they tell what was happening? Could they see her flashing eyes? Could they sense what was coming?

"Dude!" the Burgermeister called to me. "Watch it!"

But I've got this! I'm not going to let her change. I've got this!

I didn't.

As Corpse Micha and her deader entourage pushed through the wall of legislators, desperate to escape, something inside Lindsay snapped. "She's getting *away*!" she screamed, a sound every bit as terrifying and unearthly has the one her *Malum* counterpart had uttered.

Then she moved.

Yanking her hand from mine, she loped down the steps toward the gallery railing. Any spectators who got in her way were tossed aside as if they were rag dolls.

More screams, human this time.

Without thinking, I started after her. I didn't look at Helene. I didn't look at Jillian or Dave. If I had, I know what I would have seen in their faces: a whole chorus of, "Don't do it!"

"Lindsay!" I cried. "Wait!"

But she didn't wait, not even a little bit. With a wail of desperate *need*, she vaulted over the railing—her body already changing. The clothes *exploded* off of her, sending torn bits of cloth and loose threads raining down.

Then the Corpse Eater disappeared from my view.

It was twelve, maybe fifteen feet from the gallery to the Senate floor. *Not* a jumpable height, unless you're Jillian and can *parkour* it. Bottom line: you'd have to be a first-class lunatic to go over that railing without so much as a glance down at whatever lay below.

Hello. Have we met?

Someone yelled my name. Helene, maybe. I never found out.

I swung myself over, the air opening up beneath me as I fell. I glimpsed the senators' desks in their semicircle, looking like rocks at the base of a cliff. I glimpsed the faces of lawmakers staring in mute horror at the creature that had just landed in their midst. I glimpsed Corpse Micha, nearly at the chamber door, surrounded by her deader entourage, her swollen, stolen face a twisted mask of hatred and fear.

Then I landed on Lindsay's back. Or maybe she caught me. Another thing I'll never know for sure.

Two of her ten strong legs bent backward and enveloped me as they had atop the Capitol dome—pinning me against the hard, scaly skin of her back. Almost without thinking—*heck, why start now?*—I grabbed what passed for her shoulder blades and held on.

Lindsay leaped skyward, easily clearing the heads of more than a dozen panicked senators. I heard a sound like chalk breaking. Then I felt something whiz past my ear. Somebody was shooting!

There *had* to be at least one human cop in the chamber. Corpses, no matter what was happening, never used guns.

"Don't shoot!" someone yelled. "The boy! It's got the boy!"

The Corpse Eater landed in an open area right in front of the rostrum, her head rolling around and focusing on the chamber's main exit. The fake Micha was there, pushing her way through, her minions knocking aside anyone who came close. One of them, a Type Two, steeled his courage and charged back down the center aisle in defense of his boss.

Lindsay absently cut him in half.

Then, together, we launched ourselves after the fleeing imposter.

The best-laid plans ... I remember thinking.

CHAPTER 45
CRYPT

From the Senate Chamber's main doors it's a straight shot down a series of ornate, high-ceilinged corridors to the Rotunda. And Corpse Micha took that route, running with the weird, impossible agility that seemed reserved for the *Malum* royal family. All the while, she kept Deadspeaking to her toadies. It was a language that didn't lend itself to expressing emotion.

But she managed it anyhow.

"Protect. Me. Order. You. Protect. Me."

And her cronies obeyed, or tried to. Instead of running beside their boss, four of them—there were six in all—turned and spread out, blocking our pursuit.

Bad move, Dead Dudes!

With me still fastened to her back, Lindsay leaped sideways and hit the left-hand wall, shredding a big painting of some dead guy in old clothes. Then she bounced clear across the corridor, careened off the opposite wall, and somehow reached the ceiling, where she flipped over and latched on with eight of her legs.

Once there, she skittered forward, spiderlike and cat-quick, until we were directly over the four deaders, all of whom looked like they were facing down their worst nightmare.

And what was *I* doing during all this?

Fighting motion sickness and hanging on for dear life.

"Abomination!" one of the Corpses called in English.

"Yeah?" I said, looking down at him. "Look who's talking!" It probably would've come off a little cooler if I hadn't then puked in his face.

We dropped.

The first two she simply decapitated with savage swipes of her front legs. The third she cut in half—vertically—I mean, head to toe.

I still see that one in my dreams.

The fourth she *ate*. As the deader crony was engulfed by Lindsay's monstrous toothy maul and consumed, his scream of terror, inhuman as it was, twisted my already aching guts.

A moment later we loped forward again, clearing the length of the corridor and skidding halfway across the polished tile floor of the Rotunda.

Sometime during the day, the heart of the Capitol had been reopened to the public. There were people here—normal, living people—and the instant we appeared among them they scattered. Shrieks filled the huge, domed chamber and, for one horrible second, Lindsay seemed to pause, eyeing the mass of fleeing humanity. Her head rolled around me, going front to back and back to front again, her red eye studying the panicked, running figures—hungrily.

"Lindsay," I begged. "Don't."

She hesitated.

I heard something then. Not a word—more like a regurgitated idea. No, less than that. An urge.

Feed.

"Not on people," I said, hoping I sounded firm. I mean, how authoritative can you be when you're straddling a ten-legged creature from another dimension? "You can't eat living people. Just the dead."

Feed.

A balding man in jeans and a Redskins sweatshirt had stumbled a dozen steps away. He lay on the tile, crying and curled up into a tight ball, too terrified even to stand. Lindsay fixed on him the way a lion might fix on a crippled zebra.

"You are Senator Lindsay Micha!" I said, talking as fast and as loud as I could. "You *will* not do this!"

The Corpse Eater skittered toward the cringing man. Her terrible jaws opened.

"Lindsay!" I screamed. Panicked tears stung my eyes. "If you kill him, you'll never be human again!"

She paused.

Moments ticked by. The red eye swiveled around and glared at me, only inches from my face—so close that I could feel the heat of it.

I glared right back.

Then, with a frustrated grunt, she leaped over the man in the Redskins sweatshirt and bounded out through the eastern archway. There was no sign of Corpse Micha or her remaining two thugs, but that didn't slow her down. She turned sharply and hurtled down two long flights of stairs, before charging headlong into the great space directly beneath the Rotunda.

The Crypt.

But this wasn't a crypt like in *Tales from the Crypt*. Instead, it was a brightly lit room with a polished, stone floor and four big, Greek-style columns—Doric, I think they're called—which held up the Rotunda. A starting place for most Capitol tours, the Crypt's circular walls hosted various busts and statues, all donated from different states. There was scale model of the Capitol here, as well as a copy of the English *Magna Carta*.

And maybe a few deaders, too.

Lindsay and I screeched to a halt directly atop the compass in the floor that was supposed to represent the physical center of the Capitol and—perhaps—all of DC.

Nobody was around. Maybe it was closed this time of day, or maybe any tourists had cleared out in the panic that we'd started upstairs. Either way, the chamber was as silent and empty as its name implied. Nevertheless, I'd been an Undertaker too long to believe we were safe. There were tons of places to hide.

Every alarm bell I had was ringing like crazy.

Lindsay released me. I slid off her back and stood up, dismayed at how stiff I felt. My long-suffering stomach seemed totally empty, as if I had a genuine hole in my gut.

Lindsay fixed her yellow eye on me. If there was some kind of message, I didn't get it. Then her head rolled to her opposite end and she jumped away, disappearing down one of the nearby corridors.

I reached inside my jacket for my water pistol. My hand came away wet.

Broken. Figures.

Why had Lindsay left me, alone and unarmed?

Then I got it.

I was bait. She'd use me to draw out Corpse Micha and her cronies. If they *were* here, then they'd just seen the abomination leave. Once their fear fizzled, that old Corpse hunger would reappear and they'd show themselves.

A solid plan, though I couldn't say I liked it much.

Long minutes passed. No movement. No sound. I stood atop the compass, turning in a slow circle. My heart pounded.

Finally, a sticky voice said, "Looks like you're all alone, little boy."

A Type Four emerged from behind a column. At the same moment, a Type Three stepped around the Capitol model, effectively boxing me in. Both were male. Both wore power suits—the DC uniform.

"Hey guys," I said, managing a smile. Neither was particularly fresh—definitely not Corpse Micha's "A-Team." But they were still plenty dangerous, especially considering I had nothing but my bare hands.

They approached slowly, their purple-gray fists opening and closing, their rotting teeth chattering and clacking inside their skulls. But the eyes were the worst—milky and apparently sightless. They looked blind, though I knew with terrible certainty that they weren't.

My already sore stomach clenched even tighter.

Then the lights went out.

It was so abrupt and the darkness left behind so complete, that my vision needed a few seconds to adjust. Something hurtled toward me—just a flicker of movement in the blackness—and I ducked. A forearm cut the air where my head had been, the deader equivalent of a baseball bat.

The Type Four had made his move.

I couldn't see him. But I could smell him, a sickly sweet odor, kind of like rotting meat—*exactly* like rotting meat, now that I think about it. And when he moved, the stench grew stronger. Sharyn had trained us to fight in the dark. When you don't have your eyes, use your other senses.

I did that now.

Instead of retreating, I weaved around the spot where I smelled him, stepped in and gave a blind shove, causing him to stumble. He growled and clawed at me, a shape in the dark. But I slipped around him again, careful to slide my feet rather than take steps. I smelled him charge and then slam right into one of the columns, uttering a furious grunt...

...which told me right where to hit.

I drove my fist at the spot where I hoped the base of his skull would be. And I nailed it. The deader stiffened, his arms clamping spasmodically around the Doric column as he slumped. I hadn't killed him, but I had incapacitated him for a bit.

Better than nothing.

There was a loud *thunk* as the emergency lights came on, soft and red, showering the Crypt with an unworldly glow. I had just enough time to turn around before the other one, the Type Three, was on me. His rotting hands scrambled for my face as we crashed to the stone floor together.

I shoved my forearm under his chin to keep his snapping mouth away from me. Corpse juice dribbled down onto my cheek.

Where was Lindsay? I mean, what was the point of

setting bait if you weren't around to make the kill!

Then something flashed across my peripheral vision, too small to be the Corpse Eater. It was bouncing from column to column, a flurry of movement both quick and nearly silent.

The figure vaulted over the Capitol model, swung smoothly around a final column, and then delivered a kick to the side of the Type Three's head that snapped his spine in two. I actually *heard* it crack.

The Corpse fell off of me.

An instant later, Jillian asked, "You okay?"

"Yeah," I replied, sitting up and wiping God-knew-what off my face.

She pulled me to my feet.

"What happened to the lights?" I asked.

"Helene ... that weird pocketknife of yours."

An electromagnetic pulse; should've figured that. "Where are they all?"

"I'm not sure," Jillian replied. "After you pulled that stunt in the chamber, Helene sent me after you. She must have figured I was the only one who could keep up. Sorry, I got here as fast as I could."

"You got here when you had to," I said. "*Totally* Undertaker."

She smiled.

Then a dark figure rose at her shoulder.

"Watch it!" I yelled.

Jillian ducked as the Type Four, recovered from my skull shot, made a clumsy grab for her. Then, before I could jump to her defense, the girl ran straight up a nearby column, executed a perfect backflip, and landed on the Corpse's shoulders.

For a split second, the deader's eyes met mine. He looked astonished.

"Yeah," I told him. "Cool ... ain't she?"

Then Jillian, with a single hard twist of her legs, broke the deader's neck. He dropped like a forgotten puppet, and she went with him, landing easily on her feet as he collapsed beneath her.

"You *gotta* teach that to me," I said with a laugh.

"Listen," she said. "That stuff that went down in the Senate Chamber is drawing most of the attention ... for now. But I figure we got about five minutes before the whole place is flooded with security. The US government takes this building seriously."

She was right, of course.

"I have to find Lindsay," I said.

Jillian gaped. "Are you kidding me? Let's just get out of here alive, okay?"

"She's not a monster. She's a friend, and I'm not leaving without her. She's gone after Micha ... the dead one, I mean. You find the others. Tell them what's going on."

Jillian glowered. Then, with a heavy sigh, she said. "Uh-uh. I'm coming with you."

"You don't have to," I told her, meaning it.

"Of course, I do. I'm an Undertaker," she replied, also meaning it.

"You got a weapon?"

She grinned. "Will, know what I've found out lately? I *am* a weapon."

"Now you sound like Sharyn."

The girl considered. "I guess I'll take that as a

compliment, even if she *does* hate my guts. Come on, let's find your friend."

That was when my friend appeared, flying past us in a blur of legs, eyes...

...and blood.

CHAPTER 46

THE TWO MICHAS

I watched Lindsay sail by as if in slow motion. She bounced off one column before slamming into another. Then her strange body crashed to the floor, smashing the *Magna Carta* exhibit.

As I turned to her, Jillian grabbed my arm. "Will, don't!"

But there must have been something serious in the look I gave her, because she backed right off.

I ran to my fallen friend.

Four of the Corpse Eater's legs were gone. They looked like they'd been ripped right out by the roots. She was bleeding, a strange, syrupy stuff the color of muddy water. It flowed freely, soaking my pants as I knelt beside her.

Her head—that strange head of her—lolled miserably, but managed at last to fix me with its green eye.

"Lindsay," I said, my vision blurring. "What ... happened?"

A voice spoke: "*I* happened."

Corpse Micha melted out of the shadows behind Jillian. Before the girl could react, strong, dead fingers coiled in her hair, twisted roughly—and slammed her forehead into the nearest column. I heard a sickening *thump*.

Then Jillian slid to the floor, knocked senseless by a walking cadaver.

Crap, Jill. Now *you're an Undertaker.*

I stood up and put myself protectively between the two Michas. "Back off," I warned, hoping I sounded intimidating.

Corpse Micha laughed. "Or what, little man? You'll electrocute me with your amazing pocketknife? Squirt me with your clever toy pistol? Or perhaps you'll stab me with one of those saltwater syringes?" She tilted her Type Three head in a mockery of consideration. "Yes, my sister has fully informed me of your juvenile arsenal. Except you don't *have* any of those weapons just now. Do you, William?"

I tried to think up some clever response that might buy me time.

Nothing came.

One of Lindsay's remaining pincers tugged on my pants. Looking down, I saw that her head now showed its yellow eye.

Once again, something flashed through my mind—more idea than language. Then my friend's head dropped to the floor and all her remaining limbs went limp with a horrible finality.

"No ..." I muttered.

"Step aside," Corpse Micha said, advancing. We were maybe ten feet apart.

"What did you do to her?" I demanded.

"Showed her who her Mistress is," the fake Lindsay Micha replied. "She cornered me down the House corridor. So I begged for my life. I threw myself at her feet and told her how sorry I was and how I would make amends if she'd only let me." The Corpse grinned savagely. "And she hesitated … just for a moment, lowering her guard. I'm no mere Warrior Caste, little man. I'm a Royal. That moment was more than enough."

"Tough talk," I said. "'Cept I seem to remember you running out of the Senate Chamber, screaming 'Protect me! Protect me!'"

Her dead face twisted in anger. "That was before I knew my enemy," she hissed. "Before I realized how … *human* … she really was!"

This last statement hit me hard. I remembered the fallen man in the Rotunda, and how I'd managed to convince Lindsay not to eat him. I'd appealed to her human side, her sense of mercy—and had patted myself on the back for it.

But her human side was a double-edged sword.

Corpse Micha said, "And now I'm going to remove the rest of her legs."

"Haven't you done enough?" I snapped. "She's already dead!"

"No, she isn't. Merely too weak to fight. You see, little man, her form is *our* form. And it's strong, far stronger than your own flimsy flesh." She spread her arms inside her torn and soiled suit. I saw the muddy syrup soaking the fabric.

My friend's blood.

"I need her alive," the deader explained. "If she dies, then my Cover dies with her. And I *like* being Lindsay

Micha. I just need to make sure she's beyond any hope of causing further … mischief."

The idea of the real Lindsay forever locked away somewhere, a helpless cripple, while this—*thing*—that wore her face won the White House turned my stomach way worse than any ride on a monster's back.

"No," I said.

"No?"

"I said no. You've done enough to her."

Corpse Micha took another step forward. "Brave words. But courage only goes so far. Besides, I think you misunderstand the situation. While I have no intention of killing that abomination at your feet, I have *every* intention of killing *you*."

"Oh yeah?" I said, feigning a cockiness I didn't feel. "I've heard that one before. Take your best shot, wormbag."

She lunged, coming at me terrifyingly fast. Fortunately, I'd known it was coming.

I threw myself to the right. Not a step. Not a jump. A *throw*—one that sent me skidding painfully across the stone floor. At the same instant, the Dead Royal hit the spot where I'd been standing with enough force to crack the wall beside the already ruined *Magna Carta* display.

I'd hoped the collision would stun her. It didn't. Grinning, she righted herself and spun to attack again.

That's when a pair of pincers took off both her feet.

Lindsay's idea—the message she'd transmitted to me right before playing "dead"—had been simple: *Get her close.*

Helpless? I thought. *Too weak to fight? Don't think so.*

"What?" Corpse Micha screamed. "No!"

She toppled like a felled tree.

As the real Lindsay scrambled atop her, the fake one lashed out, trying to grab—and maybe rip away—yet another leg. But this time there wasn't going to be any hesitation. The Corpse Eater caught the attacking hand and cut it clean off. Corpse juice went everywhere.

Then, just to be sure, Lindsay did the same with the other hand.

Now who's limbless?

The deader, of course, felt no pain. Nevertheless she wailed, "Wait! Please! I'm sorry!"

No mercy this time, I thought. And, for some reason, that saddened me.

Lindsay pinned down her struggling, screaming adversary. Then she brought her face close. I'd expected Lindsay to eat her. But apparently it didn't work like that. This wasn't about consuming the body. This was about consuming the *Mask*.

A single word drilled into my head: *whole*.

It took only a few seconds, but those seconds seemed to go on and on. Energy—not light, exactly, but somehow bright like light—passed from Corpse to Eater. Lindsay's head begin to shimmer.

Then the fake Micha went limp, and I didn't need to cross my eyes to know that her stolen Mask was gone.

That was when the real one *transformed*.

Lindsay rolled off her Xerox, a normal woman again, her body maimed. Her entire left arm was gone, the stump bleeding something awful. But at least now the blood was human red.

"Finally," I heard her gasp. "Finally …"

"Lindsay?" I said, kneeling beside her a second time. She was naked, as usual, but I didn't even notice. It didn't matter.

"Thank you," she whispered, looking up at me.

"Hang on," I said. "You're going to be fine. Just —"

"Hush," the woman said with a thin, sad smile. "It's … all right. I'm … whole … again. I'm—" More blood trickled out the corners of her mouth. I couldn't even imagine how the damage done to her *gravveg* form had translated now that she was human.

But I knew mortal injuries when I saw them.

"Will?" She coughed.

"Yeah," I said, wiping impatiently at my blurring eyes.

"I … would have been proud … to call you son."

Then Senator Lindsay Micha died.

My shoulders sagged. My head fell to my chest. I held her hand—her limp, lifeless hand—and gave it a final squeeze before letting it fall. Finally, I took off my jacket and draped it over her naked form.

"I'm sorry," I whispered.

Small fingers locked around my throat. Gasping, I clutched her wrist, but the grip was like iron.

"I'm not," the dead woman hissed. But, of course, it wasn't my friend anymore.

It was Corpse Micha.

Stupid!

CHAPTER 47
A PROMISE KEPT

Lindsay hadn't eaten her imposter. Maybe she'd lacked the strength, wounded as she'd been. Or maybe her human half had simply gotten tired of killing. But whatever the reason, she'd taken only what she'd needed to be whole again—only what'd been stolen from her.

And had inadvertently left behind the broken shell of a cadaver, and the *thief* trapped inside.

Waiting for the body of the *real* Lindsay Micha to become available.

"I told you I'd kill you, Mr. Ritter. And I always keep my promises."

Then the thing that had been my friend leaped to her feet with lethal grace, taking me right along with her. She pressed my back against the nearest column, hoisting me higher until my page shoes left the floor—all with the strength of her one remaining hand.

I kicked. I squirmed. I used every trick I knew. Nothing worked. She was right. This wasn't some Warrior Caste thug. This was royalty.

And royalty, at least *Malum* royalty, were *tough*!

"You've cost me my Cover, little man. And I'm going to punish you for that," she purred, completely oblivious to my struggles. "But I think I'll leave your neck unbroken. That way, your body can serve as host for one of my fallen minions here. That seems only fair, doesn't it?"

I punched her in the face, putting everything I had behind it. The nose broke with a muffled crunch. But it had no effect. Zilch.

I was going to die.

Already, stars flashed before my eyes. There was a roaring sound behind my ears.

"Correct me if I'm wrong," Corpse Micha said conversationally. "Aren't *you* the boy who killed Kenny Booth? And didn't you also take a bullet meant for the First Lady of Pennsylvania? I recently met her, by the way. She still talks about you ... though, of course, she doesn't know your name. I don't suppose she ever will."

Babbling. She's killing me by inches and babbling. I'm being murdered by a babbling, preening, self-important, alien princess.

This is my life.

This is my death.

"My sister will be beside herself when she hears I've killed you." The deader giggled. "I can't *wait* to see her face! Oh, little man ... I'm afraid you're starting to go purple!" My vision darkened from the edges inward—agonizingly slowly. Her words sounded distant, as if she were down a long tunnel. "Don't worry. It's a color that will suit one of my minions just fine."

Often before, when I'd found myself right here, right on the edge of *nothing*—and it happens more than I like to think about—my mother's face came to me.

This time, however, a different face appeared. And in that face, that *beautiful* face—might as well be honest, now that I'm dying and all—I caught of glimpse of everything I wanted but wouldn't get. Heck, I'd never even be able to tell her how I really felt.

That regret was even more crushing than Corpse Micha's hand.

Then the face spoke. That puzzled my oxygen-starved brain, especially since the words didn't seem directed at *me*.

"Yo, wormbag!" the face said. "Hands off the boyfriend!"

Corpse Micha's expression changed from smug to perplexed. Her stolen eyes—Lindsay's eyes—went wide. Suddenly, blessedly, she released my throat, and it seemed as if the floor rushed up and slapped me in the face.

Lying there helpless, air rushing into my aching lungs, I watched as the Royal deader staggered and turned.

There was a Ritterbolt in the middle of her back.

She tried to reach it, but human arms just don't bend that way. Besides, half dead as I was, my vision had cleared enough to see that the syringe was empty. It was already too late.

I wanted to say something clever. But all that came out was "Uhhhnnnn."

Lindsay Micha's body exploded. She'd been freshly dead—the ultimate Type One—and pieces of her went everywhere. Blood painted the walls. Nothing at all was left behind but some bone fragments, a few scraps of tailored clothing...

...and the *thing* itself.

Dark energy, roughly woman-sized. Though it didn't have any visible eyes, or a face at all for that matter, I could sense that it was glaring at me. Hatred and fear radiated off it as the unprotected Malum searched desperately for a replacement host that wasn't there.

Then it was gone—just gone. In agony and terror. Gone.

Someone knelt beside me, cradling my head. "Will … can you hear me?"

I looked up into Helene's face.

"So," I croaked. It hurt to talk, but I did it anyway. "I'm your boyfriend?"

"Shut up," she said.

So I shut up—and kissed her. Just reached up, maybe a little clumsily, put my hand around the back of her neck and pulled her lips down to mine. She resisted, but only until she figured out what I was up to. Then she kind of fell into it. And it was nice—even if it did keep me from breathing for a little longer than I would have liked.

Finally I coughed and she pulled back. "Sorry," she said, her face flushing. Then her eyes widened. "Hold up a sec! Where's Jillian?"

"Over there," I said, pointing feebly. "Corpse Micha clocked her. We gotta—"

That's as far as I got before the lights came on.

And then went off again.

"That's Sharyn," Helene said, talking fast. "After Jillian went after you, I went after her. But there was a panic in the building, and she was faster than me."

I sat myself up, coughing again. She waited.

"I'm okay," I said.

"Anyway, I bumped into Sharyn. In all the confusion, she'd managed to get into the Rotunda with Aunt Sally. We traded. She's got your pocketknife. She's keeping the lights out so we can all get out of here."

"Good plan," I said.

"Where's Senator Micha ... the real one, I mean?"

I shook my head. Way too much to explain. Way too soon. Instead, I told her, "I really thought I was going to die that time."

"I kinda promised your mom I wouldn't let that happen."

"Yeah?"

"Yeah. Right after she hugged me."

"My mom hugged you?"

"Yeah."

I sighed. "My life's getting *really* weird."

She laughed. "No kidding. Come on ... let's grab Jillian and bail."

Except, about then, every cop in the world came pouring into the Crypt from all directions. Their guns were drawn and they looked scared—not a great combination. And all of those guns were pointed right at *us*.

"Or not," Helene said.

CHAPTER 48
THE FOURTH WATCHER

Bob Mittenzwei

When Capitol Chief of Police Bob Mittenzwei opened the door, the older of the two men viewing the bank of camera monitors turned to face him.

"So, Bob?" Senator James Mitchum asked. "What do you think of our young Mr. Ritter?"

Mittenzwei's eyes traveled to one of the monitors, on which the skinny, redheaded boy he'd just spent two hours interrogating sat sullenly.

"Kid's cool as a cucumber," he said. "I think if I poured boiling water down his throat he'd pee ice cubes. More self-possessed than most of the racketeering types I used to deal with back in Boston." He shook his head. "I've never seen anything like it."

"I have," the other man, FBI Special Agent Hugo Ramirez, remarked. "Did you talk to Helene yet?"

Mittenzwei nodded, scratching his bald spot. "In a way, she's worse than he is. Won't say a word. Nothing. At least the boy was willing to meet my eyes from time to time. *She* acted like there was nobody in there but her."

Mitchum laughed, though Ramirez didn't even crack a smile.

"These aren't ordinary teenagers," he said.

"So you've told me," Mittenzwei replied. "Look, gentlemen ... something unprecedented happened today in *my* building. More than a hundred people, most of them members of Congress, witnessed 'a ten-legged monster' jump from the Senate Chamber gallery to the Senate floor and engage in the pursuit of Lindsay Micha and her immediate staff ... all with *that* boy"—he pointed at the monitor—"riding on its back! The Architect of the Capitol is calling me every ten minutes for answers."

"I can appreciate your position," Mitchum said.

"Glad to hear that Senator, because right now I have nothing to tell her. We have no usable footage of this alleged monster, thanks to not one, but *two* unexplained EM pulses that fried every camera in the building. I lost contact with my entire staff because those same pulses took out the internal phone system, all portable radios, and every cell phone within a quarter mile! What *does* that, aside from military grade weaponry? And how do I even begin to explain any of this to Homeland Security?"

"It *is* a bit of a pickle," Mitchum admitted in what Mittenzwei thought was an Olympic-sized understatement. The senator turned to Ramirez. "If H.S. gets a hold of these kids, they'll disappear ... maybe for years."

"I can't let that happen," the FBI man replied.

Mittenzwei didn't know Ramirez except by his reputation, which had been stellar—until *something* had gone down in Philadelphia that had forced him to take "personal leave." Basically, he'd dropped off the grid. For months, nobody knew where he was. Then a couple of weeks ago he'd popped up here, in the Capitol, in Mittenzwei's office in fact, with Senator James Mitchum, one of the most powerful men in Washington, at his side—and an *incredible* story to tell.

"None of us can," Mitchum said. He faced the police chief. "What's the condition of the Birmelin girl?"

"Minor concussion. Hospital wants to keep her overnight, just for observation. Then they're willing to hand her over to Youth Services."

Mitchum and Ramirez shared a looked that Mittenzwei didn't like. Then the senator said, "Bob ... I'm sorry, but you're going to have to let these kids go. All three of them."

"Let them *go?*" Mittenzwei exclaimed. "That's impossible and you know it! This thing's too big and they're the only witnesses we've got! Look, Senator, I owe you. We both know that. I wouldn't have this job if not for you. But if I drop the ball on this, I'll be doing crossing-guard duty by the end of the week!"

"I appreciate your position," Mitchum replied. "How about this: when Homeland Security comes calling, just point them at me. And if your boss in the Architect's Office gives you trouble, send *her* to me as well. I'll settle things down with everyone."

"Yeah? How?"

The older man put a steadying hand on his shoulder. "The same way I do everything. By calling in favors I'm owed or making viable threats. Either way, I'll handle it. Trust me on this."

Mittenzwei ground his teeth. This whole day had

turned into a fiasco unlike anything he'd seen in his seven

years as the Capitol's chief of police. "What should I do with them ... Ritter, Boettcher, and Birmelin?"

Ramirez said, "Take them to Union Station. Make sure they have money for train tickets to Philadelphia."

"And don't mention *us*," Mitchum added. "Just tell them they're free to go."

"So that's it?" Mittenzwei asked sharply. "We're just going to drop them off with a pat on the head?"

Frustration made his temples pound. So much had happened! Senator Micha, another DC hard hitter, was missing, though the clothes she'd been wearing had been found on a three-week-old cadaver.

Then there were Micha's staff members, seven in all. One had been found in the Senate Chamber, four in the North Corridor, and two in the Crypt. All were comatose.

Charles O'Mally was missing, too. The Senate Sergeant at Arms, a personal friend as well as a member of the Capitol Police Board, had disappeared yesterday. A preliminary investigation had so far yielded no trace of him.

And let's not forget Rich Camp, a member of Mittenzwei's command, who'd disappeared from the Rotunda last week, leaving behind a half-crazed partner spouting stories about—you guessed it!—a ten-legged monster.

Tons of questions. Few answers.

Mitchum and Ramirez had explained *some* of what was going on—but even that little bit had stretched the limits of sanity.

And these kids were somehow in the thick of it.

If I let them go … I may never know what happened today.

Then again, do I really want *to know?*

"I understand," Bob Mittenzwei said.

"The important thing," Ramirez remarked, "is to keep this entirely to ourselves. We don't know … *can't* know … who to trust."

"Agreed," said Mitchum. "What happened in the Capitol today is going to be hotly debated for weeks, perhaps months. There will undoubtedly be a Senate investigation. That's good for us, as *no one's* better at slowing down any search for the truth than the US Senate."

Mittenzwei groaned. "Look, I get that you want to bury this thing—"

"*Need* to, Bob," Mitchum corrected.

"Okay … need to. But I've lost men. Good men."

Ramirez asked pointedly, "Have you?"

Mittenzwei eyed him. "What's that supposed to mean?"

"How many Capitol police have been lost since this business started?"

"At least three! Others have disappeared. Like Richard Camp."

The senator nodded, looking grim. "And how many of them have families, Bob?"

Mittenzwei gaped at them, his anger turning to confusion. "None."

None of them were family men. None had been with me for more than a year and a half. None had any living relatives.

"Are you trying to tell me …" He felt his face drain of blood "… that they were *them?*"

Both men nodded.

"My God!" the police chief exclaimed. "This is crazy!

How many others on my force are ..." His words trailed off.

"We can't be sure," Ramirez told him. "That's why we asked you to handle these interrogations personally."

"How big *is* this thing?" Mittenzwei demanded. "All I'm getting from you are hints. Some terrible conspiracy that started in Philly and is spreading outward. Frankly, if you were anyone else, I'd have locked you both up!"

"We can't tell you more," Mitchum said, looking genuinely sorry about it. "If we did, you probably *would* lock us up. You're just going to have to trust us for a while."

The police chief sighed heavily. Then he met his old friend's eyes. "For a while."

Ramirez turned to Mitchum. "I still think I should talk to Will. Explain things—"

But the senator held up a hand. "Not yet. I know how you feel, Hugo. And I promise you: the day is coming when we'll be in a position to reveal ourselves. But, for right now, I really think it best that we play the guardian angels. We'll continue to provide them with whatever supplies or ordinance they need, but let them think it's just you *alone* who's helping them."

"Why?" Ramirez pressed. "Senator, I know these kids. We can trust them!"

"It's not our trust in them that I'm worried about. It's *their* trust in *us*. These children have been in this struggle for a long time without supervision or guidance. They're not going to surrender that autonomy easily. We must wait until we can demonstrate conclusively that we are in a position to join the fight."

Mittenzwei listened to this exchange with growing unease. "How is it these kids have been on their own for so long?"

"Because," Mitchum replied, "unlike us … they can See."

The police chief was about to press the point when someone knocked politely on the door. A moment later, it opened to reveal a fourth man. He was young—not a day over twenty-one. "Sorry to interrupt," he said. "I wanted to let you know that the rest of them are at Union Station."

"Did they notice you monitoring them?" Mitchum asked.

"No, sir. I stayed well out of sight. In any event, they seem very distracted. They're trying to figure out what to do next."

"I'll bet they are," Ramirez said. "The Undertakers won't leave DC without their friends. That much I guarantee."

"Undertakers," Mittenzwei echoed. "That's the … street gang … you told me about."

The senator replied, "They're much more than that."

"And they're *all* kids?"

Ramirez answered, "Very brave and inventive kids."

Mitchum nodded grimly. "True. But still just children. All in all, I'm glad to have an eye into their operations."

"An eye?" asked Mittenzwei.

The senator and the agent swapped another look. Then, Mitchum explained, "We recently placed someone in their organization. We hadn't planned it that way. Not at all. But, as things turned, it was fortuitous."

"I'm still not comfortable with that decision," Ramirez said. "It's one thing to keep quiet about *your* involvement, Senator. I can see the logic behind that … more or less. But this—"

"Again, it's only temporary," the older man interjected. "Just until we devise a viable course of action, given our … handicap. In the meantime, we can be ready to act if Jillian gives us the word."

Ramirez fell silent, looking unhappy. The mood in the tiny room turned awkward.

"But I'm forgetting my manners," Mitchum announced, perking up. "Neither of you has met my young colleague here! He's from my office, but lately has been helping me on … special assignments." He motioned to the twenty-one-year-old, who came obediently forward. "Say hello to Greg Gardner!"

"A pleasure to meet you both," Gardner said.

Then he grinned.

And something about his grin sent a chill down Bob Mittenzwei's spine.

CHAPTER 49
HELENE'S LETTER

There was a *lot* of debriefing.

Once the five of us boarded the train we found a relatively quiet car and called Haven. Tom got on the line and we went over everything in detail.

I don't think he much liked what he heard.

"They just let y'all go?"

"Yeah, bro," said Sharyn. "I can't figure it either."

"They say anything to you, Will? Helene?"

"No," I replied. "We were dumped in the back of a cop car and dropped off at Union Station."

"How 'bout you, Jill?"

Jillian had a black eye and her forehead was bandaged. But aside from that, she seemed fine. "Not a word," she said. "Two cops showed up at the hospital and drove me to the train. Even gave me money for the ticket!"

"Us, too," Helene added.

"Don't make sense," grumbled Dave.

"No, it don't. Get home fast as you can."

So we did, getting into Philly around midnight and

Haven about a half hour later.

My first stop was the Shrine. But when I got there, I found Nick Rooney, the Mom Boss, cleaning it. He told me that my family had been moved around the corner, into one of the regular rooms. "It's what your mom wanted," he explained.

I went to my family's new room and found Emily asleep, but my mother awake. At the sight of me, she sort of sighed. Then she stood up and wordlessly hugged me.

"I'm sorry," I whispered.

"Me, too," she replied.

And that was that. Families are amazing.

Lilith Cavanaugh was dead, having fallen from her sixth floor office window. The local news was full of it. The Philly Police were still investigating whether it was an accident or suicide, but no foul play was suspected. At the time, the entire sixth floor had been evacuated because of a gas leak. So she'd been alone in her office. Everyone was *sure* of it.

Of course, the Queen *wasn't* dead, though her Mask *sure* was. Too many witnesses had seen her fall. As far as the world at large knew, the Director of Community Affairs was "late"—deceased, dispatched, passed on, pushing up the daisies, kicked the bucket.

Kaput!

Her body had been publicly removed and publicly processed and would be publicly buried tomorrow after a public ceremony, complete with TV cameras and politicians and speeches...

...and *us*.

The Angels had been keeping careful tabs on the body. No way were we going to pass up an opportunity to Ritter the Queen once and for all. But, so far, that opportunity hadn't presented itself. Her minions were guarding her too closely.

What little injury Jillian had suffered got Anchor Shard-ed. She was now a full-fledged Undertaker—an Angel, in fact, having proven herself in combat. Even Sharyn was starting to warm up to her. *Starting* to.

Neither Helene nor I knew why the Capitol Police had let us go.

The national media was all over the events at the Capitol, though nobody seemed to know exactly what had happened. Some were labeling it as a terrorist attack; others called it some kind of bizarre practical joke. At first, the witnesses—mostly senators—had described seeing a multi-legged monster. But most of them were already backpedaling.

Apparently, there was going to be a "Senate investigation."

Overall, Tom declared the DC mission a success. And it was, I supposed. I mean, the Queen had gotten her butt kicked and Corpse Micha was gone for good, so this one definitely belonged in the "win" column.

Except Lindsay was dead.

And so was Ian.

All of Haven still grieved for Ian. As I moved through its dank corridors, I heard his name on everyone's lips. I'd been away for a little over a week. Yet, for me, it felt like an eternity since he'd died. But for the rest of the kids, the news was still fresh.

Almost as soon as we got back from DC, Tom called a meeting and formally named my mom as Haven's new medic. The announcement went over kind of coolly, until she got up and said that, as her first act, she'd decided to *rename* the Infirmary. It was now the IAN MCDONALD MEMORIAL HOSPITAL. The Monkeys even made a wood plaque and fastened it to the brickwork just outside the entrance.

Everyone now seemed pretty okay with my family staying in Haven.

Well played, Mom.

After leaving my mother and Emily's room, I headed over to my own, hoping to stretch out on my cot and sleep for maybe three days. I kept thinking about the bed I'd had back at Webster Hall. Mattresses were nice things. I missed mattresses.

Helene sat on my bunk holding a crumpled up sheet of paper in her hands. She'd lit my bedside candle—Haven's private quarters, for the most part, lacked electricity—and its light shone on her pale face as she looked up at me.

"Hi," she said.

"Hi," I said.

She held the paper out to me.

"What's that?" I asked.

Helene scowled. "You don't remember, do you?"

"Remember what?"

Her scowl deepened. "Just *take* it, will ya? And read it?"

I accepted the crumpled paper. Then I stood in stupid indecision. Should I sit on Dave's bunk, or beside her on mine?

Finally, I sat down on mine.

"Read it," Helene repeated impatiently.

I smoothed out the single page, tilted it toward the candlelight, and read it. It was handwritten in a hasty, child's scrawl.

HELENE,

DADDY'S MOVING OUT. HE SAYS ALL THE FIGHTS ARE TOO MUCH. HE SAYS MOM NEEDS TO MOVE ON, BUT SHE WON'T. HE SAYS THAT HE LOVES ME AND HER, BUT THAT HE CAN'T LIVE HERE ANYMORE. MOM JUST CRIES ALL THE TIME. I DON'T KNOW WHAT TO DO.

I WISH YOU COULD COME HOME BUT I GUESS YOU CAN'T. I KNOW IT BUT IT MAKES ME SAD, ESPECIALLY NOW. DO YOU THINK YOU COULD MAYBE CALL MOM AND TELL HER YOU'RE OKAY?

I LOVE YOU.

JULIE

I read it twice while Helene watched me expectantly.

"Julie's ... your sister?" I asked.

"Duh," she said.

"You've never talked about her."

"You've never *asked* about her."

It was shameful but true. I'd joined the Undertakers six months ago, babbling all about my own little sister. I'd never even thought to ask if *she* had one, too. "Um ... how old is she?"

"Eleven. Sixth grade."

"This looks like a fax. Is this what you went to Quaker City Comics on South Street to get last week?"

"Two weeks ago. But, yeah."

"How long have you been ... talking ... with Julie?"

"About a year. Doug ... that's the guy you beat up—"

"I didn't beat him up," I interjected.

"Whatever. He used be our babysitter. Last year, I kinda went to him and asked him to set up this … drop, I guess is the word for it."

I could have told her that was against the Rules 'n Regs—*way* against them. Instead, I asked, "How's it work? E-mail?"

She shook her head. "E-mail can be traced or opened. Faxes are safer. We … I mean, my parents … have a fax machine. It's in my dad's office. Julie faxes her message to the comic book store. Then, once a week, I go there, pick it up, and give Doug my reply." Then, after a pause: "Or I *did*, before Doug cut me off."

"Sounds risky," I said. "What if your mom or dad saw the fax before Julie?"

"I used this code. Stupid, really … but it worked. It was gibberish, with only every third letter being important. Julie would circle them and put the message together. Then she did the same when she wrote back."

I held up the paper. "This *isn't* in code."

"No," she replied, taking it from me. Was she crying? In the candlelight, I couldn't tell. "Julie's upset. She skipped the code this last time."

"Your folks are splitting up."

Helene nodded. "Because of *me*. Because *I* disappeared. Mom just can't let it go. I've been on posters, milk cartons, supermarket bulletin boards, you name it. It's been two-and-a-half years, and my dad's had enough. He … can be like that sometimes."

"Julie's right," I said. "You *could* fax her a note. Your mom, I mean. Let her know you're okay."

But Helene shook her head. "You don't know her! If I do that, it'll only encourage her ... shift her into high gear. She's already looking for me hard ... maybe *too* hard. And I don't have to tell you what happens if she gets too close to the truth."

She didn't. I'd seen it too many times.

"This sucks, Helene."

"I know."

"What are you going to do?"

She looked at me with about a million things in her eyes. "I'm going to ask my boyfriend for help."

Before I could respond to that, we heard fast footsteps in the corridor outside my room. A moment later, the tattered curtain was shoved aside and a figure appeared, stooped and panting.

"Steve?" I asked.

Steve Moscova waved a hello, struggling to catch his breath. "Where ..." he gasped, "... is ..." he gasped again, "Tom?"

"In his office?" I suggested.

"Just ... came from ... there. It's empty."

"Try the cafeteria," Helene suggested.

Or he might be somewhere with Jillian. Like Dave might be with Sharyn.

Time's ... they are a-changin'.

"We'll find him," I told Steve, standing up. "What is it? What's wrong?"

"Wrong?" the boy asked, his eyes shining behind thick glasses. "Nothing! Quite the opposite!"

I started to ask what *that* meant, when he held up the Anchor Shard. It caught the meager candle glow and reflected it a thousand times over, filling the room with light.

"I know what this *is!*" Haven's Brain Boss declared triumphantly. "And I know how we can use it ... to *end the war!*"

CHAPTER 50
RESURRECTION

Lilith Cavanaugh

Four nights later, darkness hung heavily over Peaceful Rest Cemetery northeast of Philadelphia. A crow, which had been taking advantage of the worms revealed in a mound of freshly turned earth, sensed something and took to the moonlit sky, screeching in protest.

A moment later, a slender, white hand tore through the loose dirt, reaching skyward.

The skin was purple, the nails almost black as they clawed first at the air and then at the ground, seeking purchase. Gradually, the hand revealed an arm, then the arm a shoulder, then the shoulder a head.

The being that had once called herself Lilith Cavanaugh dragged her new host clear of the freshly dug grave. She didn't gasp or pant; she was well beyond breathing.

The Queen stood and took stock. The body she wore

was fresh, no more than a few days dead. That was excellent. What was rather *less* excellent was how much *larger* everything looked: the trees, the shrubbery, even the tombstones.

I'm in a child!

A little girl, perhaps five years old at the time of her death. Young and strong, as hosts went, but too small for practical purposes such as conducting press conferences, attending city council meetings, or even shopping for adult clothes.

Except that really isn't an issue anymore ... thanks to the Undertakers.

She spotted two men standing over yet another recent grave. They carried shovels and, even in the darkness, the Queen recognized them as *Malum*.

"You there!" she called.

They turned. Both wore weeks-old cadavers, their bodies bloating and their eyes bulging as decaying flesh released gases into their tissues. At the sight of her, the fools snarled.

Lilith went toward them.

"What are you doing here, child?" one demanded.

They don't know who I am! She couldn't project her Cover, not while wearing a body as small as this; she'd look like a circus freak with her adult head and shape trying to fit over this tiny frame. Still, they *should* have recognized her Self. That is, if they'd bothered to look.

"I asked you a question, girl!" the speaker barked in his moist, somewhat slurred voice. His vocal chords were rotting.

The Queen snatched the shovel from his hand and

impaled him with it, nearly cutting him in two.

There's your answer, fool!

Then she faced the other one, who retreated several steps, his eyes wide. "Mistress!" he said in English. "But you're supposed to have been buried *here* … in *this* grave!"

"Perhaps I was," Lilith told him, still brandishing the shovel. "Being trapped inside a coffin, I couldn't readily tell. However, as you can see, I've Transferred."

He stammered. "But … how? Where … did you … find—?"

Lilith swung the shovel and lopped his head off. "This is a *cemetery*, you thundering buffoon! It's *full* of *bodies!*"

She gazed down at her handiwork. Two minions. Both utter idiots. No doubt sent to dig her body up and spirit her away to—where?"

She picked up the second one's head and spoke in her native language. "Where. You. Take. Me?"

The fool answered at once. "Your. House. Mistress. We. Seek. Your. New. Host."

"Seek? You. Not. Find. Host?"

"Not. Yet. Mistress."

With a growl she dragged the parts of both bodies across the grass and buried them in the hole she'd dug herself out of. Perhaps they'd be resourceful enough to Transfer to one of the other nearby cadavers and dig themselves out. If not, well maybe she'd send someone back for them in a week, or a month, or a year.

Then again, maybe she *wouldn't*.

It took her most of the night to make her way home. She tried to stay clear of people, to keep off the streets as much as possible. Those few humans who spotted her and called to what they *thought* was a lost child were ignored.

One or two got close enough to see that she was dead. Those she killed.

Finally, exasperated and furious, the Queen rang her own doorbell. It was opened by her latest assistant—the same female minion who'd been beheaded by Tom Jefferson during that disastrous encounter some days ago.

"I told you to take it around—" the woman began in English. Then she stopped and, to her credit, spotted the Self inside the little girl on the front stoop. "Mistress?"

Lilith pushed into the foyer, seized the assistant, and tore her limb from limb.

It was untidy, but satisfying.

Then she piled the parts in her living room and went to the kitchen. A newspaper lay on the table. She read the front page. It was…enlightening.

From under the sink she withdrew a wooden box. This she placed atop the newspaper and opened.

John Tall's face, now a few days further decomposed, looked sightlessly up at her.

"Hello, John," she said.

"Hello. Ms. Cavanaugh."

Ever respectful, this one.

"Lilith Cavanaugh is dead," she said.

"Do. Not. Understand."

"So … while you've been languishing under my sink, none of your brethren saw fit to confide in you?"

"They. Ignore. Me."

"Do they? Well, I won't. John, I'm dismayed to report that Lilith Cavanaugh has been publicly 'killed.' That Cover is now useless. As is this house, I suppose. Without a will, it'll likely be sold at auction. I hope I was given a respectful funeral, at least."

"As. Do. I. Ms. Cavanaugh."

Lilith regarded the head of John Tall's most recent host. "You failed me."

"Yes. Mistress."

"But you aren't alone. They all failed me. I've had to dig *myself* out of a grave. Also, my sister is dead. I just read that in the *Inquirer*, which my assistant was kind enough to leave on my table before I dismembered her."

Tall didn't reply, probably didn't know how to. Lilith didn't blame him. She wasn't exactly sure what she was feeling herself.

Finally, the head in the box said, "Undertakers."

"Yes."

"Sorry. For. Failing. You."

"I know you are, John," Lilith said thoughtfully. "And, as things stand, I'm considering offering you something I never offer anyone: a third chance. My command in this world will have to change. It wouldn't do to have anyone believe Lilith Cavanaugh has somehow risen from the dead and, sadly, as we both know, a new Cover is impossible. I'll need to keep to the shadows and avoid humans altogether. I could use your help with that."

"Honored. Mistress."

The phone on the wall rang. Lilith frowned. Then she left John in his box and answered it. "Yes?"

"Ms. Cavanaugh?"

The voice, raspy and clearly dead, was unfamiliar. *Malum*, to be sure, but none that she personally knew. "Perhaps you haven't heard: Lilith Cavanaugh has passed on."

"But the Queen of the Malum *is alive and well."*

Lilith's patience, already a bit thin, broke altogether.

"Who *are* you?" she demanded.

"My name is Gregory Gardner, Mistress. Until quite recently, I served your sister."

"Then you're no ally of mine. I suggest you run ... and keep running. You might get quite far before I finally catch you."

"I could do that, of course," Gardner replied. *"But then I happen to be in a situation that you might find interesting enough to earn me a pardon."*

"Unlikely. But explain."

"Certainly, Mistress. I am in a position to provide you with the location of Haven, the Undertakers' secret headquarters."

The words were like music. For the first time, the dead little girl smiled. "Stay on the line."

She put the phone down. Then she reached into the open box and lifted out John Tall's head.

"Mistress?" the decapitated man asked.

"I'm sorry, John," Lilith said, carrying him across to the kitchen counter. "You've just been replaced."

Then she put Tall's head into the microwave, set the timer to one hour and pressed Start.

The minion was, of course, incapable of screaming—at least audibly. But his Self screamed. It screamed heartily as the radiation ate away at the already rotting tissues that were his only remaining sanctuary.

Lilith watched for the first couple of minutes, until the head in the microwave exploded like an overripe melon.

There's my version of a "Ritter," Mr. Jefferson.

Then the Queen returned to the phone and pressed it to her small, dead ear. "You have my attention, Mr. Gardner. Tell me more."

ACKNOWLEDGEMENTS

My deepest thanks go out to the Washington, DC offices and staff of Senator Robert Menendez of New Jersey for their counsel and assistance with the research that went into this novel. I'd also like to thank Elizabeth Roach, director of the Senator Page Program for her advice and insight into the daily lives of senate pages. Any mistakes I've made are mine and not theirs.

TY DRAGO

In addition to the first two books in UNDERTAKERS series, RISE OF THE CORSPES and QUEEN OF THE DEAD, Ty Drago is the author of PHOBOS, a Science Fiction whodunit and THE FRANKLIN AFFAIR, an historical/mystery about Benjamin Franklin. His short fiction has appeared in numerous venues, including the 2009 anthology YESTERDAY, I WILL ..., and he has written articles for WRITERS DIGEST. His first UNDERTAKERS novelette, NIGHT OF MONSTERS, is currently available for FREE on Smashwords.com and barnesandnoble.com.

Visit www.jointheundertakers.com!

More great middle grade titles
from Month9Books!

December 2013

April 2014

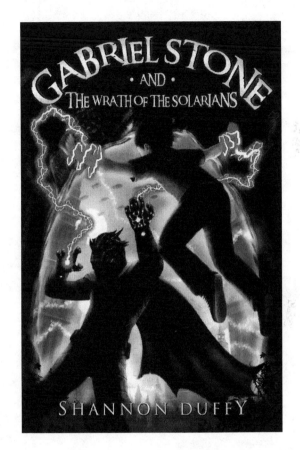

October 2014

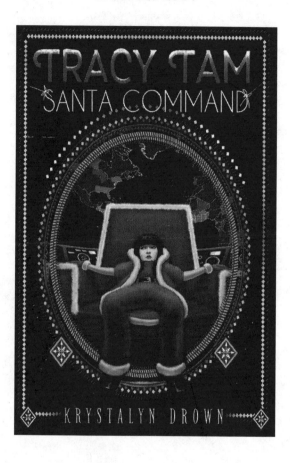